The Measure of Gold

Sarah Patten

ISBN: 978-1-7358082-0-8 (Paperback)
ISBN: 978-1-7358082-1-5 (eBook)

Library of Congress Control Number: 2020947658

Any references to historical events, real people, or real places are used fictitiously. Names, characters, and places are products of the author's imagination.

Ashland Press
18 Rosewood Ave
Asheville, NC 28801

For Rustan, Mancel, Nolan, and Dahlia

"Tempus edax, homo edacior—Time is blind, man is senseless."
-Victor Hugo

Prologue

Sweetwater, Tennessee
June 1940

My Dearest Penelope, the letter began . . .

I am hoping this note somehow finds its way to you. My cousin Manfri promised to mail it to you from London. I have heard the news of your father's death, and that you are now alone in Tennessee. I can barely allow myself to think about all that you have endured. First, the loss of your dear mother at your birth, and now this. I can only imagine the depth of your sorrow. I have thought of you every day since I left Sweetwater.

I am still living in Paris with my brother. Since the German invasion, things have become so uncertain. The whole city is frozen with shock and worry. The air is cloaked in a strained and eerie silence. With so many people in hiding or having fled the city, our streets are empty, and no one seems to know what to do.

I have decided to remain in Paris. Though I, too, feel much anguish and confusion here, this is my home and I must do

*something to fight back. I am living now with a group of alche-
mists under the direction of my brother, Fulcanelli. He is a
renowned French scientist, like your father, and he wants you to
join us here as his apprentice. The apartment is roomy at 52 rue
Laffitte in Paris.*

*When I left Sweetwater so long ago, you promised to come
find me one day. I am writing now, begging you to join me here
in Paris. I miss you, and we desperately need your help, so please
come soon and bring along the necklace I asked you to keep for
me. It is essential you give it to my brother Fulcanelli and also
that you bring as much gold as you can safely carry. These matters are urgent.*

*You have been like a sister to me, so please know that you will
not be alone. I am counting the days until your arrival.*

With much love from Paris,
Yours,
Naomie

Part I

Chapter One

Paris, France
October 1940

*P*enelope's long journey from Tennessee to New
York to Paris had been far more difficult than she
had envisioned. Bad weather delayed almost every phase
of it. Then, while crossing the Atlantic Ocean, the large,
rolling waves made her chronically seasick and bedridden.
So much time had passed that way, and while it felt good
to be on land again, the clamoring and comfortless train
ride to Paris reinvigorated her fears. She was petrified
and worn down from her nausea and sleeplessness. Even
worse, everyone she had met in her long travels cautioned
her against a deeper journey into Europe. *Especially France,*
they would say, but Penelope felt there was nowhere else

for her to go. *We will pray for you,* they concluded when they realized she would continue on to Paris despite their warnings.

Penelope leaned down to rearrange the luggage beneath her feet and felt a familiar, biting pang surge up in her. It was her first trip to Europe, or much of anywhere for that matter. She had certainly never traveled very far from her home in Tennessee, and, like some scalding, immersive bath, her loneliness and fear rose up painful and jagged from her toes, through her waist, to the very center of her being. Sad and intent, she glanced around at the kaleidoscope of fidgeting people and luggage on the half-empty train. The anxious vision soaked right through her.

So many Europeans were fleeing the war in France, and yet somehow, she was taking a train directly into its center to deliver things to the home of a man she had never met or even seen. *Who was Fulcanelli?* The question was stiff and unyielding with sharp, wild teeth. Fulcanelli, Penelope concluded, was not a French name. He must have been named after Vulcan, the Roman God of Fire, who was said to have successfully turned lead into gold. Or perhaps the name could have been related to the Latin words for lightning (*fulgur, fulgere, fulmen*). Through the grimy window of the train, Penelope traced the shadowy lineament of the French horizon with her finger. She leaned her head forward against the cold glass to try and nap. Her body ached all over from the effects of her long journey. She thought about her deceased father, her friend

Naomie's urgent letter, and the beloved stone necklace that hung around her neck.

Tawny and trim with messy blonde hair and gilded eyes, Penelope's face held a delicate, yet arresting countenance. She was a lifelong companion to the tremendous uncertainty of life, a perceptibly passionate and sinewy being. She was a loner, and she found this to be the deepest injury of loneliness, the knowledge that darkness, indeed, has a scent and that she belonged nowhere.

She had been born into this world with a job, first to take care of her father, then to forget her pain. Without dolls or tea parties to shape her childhood, the words play and work became interchangeable.

Out of the relentless loss and toil of her childhood came Penelope's tenacity, a grit that took root and wing in her body beside her intellect and imagination. Over time, long threads of sorrow and loss, life's misfortunes, joined in beside her strengths. Penelope had experienced so many sad vicissitudes in her life, and the mix of those experiences and emotions continued to move together within her like a formation of birds, traveling up, down, and right through her. Somehow her disparate parts did not collide. *Allelomimesis*, the Greeks had called it, a sort of primitive mimicry where birds would come together in unison, free and liquid as the sky. Season by season, year after year, Penelope had slowly taken full-fledged flight. She had evolved into a mishmash of hillbilly, scientist, mystic, and woman.

Penelope had left Tennessee and traveled to France because her beloved friend Naomie had written a letter pleading for her to come quickly. Polite and hurried, written in shorthand like a prescription, crinkled and well-aged in its journey, the letter's insistence had upturned Penelope's sad and quiet life in Sweetwater.

Unhinged and heartbroken from the loss of her father, Penelope had barely known what to do with the rare and mysterious letter from Europe when it first arrived. Each morning, like some relentless, circling wind, she had tossed her sad eyes to the sky in search of any answer.

"Where is Penelope? Why hasn't she come yet?" Naomie's distant, pleading voice would echo back to her.

Penelope knew about the terrible war and of Hitler and his savage destruction of Europe. She had read about the Nazi's recent invasion and occupation of France. Paris was dark, the headlines all read, yet Noamie's words were diametrical for Penelope. Penelope's lonely life in Tennessee had become so devastated, and the crumpled letter called out to her from her bedside each night like some raw matter or gypsy spirit. After all, Penelope had nowhere else to go, and the convalescence of her sorrow at the loss of her father was nearly unbearable. For weeks she lay resting and watching the mysterious letter cautiously from beneath her covers. Like a fever, Penelope's loneliness had begun to nearly overtake her until finally one day, she determined there was nothing left for her to lose, so she gathered up her belongings and traveled alone from

Tennessee by train to New York City, where she took a boat across the ocean, carrying her two battered suitcases, the necklace, and a satchel.

At each turn in her journey, from train to ocean liner to sidewalk to train again, she dragged her suitcases in her hands and her satchel across her body. The satchel contained a collection of lost and found items her father had bequeathed to her. "Something for later," his will had said in a cryptic tone. Not clutter, but things of a higher intuitive order—his book, some feathers, a vile of salt, a tortoise shell, and some quartz. They all held the weighty and ever-turbulent meaning of mystical things, and though they didn't take up much room, they occupied a lot of space.

She slid her fingers along her necklace. It was a symmetrical pattern of ropes woven around a stone. It was both ornamental and functional. When they were children, Naomie had given it to Penelope for safekeeping and now the simple necklace had been hanging from Penelope's neck for over half of her life.

At the first train station in France, Penelope was stopped by a soldier in his Nazi uniform. He insisted on examining her bags, speaking abruptly to her in German, which she didn't understand. His brow rose when he saw her two suitcases, but he then became distracted by the satchel and reached for it instead. He held the cloth sack in his right hand and opened it, shriveling his face like a raisin and pointing to the trash can.

"*Mull*," he said, disdainfully.

She thought it must be the German word for garbage.

He threw the sack back at her and ushered her past him. He was indifferent to the spell of the rattling things.

This was her first sight of a German soldier, but after she got back on board the train, and it began to move closer to the center of France, she saw other signs of the war all around her. They seemed to cling to everything like a corrosive rust. The frozen countryside was littered with tanks and smoke. As the train sped closer to Paris, she could see the rubble and burned-out farms passing by, just out of reach. Nearer to Paris, just west of the city, a whole neighborhood had been cracked open by German bombs.

There was an alarming and mundane familiarity to the devastation. Life was splayed open, vulgar and fully visible, a broken highchair, a splintered table, the roof of a bedroom ripped away and the bed still made. A cane swung from the highest limb of a tree. Stray dogs foraged in abandoned, half-burned kitchens. Near the outskirts of the city center, the neighborhoods were largely untouched, and the landscape became dense with buildings. She felt the persistent tension of anticipation in her belly as the train rolled to a stop at Montparnasse in the southwest of Paris.

Penelope quickly grabbed her bags and departed the

train station. Once outside, she had to struggle against the harsh, biting wind. The anguish of the Nazi occupation had settled in on the city like a dark cloud. It was etched into the face of each grimacing Parisian. *Sangfroid*, it was a harsh, emotional alchemy of fear and mistrust, beyond anything Penelope had experienced in her life in America. The city wore a contorted mask. Everywhere she looked the Nazi military flag hung, draped in every direction. This was the grimace of war, displayed fully in her face.

Penelope pulled the letter with Fulcanelli's address from her pocket, feeling the icy wind nip her hand. She could see scribbled words and names, yet she could not differentiate the letters. She huddled against the lantern that hung from the entrance of the train station but could hardly make out any words in the dim lighting so she folded up the tattered note and tucked it away in her satchel.

A group of soldiers looked across the street at her, pointing. She couldn't help that she had the self-conscious and crumpled-up look of a traveler, the wrong clothes, the wrong hair, the wrong walk. She was undeniably an outsider. The youngest of the soldiers licked his lips and crossed the street to approach her. His chest was like a barrel, curved staves bound with hoops and brimming full.

"*Fraulein*," he spoke forcefully. "Papers." His breath turned white in the cold air.

She propped her suitcases against her legs and fumbled

through her belongings to find her passport.

"You are American?" he questioned her in English. "What brings you here? Is this your first time in Paris?" he fired rapid questions in his tragic, stilted voice.

"It is," she replied. Her hand shook a little as she handed him her papers.

"Why are you here?" he asked as he flipped haphazardly through her documents.

"My father was a Frenchman, so I am here to see my sister," she lied, though it felt less like a lie because she thought of Naomie as a sister.

He remained silent for some moments.

She remembered that a woman on the boat across the Atlantic had warned her to say almost nothing to the German soldiers. Give simple answers in as few words as possible, and when you speak don't blink and never, never look away. Penelope faced him, her boots as fixed and thickly set as a slow-growing lichen. She saw a look of desecration in his eye.

"The sun is setting. The curfew is 7:00 p.m. If you do not allow me to escort you, someone might think you are a prostitute. Is that what your sister would want, young American?" he said in his broken English.

She shook her head no, and he gestured her to the road. She wondered if he might wish she was a prostitute as he pinched the flesh of her elbow and they moved down the street, his gloved hand tense and compressed, cold as a girder. She went with him because she didn't feel she had a choice.

"Can I help you with your bags?" he asked.

"No, thank you," she said, trying not to sound pleading. She was terrified he might ask about the contents of her luggage.

"Yanks are stubborn." His smile looked like a grimace.

She simpered tensely in return and continued to carry her suitcases down the dimly lit street. To conceal the city from bombers, the streetlights were covered or shut off. Cars' headlights were covered with a bluish paper that cast a ghostly, beryl shade down upon the cobblestone. It was a frightening effect that muffled the instincts of the night. Shadows too were swallowed by the darkness and blue tinted filter.

"The city men walk briskly here," he said. "The soldiers and the prostitutes move slowly." He spoke efficiently, adding no extra words or unnecessary gestures. He laughed aloud to himself, and he forced an unnaturally slow pace to their journey, half steps instead of whole ones. It was a syncopated rhythm, unexpected and unpredictable.

In the war, she wondered, perhaps only mixed fractions could survive, not the whole numbers. The wind and the cold irritated the hollow feeling beneath her tired eyes.

"What is the address?" he asked, with a tone of utter dismissal.

She fished around again in her satchel and read the paper aloud to him, "52 rue Laffitte."

She looked at his face again, holding his gaze for an

instant. Penelope was twenty-two years old. He was young too, maybe nineteen. He was smoking a cigarette, and his blue eyes slid from side to side in the manner of a drum, of someone caught in a shifty, deep sleep, a nightmare. He offered her a cigarette.

"No thanks," she said and shook her head before adding, "Please, I can make it from here. I prefer to walk alone."

He stopped abruptly in the street, his mouth gaping, hooks and swinging old lines. A long time seemed to pass. "But it is not safe for you," he said, without looking at her. His countenance held a certain element of instability that she found deeply unsettling. It was a mere flavor of something, the dark quiet behind the silence, a terror, a repulsion and a deep, abiding weariness.

She gathered her thoughts. "No one is safe in France, but I am just here to visit my family," she said. "My country is not involved in this war. Let me walk on alone."

He smiled a fraction of a smile. He was clearly irritated and let his arms swing heavily beside him like hanging and empty pots.

"You sound like my mother," he said and laughed, his lips trembling. "But you are wrong. I am perfectly safe because just like a shoemaker learns the art of making shoes, I have learned the skill of war. I have been taught by the best in the world. I have learned to survive and dominate. No war is that different from the next, and in this war the German army's success stands alone." He waved his arms through the darkness, mixing the air. "This city is ours." His voice seemed to echo around them.

"But, you see, I am a foreigner." Penelope pressed her lips tightly together and pinched her jacket between her fingers at the waist to keep out the cold wind that wrapped down and careened around her like a deep, purple ravine.

He raised his eyebrow, the cigarette bobbing from his mouth. "Ah, a true Yank." He said and laughed a derisive, scolding laugh. He looked at her from the corner of his eye. The cloudy night sky shone above the blackness like a silver platter. He waited expectantly, but she offered nothing. She stood silent and firm with her shadowed gaze. Finally, he snapped his heels together, saluted her, and walked off into the fettered city streets.

Chapter Two

a kind passerby had led her the rest of the way to 52 rue Laffitte, and the building now stood in the darkness before Penelope. She quickly tucked through the iron gate at the entrance and scrambled into the foyer. It was shadowy and hollow, like stepping inside a *carapace*. The walls of the building kept the vibration from the city muffled and distant. The ceiling was vaulted and cobbled with pottery tiles pressed with posies and vines. A coat rack stood upright and blooming in the middle of the foyer, like a tree.

Penelope decided to sit for a minute on a box pushed up against the wall and labeled "fragile." This city was a minefield, a curfew and Nazi soldiers stationed all throughout the streets. Such a dense, urban landscape felt alien and constrained to her. She was a country girl, accustomed to the broad forests and valleys of Tennessee. She huddled in the foyer and laced her arms together for warmth. The small room felt frigid and lonely, so she closed her eyes and thought of the warm summers in Sweetwater and the misty hills and creeks that stretched in all directions.

Penelope remembered that it was during one of Tennessee's hottest summers on record that she first met Naomie. Penelope had just turned five, and, without warning, in early May, a vibrant group of travelers poured into Sweetwater in a caravan of red cabooses decorated with ornate, yellow trim. They would stay the full growing season only to vanish in late September as quickly as they had appeared.

They were French travelers and some of the townspeople called them "gypsies." Year after year, they would come to Sweetwater and stay in bright red carts mounted on rubber tires and pulled by horses. The vehicles were also their homes, and when they arrived, they would set up camp beside the creek across from Penelope's house.

Before she would even see them, Penelope would hear their music, breezing in, distinct and full as a summer storm. The women and children were often barefoot, jangling with glistening jewelry and decorated with beads. Their flowing robes rippled in the shimmering light as they danced and sang together. They were families of travelers with exotic names like Elodie, Silvanus, Manfri,

Charity, Duke, and Penelope's beloved Naomie.

Penelope's gray-haired father, Thomas, was French as well and was entranced by the travelers. He was almost seventy years old, a reserved but affectionate man, who was gaunt and stooped forward slightly beneath the weight of his old age. Thomas was a scholar and a scientist who liked to spend a great deal of time with Penelope tinkering in his attic laboratory. Her father's merry eyes lit up each summer as he watched the travelers transform the empty land across from his house into a motley homestead, but, above all, he loved to watch them dance. In spite of his aching body and his cautious way, as their music rose up, he would lean out the window of his attic room then turn to grasp Penelope's hand, and they would dance a slow waltz together.

Each year, the rumor would spread that when the gypsies came to town, the creek would dry up and the rains would no longer come. Thomas felt unhappy about such quarrelsome gossip, so he would make an offering to the mystical travelers, sending Penelope down to speak French with them and deliver several chickens and some butter to welcome them back. Penelope liked to stay, converse, and exchange eggs from her chickens for their beadwork.

At night, as the travelers danced by their campfires, Penelope would wander down to the creek again and hide, dangling in the trees above their tents, eavesdropping on their conversations and watching them dance. Their movements were expressive, full of happiness, sorrow, fear, and delight. And they always told a story. Their favorite dance spun the tale of Circe of the Golden Tresses. A woman named Elodie played the singing enchantress and a man named Manfri, the pig. Penelope watched and laughed aloud as Manfri chased Elodie, weaving her song around him as he snorted and squealed.

"Who is that laughing up there?" Elodie paused, her voice rising up and filling Penelope's ear like smoke.

"It is the daughter of the Frenchman. She speaks our language," Manfri marveled.

Penelope flushed red.

"Why don't you come dance with us?" Elodie said, offering Penelope the long fingers of her hand. Each summer, the travelers would teach Penelope their mystical dances, and she would watch them and practice with the revival and intensity of some personal religion. From a tightly woven trot to a full stride, the puritanical rigors of her waltz gave way to a shimmy and a swivel. Driven by the rhythms of their music, the folk dances melted from the bounce and swing of the Charleston and the Texas Tommy into supple stories, mainly of love and liberty. The travelers' dances were wild and carefree and, summer after summer, Penelope learned to reveal her deepest truths through movement. The choreography of freedom had a hypnotic sway.

"At first you must conceal yourself," Manfri had taught her. "Then through movement and the heat, you slowly loosen and unravel to reveal your truest person."

His forehead was soaked in the balmy night air, "To be a dancer you must become like the seasons. You must prove to your audience that spring and summer are most startling after the deprivation of a distant and harsh winter."

The box where she sat in the cold Parisian foyer gave way a little under the weight of her thoughts, putting a solemn quietus on her warm memories of Tennessee. She opened her eyes and began to feel the familiar wave of shivering fear wash through her. She heard the letter in her pocket as it crinkled. Perhaps this man, Fulcanelli, could help her. Perhaps Naomie was just inside the door. Or perhaps Penelope was already too late. There could be nothing there at all but an empty room.

She opened the satchel her father had left her and looked at its odd souvenirs. She had brought with her so many irregular things—his book, some feathers, a vile of salt, a tortoise shell, some quartz. She clung to them like memories.

Penelope touched the necklace hanging from her neck and glanced down at the beautiful stone. It was the most familiar and beloved item she had brought along to France with her. She released the stone against her neck, uncoiling her scarf and jacket and straightening her skirt to stand. She stepped forward to ring the bell next to the door. She could hear it echo through the room on the other side of the wall, *briiing, briiing, briiing.* This was the home of the famous Fulcanelli. After a prolonged and stiff silence, a man's voice hummed through the door to her.

"Who is it?"

"Is this 52 rue Laffitte? My name is Penelope."

She didn't know what else to say.

"What is your name, again?" The door cracked open a sliver.

"Penelope," she repeated. She heard a gasp.

"One moment please," the voice said, as the door closed abruptly.

Penelope pulled the address from her pocket for reassurance. When she looked up again, a stout, mustached man opened the door halfway, reached out, and abruptly pulled her inside.

He was at least forty and his hair looked like the ruffled coat of a wild animal. His skin was dusky and his dark eyes shone like the surface of polished brass. He wore a buttoned shirt, a vest, and trousers.

"Isn't it funny how things ripen into things," the man pronounced in his French accent and reached out to squeeze her cold cheeks. He then lifted her hand to his mouth, brushed the back of it with a brief kiss, and twirled her around and around. He was downright gleeful. "This is great! But you are so late in coming! We have been waiting so long for you."

Penelope felt astonished at this welcome. "Is it true, then?" she asked. "Is this Naomie's—?" She stuttered, pausing, and looked around the room.

It was an unfinished thought. She couldn't quite find a word to describe what she saw . . . household, workshop, lab? The man stilled and gazed silently at her for a moment.

"Of course, Penelope, the truth is wii-iide." His pronunciation rang out, stretching the vowels to their maximum extent.

"I see," she said in an involuntary utterance. She felt confused, her head still spinning from the stranger's greeting.

The man was short, almost pudgy, but well-tailored with his vest and luxurious mustache. He spoke with a scuffed, hoarse accent.

She dragged her suitcases in from the foyer and closed the door behind her.

The walls of the living room were the color of cardboard, and it smelled like a tamped-out campfire. Clocks covered every wall, some upright, others sideways, some turned upside down. The whole room was contorted in this way, and they were not alone. She saw people in dusty lab coats stirring in every corner, like scientists, sponging up some solution here, clattering with some splendid machine there. The apartment appeared to be very much its own organism, so distinct from the world outside. It was like the burrow of some wild animal, just beneath the surface, and like any closed system, it seemed to generate heat, mainly from convection. The temperature was high and superbly radiant. The windows of the apartment dripped with steam.

The mustached man proclaimed with an air of formality, "Penelope, I have heard so much about you."

"And you are?" she replied somewhat timidly.

"Who do you think that I am? *Nullius in Verba*," he interrupted her loudly. Don't take another person's word for it.

"I believe you are Fulcanelli," she announced with shaking uncertainty.

The clocks chimed in choral unison. This place was both punctual and irregular.

"Why, yes. The American Penelope. You are finally here, and I am indeed Fulcanelli." He stepped forward again with warmth and solicitation.

"Naomie told me to come here." She reached for the letter in her pocket.

"Yes, of course, and, by all means, I am at your service," he responded, dismissing the letter.

"Is Naomie here now?" she asked eagerly, looking around the room again.

"No, she is not," he replied simply. "But you have traveled across the ocean. You must be so tired," he remarked with concern.

"Yes, deeply tired. Naomie told me you are her brother. Her letter indicated that I might stay here to study. Do you know where she is? She wrote to me that she would be here too," Penelope looked around again. "Perhaps I could stay the night and wait for her to arrive?" she asked Fulcanelli questioningly.

"Stay the night? Why, you should stay here as long as

you like."

"And Naomie?"

"I told you she is gone," he concluded with a hot-tempered and biting finality. A thread of a frown slid across his face. Then he looked down for a fleeting instant, reemerging with an entreating smile.

"But when will she return?"

"We are not sure," he responded.

She felt upset, but there was something familiar to Penelope about him, and his smile was a beaming thing. He had a long mustache, and his face was transparent like Naomie's, but was also lit from the inside with the same liquid luster. Penelope found it difficult to look away from him.

He quickly shifted the subject. "Naomie said your father was a hermit and a scientist like me," he said and gestured around the strange room.

"Yes, my father taught me so much."

"She also told me you are a fine dancer and a mathematician," he said. "You know math and dance have some very important things in common." He twisted the pointed tip of his mustache with his fingers as he spoke. "Both the rhythm and the cadence," he continued.

"Well, I dance mostly for fun, but I have studied as a mathematician and assisted my reclusive father in his lab my whole life. Really, I have only just begun my formal education. Naomie invited me in large part to study here with you," she said with great affection.

Fulcanelli reached out and squeezed her hands. "Yes, then, welcome," he replied.

The main floor was vast and wide-open. The room was lit by a flickering fire, and a young man wrapped in an overcoat with his back turned towards Penelope was writing feverishly at a desk along the side wall. Ten or so people were engrossed in projects and books were stacked in every corner. At the far end of the room was an ornate, mahogany cupboard that held a collection of ancient things, a phoenix, an alembic, a scale. Beside it was a piano with a pile of instruments stacked on top. Fulcanelli brought Penelope into the center of the room and grasped her hands once again with a roar of enthusiasm.

"We have waited so long for you that I hardly know where to begin . . ." he clicked his tongue against the roof of his mouth as he spoke and looked around.

"What is this place?" she asked.

"Well, it is both our home and our lab. It is dangerous for scientists to live openly in Paris," he began. "We have gathered here as a group who opposes the Occupation. We are part of the French Resistance and live together and dream up scientific ways to defeat the Germans."

He drew his hand across his forehead. On his finger was a large, gold ring. She saw that it bore the same alchemical figures as the front of her the father's book. Penelope stared curiously at the familiar symbol. It flashed against its gold setting.

"So, you are saboteurs?" she wondered aloud, looking

across the room at the motley assemblage of people and their projects. It was difficult for Penelope to envision the chaos of this apartment as an organized movement.

"Yes, in essence, so many people are gathering in the shadows like us. For us, our work here is a call to arms against the Germans. Our buildings are bombed, our streets are overtaken, our books are banned, our cities, our people, our masterpieces are stolen or in hiding. Who could have guessed the world would turn upside down like this? Though I suppose there is no use in asking such questions right now. You see, we must all use the skills we have to resist."

"Then life here must be quite a dance," she said and paused, reflecting. "You know in dance, you should never look behind you or down at your feet or else you will likely stumble," she added.

"Indeed," Fulcanelli smiled and tapped a tango with his feet. "Certainly, in times like this, you can only look to the next day, and, of course, remember to take nothing for granted. Here, in this apartment, we believe no idea can be too radical."

"Then what schemes are you working on?" she asked, rubbing her hands together in excitement.

"Yes, I will get to that, but first I want you to meet someone—Lucien," he called out towards the man huddled at the desk. "Take a break from your work to come meet Penelope. She has finally arrived!"

The man at the writing desk stood up abruptly. He

was alert and upright in his posture, but his clothes were ragged. He leaned forward and reached behind a clock to return some papers to a hole in the wall. When he swung around to face Penelope, she felt the instinct to turn her head away in retreat but did not, and in an instant, his intrepid stare enveloped her with a prickling static. He looked at her, his wide eyes diving into her flesh the way air can penetrate through to the bone. The effect was startling, and some familiar part of her transformed like a landscape tipping into springtime. She watched as the whole room seemed to dilate and contract around him.

Lucien was tall with hollow cheeks and a determined, handsome face. He looked to be about thirty. Striding towards them, he gently placed a kiss across both of Penelope's cheeks with a peculiar intimacy.

"Welcome," he said. His gray eyes were lit like lanterns, his gaze and touch full of sensation. "I have heard so much." He spoke deliberately, and his comment unsettled her.

"But how could you know anything about me?" she blurted out in her fatigue, drawing away. Her words hung in the air like calipers, measuring the narrow distance between them.

"From your beloved Naomie," he coaxed her.

"I see," Penelope cautioned and paused to look around the strange room. "And where is she now?"

He hesitated, meditatively jutting his lower lip out a fraction and glancing at Fulcanelli.

"Don't worry. She has only told me good things about

you often." He seemed to want to say something more but did not.

Lucien was unshaven and had the dusky and rough complexion of hewn wood. Penelope watched as his unspoken thoughts veiled his gaze like some intricate filagree, the same way steam decorates and freezes along a winter window. Her mind retraced the precise places where he had kissed her along her cheeks. She offered him a quiet smile, and he seemed to redden.

"Penelope, Lucien," Fulcanelli broke in. "Please sit down. You must be tired and need to rest your legs after such a long journey." He gestured towards a scattered collection of chairs behind them.

They stood together, scarcely listening.

"What are you waiting for Penelope?" Fulcanelli barked impatiently. "Are you like Lucien? Do you not yet understand the importance of rest?"

Penelope took a half-step backwards then gestured behind her. "Of course, I will gladly sit, though I was wondering where I should put my bags?" Penelope asked. "I'm afraid they are in your way." Her suitcases rested in the center of the busy room, fixed and worn as a milepost.

"They are not in our way at all," Fulcanelli reassured her. "In fact, quite the opposite. We have also been awaiting the gifts that you bring to us." He pointed to her luggage. "What's inside?" Fulcanelli asked with a child-like innocence.

Penelope nodded and led Lucien and Fulcanelli to the

center of the room.

"This suitcase contains some trinkets of gold for you that Naomie asked me to bring," she pointed to the larger bag. "I could only bring a small amount. It is scarce and hard to find."

"That will do."

"I'm sorry I could not bring you any more than that," she said. "I know you must need the money."

"Oh no, do not be sorry. We don't want the gold for its value in currency," Fulcanelli responded with a hint of frustration.

"Then why do you need it?"

"For our experiment," he stated flatly.

Penelope's questioning eyes darted from Fulcanelli to Lucien and back again.

Lucien responded gently, "We are taking some bold and unorthodox steps to fight the Germans."

Penelope's eyes cut from Lucien to the large suitcase standing between them.

"Fulcanelli believes that science, specifically alchemy, can win the war and free us. We hope to save many lives," he continued.

"But—," Penelope began.

"But what is alchemy?" Fulcanelli interrupted. "It's complicated. Particularly, in this city in this time."

"No, I wasn't going to ask that at all. I was going to ask how you planned to break down pure gold for your experiments. I have done it myself only one time before."

Fulcanelli and Lucien exchanged a discerning glance.

Penelope had discovered alchemy as a child with her eccentric father. Growing up she had studied the works of the great Basil Valentine. Together, they read *The Twelve Keys of Basil Valentine* again and again. It was as much art and poetry as science, depicting each of the twelve steps to make the Philosopher's Stone. Their study of the stone led them into the more esoteric dimensions of medicine and faith as well.

As an older man, her father, Thomas, had even written his own alchemy book titled, *Ex nihilo nihil fit.* It was a leather-bound, weathered book, engraved with the curious picture of a naked man and woman at the base of an elaborate tree. He had spent years gathering the essential ingredients for his strange recipes and organizing them in his lab—ammonia, hydrochloric acid, nitric acid, all kept in bottles her father had labeled so carefully and set high out of reach. For Penelope and her father, the process was part play and part science. Then, there were the ground-up minerals: the sulfur, cinnabar, and hematite. They had spent whole summers collecting other ingredients from the forest—micah, chalk, the resin of a pine tree, lichen, some wax, and a drop of dew. After a long and belabored search, Penelope had even discovered some locust wings in the piles of dust beneath her father's unkempt desk. She had been mixing strange scientific and alchemical potions with her father for as long as she could remember.

Penelope had even brought the heavy alchemy book along with her to Paris because Penelope's father considered *Ex nihilo nihil fit* to be his magnum opus, and it was written in his handwriting. Its final chapter culminated in a recipe Thomas supposed would have saved Penelope's aged mother from her postpartum hemorrhage and untimely death—he called it The Golden Pill. Her father's notations in the book had described the legendary pill as explosive and dangerous, warning that the slightest misstep could torque it from life-giving to life-taking. *The potency of the recipe was such that even the salt of a sweaty palm could taint it,* he wrote.

"You must distill it down to a crystalized powder and coat that pill in gold?" Penelope had asked her father one day.

"Yes, but the mere warmth of a moist and nervous hand could upset the concoction's volatility and unleash its destructive potential," Thomas had stated firmly.

Thomas had an unusual manner. He was odd, yet handsome, with one eye larger than the other and a large nose that curved slightly to the left, giving his countenance an asymmetrical look. Gravity and age had stiffened his lower back and pitched his balance forward through his bent knees.

"I thought my mother died because she was too old to give birth. A golden pill would have saved her?" Penelope asked.

"Yes, a pill encased in gold," he replied slowly, nodding his head with conviction.

Penelope didn't know if it was delusion or science, so she had sat on the floor of her father's lab, shakily clicking a dropper into the rim of a glass flask to melt the gold, imagining the ever-flawless effects of swallowing down a gleaming and golden pill, like swallowing the moon.

"We won't need to break the gold down to complete the experiment." Fulcanelli's voice broke through her memories. "Some believe copper sulfate or potassium nitrate would work in place of the gold because of the restrictions of the war, but I suspected that kind of shortcut wasn't a part of the ancient recipes. So much of science is about precision and procedure."

Lucien nodded, adding, "We also thought the problem with our experiment was that one of the thermometers was somehow broken. There were so many subtle steps and details that it was difficult to gauge."

"But once we saw the results, we knew," Fulcanelli said.

"Knew what?" Penelope asked.

Fulcanelli continued almost mumbling as though he were talking to himself, "Knew that our premise was over-simplified and flawed. We were thinking about the experiment backwards. But here is the tricky part: we had been working for months and months, and it was clear from the instructions Lucien had translated from the papers that the first step would be to make the metal sprout."

"Like a plant?" Penelope was trying to understand.

"Exactly," Fulcanelli replied. "Then, I went to bed one night and dreamt quite vividly that I dug a hole, planted my tooth in the ground, and an entire tree grew out of it. It was then that I understood the error, so I came into the lab that morning and dropped it in."

Lucien's whole body caved in defeat, "For so many months, I had gotten the translation wrong by just one word. I thought the symbol was an alloy. We were looking for two things, not one."

"Dropped what, where?" Penelope challenged.

"His gold tooth," Lucien answered. "Into the solution we had mixed."

Fulcanelli smiled and, looking directly at her, pulled his cheek to the side to reveal a large gap in his teeth.

Penelope laughed out loud so hard she threw her hand to her mouth to stifle the noise.

"It's difficult to even describe what happened after that," Fulcanelli remembered.

Lucien continued, suppressing his own laughter now too, "The gold tooth sprouted almost instantly."

Fulcanelli interrupted, "Into a beautiful crystalline structure that the ancient alchemists call Philosopher's Gold. It's a powerful phenomenon, the basis for many of Newton's esoteric experiments."

Penelope attempted to regain her composure.

Fulcanelli spoke crossly, "It's not funny Penelope. You

can laugh with me but you must not laugh at me. You see, so many modern scientists group alchemy as pseudo-science with such areas as magic, superstition, and astrology. They allow its mystical aspects to surpass its chemical aspects. They dismiss our work and fail to see the whole point." He waved his hand around the room and a sweat of passion broke free from his brow. His voice grew louder, "Isaac Newton was not so naive and arrogant. The metallurgic terms, the spiritual terms, and the metaphors drive so many lesser people away. The gravity of it scares them. But in turning their backs on us, they misunderstand the fundamental truth of what is happening."

"I am so sorry for my laughter. I am tired and your display of teeth caught me off guard," she spoke entreatingly. "So, what is it that you believe this experiment will do exactly?"

"Though we have been unable to replicate it, Fulcanelli believes in a type of transmutation that he thinks could change the world, certainly change the tide of this war in an instant," Lucien began. "So many people believe that alchemy is about transforming lesser elements into gold to obtain wealth and power. They think of alchemy as some sort of hoax or joke to be mocked. Their greed has blinded them. Alchemical transmutation is everywhere. When a piece of wood converts to fire, that is transmutation. Isaac Newton was transfixed and alarmed by this principle. He wrote thousands of pages on the subject of transmutation and never published one. He feared it was an idea that was too alarming to be revealed to the world. He even encoded his work on these concepts in a mysterious language," Lucien spoke and pointed to the papers on his desk.

He continued, "In those papers, Newton references a friend of his who made claims in a vague account that in mixing mercury and gold and an unnamed element at room temperature he created energy, some type of cold fusion it would seem. Fulcanelli believes that this finding is possible. He believes that gold is a seed of the sun and that through the proper manipulation of gold a type of cold fusion could occur that would create abundant energy without having to ignite or sustain the reaction. Many scientists think that our experiment is a type of magical thinking, but we believe that—."

Fulcanelli interrupted, "Our life depends on it."

"Thus, the gold," Penelope interjected, smiling broadly.

"Indeed," Lucien said as he inched close enough to brush against her arm.

Fulcanelli stepped forward between them, his eyes wild and intent.

"And those are Isaac Newton's actual papers?" she said with a questioning excitement.

Fulcanelli nodded fervently, pressing his shaky finger to her lips to quiet her. "Enough about the papers, my dear. What about the necklace?" Fulcanelli's smile had an electric, almost disconcerting current. "The necklace is also what we have been waiting to see."

"Yes, we've been long expecting it," Lucien said, with

great intent.

Their comments betrayed some larger conversation she was somehow a part of but had not been aware of. She looked up at Fulcanelli with a wide-eyed and questioning gravity.

"You have? I must say, I don't understand why the necklace is so important to you." A feeling of suspicion rose up in her and she took a step backwards away from them.

"When Naomie told us that you were coming, she told us you would bring a gift of some gold and a necklace too," Lucien responded. "The necklace is essential to the work we are doing." He spoke almost repentantly. "The war progresses and yet, for us, there are so few resources and everything is running behind."

He was no longer looking at her but was looking at the pendant that draped down from her neck. She covered it with her hand protectively.

"This one?" she questioned with feigned indignation. She was no longer sure she wanted to give it up along with the gold.

"I believe so," he said, looking towards Fulcanelli.

Fulcanelli nodded twisting his odd ring upon his finger.

Her heart was beating uncomfortably fast. Naomie had given the necklace to her as a gift so long ago. It was the one constant thing she had possessed, a reminder of their friendship.

"But where is my Naomie? I was planning to return it to her." She looked around the room full of strangers.

A young scientist was tinkering with what seemed to be a capsule of some sort. She watched him, her eyes tense with curiosity. "Plus, I need to rest first," she sighed with exhaustion.

Lucien touched her shoulder with his hand. "We understand," he responded and stepped between Fulcanelli and Penelope. "Your trip must have depleted you."

Fulcanelli bore the disappointed look of a child whose toy had been put away upon a high shelf. He turned and withdrew from the room abruptly.

Penelope continued to suspiciously eye the man across the room from them tinkering with the strange capsule.

Lucien watched her gaze and remarked, "You will meet him another day. His name is Philippe, and he is building a time machine," Lucien commented gently as if he could hear the questions of her mind.

"Is that mathematically possible?" she questioned.

"Doubtful, but for Fulcanelli, the more radical and far-reaching the idea, the better. He likes to stretch the bounds of what is possible in science." Lucien smiled. "However, some of our projects are more reasonable." He pointed to a stack of boxes decorated with a skull and crossbones labeled "Explosives."

He led her down a long hall, past the kitchen and a stairwell to a back room filled with empty cots. "Rest now, but please know we are hoping that you will stay here and join our scientific insurgence," he continued as he handed her a blanket.

This place was a remote island of ideas and experimentation, the type of refuge of like minds that she had always longed for, the highest use of a mind like hers.

"I believe so," was all she said in response, but Lucien couldn't tell whether she was talking about her need to take a rest or his invitation for her to join the French Resistance.

Chapter Three

The next morning Penelope awoke with a start. She had slept surprisingly well on the uncomfortable cot. Her fatigue and the strangeness of her circumstance had simply overtaken her. 52 rue Laffitte was a world apart. Practically overnight, without performing any real task or function, she wondered if she had officially transformed from traveler to saboteur? A queasy hunger swirled low in her belly as her realization took hold. Was she now a part of the French Resistance?

"Let her rest. I believe she meant what she said," she overheard a man whisper. "I will talk to her," the voice concluded.

While there were at least ten people in the lower level of the apartment, Penelope felt certain she was still the only woman, so she sat up and looked around to see who was speaking about her. There were a handful of men stirring beneath blankets along the shadowed walls, and the remaining four were eating by the window. With so little food and space to sleep, there seemed to be a breach in the room between the weary and the hungry, and as the morning sun drew across the floor, the breach widened. No one seemed to want to stand in the light of the window. Fulcanelli and Lucien huddled in the middle of the room. Fulcanelli was preoccupied, twisting his ring nervously and paying scant attention to the activities around him.

Lucien glanced over at Penelope and stepped towards her smiling, "Good morning. Can I bring you anything?"

"No, thank you though," she responded, her blanket still draped across her.

"Did you get some rest?"

"I did, I suppose," she reflected looking around. "You know, somehow I managed to convince myself that it would be different here than in Tennessee."

"How do you mean?"

"I came here, in part, because I thought things would be easier."

"In Paris? Now? What do you mean?" Lucien looked at her, slightly stricken.

"I guess I thought I might shake this terrible feeling," she concluded.

Lucien paused, reflecting, "Yes, Naomie told me about the loss of your father. I am so sorry."

He offered her some warm tea.

"At the very least," she nodded, blowing into the steaming mug. "Gone are any illusions that I can ever go back home." She held the mug closely.

"So, you have decided to stay with us?" Lucien said with a hint of delight.

She hesitated. "Yes, I suppose." She then nodded. "Plus, I don't think I really have a choice."

"Indeed," Lucien gazed down at her quietly.

After a few moments, Fulcanelli approached and broke in with a stuttered urgency, "Penelope, it is essential that we see the necklace very soon."

Lucien stepped between them and squeezed her shoulder reassuringly. "I know you are just waking up but would you mind?" Lucien asked. "He is quite impatient to see it."

She looked towards Fulcanelli and nodded reluctantly, reaching to touch the necklace with her hand, "I suppose, but?"

"What are your concerns?" replied Lucien, his eyes entreating hers.

"I suppose I'm afraid to lose it. It's something familiar, and I have become so, so—fond of it." Her words cut to the center of her precise loneliness. It felt wrong to simply hand the necklace over to these strangers.

"I know. It was so unfair the thing was given to you for safe keeping in the first place," Fulcanelli ranted loudly. "It must have been so much to have to guard and protect it all this time."

Her voice caught in her throat. She didn't understand what he knew about the necklace or why he was using such dramatic and protective language surrounding it. Naomie's gift and promise had meant so much to her, but what could it possibly mean to these men? And what else did they know?

She thought back to the afternoon she had first met Naomie as a child. The colorful caravan had arrived in town once again, and Penelope wandered down to welcome them and deliver her eggs. However, when she arrived, the camp was empty. She heard a commotion and looked around to see the weary travelers gathered down by the creek. They were frantically jumping and shouting at the water's edge. Naomie, with her dusky eyes and hair wrapped high upon her head, had fallen in the water and was struggling to stay afloat. Penelope dropped the eggs to the ground and ran into the water. Naomie was a few years older than Penelope. She was tall and solitary and reminded Penelope of a spindly mantis. She wore long dresses with elegant scarves that zig-zagged down along her long, thin legs. Today, Naomie was dressed in layer upon layer of bright scarves and silks and pushed Penelope away at first, so Penelope had difficulty grabbing her around the waist and drawing her toward shore.

Naomie coughed and spurted as the crowd slowly dispersed, leaving the two girls alone on the bank of the creek.

"How did you fall in?" Penelope asked.

"I saw something sparkly at the bottom of the pool," Naomie responded and looked away from Penelope.

"The water is quite beautiful," Penelope reassured her.

"My father and I call it The Jewel. It sparkles everywhere," Penelope continued, shaking the water from her hair, gesturing wildly with her arms to add emphasis to the inadequacy of her words. Shimmering white and gold light flashed from the pooling water in the sunshine.

"That's the one," Naomie responded, pointing to a glimmering rock at the bottom of the creek bed. She gestured and squinted.

Penelope looked to where the girl was pointing and dove back down into the creek. When she rose up again, she climbed out of the water and poured a handful of micah out over the large rock beside Naomie. She brushed her hands through her hair to squeeze out the water. "Look. It's like gold."

Naomie knelt down, picked up a piece of the small rock, and examined it.

"No, Penelope," she responded sharply. "Don't be mistaken. It's nothing like gold." She paused for a second. "This is fool's gold," Naomie said, staring blankly at her. "Don't waste your time. You must learn to know the difference."

"It looks just like gold though," Penelope said and rubbed the micah against her hair.

"No, it's very different, because, you see, gold is like

blood. It contains a part of everything essential in nature, but it's also dangerous because it makes people greedy." She stared intently at Penelope. "Real gold is both soft and hard. It's malleable. Fool's gold is flaky because of the sulphur. It's hard and will break rather than bend. In minerals, like people, these differences matter. You need to learn to tell them apart."

Penelope crumbled the micah into her hand and swirled it around with her fingers. She opened her mouth and licked her finger drawing a gold streak down the middle of her tongue. "It tastes like dirt."

"Why did you save me?" Naomie asked abruptly changing the subject. "You see . . . I didn't want to be rescued." She spoke sharply.

"You would have drowned then." Penelope spoke with a delicate concern.

"Yes, that was the plan because my father is going to sell me off in marriage to a nasty man." Naomie's father, was an older man with a long chin, and a thin, tufted beard wound into a sharp point. "My father is a traditional Romani. He will get paid a large bride-price for me."

As she spoke, Naomie fell to her knees in a suppliant prayer for help from Penelope or the creek.

"But you are barely older than I am!" Penelope exclaimed.

"He doesn't care, and once I am married, I will never see my family again." Naomie's eyes pooled with tears. "You wasted your time saving me because when you leave,

I will just jump in the water all over again," she concluded.

"Then why don't you just run away instead?"

"No, if I run away, I may find some worse situation than my own." Noamie cautioned and grasped the stone necklace that rest on her chest. The necklace's rope was a concentric arrangement, circles overlapping circles, countlessly shadowed in all directions, the intricacy of a burning candle.

Penelope paused for a moment, regarding Naomie's arresting pendant.

"I know I can think of a better solution than your death," Penelope pleaded. "Can you give me some more time though to come up with a good plan?"

Penelope would do anything for Naomie, and her letter's urgent request for Penelope to return the necklace to her brother was clear. She turned back towards Fulcanelli and hurriedly unclasped the necklace before she changed her mind. She pulled the rope from around her neck, releasing it gently to him.

It was the simple laws of alchemy—heat exists and all thermal systems always tend towards equilibrium. Penelope had studied these concepts and had orchestrated these experiments with her father. In her inscrutable heart, she knew she had come to France to hand over the necklace alongside the gold, but with Naomie missing, she felt the stifling oppression of her loneliness rise up.

"Here," she said, as she reluctantly withdrew her hand. She felt a prickling cold run through her fingers as they all gazed into Fulcanelli's palm. It could have been the reflection of the copper chandelier from the ceiling, but the necklace too seemed to have a heat, a pulse, and a soul's complexion.

Fulcanelli held it up like a prism, outlining its edges with his finger and handed it to Lucien with a prolonged and binding smile. Lucien held the necklace in his hands, unraveling the rope from around the stone. Molecular motion, touch, transmutation, the sensation of release overwhelmed her and Penelope was amazed by how quickly the carefully braided ropes of the knot fell away into disorder, releasing a simple rock. The stone was bright blue and dotted with spots. It was still stained with her blood from injuries past. The more she stared, the more she became frozen in her spot, watching it the way a scientist watches mercury fulminate, hoping it was less explosive than it felt.

Lucien turned and quickly stashed the stone within the same hole on the wall above his desk where he kept the papers. He released the stone the way a hand releases a hot coal to the fire.

The building swayed and warmed as Lucien returned the clock to the wall. The hole seemed to have an aptitude all its own to imbibe then imbue and swallow things down within its walls, causing the inward to turn outward. It seemed more mouth than hole, more belly than wall. What had she seen? Her vision wavered, her vessels contracted with tension and excitement.

"It's like poetry," Fulcanelli said to a man across the room. "The universe possesses so much magic. Put your ear to it and tune in. Energy, too, has a rhythm and a cadence."

She looked around and saw another man across the room from her constructing a flashlight that seemed to release a kaleidoscopic pulse.

Fulcanelli watched Penelope curiously studying the flashlight.

"His name is Professor Durand, and he hopes that when it is shined in an assailant's eyes, it will cause vertigo and nausea. Just think, a flashlight as a weapon," he explained, chuckling. "At least, we hope. After all, these are our scientific barracks," Fulcanelli turned back to her and gestured. "This is a war of science too. Please come, follow me," he said and ran to the charts that hung across the room.

"$\Gamma = (ZL - ZS)/(ZL + ZS)$," Fulcanelli quickly wrote on a chalkboard. "ZL is the load and ZS is the source," he concluded, as he hunkered down behind the boards, like a boy peeking out from behind a privet.

Penelope stepped towards him. It was the reflection coefficient. It measured the difference between the incident wave and the reflected wave. Penelope racked her mind for the answer.

"There are several other ways you can calculate that," she responded, though she really wanted to know where

Naomie had gone and if she was coming back. She had not yet asked enough questions about her beloved Naomie.

"I am so glad to see that your eyes are wide open to all of the possibilities," Fulcanelli smiled.

The room was a mix of things, a cauldron, cathodes, catheters, solutions of liquid and piles and piles of papers. It was a controlled chaos, a dormitory and a lab, a double-blind experiment of a long duration, and in the midst of it all, there was Lucien. He was wholly consumed once again in some project at a desk beneath the clock where he had hidden the stone. Like a scribe of some ancient text, he appeared to be translating words. There was a bundle of old, wrinkled papers stacked on his desk. They reminded Penelope of her father's alchemy book because they too were discolored and covered with rudimentary drawings and rough handwriting. A pen in his hand, he remained still as a stone, tucked in his adjacent corner and fully absorbed in his translation of these mysterious, crumpled and yellowed papers. He seemed indifferent to the chaos around him.

"I'm sorry, Penelope, excuse me for a moment," Fulcanelli said as he wandered across the room to grab a tool.

As she turned to watch Lucien again, his eyes shifted their focus from his papers to her. As he stared at her, his expression was fixed somewhere between anxiety, pleasure, and sorrow. His gaze was pure rapture.

"Chemistry is always changing," Fulcanelli said as he

returned to her side. He cast his iron gaze towards Lucien. "I can't believe it," he teased, laughing aloud. "Have you noticed how he watches you? He can't seem to look away. I've never seen Lucien distracted from his translating, not even for a moment." Fulcanelli twisted his ring on his finger once again. "He must be even more excited than I am to have you here. He's usually so caught up in his work that you'd think he was having a real conversation with Isaac Newton," he concluded. Fulcanelli smiled at Lucien. "In science, the point of view is always shifting and turning. Lucien is racing against the elements of war and science, trying to stay with the shift. We all are." Fulcanelli spoke with an almost fevered, sanguine anticipation.

"Then perhaps I can help him with the translations?" Penelope asked haltingly.

"We shall see," Fulcanelli responded with caution. "Perhaps."

A dazed sensation of euphoria soaked through Penelope as she watched Lucien. Fulcanelli could see that Penelope too could not turn away. Although she was an inveterate loner and a mystic, the touch of Lucien's eyes stirred a new and singular feeling within her. She could almost taste the sweet, slow melt of its confection. It was the word that she had forgotten, the opposite of loneliness. Pliant and soft, the distance between them drew her in more deeply.

She felt a natural curiosity about the papers too and Lucien's devotion to them. As he returned to his work, Lucien seemed utterly caught within the web of his own thoughts. The whole curvature of his body huddled above the papers and balanced there, like condensation. But his hands were molten, intently gliding from scribbled word to scribbled word. He appeared to touch them all at once. His movements, both lithe and gritty, stirred her. As she stood in silence, she felt unfamiliar questions crystallize within her.

Fulcanelli cleared the hoarse croak from his throat, and she turned back to him abruptly. Fulcanelli was her teacher, and there was no time for self-reflection. Already he was asking her to determine the number of particles per unit volume. Did they move from weaker to stronger parts of the field, or would they move from stronger parts to weaker ones? He was asking her, and she didn't yet know the answer.

Chapter Four

Fulcanelli's scientific skills were so renowned by this time that the German and the Allied armies wanted to benefit from what he knew. He was an aristocrat, an architect, an engineer, and a chemist, and he was spoken of with reverence, adding a great mystery to his existence.

He slurped down his cold, sugared coffee and looked up at Penelope's equations. "Take a break and rest for a moment. The questions should be simple, my dear."

She had already learned in her first few weeks of living at 52 rue Laffitte how Fulcanelli enjoyed speaking in riddles. The apartment itself twisted up two levels like a maze. Penelope scratched her head and looked out at the rain falling down outside of the window. The streets of Paris were silent.

Penelope and Fulcanelli watched a stray dog nose his way down an alley. A few moments later, a young girl scurried down the street alone, clutching an oversized bag to her chest. She stumbled on the cobblestones as she hurried by.

Penelope turned to Fulcanelli, "Do you think that little girl needs help?" she spoke with a high pitch of concern in her voice.

"I doubt it," he replied.

"So you do not think she is a runaway? It is raining outside, and she wasn't even wearing a coat."

"No, most likely she is running as fast as she can back to her apartment after an errand because she is just as scared as the rest of us," he stared at her blankly. "If you ran after her and tried to help her, it would only draw attention, and you would most likely scare her even more."

Penelope wanted to argue back, but she worried he was right. She sighed. "I think that girl is the first child I have seen since I arrived in Paris," she said. "Where are all of the children?"

Fulcanelli looked back at her with distracted concern.

"Most children are not allowed outside of their apartment or their families have sent them out of Paris altogether."

Fulcanelli's mind had abruptly shifted to another thought. "Get back to your equations while I go fetch us some coffee." Fulcanelli said then turned back to Penelope "And while I'm gone, don't get any ideas about running after that little girl. Some runaways don't want to be rescued." he joked, shuffling out the door of the main room, down the hall to the kitchen.

Penelope looked out the window at the street again in search of the young girl and remembered the first time Naomie ran away from her home in Tennessee. She had asked Penelope to go along with her.

Penelope was only ten then, and her skin was as unblemished and translucent as tissue and her eyes were a burning, pale copper that always seemed to be peering out from behind something large and in the way. She had the thick, wild hair of a lion.

The girls had packed a small bag in the middle of the night. They met along the main road and followed Naomie's cousin Manfri down along the train tracks to the dense forest at the edge of Sweetwater. Manfri, with his bald head, broad, gap-toothed smile, and a sparse goatee, was huddled with a group of a travelers, waiting there for the next slow train to ease on up the hill.

Penelope watched as her friend Naomie chased her cousin and swung her bag at him, the two of them laughing. Teasing, Penelope knew, was a potent form of love. She looked up and down the empty railroad tracks, feeling the prickle of excitement rise up in her. The coalescence of her fear and excitement reached down into the depths of Penelope. She thought she could help her friend Naomie break free from her cruel father, but she worried about her own kind, lonely, widowed father sleeping soundly at home.

"Where are we going and when are we coming back?" Penelope whispered naively through the night air, wringing out her hands in despair. Naomie reached for her and Penelope leaned her head onto Naomie's shoulder. The two girls were nearly inseparable.

Penelope's face was crowded with worry over her friend's predicament.

"I won't be my father's prisoner anymore," Naomie reassured her.

They heard a distant train whistle and the small crowd of drifters formed a line. As the train slowly approached, one by one, the travelers scrambled up onto the front ladder of the last boxcar as it was pulling through. Penelope stuck close to the back of the rattling car. She sat near to Manfri and Naomie and listened to the other travelers' chatter about finding work. As the train rolled out of Sweetwater, Penelope could feel the velvet scent of the thick forest wash over her.

"You see, riding the trains is an art," Manfri said.

As Manfri was explaining the rules of the road to his cousin, Penelope shuffled closer and wiped her tired eyes with her arm.

He spoke up so she could hear better. "First of all, you girls need to understand the difference between a hobo, a tramp, and a bum."

"What's that?" Naomie asked.

"A hobo travels for work," Manfri responded.

"That's you then," Penelope said, and he shook his head.

"No, I am a traveling dancer," he replied.

Penelope felt confused, "But—"

"A dancer is a little different than a hobo," he interjected. "And a tramp travels but won't work."

"What about a bum?" Naomie pursed her lips.

"A bum won't travel or work," Manfri said.

Penelope was absorbing it all. "What are we then?" Penelope asked her friend.

Naomie shrugged.

"Runaways?"

"Hobos don't like to stay in the same place too long, and they don't live a certain way just because everybody else does, or someone tells them to."

"Well, I like that," Naomie said, her eyes brightening.

Penelope scooted in closer and sat steady as a stone.

Manfri took a long sip from his jar of clear liquor and began again, "There's some simple rules to remember about the trains though, to keep safe. First, when you catch a boxcar, jump for the front ladder. If you jump on the one at the rear and miss, you fall between the cars and under the train." He scratched his head. "And you'll die."

He continued with tips on how to sleep while standing up, how to avoid getting locked in a boxcar, how to ride on the exterior of the cars, how to judge when a train is about to leave, how to read the hobo signs and, most importantly, how to avoid the bulls.

"The bulls are mercenaries hired by the railroad to keep us off."

"Like railroad police?"

He nodded.

"The bulls," Penelope whispered over and over again to herself as the train picked up speed, racing farther and farther from Sweetwater.

Penelope heard the clatter of a plate drop from Lucien's desk to the floor. She wandered over to him, gently approaching his mess of papers.

"Is everything okay?" she asked.

Once again, he had barely eaten his lunch that was now splayed across the hardwood floor. She reached down to clean up the mess.

"Do you want me to fix you another plate?" she asked.

He shook his head no and drew his hand to his forehead. "I can't. I can barely swallow it down," he replied.

She looked at him with concern and was about to respond but he interrupted her.

"Can I ask you a question?" Lucien asked visibly frustrated.

"Certainly."

"What does it smell like in here to you?" he asked gesturing at the apartment.

Penelope smiled and laughed.

"With so many of us living in close proximity, I guess it depends on the day," she replied. "Sometimes it smells like a cave, sometimes like a bathroom. Mostly though, it smells like smoke and warm bread."

"I see," he said.

"Why do you ask? Does it really matter?"

His face was tense with concern. "I suppose there is still a bakery in the building beside us, but, lately, I can't smell the difference. I am terribly bothered to think so, but it's like my olfactory senses are broken."

"Or maybe they are just jumbled," she said. "It can happen."

She looked around the room. "What about this?" she reached to the table behind her and lifted an ashtray to his nose. "Do you smell anything?"

He shook his head from side to side slowly.

"Nothing," he concluded sniffing the air around it.

She looked around the room again.

"How about this?" she drew a half-empty cup of coffee beneath his nose.

He shook his head. "I don't understand what's wrong. It scares me to lose one of my senses like this."

"Here, step over here, sit down, and close your eyes," she gestured to the couch. "I think I can help. Just give me a minute." Penelope wandered table to table, grabbing things as she went—a bundle of tea leaves, a candle wick, and a wooden box. One by one, she waved the items beneath his nostrils. He seemed indifferent to the changes, so she lifted the crook of his elbow to his nose.

"Now breathe in deeply several times," she urged him.

He breathed in his own scent and exhaled a sympathetic hum.

"Okay, now wait a minute and let's try once more," she said lifting his arm again, then waving the cup of coffee beneath his nose.

His eyes opened wide with delight. "There it is! I can smell something!" he exclaimed. "How did you do that?"

"It's a simple trick I learned from my father in his laboratory. The smell of your own scent creates a sort of baseline habituation. It resets our brains somehow."

Lucien stared at her in distant wonder. "I am speechless," he said, holding her gaze. "Thank you," he concluded and leaned forward through the veil of her hair to hug her. As he pulled her close, he seemed to draw in the delicate scent of her neck. Her eyes widened as he narrowed his breath so close to her skin, almost but not quite touching her. She froze in the intimacy of the moment, and when he finally drew away from her, he exhaled a deep and full-throated hum. The noise sent a twisting, warm pleasure up through her chest, along her neck, and cast a tingling, red flush into her cheeks.

"Perfect," was then all that he said and some part of her surrendered.

They stood quietly together until Fulcanelli broke in. "I've returned," he proclaimed. "Here is your warm coffee." He handed it to her.

When she finally mustered the courage to turn back towards Lucien, he was stationed back at his desk, once again working feverishly over the translation of Newton's papers. A man on the other side of him was building a giant magnifying glass to write messages onto grains of rice as a means of discreetly passing information. Another scientist made origami planes out of Resistance propaganda, folding the paper over and over again on itself. He then flew the planes across the room and measured the distance. Yet another scientist carved and hollowed out decorative woodcarvings. He would then mix explosives to stuff inside his wooden trivets to place near railroads. The residents of the apartment were looking for both large and small, yet vital, ways to disrupt the Germans. One pharmacist concocted an itching powder and a deodorant to cause a blistering rash. He planned to distribute his goods directly to the German soldiers.

Day after day, mysterious and primitive people came and went at 52 rue Laffitte. They carried the iron tools of lapidaries, band saws, trim saws, grinders, engraving secret laws into gems—all of them enveloped in the drama of the silent, scientific war. They called themselves the Royal Society.

"To think continually," seemed to be the motto. They rarely ate or slept; nothing could divert them. A whole carnival of ideas and experiments were welcomed there, no idea too great or too small. And when a discovery was made, they moved on quickly to the next task. There was no time to waste. The war held them all together in this great effort of scientific subversion to the Occupation.

"Okay then," she asked Fulcanelli, "Was mathematics invented or discovered?"

"Penelope, first you must step back a minute." Fulcanelli's glasses joggled on top of his head as he spoke. "Understand that nothing within the universe is as it appears to be."

He led her over to his worktable. Small birds carved from different pieces of wood were scattered among maps, books and disorder. "Alchemy is science as much as intuition, and it is always the simplest answer."

"Okay, then let's take a simple parabola, for example. Any object thrown, travels in a parabola. From the beginning of time, it has been this way and it's not just any arch. It is always the same specific mathematical criteria."

Fulcanelli pointed to the sky. "Only in Euclidean geometry," he said. "The missiles travel in that same arched curve. That is an observable geometry. Call it God. Call it science. It is observable and easy to replicate. It was there before math. How is this not as it seems?" he continued.

"But Galileo didn't account for the Earth's curve," she said, challenging him. "Only Newton did. By the same principal, a bullet shot and a bullet dropped will reach the ground at the same time. That truth was hidden there too, in the same line of thinking, in the same observations. What else could be there so visible that we just can't see it?"

"So what is it then?

"Neither, both. Mathematics is both abstraction and persistence."

"But why?"

"Because the universe is always in motion."

She looked at the ground.

"Try a chemical garden." He brushed the wooden birds to the side. "When you add copper sulfate or iron sulfate to water glass, something unexpected happens."

Water glass was a glassy mass of fluid, clear lotion, neither liquid nor solid. She picked up the brimming beaker that was filled halfway with it and examined the specimen like a primate. First smell, then touch, then taste. Penelope liked things that were primary, yet neither normal nor expected. Fulcanelli took the jar from her hand and poured it into the iron sulfate.

She rested her chin on the table and nodded as she watched the colorful plants emerge and begin to grow upward in the solution.

"It's the same way ice emerges from water or syrup drips out from our trees," she observed. "Life can't help but ooze out from places."

He smiled down at her, and she leaned in towards the jars. The towers of life swayed in the water, rising and dividing, as though they were real plants in real bloom. "A crystal garden," Penelope said, continuing to marvel as she gazed steadily through the glass container.

"Make no mistake," he said finally. "Alchemy is full of

miracles." He shook the jar of towering crystals, breaking them into swirling bits and pieces, "It can also topple monarchies." Some of the towers involuntarily fell to the bottom of the jar and others toppled against one another like pretzels piled up and down on themselves.

"Then what of truth? What does alchemy say about truth?" Her eyes were transfixed on the swaying water.

"War is an unnatural vibration, but truth is a natural vibration." This time his words washed over the room, the walls taut with tension. "Well, for instance in music, let's take the note of C minor," he continued. "That note is the anthem of heroic struggle and emotional force. Take Beethoven's Symphony No. 5."

He began to hum the piece, then walked to the piano and started to play while continuing to speak, "It's a narrative about heroic struggle. From C minor all the way to C-major coda. It's the vibrational furnace that heats. It's the triumph of the hero." He played on while she listened.

"Do you hear it getting faster and louder? Such insistence. Such nobility," he continued.

Penelope closed her eyes to listen.

"You see, the key of C minor does its job perfectly here. Now go to the window and look out at the street."

Penelope walked to the window and looked out at the shrunken and silent city.

"What do you see?"

"I see sidewalks, streets, apartments, shops, buses, parks, cafes. I see three men standing in front of our building. I see armored vehicles parked in the streets. I see foreign soldiers and bureaucrats."

Her heart leapt into a parabolic orbit, as Lucien moved to the window close beside her. He was there, standing with his fixed gaze and arms crossed. She met his eyes with hers, and he reached to rest his arm across her shoulders. The sensation of his touch trickled down her back like warm water.

Fulcanelli closed his eyes and continued to play. His hands and body moved through the air almost weightlessly. "What do you feel now?" he offered.

She paused. "I think it's hope," she said, wondering aloud.

"The song's beauty and importance make it the perfect backdrop to the war. But why?"

"Because of its emotional force," Lucien began.

"Exactly, but why? Or more important, how?"

"Mathematics, meter?" Penelope asked, but she was more confused than ever.

"Think, Penelope," Fulcanelli blurted out. "We don't have time for this. You see, humans are the weakest of all of the animals because we so rarely see a clear purpose for ourselves. A fish is born to swim, a bird to fly. We travel, we learn from our elders, we learn from books, from mentors, and we discover truth as it comes available, but it is never readied for us on a spoon." With that he twisted the ring on his finger as he spoke. "You are a dancer and a talented mathematician and alchemist. You see the world in movement, numbers, and formulas. Beethoven saw the world through the math of music. It was his journey of how and why." Fulcanelli's complexion became marbled, and his speech stuttered by the force of his emotion. "True alchemists don't learn to turn noble metals into gold simply to become rich, they do it to discover gold themselves." His wild eyes were on her, and she felt as if the room had begun to spin.

He rose from the piano, and Lucien retreated to his desk.

Penelope felt tears brimming in her eyes and moved away from them both.

"This is too much, perhaps." His brow knit with concern. "Please sit. You look weary."

"And what about your sister Naomie?" Penelope deigned to ask once again. "I came to Paris to find her and she is gone. Where is she? Why won't you tell me where she has gone?" she cried out to him. Tears poured down her face.

Fulcanelli paused, shook his head, and handed a cup to her. She looked over at Lucien. She had felt him glance her way with question and concern. But he hesitated, and then returned abruptly to his work.

"I can't discuss this with you now," he said, still shaking his head.

"You always say that," Penelope swallowed down her tears angrily.

Fulcanelli turned and walked back to the piano.

After a few moments, Penelope took a slow sip from the

cup and found the taste was floral and spicy. She drank it down. "Mulled wine," she burst out.

"You have had this drink before?" Fulcanelli asked.

She nodded, "With your sister perhaps." She wandered back to the piano. Naomie had not been alone in her love of this special drink. For Fulcanelli as well, it offered relief.

"Only we know life has a flavor," he said, smiling and winking.

"Naomie always said that the earth spins like a toy top, and if you drink too much, you start to feel the spin too intensely."

"To my dear sister Naomie, and to the great spin," Fulcanelli toasted Beethoven, Naomie, and the shrunken, gray horizon of the occupied city.

Chapter Five

The stone from the necklace was a heterotroph, and Penelope could hear it howling from behind the clock-covered walls. The sound was a high frequency, like the scratching of an animal, and it kept her awake in the strange apartment. She wandered from her bed to the lab. There was a flickering candle and though, at this late hour, she could not hear anyone, Lucien was stationed in his chair, with his back to her, writing and petting a small bird as it hopped along his desk. He was wearing a dark blazer and his hair was shaggy. She spotted him as he affectionately chided the bird with his finger while it stepped across his beloved papers. She cleared her throat so she wouldn't startle him, but he had already cast his gaze across his shoulder. He always seemed to sense Penelope before he saw her, and the effect was immediate and galvanic. Lucien's neck flushed, and he turned speechlessly to fully face her.

Gray-eyed and handsome, his appearance was deftly balanced by an unnamed solemnity, like a castaway or soldier. By the looks of him, it was clear that he had endured some calamity which he could not shake.

"I'm sorry, but do you hear it?" she asked, breaking the silence.

He had no response, so he just watched her cautiously.

"That horrible noise?" she asked.

He raised his hand to his mouth and still said nothing, watching her ponderously. He seemed to be wandering somewhere in his mind, motionless, just out of reach, close but so far.

"Can you at least bring me the stone?"

"I'm sorry," he said at last. "Why would you need it?"

His voice was low and pleasant. He placed the small bird in its cage alongside his desk.

"Because I can't bear the noise any longer. Can't you hear it?"

He shook his head, "No, I hear nothing at all."

She gritted her teeth in frustration.

"Here," she said, covering his eyes with her hands and pleading once again. "Listen."

His whole body seemed to lean into the warmth of her delicate touch, enveloping him almost completely in the charcoal of the night air.

He waited a moment before tensely laughing and said,

"I think I do now."

It was bleating and high, a noise with an animal's cadence. Lucien walked over to the wall and reached behind the clock into the hole, moving his arm around and around until he found it. He pulled the stone from the plaster and laid it on his desk beside the crumpled papers.

The room was dusky, but the stone seemed to rattle and blather like a teapot releasing its steam. "What is happening?" Lucien asked, taking a half step back and brushing his hand along his neck.

Penelope stepped towards the stone and touched it with her fingertips. This seemed to console it, but when she lifted her hand away, the noise began again. The stone was uncomfortable and hot, with a low tremor and neither Lucien nor Penelope knew how best to settle it fully. She picked it up and pulled it against her chest.

"Perhaps it's cold," she said aloud. She huddled her hand over the stone to insulate it. She looked up at Lucien who was watching her.

His eyes were absorbing and boyish. He seemed amused, pulling a handkerchief from his pocket.

"A blanket, perhaps."

It was the first time she had seen him fully smile.

She snatched the handkerchief from his grasp, smiling back at him and carefully swaddled the stone before returning it to her chest, laughing and rocking it like a newborn baby. The beat of her heart seemed to soothe it. "It's lost its light," Penelope said as she peered down at the stone with concern. When she first touched it, she had felt its heat and seen its luminescent glow, but now it had dimmed from turquoise to a dull blue. It felt more regular, like a nondescript and simple stone, nothing pulsing, nothing alive.

"Shall I get some water?" he asked.

"Perhaps."

He was standing so close beside her that she could feel his body's warmth. It was simple conduction, she told herself, that made her shake a little. He ran off to the kitchen and returned with a glass. She reached for it, but her trembling hand fumbled, and it dropped, shattering loudly on the floor, spreading shards of glass and water in all directions. Penelope gasped and dropped to her knees, sweeping up the glass with her free hand.

"Stop. Stop," Lucien pleaded. "Let me get a broom."

By the time he came back, she was bleeding. Shards of glass sprouted out of her hand like the quills of a porcupine.

"You have to be more careful," he scolded as he pulled the glass from her fingers. "All of the doctors are in hiding or with the soldiers. There is no one to sew you."

She looked up at him, at the brooding look on his face. She felt an inward confusion in the moment. While her hand throbbed with the pain of the cuts, she felt a peculiar, inward delight at his attention. "They aren't deep," she said as she placed the rock on the desk beside her. He reached forward and brushed the hair from her face, gently tucking it behind her ear.

"Here, hold your hand in the light," he murmured.

She kept her hand hovering above the stone but in the candlelight. He retrieved tweezers from his drawer to remove the pieces of glass from her hand. He had to change the position of her palm to get to ones that were resisting. A tiny flume of blood fell from the tip of her finger to the stone below—and like a spongy mollusk, its asymmetrical pores absorbed the blood. The change was so subtle at first, they hardly noticed. But then the stone turned from a grayish blue to turquoise and bronze. What they saw next broke all of the laws that they knew of science. The stone acted as if it had been woken up, and a brocade of vessels, like silver thread along the seam of a quilt, began vibrating with a heat, and the handkerchief fell away like a bandage. They felt the air turn static around them.

"What's happening?" Penelope asked.

Lucien was still holding her wounded hand and didn't speak for a few moments.

"I've never seen anything like this before" was all that he could say, still touching her.

Penelope's hand was barely bleeding, but a few more drops fell onto the stone. This time the rock's surface seemed to crackle like the sun with the faint smell of a lemon.

"It's the blood," she observed.

The candle flickered as the stone continued to transform itself.

Lucien stared intently at the strange actions of the

stone. Neither of them could muster a word, and the more they stood together holding hands, the more aware they were of the heat that was exchanged between them.

Penelope's palm was throbbing now, and the cuts were inflamed. She winced as he squeezed her hand tightly.

"I'm so sorry," he said. He lowered her hand to touch the stone and said, "Here, try this." She was surprised that instead of feeling like a hard surface, it felt fluid to her touch, like grabbing the soft middle of a pillow. But when she looked down, the stone was dry and hard.

"The rock feels watery, like mercury, to the touch," she gasped and fought the urge to pull her arm away.

They watched her hand as the inflammation of her cuts shrunk into nothing, the way the waves left by a pebble thrown in a pond dissipate and then disappear. The longer she stayed touching the stone, the more the lacerations faded into the horizon of her hand. First, they became shadows and then slowly, no more. She started to cry, and he drew her hand away from the stone into his embrace, letting the fiery sensation subside. Their eyes remained fixed on the stone, huddled together, and Penelope was shaking with fear and excitement.

"Hold still," he said, as he lifted and wiped her hand with the handkerchief. "It's amazing." He couldn't find a sufficient word. He hoisted her off of the ground to him, his hand still holding hers, his other arm steadying her waist.

"How strange" was all she could think to say.

"Confounding," he responded, releasing her abruptly, uncertain of what had just happened.

They turned from each other back to the stone.

"It's gone quiet now. I don't hear the hum any longer."

"Perhaps we should put it away," he added, softly.

She nodded, and he wrapped the stone in the handkerchief and tucked it away in the wall behind the clock.

She was delirious with fatigue and wonder, but she did not want to go back to the dormitory room. She didn't want to leave Lucien. The night possessed an innocent, magnetic pleasure to it that she found new and consuming. She looked down at his desk.

"What are you studying here?" she asked.

"I am translating some of Newton's papers," he said. "Specifically, the idea of radioactive decay. There is life in things that seem inanimate. It's just that the language is so coded that the translation is . . . "

"Impossible?" she asked.

He nodded, smiling, "slow."

"I understand. I am self-taught from my father's books and piles of other, old books from his study. I was so bored that I read them over and over again, cover to cover. My favorite one was Newton's *Philosophiæ Naturalis Principia Mathematica*. For some reason, it came easily to me. I felt at home with the subject matter." She paused reflecting for a moment, "I think I could help you if you will trust me."

Once again, the air knotted between them. It could have been his intellect, or perhaps the violence of the war, but it was clear from the crowded look upon his face that Lucien did not trust anyone. He was smart and proud, but more than anything, he seemed to move with the plumb and stiff deportment of a soldier.

She had found Newton's *Principia* in her childhood home. In her father's lab there had been books, stacks and stacks of them. Books about basic math, about geometry, and about calculus; ancient books, crinkled and leather bound. There were also journals and diaries with looping letters filled with the excitement of cursive and time spent ruminating, stories about her father's more bizarre scientific experiments. The journals contained his drawings of alchemical symbols, of the anthropomorphic properties of base metals, of herbs, and the faces of other ancient scientists.

After her father had died, Penelope had come to understand his esoteric journals more fully. She discovered that loneliness, like the metals depicted in his drawings, was a basic element of life and it had a distinct odor and a flavor, the smell of a soggy basement, a bitter root buried so deeply. She also found that it was best to wear her loneliness like an enamel. There was no persuading lonely. It just was. It was greedy. It motivated people to act in strange ways, like a hardened fever whose only salve was a tender and uncomplicated love.

Since she left Tennessee, she was alone but for science

and math. The number one was lonely, but 1+1= 2, she felt deeply. She liked addition far more than subtraction, and basic math was unchanging. There were whole numbers, Roman numerals, prime numbers, fractions, decimals, ratio and proportion, percent, measurement, sequences, patterns, and graphs. And she loved geometry. The angles of a triangle add up to 180 degrees, always, every time, no matter how many times she did it. Shapes stay where you put them. They were unmovable and unmoving. Penelope liked it that way. The ruler and compass became like an extension of her. As a young girl, she would go to the creek and draw beautiful flowers and trees, the mathematical symmetry of nature intoxicating beyond what her father, Naomie, or any book about science and alchemy had told her.

"*Principia* is my favorite as well," Lucien noted with interest. "What was it that you loved about it?"

Penelope reflected for a moment. "I loved it because I had never learned how to deal with things in motion. I was familiar and comfortable with a fixed world, not the one around me that was ever-changing. How fast, how far? *Principia* held a study of change. I like how it described how calculus could explain planetary motion, the shape of fluids, the earth, and the motion of things." She continued, "Its language challenged my sense of what was possible in the world. What about you?"

Lucien began, "I like how the book is made up of obtuse writing, and rambling equations. I have read it over and over again. When I was younger, I did not have many friends and had not taken on the true language of the world, so to me, Newton's tome became a good, good friend. I felt I understood him," he observed. "Because of the Great Plague that had ravaged Europe, Isaac Newton had been forced to return home to study, and during this time he invented calculus, developed his theory of light and color, and published *Principia*. I, too, was a loner." Lucien recognized that he shared with Newton an abject solitude that fueled big questions.

Penelope pushed Lucien's arm to the side and examined the papers. For both Lucien and Penelope, knowledge was their greatest companion. Lucien was deciphering a small, lost collection of twenty or so pages of Newton's esoteric papers, which Fulcanelli had found in a library years ago and stashed away in his pocket. He and Lucien had spent nearly a decade trying to translate them, but the words were dense and jumbled like a puzzle. Penelope's eyes lit up with focus and slid from the papers to Lucien's notes again and again. There was a familiar intimacy to Newton's handwriting and drawings.

"I believe this symbol is a notation for home," she said, pointing to the tomblike drawing on the crumpled papers. "You have indicated cemetery, but I believe the word is home."

He seemed alert and impressed, almost eager, "I must check with Fulcanelli before we can continue. These are very unique papers and I must ask his permission to share them with you." He drew his pen into his hand and wrote the word "home" along the margin of his notes. Penelope liked the rigid smallness of his handwriting. The letters fell tightly along the page like the compact script of a typewriter.

"And where is your home?" she asked.

The word had a disposition.

"In the north," he replied. "My mother and sister still live there." His tragic look told her that Lucien, too, had experienced loss. It was something in the withdrawn and furrowed look of his forehead. "My mother is a seamstress, my sister a nurse. And you?"

"My family is gone," she said.

He looked at her, perplexed.

"I lost my mother the day I was born, and my father died before I left Tennessee," she concluded. "Everyone I've ever loved seems to slip through my fingers . . . " she added, fumbling with the papers on his desk. Her sorrow knotted around her throat. She looked down at the papers. "Except Newton, in mathematics—if all of the senses are diverted, the numbers remain."

Lucien frowned with concern and nodded gently, pulling bread and cheese from his drawer and offering her a plate.

She continued, "It seems the whole premise of the Royal Society is the belief that the numbers and science will help us prevail over the Germans. For Fulcanelli, it seems to be a race of math and physics as much as it is a race of tanks."

Lucien listened with a curious patience that comforted her.

She checked her hand, touching the places where the stone had erased the wounds. It was fully healed, as though it had never even happened.

"Math doesn't really explain what transpired with the stone though," she observed.

"Alchemy does," Lucien stated. "The Philosopher's Stone, *Chryspoeia*, the Elixir of Life, all alchemists agree that it exists even though they disagree about what it is and how to make it. They say it is made from the four elements, and when they come together, that is the precise, mystical place where alchemy diverges from pure science. Newton spent his private life seeking out this knowledge. Fulcanelli too."

As he looked at her and continued to speak, he reached forward to touch her hand. Penelope felt the potent unrest of Lucien's gaze, both languid and mineral like the stone.

Chapter Six

The stone from the necklace stayed safely hidden behind the clock in Fulcanelli's apartment. Penelope had come to realize that she missed the mysterious rock necklace and felt a sense of loneliness without it. In the silence, important questions had emerged. What had become of her life in Tennessee? Like everything, that too had slipped from her grasp, and every time she thought of it and her uncertainty about Naomie's whereabouts, she felt the crushing rush of blood to her head, like a stifling migraine rattling up and down her neck. Yet every time she brought Naomie up to Fulcanelli, he abruptly left the room.

She spent most days in Fulcanelli's office reflecting on Naomie's distant and troubled life in America. She considered how Naomie, like Fulcanelli, ran away from things.

She remembered when they had jumped the train out of Sweetwater together, Naomie running from her father. Penelope was so young then, and she remembered how town by town the boxcar filled with more people, all talking about the latest stories.

Looking out the slats of the train car, Penelope spotted the hobo signs littered along the rails: two shovels meant work was available, a face perched in the crease of an X meant a doctor, and squiggled teeth suggested a fierce dog. The sparse language of the road was everywhere. She heard it in their spoken stories as well. So many of their tales were polished with liquor, and everyone had one.

The style and tendency of the stories, as it happens, drove the logic of the hobo's language. It was strictly utilitarian—about safety, work, food, and shelter and happened in as few words as possible.

The language of science and the war was similarly sparse and coded, so Penelope poured herself headlong into the familiar experiments Fulcanelli had left splayed out and half-finished on his desk. She stood quietly measuring and heating materials for an experiment Fulcanelli had started from her father's alchemy book.

So focused on properly preparing the solvent for the

experiment, she hardly noticed Lucien approach. "You're more fascinating than anyone I have ever met," Lucien whispered quite simply, stepping close beside her.

There was a prolonged and uncomfortable silence. She had thought it was Fulcanelli returning to his office to help her prepare the solvent and was surprised to see it was, instead, Lucien standing there watching her. His words sparked some unfamiliar feeling within her, and she swallowed it down in a nervous gulp.

"That can't be true," Penelope replied, her mind was turbulent and her words barely audible.

Lucien was not only a mathematician; he was an alchemist. A refugee, with dark circles hanging like crescent moons beneath his eyes, from having spent four long years during his childhood living under the boot of World War I, he had a look of sad intensity about him. The violence in his own town of Somme had been shattering, his town's innocence all but consumed, melted down like the metals the military mined from their hometown and repurposed to rule over them.

"Words matter to me so I mean what I say," he explained, turning to reach for her hand, but the clock above him chimed loudly, startling them both.

Penelope looked up at Lucien, shaking internally and somewhat tongue-tied. She didn't know how to express what she felt in her heart, so she turned her attention to the clock, concentrating for a long time.

"I wonder, have you ever noticed that this clock is out

of beat?" Penelope responded at last, her eyes filled with purpose, a pinkish tint now clouding her complexion. She pointed to the banjo-shaped, walnut clock that hung on the wall above Fulcanelli's desk.

"I don't understand, what you mean?" he answered immediately, looking at the clock with a renewed curiosity.

"I mean that the clock is going tock-tick, tock-tick instead of tick tock, tick tock," Penelope said, as she turned towards the clock.

"I've never known it to be any different than that," Lucien added. He stood still as marble, staring at Penelope with a sort of blanched immobility. It had never occurred to him that time also mandated a chime and a perfect pitch.

"It is so quiet in Paris that my hearing has become particularly strong," Penelope observed.

Lucien looked directly at her distinct and distant gaze. She was arresting, something exceptional to behold. Her eyes were a shade of copper that reminded him of the precise way clouds can reflect the changing light of the evening, and for Lucien, she possessed that unmistakable and searing wilderness, the kind that sets fixed things free.

"Thanks for telling me. What can I do about it?" Lucien said.

"It's easy. Well . . . first, do you have a matchbox?" she replied with emphasis.

Lucien leaned over and reached into a drawer.

Penelope rose up mechanically and grasped the box from his hand, turning to slide the matchbook under the left side of the clock. The pendulum swerved, then the clock settled into a regular rhythm. Lucien stood and watched in awe.

"Ha!" Lucien laughed out loud. "You did it! A matchbook is all it took. It couldn't have been any easier." He looked at Penelope, his mouth wide with wonderment and surprise.

"Tick tock, tick tock," Penelope sang along, smiling. "You know, you can do so many things, but you cannot halt the passing of time," Penelope remarked, as she poured the contents of Fulcanelli's experiment from one flask into another. "If we stopped time, we would, quite simply, lose our bearings," she continued as she closed her father's book—which was filled with various recipes— and set to mixing more things in bottles. "And time has a definitive rhythm."

The title of her father's book was engraved *Ex nihilo nihil fit.* Nothing comes from nothing.

"Yes, then that means time must come from something," Lucien pronounced, pointing at the book's cover. "Or someone."

Penelope's eyes widened, swelling with aggravation.

"What do you think the drawing below it means?" she asked. "It is a man and a woman at the base of a tree." She traced the image with her finger. "The tree sprouts into many branches above them, and there are words on the leaves of the branches."

"Oh, yes, that one is fundamental. That one is a picture

of the four elements, of fire, air, water, and earth." Lucien reached out to the table and pulled the jars of salt, mercury and sulfur towards him. "The balance of male and female." He held out a jar of sulphur. "Sulphur is the male element." In his other hand, he held the mercury. "And mercury is the female. If you balance them perfectly, you have health and harmony. You can achieve pure gold."

Penelope leaned over the elixir that was bubbling and steaming on the counter, "How long does this concoction need to boil?" She turned her face away from the rancid smell of the steam.

Lucien drew the recipe book near to him and opened it again, unbending a fold in the page and pointing his finger at the text.

Penelope's eyes narrowed on the scribbled writing, "It says something about boiling it until the bitterness is released, but I don't see anything that says how long that will take."

"Sometimes it is more rapid and sometimes it is less rapid. It depends on so many things. Are you bored with this already?" he asked with a low tone of humor.

"Not at all," she replied. "Card games are boring to me. No, I'm filled with anticipation. I am just impatient to learn." Her eyes were wide and nervous.

Lucien responded, "A lot of alchemy is about waiting. Time can vary pretty dramatically with these potions. You cannot become overeager and rush the process. There are a lot of factors that affect the rate of change in the potions, the temperature of the air, the humidity, the concentration of ingredients, even the type of heat used can play a role. Are you having second thoughts?"

"None at all," she concluded, casting her eyes at him. "It's just that sometimes this book seems less like a prescription for tonics and medicines and more like a cookbook." She flipped through the pages. "What's the difference between alchemy and fixing a meal?" Penelope spoke in a teasing yet defiant tone, her fist pressed firmly to her hip.

"Well, think of it," Lucien said. "Yes, alchemy began in the kitchen. It's the heat that transforms things for cooks and alchemists. But then the paths diverged. Alchemists did things like use heat to transform sand into glass, and cooks used spices and heat to create flavor."

"But who are they? Who are these mysterious alchemists?" Penelope continued, now leaning into the wall beside the clock.

"They are artists, scientists, doctors, farmers, soldiers, anyone. We are all alchemists in a way." He pointed out the window to the people on the street. "You can never tell. It's really anyone who wants to know about transformation and discovery. And there have been lots of unexpected discoveries along the way by unexpected people. Alchemists can boil certain plants to make stains and dyes. They can marry metals."

"Is it primarily about function then?"

"Sometimes, it is. But most profoundly, it is about the state of the soul."

Penelope paused to ready her tongue, realizing that she had so many unuttered questions gathering within her. "How does metal have anything to do with the soul?" Penelope pursed her lips.

"I have a friend who is inventing invisible ink for use in the Resistance and another who is trying to figure out how to calculate the weight of a soul. There are so many beautiful and varied questions to ask about the world. Wouldn't you say that there is no remedy for the heart's imagination?" Reaching out, he swept the hair from Penelope's eyes. "And thank goodness there's not. Our infinite curiosity defines us. Questions are what haunt alchemists the most, and the questions are limitless, especially when it comes to the laws of nature and disease."

His words crowded the office, hanging in the air just above the clinking, bubbling of the steaming bottles.

"Then what of Naomie's magical stone?" Penelope grumbled, her eyes cutting towards Lucien in a diagonal gaze.

Lucien pretended he hadn't heard her and grasped a cylinder filled with some chalky powder. The word "thistle" was engraved on the outside, and he handed it over to Penelope along with a vile of some cobalt liquid.

"Enough questions. Go find Fulcanelli and get him to show you where to store these," he told her, gesturing to the hallway. Penelope stepped towards the door, her gaze searing. Her heart was filled with so much she still needed to say, and she hoped desperately there would be a time when she could say it.

"Tick, tock, tick, tock," Lucien continued to sing softly to himself as he watched her walk out through the door to the hallway, his fingers touching the wall to feel the beating pulse of the clock.

Chapter Seven

The collaborating French government proclaimed loudly how Paris was "free," "open," and had been "spared," so reassured residents who had fled during the summer, returned during October and November. They entered into a Paris where life held all of the silence and tension of an empty stage readied for a grand production. They were hungry and scared but relieved their city had not been destroyed. The stress and lassitude fed their deep denial.

With the Occupation still new, many Parisians lied to themselves outright, somehow believing that Paris was not a part of the larger war. German soldiers filled the streets. Food had been rationed for months. There was a curfew, and the city was mostly empty of traffic. Yet somehow residents still deluded themselves. With the absence of cars and the city's bustle, the streets of Paris were eerily silent. The noise of a forbidden radio broadcast or an argument could be heard blocks away. Bicycles and back alleys had become the fastest, safest way through the complicated city streets.

Penelope had been in Paris for almost a month, yet she had not left the apartment. Fulcanelli would not let her. His most recent project was to create a pamphlet to distribute throughout Paris that gave information about the horrors of the Occupation and listed simple acts of defiance that Parisians could participate in, ones that did not require violence or complicated gadgets. Penelope would study with him and help him create the brochure. They disguised the information in a playbill. All the work was done by hand.

Fulcanelli hoped that his playbill might help awaken Parisians to their dire circumstances. Hand-printing the playbills was tedious work for Penelope, but it provided an easy break from the dark, pursuant questions of loss and her distant life in America. She was so busy during the day that memories of her life in Sweetwater mostly only came at night. She missed her kind, diligent father. She missed the smell of her old house. She missed Naomie, and she missed the necklace so much. Some nights, instead of sleeping, she would stare at the ceiling and replay over and over again in her mind how both Naomie and the necklace had saved her life when they had tried to runaway together on the trains.

She recalled how she and Naomie had watched from
beneath the blanket as the two bulls had rounded everyone up like cattle and herded them in front of the small
railway station. The girls peered out through the hole of
their hiding spot as the night fog surrounded the small
crowd. There were thirty or forty hobos, and they were
told to kneel and remove their clothing. Two of the men
made a run for it, and a couple of shots went off. One of the
men fell to the ground, twitching. He was older with gray
hair. The bull approached and began kicking the downed
man repeatedly, until he stopped moving altogether. The
other man was never seen again.

The bulls shook out change from the hobo's clothes
and gathered all of the money they could find. Penelope
was overcome as she watched Manfri stripped, baited,
and heckled. Soon enough, as Manfri's hobo stories had
proclaimed, the prisoners would be marched half-naked
to the cotton fields where they would be sold to a farmer
and forced to work for free. The men likely had already
pocketed the cash and made the deal, promising to bring
twenty or so workers back from the rails to the farm.

The bulls rolled a cigarette to share between them, then
hiked up their trousers and lifted up the body of the unconscious hobo and dropped him across the tracks. They
would claim as their alibi that another poor, drunk had

fallen beneath the train, his body too mangled for anyone to notice the bullet hole. No tears shed. The cold-hearted tyranny of it hung in the air and Penelope, stitched to her spot in the boxcar, paralyzed, could not stop sniffling.

A nearby train quickly jerked away and drove over the limp body. Human life, rolled to the side and then run over. Penelope could not restrain herself and gasped out loud, the high-pitched voice of a girl ringing through the metal with a stark and hollow clang. The bulls looked up towards the sound of her hollow voice still hiding beneath the blanket.

"It looks like we missed someone," one of them said.

Penelope was scared and drained white. The night air was black and silent, and Penelope's breath bobbed like the needle of a sewing machine.

They heard the clunk and drag, clunk and drag of a man approaching, the lone steps of a man with a slight limp. "We heard you. We know you're in there," his voice echoed around the empty boxcar.

Penelope could feel him standing right above them, kicking around at the thin blanket covering them. Naomie's whole body was now trembling, she held tightly to the rock necklace around her neck. Naomie squeezed the necklace more firmly as he lifted the blanket from around them.

He had a beard, only one good eye, a knife and rank breath. His mangled face and eye epitomized brutality and indecency, and it caused Penelope to shudder. This was his world and his reason for being, and now he fixed his one boiling and blood-shot eye upon the prize before him.

He grasped the girls by their hair and dragged them out of the rail car. Penelope's vision was blurry, and her head ached, but she saw that Manfri's nose was now bleeding, and he had been crying so hard tears covered his face and reflected the moon's light with a subtle cast of silver. The bull pushed the girls into line with the others. Another train came through the station from the opposite direction and pulled to a stop behind them beneath a mossy tree.

"Are you okay?" Manfri whispered down to them, a drop of blood still careening down his face.

The girls nodded their heads, hearts racing.

"Listen to me carefully," Manfri said. "Stand behind me. I am going to distract them, and then I want you all to go get behind that tree. Hide there. Climb it. Then jump on the top of that train before it pulls away. It will take you back home to Sweetwater. Do you understand me? Jump on the top of the train and don't look back. Do you understand me? Do not look back."

The bulls approached slowly.

"We almost didn't notice you," the bull said, chuckling to himself, his heavy leg dragging.

He pulled a small notebook out of his pocket, "How old are you?"

"I won't ever tell you," Naomie replied angrily.

He wrote down something in his notebook and leaned

his head back. "Little girl, these rails are full of secrets." He smelled like liquor. "Every one of them hobos has a secret." He pointed at Manfri. "You see, you never can get a straight answer from a hobo."

Naomie glared back at him. Manfri fixed his eyes to the ground.

"Well, it seems to me, you've got some secrets too," Naomie huffed and pointed her chin to where the dead hobo's body now lay, vacant and mangled.

The bull let out a howl and grabbed Naomie by the hand, jerking her angrily out beneath the sky. "Don't disrespect me." He squeezed and twisted her forearm so forcefully her bones began to warp. Penelope knew he wouldn't stop until he broke Naomie's entire arm.

Suddenly, with an abrupt yelp, Manfri fell to the ground, flopping blindly and jerking, convulsively.

"Stay down," the bull pushed Naomie to the ground and lurched towards Manfri, who gave Penelope a forceful look, beckoning them to run.

"Don't look back," Manfri mouthed.

The girls made a quick dash towards an old, gnarled willow tree. Carefully, slowly they backed away into the shadows. They slipped behind the tree and swung into its branches, climbing higher and higher. The tree was like a hoary cobweb, draped with moss and old age. Its limbs creaked with the soft weight of the girls.

They climbed all the way to the top and discovered that just below them was the gleaming bright roof of the other train. Penelope could see a spot in the middle, right where they needed to land. She looked down at the ground, at Manfri who was still shaking and carrying on, and then back at the train. She closed her eyes and jumped, landing with a decisive thud on the top of the train. Naomie dropped down beside her. The noise was jarring and unmistakable, and she could hear the bulls searching frantically for them along the tracks that surrounded their train. They lay down against the metal roof to hide and felt the train jump a little. As it lurched forward in preparation to leave, she could hear the bulls rushing about in search of them.

"There they are... on the top of that one. Right there," one of them shouted.

Penelope grabbed her friend's hand more tightly. She could hear Manfri screaming, "Leave them. Leave them. Let them be."

The girls faltered as the train skipped forward again. She heard the sound of a man breathing and climbing up the side-ladder of the train. She saw the claws of his grease-darkened fingers clasp the edge of the roof beside her.

"Don't let the others get away," the man screamed even more loudly to the other mercenary.

In the chaos, Penelope looked down to see Manfri and the other hobos race away and scatter into the woods around the tracks, disappearing into the inky darkness.

The man's other hand reached up, gaining better

purchase. His head started to rise up over the lip of the train car roof. Penelope could see the crown of his head ascending towards them as the train began to roll forward. He grabbed Penelope's wrist and started to drag her off of the train, tearing her away from Naomie. Penelope felt the sharp clawing of his nails dig into her skin. She scrambled to find a hold as he pulled her towards him.

Naomie drew the rock necklace from around her neck. With all her might, Naomie rose up beside Penelope, kicking him with her feet and swinging the necklace at his hands, losing her balance and missing, nearly falling backwards off of the train. Naomie regained her balance and swung again, and again, harder, better, more focused, this time cracking his fingers and knuckles, head, and eyes as he pulled his full bodyweight up and over the lip of the roof. Finger by finger he lost his grip on Penelope's wrist. He yelped once, then twice.

His screams of anger and pain rang out through the rail yard. With one final kick, Naomie knocked him from the roof of the train, and his body fell down between the cars to the rails with a prolonged and agonizing scream. There was a pronounced and hollow crunch of his body beneath the weight of the slow-rolling train, but neither girl looked back. Manfri had told them not to look back. As the train gained speed, Naomie grasped Penelope and the necklace and held them close. Penelope saw how the rock necklace swung to and fro in Naomie's hand. It seemed to have a life of its own, rhythmic, pulsing, and warm to the touch.

As the morning light rose around them, Penelope looked out from the roof of the train at the countryside spread out along the horizon ahead. There was a brocade of forests, pine, hickory, oaks, and other hardwoods and deciduous trees. There were barns and narrow, bronze valleys with rivers, flumes, glens and far-flung waterfalls. Penelope watched a great blue heron cruise along beside the train with its deep, methodical wingbeats. They both seemed to float with forward movement.

She saw more birds poised and statuesque, motionless by a creek or a marsh. The birds and the trains were nothing if not deliberate. She heard the whistle as they slowed through the towns, the lights of the farmhouses in the distance. Still terrified, she imagined what it must be like in her own warm house with a fire and breakfast, her father thinking she was still asleep in her bedroom. She was thankful they were almost home and hugged Naomie close.

"I would never let anything happen to you," Naomie wept as she spoke, and something deep and permanent was forged between them. "We are like sisters now."

When Penelope finally finished hand-drawing all of the playbills, Fulcanelli and Lucien invited her to come to their private lab. No one else in the apartment even knew the room existed. Within Fulcanelli's private quarters, there was a hidden staircase tucked away in a rear corner.

"We need your advice on something," Fulcanelli told her.

Lucien stashed his notes beneath his arm.

A door hidden behind Fulcanelli's dresser led to a lantern-lit and windowless attic space. Lucien offered Penelope his hand as she climbed up the dim and gabled staircase. A plaque at the top of the stairs read, "Pigeon Loft." She ducked beneath it and released Lucien's grasp as she entered the room.

In the tiny space, scientific paraphernalia cluttered a large table. Shelves lined the walls where windows could have been. Jars, labeled in a cursive script, rested evenly spaced along the shelves. It reminded her of her father's lab. Penelope quickly recognized the bottles from her life in Sweetwater. She knew the intimately flawed etchings of Naomie's handwriting. Stepping over the broken debris of countless failed experiments, she walked across the room to touch one of Naomie's bottles. Like the rush of some ebullient song, Penelope's spirit lifted. She turned smiling to face Fulcanelli and Lucien. Fulcanelli shook a flask vigorously in his hand as Lucien wrote down the results. They were reviewing the results of their experiment. Their countenances bore the look of weary frustration as they began Newton's muddled experiment again. Trial, error, adjust, repeat, that had been their pattern for over two years.

"I had no idea this room was here," she gaped around her.

"Secret spaces are essential to life in Occupied Paris. People who are aware of the dangers of the war are building hidden spaces like this all over the city. Paris is becoming like a rabbit warren or a maze of caves."

"Plus, we cannot risk any interruptions with this work," Fulcanelli said. "We are not making enough progress yet," he added with aggravation in his voice.

Lucien moved to the side to create space as Fulcanelli reached out to draw Penelope between them.

She set Naomie's bottle down. With Lucien in such close proximity, she could not settle her zig-zagging mind. Her heart raced. The mere existence of him so near was both confounding and stultifying, a near constant reminder of her persistent feelings of loneliness.

Fulcanelli gazed hypnotically at the bottles before him.

"We have determined that we are stuck. We were hoping that you might join us," Lucien spoke softly to her. "Can you spend your afternoons in here with us and help me translate the papers after dark?"

She nodded, "I believe so."

He squeezed her arm with delight.

And so in the stillness of each night instead of sleeping and dreaming of her lost home and friend, she would slip into the secret room to help Lucien with his papers. In many ways, she spoke the language of alchemy better than English or French. She liked the rudimentary drawings and the old-fashioned words that freckled every page. Some of the material on the papers was smudged beyond recognition. Those words had to be blindly guessed at, a feat of deduction and imagination that suited Penelope's unique mind.

"I think that the word is shell and not crystal," Penelope said and pointed to the page. "And this other word is powder."

"Why would you think that?" Lucien responded. The steely glimmer of his eyes rang through her.

"Partly, it's a guess, but it's based in the logic of simplicity. It seems to me Newton is saying that in order for the seeds of the rocks to become accessible, you first have to break open the shell. Think of it as a barrier. That barrier needs to be acted upon by a powder to release what's inside. He calls it the powder of life, perhaps it is some type of nitre?"

"What do you make of the word air, right here beside. Both air and powder together?"

"You have to remember that Newton's whole thinking is a natural philosophy that is derived from our basic questions about matter and how it interacts. In the beginning, before time, there were just the elements and those elements mixed together with something else, something mysterious, to create geography and life, to ignite everything that we see and feel."

She spoke in the slow cadence of rippling waves. Her words washed between them. She knew from her travels across the Atlantic that there was nothing lonelier to her than the ocean, except perhaps this apartment. She paused and looked at Lucien as she spoke, trying to contain her emotions. Penelope saw and felt things strongly. She was worn down by the loss of her father, the upheaval of her strange new life in Paris, her questions about Naomie's whereabouts, and the intensity of her inestimable connection with Lucien.

So much time had passed, and she still woke with the cold and aching nightmare of her father's passing every day. She wanted to share her fears with someone, but Lucien was so new to her and, in spite of her strong feelings, she wondered if she could really trust him, if she could ever truly know or understand another soul.

She gathered herself and continued, "The translation to me says that some aerial powder is needed to ignite that spark and crack the inert shell or covering of those elements. It seems to be a central ingredient to Newton's process."

Lucien wiped his hand along his desk and blew the dust from his palm into the air. The particles flashed in the light of the candle. He drew closer to her as the dust settled between them, so close that she thought he might kiss her. She could see an inner conflict of desire written in his face. "You are keen," he said softly into her ear. "Naomie spoke about your mind. She said that you were gentle and wise."

"Just think, a mote of dust could ignite the universe . . ." Penelope laughed.

His hand slipped beneath the frayed, untucked edge of her blouse. She could feel his warm hand nearing the skin of her belly but he seemed to stop himself.

"What else did she say?" Penelope wondered aloud, her lips tense.

"She said you had an early knack for your studies, that you loved history and philosophy—but especially math, chemistry, and physics. She said that you were sweet and deft like your father." He continued, "She said that you were watchful and quiet but playful. She went on and on about your sense of adventure, but she said that she was your only friend and that made you imaginative but somewhat lonely and stoic . . . "

Penelope's eyes widened. "So, I guess she told you everything."

"It would seem, because she talked about you continuously. She told me so many things—but there are some things that I did not know." He seemed ponderous, virtually stricken by the conflict of his mind over his emotions.

"Like what?"

His gaze broadened then contracted.

Penelope smiled up at him sweetly, and his brow softened.

"She did not tell me about your strength and your graceful figure," he said, adjusting in his seat so he could see her more fully. He reached out and lightly touched her face. "She did not tell me about your fine nose, your full smile, and the softness of your skin." He moved his hand down along her neck, "She did not mention your hair or your copper eyes . . . and never once did she tell me about the pale birth mark along your neck . . . the scar along your ear . . . or your beautiful face." He paused. "Which upon closer inspection, I have determined is perhaps the most beautiful I have seen."

His words stirred her, but his expression still wore a mask of calamity. He drew his hand away, squeezing his fingers into a fist. His knuckles whitened, and his mind clouded over. He somehow managed to believe that by some personal mastery or deportment, he could suppress the emotions rising up within him.

"What's wrong?" she asked, reaching out to soothe him. "I was hoping you might kiss me," she confessed, reddening.

"No, you see, I would but I cannot." He shook his head and pulled farther away from her.

"But why?" she leaned towards him hopefully.

"Because," he said and paused to gather himself.

Without thinking, she drew her arms to him the way the wind streams towards the clouds in the sky, fluid and certain, but he nudged her away.

He fixed his jaw. "Because you are part of the Royal Society too," Lucien concluded turning his back to her. "And there is a cruel war outside."

"I see," she muttered.

But she did not, so she swallowed down his words like a shard of glass and stood up. As she hurried out of the room, tears ran down her cheeks. It was the conflict of self-repression, deeper than anything she knew outside of the slow execution of her vast and lonely heart.

Chapter Eight

While the Royal Society was doing its best to adapt to the new circumstances, the Occupation was all around them. Soon after Penelope arrived in Paris, Professor Durand left the apartment to retrieve money and food from his daughter's home several blocks away, and he had never returned. He was a renowned physicist, beloved professor, founder of the Royal Society, and Fulcanelli's close friend. When Fulcanelli contacted Professor Durand's daughter, she reported that he had been arrested at her home and interned. The professor's experiment, the vertigo inducing flashlight, sat in a box in the corner of the main living area, suspended in time and place. Fulcanelli had sent his friend on the errand, and he felt a near continuous blinding regret. It was not the first time since the Occupation that Fulcanelli had underestimated the situation.

The collaboration between the French government officials and the Germans rested on a balance of terrible things. The government tried to maintain the illusion that everything was just the same as before the surrender of Paris, except now there were German tanks and soldiers continuously patrolling the streets. Resistance groups like the Royal Society were emerging, but the German reprisals against the newly forming groups were brutal and swift. It was clear that one of Professor Durand's students had betrayed him to the police.

The situation escalated as demonstrations against the arrest of the beloved professor began. Students and teachers from his university organized to lay wreaths at the feet of the victorious statues throughout the city all day. Groups appeared and then disappeared, defying the German injunction against crowds gathering. By 5:30 pm, at the statue of George Clemenceau on the Champs-Élysées, five thousand people had gathered with flowers to defy the occupying forces. Soldiers armed with machine guns cleared the area. Military cars chased the crowds down alleys, arresting the students and closing off access to the area. The collaboration was a vicious disease that yoked the city and sent Fulcanelli into a frantic, obsessive journey to somehow, mathematically break the hold of the occupiers on Paris.

In the month after Durand's arrest, Fulcanelli's face bore the listless pallor of fear and agitation. He cast equation after equation about radioactive decay in Penelope's direction. Day in, day out she would huddle in a corner at a desk, or in the attic lab, barely eating or sleeping, striving to keep pace.

Exhausted, she wandered to the kitchen to find Fulcanelli.

"Have you finished the calculations?" he asked with irritation, swirling his tea with a spoon.

"Yes, and I have some questions." But then she stopped and wasn't able to put them into words.

Fulcanelli watched her a moment, noting her solemn and hunched posture. "It is a lot, I know. I have been relentless. Since the capture of Durand, I am feeling the pressure of time and loss." He seemed to look out into some wilderness within his mind. "You must be lonely for your life in America. If you need a break, I understand."

Penelope poured a cup of hot tea and sat down beside him, "I am terribly lonely," she said, "but the work has been a fair and quiet companion."

"The war is overwhelming," Fulcanelli said as he warmed his hands above the steam that rose out of his mug.

Their conversation was interrupted for a minute by the rhythmic click of Parisians' wooden shoes hurrying along the cobbled sidewalks rising up through the kitchen window like a haunted, hollow symphony. The silence of the city amplified these strange, new noises. Rubber was for the war, not for shoes any longer. The boots of the German military rung out to a different cadence.

Penelope stared blankly ahead.

"There is a whole, vibrant city beneath the blanket of this war. It is still there. The art, the dance, the music still survives."

His words stung, and she could only think of dancing with Naomie and Manfri by her beloved childhood creek.

Night after night in the summers, Penelope had danced with Naomie and her family in Sweetwater. By listening carefully, she had come to understand the French they spoke and the dances they choreographed, then she would practice in her room at home. She had learned to tuck and roll her belly just like Elodie, her arms rising up in the air, her hips swiveling, and when she was finally brave enough to show them what she had learned, the gypsies were shocked to see the moxie and pure artistry of her movements.

"She's got the gift," Manfri had said, as he tipped back her chin and asked her to balance a sword along the bridge of her nose.

They discovered that her knees and hips were limber as sap and so they also taught her to do the contortionist tricks—lay her chin on the ground and drop her feet over behind her head, to stand and wrap her leg across the back of her neck. She wasn't aware of this, but they needed her to draw the crowds. Her paraffin skin, her golden braids swinging like tassels, her eyes wide and open as an atrium, shining like copper, caught people's eye.

It wasn't long before they had loaded Penelope in the wagon and took her to town with them to perform. Elodie would use some of her delicate scarves to wrap Penelope like the bud of a blossom, and Naomie, Elodie, and Penelope would dance while the rest of the band clapped and played songs around them. Inevitably curious, crowds gathered while Penelope circled Elodie like a satellite. Manfri had taught her to bat her eyes and always let her gaze linger on the people in the crowd, until she felt a vibration in her chest like a flutter.

"Then, you have their attention," he had told her.

Returning her focus to Fulcanelli, she answered him. "I know virtually nothing at all about Paris. What is there to know?"

"So much." Fulcanelli said with evident alarm. "First of all, there is the art." He raised his arms wide, his eyes smiling.

"The art?"

"Yes. It's transcendent," he stated with an unblinking certainty.

She looked out the window of the apartment at Paris.

"It's dreams become real, my dear," Fulcanelli said. "In architecture, painting and writing."

More than anything, Fulcanelli loved the paintings.

The mangled surrealist images appealed to him; his own worldview was a juxtaposition of accepted truths, the scientific and the mystical. He told her about the paintings of Dali, Miro, and Magritte. He spoke of it as a revolutionary movement born of war and suffering, dreams, and nightmares. He told her that the surrealist artists never shied away from the incongruence of life. So much like Fulcanelli, they celebrated those splintered realities.

"So then are most people quite simply blind to it?" she remarked.

"The art or the transcendence?" he chuckled to himself. "In other places, art can be forgotten but not here."

"And why is that?"

"Because Parisians understand magic and the profound uncertainty of life." Fulcanelli flushed slightly with the strong emotions of his words. "The word for it is passion. It is part of life here. The art is a by-product of the abundant passion."

Penelope drew another silent sip from her teacup.

Fulcanelli lowered his eyes with a look of deeper concern, "Do you need to rest, Penelope?"

"No, I am not tired in that way," she responded. "Mainly, my mind is tired, and I want to take a break for an afternoon. I would like to see Paris, but I am afraid it is not safe. I am afraid the Occupation has taken it away, the art, everything."

"The Nazis have taken nearly everything. In Paris, they came for our art first so there is little left that is not hidden, but there is one secret place where you can go." He smiled and waved his fingers in the air like Chinese lanterns. "You can find more art there than in some of the most famous museums in the world. But you cannot tell anyone," Fulcanelli said with a playful smile. "Soon it too will be packed and taken away for hiding from the Nazis. But I can arrange for you to see it today, if you would like."

She nodded fervently.

"Lucien," he called out, the sound of his voice blooming room to room.

There was a silence, then the staccato of Lucien's dutiful footsteps approaching the kitchen.

"What is it?" he asked, his words filling the silence.

"Would you like to take Penelope on an outing today?" Fulcanelli questioned.

Lucien appeared taken aback.

"Yes, very much." Lucien's voice abstained as the pliable flush of emotion washed up along his neck. Fulcanelli handed Lucien an address, which he noted before tucking it into his pocket.

"I am afraid I have allowed my inward troubles to stifle her," Fulcanelli said with a mixed despondency. "I am sorry, Penelope. Just be careful when you leave the apartment. We have already lost two people to the Germans."

"Two?" she paused. "But who has been captured besides the professor?" Penelope turned to face Fulcanelli.

Fulcanelli and Lucien exchanged a look of injury. At first, neither responded.

"Who?" Penelope demanded.

"Naomie," Fulcanelli cried out. His words landed like the renouncement of something naked and true.

The name released against her like a sharp blade of wind. "My Naomie? Your sister?" Penelope gasped. "Why am I just hearing about this now? How long ago did this happen?"

There was another prolonged and sucking silence. It was the pronounced silence of some heavy emotion falling, like when a body, passing through its position of equilibrium, is about to hit the ground, when gravity can do no more work upon it, and all energy is kinetic, with no more potential. Penelope's eyes burned with sadness and fury as she thought of Naomie trapped, dirty, and scared in the hands of the German soldiers. Her jaw was locked with fierce emotion, and she could not speak out the many unutterable questions that swelled up inside her. Her lonely knees gave out and her body swayed.

Lucien rushed to her, and Fulcanelli looked stricken.

"Just before you arrived. She was waiting in line for rations. She was taken off the street in broad daylight." Lucien responded softly, holding her arm to steady her. Although she understood the words he was saying, she could not quite accept them.

Fulcanelli whimpered with crushing solemnity, "It's my fault. I sent her on the errand. I should have known better." He seemed almost paralyzed with emotion. Penelope bit her lip and remained silent. His despondent look scared her. She was afraid of what else he might say.

Fulcanelli turned and left the room abruptly.

Penelope pulled away from Lucien and stepped towards the window, looking out at the dark clouds clearing. She could see the sun shining back with a heartfelt indifference.

"I'm sorry," Lucien said, giving her a forceful look. "I know it is a lot to comprehend, and there's no way to anesthetize this pain." His eyes were clear and beckoning. She stared out the window in silence a long time before he moved in close again, almost genuflect before her. "I'm sorry to bother you, but if we are going to the Deschamps' house, we must go now before it gets too late," he said, his voice expressionless, his hand reaching for hers.

Close then far, Lucien was mercurial as the ocean. Her heart rose and fell with his tides. She said nothing, reluctantly refusing his hand, and turned to walk towards the main door of the apartment. Lucien followed behind her. At the door, Penelope paused attempting to stifle the impact of what she had heard.

"Why did they take her?" she whispered to Lucien.

"They are trying to find Fulcanelli," he replied. "It is my belief that they hoped she would tell them where he is hiding."

"And where is she now?" she said in the hollow tone of cavernous sorrow.

"We know she is alive, but we are not sure where she is." His words jarred her.

The rains had stopped, and as they stepped through the apartment door into the foyer, Penelope felt the pull of her loneliness. It had the feel of sandpaper along her skin.

As they stood in the cavernous foyer, she paused to brush away her long hair, roll the sleeves of her coat, and tighten the belt at her waist before stepping onto the street. She was trying to stop herself from remembering that it was here, outside on the streets, that Naomie had been taken. After all, Fulcanelli had promised her that art could set a person free.

Chapter Nine

*P*enelope and Lucien walked through back alleys
cautiously, quietly for several miles into the 11th
Arrondissement of Paris, along a residential street, to
number 48, an exquisite mansion with large, carved doors.

"This is the place?" she gaped in wonder.

"Yes," Lucien said. "The house has been abandoned.
The family fled France before the war. Unlike their neigh-
bors, this family was unknown and excessively reclusive
in Parisian society, thus preserving their exquisite art collection from the Nazi looting. The collection remains safe
and is largely unknown."

Penelope looked up at the stately mansion. She was
expecting something hidden, or underground, not this

ostentatious display, right in the middle of Paris.

"It's so fancy," she said.

"No fancier than any other building along this street. But inside is like a *petite* palace of Versailles," Lucien commented as he pulled the key from behind a stone along the facade of the building, unlocked the tall gates, and pushed them open.

They wandered slowly through the mansion's front doors, twisting the lock behind them. Lucien looked notably relieved. Locked inside the stone fortress, he felt safe again, and like the chain reaction of an illness as it abruptly retreats, his whole disposition lulled. At ease, away from the constant scrutiny of Fulcanelli and the streets of Paris, he seemed to shift back into some truer version of himself. The inflection of his mouth and body moved with a renewed hopefulness.

Behind his eyes, Penelope could see a berm of unspoken thoughts begin to give way, one tear and then another. Since the Occupation began, grave and heavy secrets had accumulated inside him. His life and emotions were caged by the war, as a Parisian, as a scientist, as a person; yet the false safety of this locked door could not balance out his feelings of loss. Lucien, too, knew the woven, textured pain of loneliness, and he wore his suffering like a mask.

"We can stay here as long as you like," he reassured Penelope as he wiped the damp tears from his face.

She was speechless. His emotions stilled her. He turned away from her to face the room. She had never seen anything quite like this home, with its gilded frames, marble, silver tea settings, and tapestries in every direction.

Every aspect of the house was artistic. "This was someone's home?" she asked, as Lucien led her past the gilded stair rail into a large drawing room, which faced a garden out back and had views into a park beyond. The room was decorated with white-and-gold oak paneling and a portrait of a pink-cheeked noblewoman dressed in striped satin.

"Yes, but this is a painting by Marie Antoinette's court painter," Lucien remarked. "So, it was not an ordinary family or home."

She thought of her home in Sweetwater, its simple, bare walls and broken places.

Lucien stepped forward to untie the knot of her coat and remove it. As he approached her, he was strangely watchful and reticent, taking his time to unbend the knot, drawing her hair carefully to the side as he stepped behind her to pull the coat from her arms. He draped her coat across the arm of a chair, alongside his.

Penelope continued, "I cannot imagine living in a place like this," she said, laughing.

"What is so funny to you?"

"The home I grew up in was nothing like this." Her merry words sounded out of place in the formality of the room.

"What was yours like then?"

Lucien stood closely beside her in the vastness of the

house. She felt more uncertain in his presence than usual.

"My home was a simple farmhouse. It had so few decorations." She reminisced about life alone with her kind, distractedly brilliant father.

"It sounds perfect to me," he coaxed, nudging her elbow.

"It was," she laughed and smiled shyly back at him.

"But what became of this family?" she shifted the subject. "Why don't they live here now?" she continued.

"This was the private home of the Deschamps banking family. In the 1800s, many of the bourgeoisie built mansions here around the Parc Verdun. The park was vast and very exceptional, so large that it used to be a hunting grounds for the rich." He drew back the curtain and gestured to the green park outside of the window.

Penelope leaned beside him and saw a lake surrounded by a forest of trees in the distance.

"It was a playground for the wealthy Parisians. So many trees, but there were also artistic elements hidden in the park, Corinthian columns, a Chinese bridge, an Egyptian pyramid."

"All of those things inside that park?"

"Yes. It was a time of opulence, of saying yes to more and more and more. The residents were drawn to the theater and drama of the park. They spent much of their time there."

"Only the wealthy?"

"Well, no. The alchemists loved it there too, but for different reasons."

Penelope looked up at him with a diligent curiosity. "What do you mean by that?"

She remembered the forests and hills of her town and was astonished that a forest could contain such man-made ornaments as columns and a pyramid. Looking out from the window, she saw no trace of these monuments.

"Deschamps and his wife were alchemists too. It is in actuality a very profound space in alchemy. An important Italian grotto is there that is quite significant, and there are other magical elements as well."

She looked up at him, perplexed.

"Penelope, Paris is a very mystical city in many, many respects." His voice was half caressing, half demonstrative. "Much is hidden here in the architecture of the buildings and the parks themselves. Not everything is as it seems. So much of this city was built this way, with this intention."

She looked at the mysterious park out the window, the mist clung-low to the greenery.

He continued, closing the curtain and turning towards Penelope, "Deschamps was a secret collector of furniture and art. He built this house for his wife, but tragically she was killed while traveling during World War I. Deschamps was so devastated he shuttered the house and hid inside with his art."

"Then why does Fucanelli know where they hide the key?" she asked.

"Deschamps' daughter, Faustine, is the sole owner now, and she is a friend of Fulcanelli's."

Penelope followed Lucien from the large drawing room to the dining room that also overlooked the garden and the park. A linen-draped oval table was set for eight, as though dinner was about to be served. She pulled out a chair and sat down. "It is a family home that is frozen in time," she said and looked up at him.

"Sometimes the past is too insurmountable." He readjusted a spoon along her place setting. "That was true for the father, so he abandoned the house after much sickness and distress and asked that nothing be changed. This is the same table his wife had set for dinner the night when she was supposed to return."

Penelope's heart sunk, astonished, and she withdrew her hands from the table abruptly. "What will happen to it?" she exclaimed.

"After the war, we will have to see. For his daughter Faustine, it is her family home. But she is Jewish, and Fulcanelli worries her social status will protect her for only so long."

"Why hasn't she gone into hiding or left the country?"

"Much like this house, she is hiding in plain sight, at parties, on hunting trips. She is still very fluid in the limited social life of Paris."

Penelope got up from the table with delicate ease, and they wandered the labyrinth of rooms. She felt equal part sorrow and beauty, and yet this place was still a refuge from an intolerable reality that was visible from every window.

They wandered into a large study, with a tall gold-framed mirror flanked by a pair of gauzy tapestries depicting rustic scenes.

"Is her father still living?" she asked.

"No, he died recently."

They were quiet, taking in the room. Penelope watched Lucien in the mirror. His face was boyish with a soft complexion and large eyes but his intensity defied it all. He looked more exquisite to her than the room. She felt an unfamiliar binding hunger when she looked at him, a curiosity and pull both strange and frightening to her. It was clear to her that every time they entered a room, he too saw her first and most fully. When his eyes met hers in the mirror for a fleeting second, she reached behind and grasped his hand with intention, lacing her fingers alongside his with tender affection. Lucien smiled quietly.

They wandered hand in hand into the dimly lit main bedroom. When Penelope saw the Deschamps' family tree displayed above the bed, she released his hand and walked immediately up to the image. She reached forward and traced the branches with her fingers, touching the lines, following the main branch to the mother's name.

"The tree of family life," Penelope said, lifting her eyes to Lucien. "Fleur Deschamps," she mouthed the name of the mother. She felt the sadness of the house well up in her like some high elevation, her eyes brimming with tears.

Lucien nodded.

"And this was their room." She touched the bedspread,

the pillow, all the intimate details of the bedroom. She wanted to touch it all, absorb it vapor-like into the deepest part of her. She thought of Naomie, her mother, and her father. She understood this story too well, the story of this family, and of the fractals of its broken family tree.

She stepped past the bed to the window and winced visibly as she drew her hand through the curtains and looked out the window towards the mysterious park below, pausing a moment to watch the birds as they flew tree to tree. Lucien was standing close, watching her without saying anything.

She turned to him. "Tell me more about your family," Penelope said, a feeling clinging low in her belly as she spoke.

He responded in a gentle, cautious voice, "Well, my mother and my sister live in northern France."

"Yes, you have already told me that. What else?" she said with urgency.

"My house too was nothing like this house. My father was killed in the war. He was a farmer. We lived in the north near Somme. It was during the Battle of Passchendaele, in July of 1917. My father was leading a group of men across a river when they came under heavy fire. We were told he drowned in the river trying to rescue his comrades. I was a boy then. Since the war, I have hardly seen my mother or my sister. It is best that way. Their connection to me now would only endanger them. Love can sometimes be fatal here."

He smiled sadly, the scent of some fond emotion washing over him.

"I disagree," she said, but he stopped her. Reaching forward he grasped her hand and pulled her towards him, brushing his forehead against hers. He smiled down at her, releasing her and abruptly shifting the subject as he led her into the next room.

"Do you want to see my favorite room?" he asked.

She jostled his rangy frame teasingly with her elbow. "Why do you keep pushing me away every time I come close?" she asked.

He closed his eyes with visible frustration. "Because I have to for your sake and mine. I am afraid to be close to anyone. Penelope, look at this house. Is this home not a monument to the age-old tale of how love can break you to pieces?"

He took another step backwards. Lucien was a man of measure and control. He straightened his shirt. He wore his candor and self-discipline like a protective shell.

"Has love broken you to pieces before?" she asked.

He closed his eyes, not responding.

She asked again.

"Yes, once before."

"Then tell me," she beckoned him.

"My fiancée died in a train crash over five years ago. Tragedy makes no allowances for love."

"So . . . you have determined that loving is no longer worth it?"

"Essentially. The equation of love and loss is too difficult for me, particularly in times of war."

"And you believe you are in control of love?" The only thing Penelope knew about romantic love was from stories. She thought of it as an involuntary fever that rose up.

Lucien's face was fixed with determination as he responded, "I have experienced it only once and it nearly destroyed me. Now I have successfully avoided it for over five years."

"Then what is this thing between us?"

"I do not know." His voice sounded plaintive.

"Well, I am curious and I have my suspicions. Let me just say that I believe you have miscalculated," she stated, smiling in her defiance. Her high voice rang out through the quiet house like a silver toll as she strolled out into the hallway.

"I see." He seemed stunned and touched by her candor and wide-open curiosity.

"Have you seen enough art for today?" Lucien challenged.

"No, not nearly enough," she wondered if she had said too much.

She ran ahead of him. He followed behind.

They stood in front of another painting down the long hallway. It was a pastoral scene of a couple embracing. The woman's blouse was cut low and sensuous. Penelope had not seen such warm-toned flesh and sexuality so freely displayed since looking at her father's alchemy book. As a girl, she stared at the book and wondered why those pictures made her feel so strange. She felt as though she was scratching at the surface of something vast and important, the same way the waves of the ocean rise up and then draw in and obscure the content of their salty waters. A certain watchful heat surrounded the room as they continued to look at the painting.

"How very beautiful!" she remarked with a trace of melancholy in her voice.

Lucien grazed her sleeve as he passed by. The sensation terrified her, sending blood up her neck in an instant, almost painfully. Then, it seemed a long while that he stood even more closely beside her and continued to study the painting. The silence was uncomfortable—yet, when she broke it and turned toward him, she realized he was watching her and not looking at the painting.

"He looks at her with such . . ." she stumbled to find a French word to describe the man in the painting.

"Passion," Lucien offered with a haunting clarity.

"No . . . it's yearning, I believe." She hadn't been able to look at him when she said this. Standing in this house with Lucien, she felt the discomfort of her own longing and knew he felt the same.

"Do you think artists are alchemists too?" she asked, attempting to divert the prickling sensations coursing along her skin.

"Very much, the artists are fighting their own war," Lucien told her. "They are refugees, spread everywhere, like the scientists . . . like us."

His words were pronounced distinctly, like his gaze. His attraction at the sight of her was palpable. It was like a type of distress but pleasure, blistering hives of emotion ran up and down his neck before they disappeared in the late afternoon light. His face flushed, and he stopped speaking, sensations flickering. There was a prolonged and watchful silence.

Then what had begun as a stir in his distant mind emerged, like a reflex, and he reached for her, pulling her close to him and pausing there. He first drew his fingertips gently along her lips, then he drew his face towards hers and kissed her. It was a long kiss with a yearning and passionate steadiness. The effects were incalculable, both liquid and gold.

Chapter Ten

"All substances are composed of the four elements of nature—Fire, Water, Air and Earth." Fulcanelli was stuffing explosives into a dead rat. He was referencing Newton's esoteric papers.

"God is efficient, Newton believed this too," Penelope said with a hardened clarity.

"Simplicity is always where you begin . . . and end," Fulcanelli added.

"And the rats?"

"So simple . . . so efficient. The defeat of the occupiers will not be built on one thing alone but upon the sum of many things." Fulcanelli wrapped a blanket around his shoulders.

"Let me see," she reached across and grasped one of the limp vermin. "How does this relate to alchemy?" she asked.

"Fire can be one of the most potent agents of transformation in alchemy," Fulcanelli pulled a knife from the table, "First you cut open the rat, discard its guts, then you fill it with plastic explosives to make it look like a rat again, then you sew it like this. It's simple. The rats are everywhere." He was demonstrating his method to Penelope, a small fuse extended from the rear of the rat. "They are in every gutter and so obvious they are as invisible as the clouds in the sky."

She nodded, looking around.

"Not only do the rats blow up erratically," he continued, "but we have circulated rumors about the exploding vermin throughout the city, and the German soldiers are afraid of every rodent they see, living or dead. This, too, is a type of subversion."

Fulcanelli had recruited a small group of the Royal Society to make rodent bombs. Penelope's job was to drop the rats at specific sites around the city, wherever there was coal to be distributed to the military. The rats, unnoticed, would be shoveled into an industrial furnace and would explode, further dismantling the war infrastructure. At least, that was the idea.

"As a woman, you will be less noticeable," Lucien said as he approached the table. He grasped her long braid and skillfully untied it, shaking the hairs gently between his fingers and watching it unfurl, twisting it into a bun and pinning it at her neck. "The less decorated you are the better." His touch was seductive and comforting but his voice was harsh, almost scolding.

Penelope raised her head and drank in the moment like a shot of elixir. She had spent her life undecorated, having worn neither feather nor ribbon, no fancy dresses, and outside of the stone necklace, no jewelry. Her braids were her only luxury, and no one, other than Naomie, had ever woven or unwoven her hair. Lucien's touch had made her stir as a cascade of memories of Naomie's summers in Tennessee came back to her, both of pain and delight. He drew his finger slowly along her shoulder and goosebumps rose up and down her arms, reminding her that in life, there was no method to emotions or memories, no choreography; and ultimately there could be no relief.

"There are large and small military sites all over Paris," Fulcanelli had said. "Tons of them. We have made a map for you both to study." He sipped from his cup and looked straight through Penelope to that place people look when they are thinking of something distant and painful.

"It's so simple it could work," Penelope responded.

"As I said, the less decorated the better," Lucien repeated, still combing his finger through the stray hair that fell out of her bun and along her shoulder. The loose tone of his words hit, but his touch lingered on her skin like a tonic, every molecule tingling, igniting along the places where his fingers had been. With so much of her soul in motion, her blood rushed involuntarily to her face.

Lucien had spent weeks poisoning rats in the gutters then harvesting them like apples from a tree, storing them in a satchel that hung from the window beside his desk in the frozen, December air to prevent them from decomposing.

"The best outcome is injury to the war machines," Fulcanelli said. "The war would be nothing without its trains, its factories, its soldiers. We are going to bury the machines." It was all about injuring the engine and the chassis of the war, and the Royal Society's thoughts on what that would entail.

Penelope and Lucien disguised themselves as an older couple, so they could move more freely through the city. They spent weeks strolling, arm in arm, site to site, Penelope dropping the rats from a hole inside her bag.

"Can I show you something?" Lucien asked her early one morning. "It is only a few blocks from here, near the river."

She nodded as he pulled her down a narrow street. "This city is a labyrinth," Penelope observed, looking up at the majestic buildings that surrounded her. Paris felt frozen in time. These were the streets of Joan of Arc, of Napoleon. She felt disoriented. "You seem to know your way very well," she commented.

"Yes, I do. I have lived here since I was a schoolboy. My mother sent me to school in Paris after my father died," he replied, as they turned down another even more narrow, cobbled street. "Walk slowly and look down," he urged as a commotion at the end of the street erupted.

They kept walking forward, and he nudged her away from a Police Nationale vehicle parked in front of a building. The car door was open and a woman and her young son were struggling not to be pushed inside.

"Don't look up. Keep walking," Lucien whispered.

As they crossed the next intersection, the police car sped past them.

"What was that?" Penelope said, her voice strained.

"They are Jewish. It was a raid."

"Then we must go to find and help them."

"We can't. Then we will be arrested too. We must try another way," he spoke sharply. Lucien's eyes looked weary. He continued, "The Germans have been unscrupulous invaders of our city. Parisians are known for our freedom and yet we can do nothing to protect that family. We are powerless."

She thought of Naomie and wondered if she had fought as fiercely against her abductors as she had fought against the train bulls as a girl.

Lucien's face was stricken. Dressed in the disguise of an old man, he looked both old and young. As a Frenchman, the powerless self-abasement of the Occupation tore through him. His only mechanism was his devotion to Fulcanelli and the Royal Society, so he bowed down to Newton's papers daily, almost religiously, in a fevered and desperate hope to discover some purchase there, some way to shift the story of his own defeat.

The facade of Paris and its monuments had been spared by the Germans during the invasion, but the violence persisted. The Occupation inflicted a more discreet and symbolic type of assault than bombs. It was a shadow that darkened the city not only through the array of truncated freedoms and starvation tactics, but through gross emasculation of its revolutionary and liberal culture. The daily habits and restrictions of life in Paris wore Lucien down. The Occupation was a type of psychological deconstruction, deeper than any bomb because it was from the inside out. True progress would take time, he told himself.

"What will happen to that family?" Penelope asked.

"They will split them. They will kill them. They do not care."

"Then we must act fast," Penelope cried out.

"Then they will kill you too. You must be patient."

They followed the cobbled streets in silence until they arrived in front of a nondescript building wrapped in barbed fences.

"What is this?" Penelope asked.

"This was my art school. My life in Paris began here," he looked up at the building. "It has been gutted."

"What is it now?" she wondered.

"Mostly empty it seems, but Fulcanelli told me it is being converted to a barracks."

"How ironic," she commented. "So, you are an artist? Why didn't you tell me?" she added with approbation. She felt hurt he had not told her.

"It's not something I like to talk about," he flushed.

Penelope looked sternly at him.

"Just like you have never told me that you are a dancer, only Naomie told me that," he said, eyeing her closely. "So yes, I am a painter."

Her face tinted. "What kind of painter?"

"We call it avant-garde."

"What does that mean?"

"It literally means the line of soldiers at the front of a battle. It means that my art is a pursuit of authenticity, that my work can be controversial. As avant-garde artists we see ourselves as a vanguard of soldiers ahead of authentic and necessary reform within society."

"I see," she nodded. "But specifically, what do you paint?"

"I paint people, then I remove some part of them to rob them of their deepest humanity."

Her eyes widened, "What parts of them?"

"Sometimes it is their eyes, their mouth, sometimes it's their hair, their legs, their hips, anything. It depends."

"I would like to see your paintings," she exclaimed.

"You cannot. Their content became too dangerous for my family. After the invasion, I had to go underground. The paintings are hidden. I have promised myself that I will not paint again until the war is over, until I know my mother and sister are safe."

He stopped and looked down at her. He grasped a loose tendril of her hair and brushed it away from her face. Bit by bit, she let the pleasure of his touch seep in like an oil. "The faces I paint are a mirror to the larger picture of what is going on."

"What is your inspiration?" she said.

He sighed deeply. She felt inclined to reach for his hand and lace her fingers with his.

"Days after I found out about my father's death, I rode my bike to the Somme River where he had died to try and find him. I didn't believe what my mother had told me. I climbed down from my bike and wandered up and down through the aftermath of the swollen river, looking for any sign of my father. After the battle, the Somme had an entirely new landscape and topography. It looked rabid, frothing at its edges. The mountain of debris was endless, and in a disaster of this scale and scope, it was hard to know where to begin."

He pulled her down the street as he spoke.

"I was a boy impatient for some discovery. I was a child, so I was not adept at guessing, pilfering through the sucking pig pen of war and river, turning over things to find some trace of my father. I couldn't apply any mathematical logic in it. This was a tragedy that was not subject to any laws or alchemy. It was random and chaotic and painful, a military car upside down along the gully, a dead horse, a bag of someone's rations, a shoe, a sock, and trees, walls and walls of trees frozen in the mud."

They crossed another avenue as he spoke, "I waded through the outline of the swimming hole I used to know well. It looked like soup and I noticed someone was floating there, face down in an eddy. All I could see was the back of his overalls, a denim x across his back, so I waded out headlong to him and dragged him by his straps and floppy arms to the shore.

When I rolled him over, I pressed my ear to his heart as if that would somehow matter. He clasped a gun in his frozen, stiff hand, so I freed the gun and tossed it beside me. I grasped around at his cold and bloated hands, and when I finally looked up to his face, I saw that nothing was there. Instead, it looked grotesque and mangled, fish-eaten, the way acid acts upon water and its suspended impurities, carbonizing them, coagulating and melting them into a mass," he said, swallowing hard.

He continued, "Whoever this man was, he was unrecognizable now. No one should see a man like this. Still I wanted to know his name to make sure it wasn't my father, so I dug in his pockets to see what I could find. In one, I found almost nothing but a pouch of soggy tobacco and some wet matches. In the other, I found a pocketknife. I kept everything but the tobacco. The back of the knife was etched with the name Douglas. I remember wondering if someone would find my father the way I had found Douglas and brush his hair from his face to close his eyes. I looked at him carefully and dissected his mangled features the way a scientist would cautiously and delicately disarm a bomb. I wanted to know his story."

He was crying. She looked up and could see the wet

tears falling from his face, shining there. After examining them momentarily, she leaned forward and wiped his tears away with her finger. She drew her damp finger to her mouth, swallowing them down. She wanted to understand. The tears had the unexpected taste of something embroidered, the flavors delicately touching all parts of her mouth. She closed her eyes and imagined her home. She opened them again and saw Lucien.

He looked at her, his eyes damp and hungry.

"What happened next?" she asked, barely able to form the words.

"I decided to bury Douglas in the soft, sucking mud beside the river. It almost pulled me under too. My study of art and alchemy has helped to release me from the gripping pain of that memory."

A German patrol passed by them, so arm in arm, they continued to walk away from the barracks in a pregnant type of gravity and silence. The war had diminished the vibrancy of city. The cacophony of life—buskers, beggars, cars, walkers, and street vendors was muffled. The city was quiet now.

Alchemy's greatest achievement, beyond math, beyond magic, beyond art, was to mix things, distant self with distant world.

Chapter Eleven

*I*t was mid-afternoon when the bomb exploded, filling her handbag brimming with dead rats with smoke. Penelope and Lucien were on one of their daily strolls dropping the explosive-filled vermin throughout discreet German military sites in the 8th Arrondissement.

"Merde! Merde!" Lucien said as he grabbed a rag from his pocket and put it to Penelope's eye.

Her eye was gouged and burning with a chemical debris from the explosion and bleeding badly. She looked down at her feet and shuddered. "Lucien, Lucien," she cried, "there's so much blood." It was like looking through a gossamer veil.

Scared, Penelope clutched the bag more tightly, wafting the smoke of the smoldering vermin all around her stinging arm, rattled with shock. Her disbelief and fear moved

through her with a fluid animation that she didn't anticipate, as if they too possessed both instincts and ardor. She
feared the pain from her eye might consume her. Lucien
grasped Penelope by the wrist, pulling her down the street.

They ducked into an alley. He grasped her face, and
said, "I need you to drop the bag." Her knees wobbled, and
she was aware that the bag was as heavy as damp, soaked
wood.

He was speaking slowly, but, frozen in shock, she
clutched the handles of her handbag even tighter alongside her. The smoke and the ringlets of her hair clung to
her blood-soaked face.

"No. The water," she said in a moment of clarity, pointing across the avenue to the Seine. He nodded, and they
dashed across to a bridge. She leaned over, and when
she dropped the smoking bag into the current, it let off
a putrid smell of burnt hair and fireworks. The bag sank
and disappeared, leaving a thin trail of smoke behind it.
Penelope grasped Lucien's handkerchief and pressed it to
her eye, tucking herself into his coat. Her face was going
numb from the pain.

"We need to hide," he said and ushered her back towards
the street. "We can't let them see us."

As they stepped back onto the sidewalk, a group of
German soldiers was coming down the road to investigate
the commotion.

"If they see you are bleeding, they will know it was us."
He pulled her closer.

There was nowhere to turn, nowhere without the vexing presence of soldiers. A woman standing in front of her storefront pointed to them, "It was them. They exploded something," she yelled out.

Penelope and Lucien turned away from her and walked briskly in the other direction. As they scuttled back across the bridge, Penelope could feel Lucien's heart racing through his shirt. She felt scared and reached for his hand.

Her eye was throbbing with pain. The soldiers were following them and yelling, "*Halt!*" their voices pulling at Penelope and Lucien like a riptide. There were at least ten of them, and others were following in cars. Penelope knew they were outnumbered and outmaneuvered. All they could do was find somewhere to hide.

"Come here," Lucien said as they wheeled around a corner and ducked quickly into a cinema. The door was open, but the box office was closed. The lights in the main foyer were off, everything dark and empty. They sprinted down the hallway of the theater trying to open door handle after door handle. At last, Lucien pulled one open to a bathroom, and they ran inside. He shuffled Penelope inside the wash closet and closed the door tightly.

"Wait here until I knock," he said. "Don't make a sound."

Her heart was racing. She shrank against the cold, kettle wall of the bathroom. She could hear Lucien wash the splattering of her blood from his face, drawing cold water into his mouth trying to smooth out his breath. Penelope had forgotten the even sound of water rushing from pipe to sink, which was suddenly interrupted by the loud rustle and canter of soldiers who had followed them into the cinema. Lucien took one deep breath before he stepped out of the bathroom. He started to whistle a tune with a nonchalance that defied the moment.

"There he is," cried one of the soldiers from down the hallway. "Seize him!"

Penelope heard the distinctive, canine sound of a pack circling, followed by a blank thud, and she knew Lucien had been thrown against the wall.

"Where is the girl?" they yelled.

"I do not know what you mean. What is happening? What girl?"

"Do not play games with us. We want the girl with the bag."

Penelope heard a blunt object smash against the bathroom wall. Sounds encircled her, as if she was standing inside a cave.

Then she heard the door to the bathroom open, and she peered through the cracks in the wash closet and saw a lumbering, clumsy man wander through. He was muttering under his breath, and she could see his briny eyes. He was poking things with his gun as he ambled around, yet he took a moment in the mirror to smooth his hair.

"Have you found her?" someone yelled in the door.

Penelope stood motionless against the wall. The words impaled the air around her, and she realized she was stuck. There was no way to escape. She saw the soldier pause as he again looked at his reflection and then turned toward her closet.

"No," he yelled back, twisting the doorknob with his hand and then abruptly pushing it open with his gun.

She squeezed behind the door even more tightly. She was desperately hoping he wouldn't push any harder, but the gun lacked the sensitivity of a hand, so he didn't notice the soft resistance of her chest and belly as the door pressed against her.

"She's not in here," he yelled, this time over his shoulder and turned back to look at himself once again.

She had no choice but to wait it out. The closet remained her tiny prison, and her eye throbbed like a boiling pot. As he walked out of the bathroom, her knees gave out, and she sunk slowly to the floor.

A soldier outside screamed, "Get to your feet," and she could hear Lucien scrambling, clawing at the wall with his hands. She heard a smashing sound. The noise quivered against the wall then fell to silence. She could hear Lucien, trembling and breathless.

The lights of the bathroom flickered and then went out. Penelope closed her eyes to shield herself from the dark pitch of the blackness. The city had become a living shadow, no light, darkness pervading every corner.

Her father had long ago taught her the importance of the dual nature of light, of Newton's rings, of constructive and destructive interference. It was Newton who first proposed that light was made up of tiny particles working together. When they added to each other in constructive interference, there was light. When they collided in destructive interference, there was obscurity. War is a disease, she thought to herself. She pressed her face into the wall, wishing with all her might that they had beaten her and not him.

More soldiers entered the theater, "Let's try this again. We must speak with you. And where is the woman?"

"You must be mistaken. There is no woman," Lucien replied.

"The woman with the bag."

She could hear as the questioning and the violence continued. The officers wanted to know if he had heard the explosion and why he smelled of smoke.

"Here, take my jacket. There is quite a bit of money in the pocket." He tore it off his body. "You have taken everything else. Can my family and I not even have a fire to warm us? Is that now illegal too?"

His sarcastic tone only provoked them into beating him more viciously, and Penelope could hear the blank and vacant thud of his body as he fell to the floor again. They checked the jacket pocket and were pleased by the pile of money. They didn't want to have to carry him so they took his money and left him there. She heard them murmuring and laughing caustically as they clambered down the hallway and out into the street. The brutality was rife, the infestation complete.

When Lucien finally was able to stand and knock

on the bathroom door, he was as pale as paper. He was bruised and bloody. They sat on the floor a while and huddled together. He kissed her hair. He held her tightly and tucked her hair behind her ear over and over again saying, "They are like monsters, horrible, terrified monsters. These are their sick games."

There were no real words to say, only nervous vexation. By the time they finally gathered themselves to walk out the doors of the cinema, it was dark outside, and no one was in the streets.

"The violence, I don't understand," she cried out. "They seemed to enjoy it. Their minds are diseased."

"Don't try to diagnose them. We are not doctors. We are alchemists. Our only work is to separate the impure from that which is pure, to draw the chaos from the harmony and find the magic. We cleanse, dissolve, freeze, congeal, purify, marry and distill. We sometimes join things and sometimes separate them, but when we rise, we never fall."

The whole city seemed buried alive by the cover of night.

He turned in the opposite direction of the apartment.

"Where are we going?" she asked. "It is past the curfew."

"To an important place," is all that he said.

Lucien led her to a palm grove in the center of the city, a courtyard surrounded by an arcade of ornate, white columns and palms. The rounded arches opened into a cloistered court. It was like walking into a prism, an enigmatic oasis with large palm trees lining the perimeter of the courtyard. There, the dim light of night seemed to undergo some sort of refraction, like stepping to the inside of a soap bubble, the rainbow partially polarized around them. There were large statues of Eros, Diana, and Venus. There were large bushes and at the center of the palm grove was a marble fountain. The whole scene was like a fresco of an aviary, with birds perched like the abundant and laden buds on the fronds and branches of the bushes and trees. The birds made a sound that was an unencumbered emulsion of things, both refined and disordered.

Without speaking, Lucien led her to the fountain and pulled the handkerchief away from her eye to get a better look. He pulled a small piece of debris from her lower eyelid with his trembling hand. He touched the delicate pallor of her eye. His finger stuck to the infection of her eye like flypaper, and yet there was something almost fluvial about the exchange between them, a natural flow that was beginning to seep into the places the war had so readily hollowed out.

"Can you see?" he asked.

She shook her head no, "Not from this eye. It's gone black." It was terrifying for her. The darkness settled like a sediment around her.

"Can I ask you something?" She could feel the warmth of him beside her.

"Of course." He scooped a handful of water from the fountain and splashed it into her wounded eye.

"Why did Fulcanelli want my necklace?" She felt a

rushing and a tingling sensation, as he splashed another scoop. "What's he going to do with it?"

"Is that okay?" he asked as he splashed more water into her eye.

She nodded.

"It wasn't the necklace he wanted, but the stone inside of it." He splashed even more water to her eye and asked again if she was okay.

"It feels good," she sighed. "But my face is tingling. I don't understand what is happening?"

"Close your eye for a second," he requested.

From the darkness of her eye, she saw numbers and the sun, a flicker of light, then dark, then an exquisite pink, the sky becoming the pinkest aquifer. This caused her to gasp for breath.

"Alchemy can do more than just make gold. Here, lean forward," he said. Lucien poured more of the water around her back and neck where the blast had burned her.

"You must not eat or drink anything until the eye heals completely," he said. "Go ahead, take a breath, plunge your face in and then open your eyes as wide as you can."

She was confused but leaned forward and submerged her face all the way into the cold water of the fountain as he requested. Opening her eyes, she let the water wash over them. At first, she saw only a blur of things, but then she saw numbers and the numbers merged into the pattern of a flower, and she saw the flower bloom. She quickly pulled her face from the waters, reeling.

"What is going on here?" she looked up at him, terrified.

"I told you about Parc Verdun and the alchemical mysteries hidden in the architecture there. Well, this park is no different. It's one of the many secrets this city holds. The water from this fountain heals. Paris has many of these sites. Don't be afraid."

She bent forward and continued to soak her eye in the shallow, cool water. As she looked down, she could see the clumps of her dried blood drawn and swirling down to the bottom of the fountain, a jelly. It was pure magic. They gathered and bobbed there like a handful of rubies, coagulated and shimmering beneath the water. She could not look away.

When she finally came up for a breath, Lucien was close beside her, and she could see him altogether more perfectly, his face decorated with swollen bruises, a kaleidoscope of black and purple. His left eye was languid and weepy. He had taken his shirt off and was trying to wash the red stains from his skin. His efforts were prolonged and meticulous, and when he looked toward her, his eyes did not retreat from hers. She felt it all the way to the dusty molecules of her bones, her frightened eyes, the long drapes of her hair. She watched the purple lines of his bruises, like small purple flowers sprinkled across his back, fade away. She wanted to touch them all. She wanted to smell and taste their perfume. Their gaze was equally prolonged and thorough, some rich ceremony, like overcoming something and casting it away.

Waves do not travel in straight lines, she thought. They move together. She was trying to distract herself from the emotions crowding around her.

"Explain this to me?" she beckoned.

"There are these magic places where nature is inverted." His swarthy complexion drew him into the shadows. "The alchemists and shamans know these places. There are maps of them."

She felt a vestigial flicker of pain in her eyeball, and without hesitation Lucien scooped another cup full of water to her eye. His touch had a vibration, like being inside a beehive.

"The math is inverted. Love and magic can do that in the world."

She reminded herself that she was there to study. She watched him move with a solitary hunger. He was both masterful and clear, and so without thinking she pulled his head to hers. She kissed his cheeks, the corners of his eyes, his forehead, a thousand kisses seemed like barely enough. These were silent instincts, and so he reached around and lifted her off of the ground, kissing her mouth deeply, expanding, expanding the way water turns into steam, of one thing becoming quite another.

Chapter Twelve

$\mathcal{F}$ulcanelli remained shuttered in his lab and office, closed away. After hearing of Lucien and Penelope's near disaster, he spent the whole night in the half-awake and sweating bath of a disjointed, early dawn nightmare. For days after, he stayed half-bathed in that paralysis until he finally seemed to wake from it and invited Penelope into his private quarters for a visit.

"Bring the papers," he had said, as though things might return to some state of routine once again.

Penelope entered his lab with a cup of warm tea to soothe him, and he described to her how a light rain of insects had been falling on him through a crack in the window, an alluvial covering of segmented animals with hardened exoskeletons and jointed limbs. He asked her to check the ceiling for a crack above him. She didn't see a crack, or even any insects, only the rain falling down outside the window.

His thoughts still bore the bramble of a fitful mind, and he then began to refer to the insects as soldiers. He had meant to say they were insects, centipedes, scorpions, millipedes, spiders, and that those leviathan images had wrestled from his mind onto his body. Or perhaps it was the other way around. He didn't like to acknowledge his emotions, and instead he left the room to shower and scrub his body, shaving away his mustache without a mirror. When he returned from the bathroom, he looked wild and unsteady.

Penelope handed him the papers. "Here they are," she offered. "What else?" She spoke softly.

His agony had transformed him.

"They have taken Naomie from outside the city to a work camp in Germany," he began. "I have just learned this, and I am afraid I must surrender the papers and myself to the Germans. Otherwise, they might kill her there."

Penelope felt his words dissolve into her. She searched the floor, the ceiling, the air for some better answer than the one she knew. Nothing could replace them.

"They will kill her, even if you do," she said.

"But she is my sister," he replied, clearly in agony.

"And she is like family to me," Penelope responded, her voice low and barbed. This was the first time she had ever uttered the word "family" in relation to Naomie. "Family" was a word that was both commodious and distant for Penelope. "The Germans know very well that she is your sister, and this is the very trap they have set for you."

She reached forward and grasped the papers from his hands. "You are wrong about this. Rest here until your mind is clear."

She raced out the door of his office, through the apartment to the main room, and set the papers on Lucien's desk beside him. She could hardly speak. The news of Naomie's transfer to Germany tightened along her diaphragm like a biting corset. Her eyes were endowed with a familiar manacle of loss that was beyond tears and words.

"What is it?" Lucien looked up at her, his face strung tightly with concern.

She steadied herself against the desk.

"Don't let Fulcanelli touch the papers," she said in a matter-of-fact manner. "He is considering giving them to the Nazis in an attempt to free Naomie."

Lucien slid his hands to his face in an inward fit of fear. "We must hurry then." He sat up, turning away from Penelope, and readjusted the papers on his desk, stirring his pencil across the page in a tumultuous manner.

Penelope thought of Naomie and her slight build, and of Naomie's gypsy spirit trapped in the haunted, brutal camps, unable to leave or retreat. These German camps were run by true, living monsters. Penelope couldn't contain her tears as her mind crossed over into a new place of sadness and silence.

Penelope sat down beside him, her face alert and angular. She was becoming thinner every day from hunger. "Can I ask you a question?" she interrupted his work. "Why did it take so long for you to tell me about Naomie?"

His brow furrowed. "What use is it?" he said stubbornly, his voice almost surly. There was something about her question that aggravated him.

"Naomie was like a sister to me. I traveled here to see her. I deserved to know."

"Exactly, she felt like you were her sister too, and when we told you, it hurt you, so what good was it? You had just lost your father. We were trying to protect you. Naomie is still a prisoner regardless."

His face was certain and ready, like a cork drawn. Lucien waved away a ragged fly buzzing near him.

"Whether or not Naomie is caught by the Germans, it hurt me not to know. She is caught and therefore so are we, that is the whole point." Her voice shook as she spoke.

He reached forward and pulled a long tendril of gold hair that had fallen onto her dark blouse. "Yes, we are caught, but some get released," Lucien said, tucking the golden thread into his pocket. "Yet somehow our slow death can be clarifying. War accelerates this whole process. It is in some ways illuminating. You can differentiate things more clearly."

"You know that you can't save Naomie or me. You can't protect your mother and sister," she responded. "It's a fallacy to think you can. Only the abandoned dogs and cats roam free and hungry. This whole city is bewildered. Everyone's lives here are turned upside down. Nothing is fixed or certain."

He looked away from her. He was restless, his eyes scanning the room. That morning, he had heard rumors of more police raids.

"That's right." He gazed up at her. His words punctuated the air. "The story I told you about my fiancée was only half true. It is true that she died in a train accident. But what I didn't tell you, or anyone else, ever, is that I was on the train too, but I didn't wait for her. I jumped ahead of her and survived." He said, leaning forward towards Penelope, almost falling to his knees.

Her eyes stilled upon him intently. She reached forward and held his face with her hands. His mouth was tense with shame. For five years he had held this secret, and the burnished guilt of the half-truth had ground him down. He still carried the loss of this woman, like a wounded man with a limp.

"So, yes, I understand that," he concluded. "I lost her forever, and since then I've tried everything I can think of to protect the people I love, and none of it is working. I didn't want to tell you about Naomie to spare you from the pain. I couldn't bear to watch you suffer helplessly too. She is gone and there is nothing we can do. The Royal Society is starving, broke, and no closer to completing the experiments from Newton's papers. Tell me, is there something I haven't thought of?"

She racked her brain for an answer. "It's just—" was all she could think to say. "I'm sorry," she concluded.

She felt his sorrow reverberate through her and hoped she might find an answer. She tipped forward and brushed her lips against his cheek, her hands caressing him. As she drew back, he pulled another strand of her hair from her shirt and stashed it in his pocket.

"Why do you want my hair? Do you need it for some experiment?" she smirked.

"No, not at all, I keep it because it reminds me of you," he said with sincerity, tossing a shy glance up at her. He pulled a collection of them from his pocket, his face flushing as he turned back towards his desk.

There was no remedy for the effect his words had upon her heart. Penelope stilled as her longing took shape, a type of involuntary surrender. Unlike the hunger of an empty belly, his words overflowed all around her, soaking into everything she touched, spoke, and thought she knew.

Chapter Thirteen

*S*ince the explosion, Lucien had become more mercurial, one day close, then distant, then close again. Penelope didn't know whether it was his fear, his urgency to finish his translation of the papers, or some private doubt that had driven him so far. She wondered if he had made some solemn promise with himself or Fulcanelli to distance himself from her to keep her safe. Either way, the estrangement was palpable and excruciating, like the severance of some new part of herself.

"Please, you're becoming so thin. Can you just take a break?" Penelope urged Lucien.

Terrified and electric, since the explosion, he worked at his desk night and day. "I need to decipher this," Lucien pointed with exhaustion to a series of rudimentary drawings that seemed to demonstrate the way salts could be made to precipitate themselves from a solution. "But I cannot even find my pen." He looked around in frustration.

"It's magic," Penelope observed. She was looking at the papers and winding her fingers through the silky catacombs of her hair.

"No," Lucien said, shuffling his feet in protest. "Alchemists are very different from magicians."

Penelope closed her eyes and put her fingers to her temples, pretending to focus. "Ta Da!" she said and pretended to pull his beloved ink pen from behind her ear.

Lucien smiled and laughed, as she clapped an explosive cloud of dirt and dust from the desk into the air as her grand finale.

"At its worst," Lucien said, "magic is just a sleight of hand, a word people use for that which cannot be explained." He grasped the pen from her hand. "Really, it's just that nature has secrets to discover. You can't force them. They must yield themselves to you."

"Like the discovery of sodium sulfate," Penelope said, looking at the assorted drawings strung out along the page of the papers. The haze of the dust was beginning to clear.

Lucien sighed loudly, pursing his lips. He closed his eyes, his face a tense, warm hearthstone. Since the explosion on the street and Naomie's transfer to the German work camps, he was not in the mood for joking around.

Penelope spoke in a more serious tone. "Like understanding the elements of nature..." The sounds came from a distant place in her throat.

He watched her with no response.

"And love," she continued.

Love. The word protruded into the room.

"Yes, that too." Lucien flushed a fantastic shade of ruby.

"But what about love, Lucien," Penelope asked. "What does alchemy say about love?" She continued to weave her fingers in and out of her hair.

Lucien could hear passion's falsetto pitch rising in Penelope's voice. He could feel Penelope's nervous feet swirling beside him in both fear and pleasure, her index finger flexed white to grip the chair.

"What about love?" Her voice climbed higher.

The apartment echoed with a tense silence.

"Alchemy says it's transcendent, like fire," Lucien responded, finally. "Love is the agent that ripens people. It awakens them." Lucien's voice slowed. "But as I've told you already, it's too risky," he concluded, turning back to his papers once again. He waved her away. It was as though the apartment air thickened around them. Penelope nodded, then quietly left the room.

Penelope had to remind herself she was here to be a scientist and not a lover, and she had come upon her feelings unexpectedly and unknowingly, having never felt such friction in her heart before. She wiped the tears from her eyes and steeled herself as she walked down the hallway into the kitchen.

A woman named Vera, a member of the Royal Society, who came and went from the apartment once every week, greeted her at the sink.

"Are you okay?" she asked.

Penelope nodded, her eyes were still filled with warm tears.

"I guess you heard about Naomie?" she determined.

Penelope nodded once again, unable to speak.

Vera studied her for a moment.

"And perhaps something else too," she added, pausing for a moment. "Penelope, forget this mad house. This place is so crazy. If you really want to help her, Fulcanelli is wrong, you don't need alchemy, you need a plan. You need money and resources from outside of Paris. Do you know about the British Intelligence?"

Penelope shook her head no.

"The *SOE*, or Special Operations Executives, was created to help assist the Resistance. It is part of the British Secret Service but is designated to help fund and train subversive groups within the occupied countries. You should join the British *SOE* and be trained in subterfuge to steal secrets from the Germans," Vera said.

Vera was British, and she was the only other woman in the Royal Society. She had pale skin, short brown hair, and a full face. She repaired Resistance radios and soldered together discrete antennas that she distributed in the neighborhoods. She came to 52 rue Laffitte to help her boyfriend Philippe build his death ray machine.

"The Royal Society is starving here in this apartment. Each week grows bleaker and bleaker. These men are clueless and blind. They are like mad scientists. If you need money, the *SOE* has plenty," Vera told her. "They will take you and send you back to Paris well-trained as a saboteur. I have heard they are looking to work with more women now because they realize that it is easier for us to blend in." Vera spoke in a delicate voice. "We can travel with money, radios, and explosives buried in our coats, or in shopping bags and in purses without inviting as much suspicion." They were in the kitchen, and Vera concluded in strategic whispers. "Women will happily create havoc for the Nazis." She paused, "The *SOE* may even know how to help Naomie."

Penelope listened intently, and she peppered Vera with questions through the remainder of the day and well into the night. Perhaps, Vera was right. It seemed pointless for her to remain indefinitely isolated in this apartment in Paris. Time was running out. Her tired eyes burned as she thought of Naomie trapped, dirty, and scared in the German work camps.

It was late at night when she finally wandered into the bedroom from the kitchen. She could see Lucien awake but resting on one of the cots.

"What are you doing here?" she asked him.

"Looking for you."

He had been so vacant lately, but yet in spite of her apprehension, she reached for him and sensed his jaw soften to her touch.

"I need to rest," she whispered. "I have a lot to think about."

He laced his fingers in hers. She knew that sometimes he felt he had to touch her and other times he felt he couldn't. Lately, his heart seemed to swing like a pendulum.

"Where is Fulcanelli?" he asked.

"I'm not sure."

"I thought you were with him."

"No, I was catching up with Vera," she whispered. "Where did you put the papers?" she continued, fearful that Fulcanelli might find them and make his way to the Nazis.

"I hid them in the piano," he reassured her. "He would never think to look there."

Lucien's voice was drawn and tired, and his gaze was knotted with concern. She lay down beside him and drew her face to his. He tilted his head forward and grazed his lips against hers, pressing into her, caressing her face with his hand.

"Please be patient with me. You know Isaac Newton said once that 'genius is patience.'" His voice circled around her.

"As is love... and loss," she concluded.

But she didn't feel she could be patient any longer. She didn't understand the feeling of love in this way, and it scared her enough that she suppressed it as did Lucien, and pretty soon they were talking about the attributes of mercury and numbers, stiff and decimal-laden numbers. Somehow the question of infinity was easier for them than the question of passion and love.

"The Philosopher's Mercury has five long stages,"

Lucien observed. "If we could decipher the translation and start tomorrow, it would still take us almost a year to make it." He was right. The translation of the papers was only the beginning. The experiment would take years to complete, at best. Frustration rose up in her. How could such efforts or the explosion of stuffed rats end the war?

Her body was tense with frustration. Penelope had left a great deal of innocence at the altar of her home in Tennessee. What emerged from time to time was a lack of hope and a reluctance to rely upon others. Such a gaping hole drove her to a taut distance and a sadness, particularly in the night. Having lost so much in Sweetwater, Penelope had long ago been baptized into the world of the undecorated and most lonely. Lucien misunderstood her remoteness in this moment.

He looked into her far away eyes. He could see long valleys of sadness there, so he wrapped his arms around her, kissing her so passionately that it cast away the lonely chill that had enveloped them that night.

Penelope had so much to say, but with her feelings so strong she could not think of the words. Instead, she drew the blanket over them and moved closer. He grazed his thumb along her cheek and tipped his troubled forehead into hers. They rested there for a long time, as his breath moved beside hers with a slow cadenced beauty. Evening poured in through the window. Along his back, she could see the shadows of the night stain his skin, spreading like bruises on the landscape of some continent or ocean. She ran her fingers along his ribs in a disorderly sort of way, the tips of her finger grazing over theoretical mountains and valleys to see how her turbulent touch would reshape his close but distant world. She closed her eyes and pretended she was in the ocean rising and falling in the waves. There was nothing lonelier to her than the ocean. She twisted her hair into a crown upon her head, finger by finger he laced his hand in hers. He was exhausted and didn't have to say anything at all, but she knew he loved her too. He gazed at her and held her close, kissing her hair and face, until in a moment of timid happiness, they drifted off to sleep.

Chapter Fourteen

*P*enelope awoke to the smell of licorice and saw
Fulcanelli standing with a cup of fragrant tea
above them, shirtless and declaring that he needed to
show Lucien and her something outside the apartment. He
wanted them to hurry and meet him at the front door of
the apartment shortly. Penelope was so distracted by the
many scars and scratches on Fulcanelli's chest and back
that she could hardly hear his words. There were dozens
of them on his torso. She wondered if it was his father who
had hurt him that way. They were the full-blown, disjointed constellations to his life, a conduit to some dark,
unspoken pain he continued to nurse, a wound no bandage could contain.

Penelope and Lucien reluctantly awoke, dressed,
and met Fulcanelli, who was now wearing a shirt. They

followed him into the aching dawn of the city. The early morning sun made the buildings a blurred and nostalgic shade of rye.

"It shouldn't have happened that way," Fulcanelli said, speaking to them for the first time about the explosion. His words seemed to make his teeth grind. "I'm sorry. I should not have put you in danger like that, I take full responsibility. I can hardly sleep. I can hardly forgive myself. It was so reckless and careless of me. It's just that the Germans seem to take everything but the solitude." He held his body in the half-defeated posture of a dishrag, "Before they come for us, I must take you to Notre Dame," he said.

Fulcanelli had told Lucien to bring some other papers that were hidden in the strange hole in the wall. The papers looked like architectural drawings of the cathedral. Penelope wondered what other relics were in the hole besides the stone and the blueprints.

"Be careful with them," Lucien said as he handed her the papers.

She stashed them in her shirt and blindly followed along as the sun slithered smoothly up the sky. Without his mustache, Fulcanelli looked a bit like a stranger. In truth, Penelope knew so little of his life except that he had traveled around the world at least twice, and on his second voyage, he had acquired smallpox near a cathedral in Norway, and that had forced him to seek refuge in a monastery. There he learned about Gothic architecture, and there he learned to play dominoes and was allegedly baptized. She also now knew that Naomie was his only sister.

"Light alone creates color," Fulcanelli said as they scurried towards the cathedral. "Red, orange, yellow, green, blue, indigo and violet. Isaac Newton liked that there were seven. He noted that seven was special because he believed a correlation existed between colors, musical notes, and the days of the week. After all God had rested on the seventh day, identifying it with completion. The rigor of human emotions left no room for anything less than seven."

The five senses were quite simply not sufficient, Fulcanelli believed, and he constantly sought more. "It's the power of refraction," Fulcanelli concluded as he pointed to a place where stained glass used to hang. "In Gothic architecture, like in love, the secrets are in plain sight."

Fulcanelli was explaining how the stained-glass windows had been removed from the cathedral to protect them from being destroyed during the war.

They paused to look around at the inside of the great cathedral, while Fulcanelli continued his lesson, "This building has stood watch through the centuries. It saw us through ordinations and revolutions. Napoleon, King Louis, Joan of Arc. Notre Dame is one of the world's most perfect and prominent examples of Gothic architecture. Each stone, you must remember, is hand sculpted. It alone will remain after this war too."

Penelope tried to take in any of one of the five-story towers, in addition to the cathedral in its entirety. She had never studied anything like this so closely, that merger between art and the divine. They continued to examine the building's facade, the swooping columns, the large, dark doorways, the trifoliated arches, the tremendous towers with dark, slate roofs. She thought of the forests and hills near her house in Tennessee.

"Man can do this," Fulcanelli said. "Of course, time and man can undo it as well. It represents those tensions too. This cathedral tells as much the story of human creation as human destruction," he continued. "In the two hundred years of its creation, so many fools and wise men had their say." He spoke about the cathedral's desecration during the revolution, its statues beheaded, parts of it torn down. "They used the cathedral to store food," he told them.

Food, she thought. The Royal Society was nearly out of money and starving. Hunger was a gradual change. She thought she had learned about hunger during her travels across the Atlantic, but she was wrong. In Paris, she had to endure the endless hunger of her belly. Along with it came the deep vibrations of her heart. Standing next to Lucien, she felt the stifling oppression of her love for him. She felt empty of so many things, of food, of warm touch, of love and mostly of words.

They stood below the western front of the cathedral. Its two giant towers rose up in geometric progression. The famous bell of the south tower, hung with terrific loneliness in the blue sky.

"The hieroglyphics of alchemy are written throughout this church," Fulcanelli told them. "Every calculation had to be worked out precisely for it all to balance together so perfectly."

"What are these?" Penelope asked, pointing at the doors ahead of them. They were decorated with panels depicting the universe, mimicking the cycles of the sun, rising from January, descending to December.

"Those are the portals," Lucien responded lethargically.

"Theologians are always striving to reconcile the largeness of the universe with the smallness of man," Fulcanelli observed. He watched with delight as she traced the door panels with her fingers. The wood bore a cold neutrality.

"This is a monument to the accumulation of humankind," he continued, "our knowledge, our art, our history. Each pulse of history leaves its mark. We are in one of those times now." He paused and scratched his chin. "One day, I hope, you will see the wheel window. They have taken it down for now, but it is a great masterpiece. The south rose window was a gift from a king, eighty-four panes, divided into four circles. The first one has twelve medallions, and the second has twenty-four. A third circle is made up of quadrilobes, and the fourth circle has twenty-four trilobes medallions. This window features the symbolic number four, along with its multiples, twelve and twenty-four. It is called the rose window because of its similarity to a multi-petalled rose."

"What is the significance of the rose?" Lucien said, without meeting Fulcanelli's gaze.

"As you know, numbers and patterns are always of metaphysical significance. This is no exception. The whole design of the church is about geometry and proportion, the number of pillars in the choir, the ratio of the levels of the windows. You should go to the library and look up the mathematics involved in the architecture of this building. It will astonish you. I brought a simplified version of the blueprint along with us. I believe Penelope is carrying the papers with her."

Fulcanelli looked up at the enormous scale of the church. "The circle symbolizes unity, the flower symbolizes life, the repetition of pattern is duality, the triangle transcendence, and so forth. The mathematics explains it all."

Penelope felt the prickling papers tucked inside her shirt. She had noted that the drawings were written in Fulcanelli's handwriting. She looked to where the window had been. She could feel Lucien's gaze prick upon her neck.

"All great buildings mimic nature. The pyramids, Babel. They grow and change over time like a plant," Fulcanelli continued. "Many of the parks in Paris are the same, the architecture mimics the natural secrets we so easily overlook in our day to day." He smiled and chuckled to himself, causing his whole body to vibrate as he laughed, though his face was still lettered with strain and confusion.

Penelope wandered up the stairs and into the towers of the great church. She was trying to keep her balance while she watched Lucien and contemplated how in this communion of the soul, rock, and earthen soil, the walls could be so steadying and yet so cold and unresponsive. Perhaps she would have to go to the library to learn more about the chilling logic of it.

They continued to climb the stairs, and Fulcanelli remarked that in Greek mythology *Ananke* is the human heart. This word too was etched into the wall of the cathedral. Penelope traced the cold letters with her fingers.

"*Ananke* is the Greek word for Fate," Lucien offered. "In mythology, she was the daughter of Hydros and Gaia, and she held a spindle, having emerged with the formation of the cosmos, the mother of the Fates. She and her consort Chronos were said to have cracked open the universe, separating it into its pieces, and encircling it in a rotation of earth, the heavens, and time."

He touched Penelope's hand, confiscating her gaze for a private, burning second, making her feel taller and more beautiful. *Is this what love does?* She wondered. She felt startled and scared and tasted the salt of desire in her mouth. Her emotions usurped her thoughts.

She hadn't been thinking about *Ananke*. She had been thinking about covalent bonds and acids. "Co," to share, those chemical bonds or connections were the basis of all living systems, a pair of electrons shared by two atoms. An acid, she felt, was any incomplete molecule that was thus capable of accepting electrons, and bases were the perfect donors. Her mouth tasted like the ocean. She could quantify growing old, but she couldn't fathom love. She worried that her bond with Lucien was covalent.

Fulcanelli interrupted her thoughts, "It's a word that marks the merger of fate and love, the human heart and the cosmos, and she dictates the path of one's life."

"*Ananke,*" Penelope repeated in an aching whisper.

Lucien looked down at her, quickly looking away.

There were cracks in the walls. She traced those with her fingers. Her questions gathered around her.

"Come see this!" Fulcanelli shouted from the stairs above, and they followed his voice up to the spot between the towers to the Galerie des Chiméres. The gargoyles were everywhere, some built to drain rainwater off the roof and others for decoration. All of them scanned the city below, animal and human figures, half-man and half-animal with beaks, talons, snake tails. They were grotesque, scary, ponderous creatures, and they were everywhere at this height.

"They each seem to have a story," Penelope said. "And a personality. It's like you are meant to come and visit them."

"The artists spent years following Viollet-le-Duc's designs." Fulcanelli offered.

Penelope looked out from the tower. They were indeed on an island in the river, with it weaving like a thread through the giant city. She could see the palace domes and the flying buttresses of the cathedral itself. From this vantage point, she could see that the whole city was veiled in the shadow of the war. The edges of Paris were filled with destruction and rubble, tanks and burned out cars. The city-center and its people looked abandoned. The Parisians said it was, *"La ville sans regard,"* where no eyes could meet. Penelope too felt stranded there, alone.

Fulcanelli gestured for Penelope to hand him the papers, and she unfurled them in front of him. "This was one of the first Gothic cathedrals. The Gothic design required thin, high walls and as the cathedral settles the walls began to push outward and crack. The buttresses were built to stabilize the structure." He then paused, a fermata taking hold. It was the prolonged tone of silence, and the duration unsettled her.

She looked to Fulcanelli and saw he was looking up the river and his eyes were focused on the Eiffel Tower. She noticed a large structure with a glass roof.

"What is that?" Penelope wondered aloud.

Lucien answered, standing beside her. "It is the velodrome for racing cycles, but the glass roof has been painted dark blue to avoid the bombers."

Fulcanelli remained silent.

"What is it?" she asked.

"It's a trap," Fulcanelli said, looking at them with sharp concern. "The Nazis have started to turn it into a holding pen for the Jews." His lip began to tremble with emotion, and his eyes wore the look of high fermentation, something was brewing.

"We believe they held Naomie there for a time," Lucien said.

Penelope felt his words congeal around her.

"The Resistance have told us it is going to happen," Lucien remembered. "Someday, the Reich will come back for a mass imprisonment of Jewish men and then the women and the children."

"They will split the families apart and take them to the camps like Naomie."

"No, how can this happen?" Penelope cried out and turned towards the stairs.

"It's this war," Fulcanelli said. "I have spent my life looking for the mathematical structure of reality, scouring numbers and equations, but physics has remained silent on the question of both love and war." He grew sullen and looked out into the river's refluent waters. He stood somewhat crouched, clinging to the cold rails of the cathedral. He had crossed over to another side of silence and seemed to have no words left.

As she observed him, Penelope, impoverished, with so little food and so little hope, suddenly became resolute. She decided she would go to London to find the *SOE* as Vera advised. She would bring back money and resources. She would have to find a way to talk to Lucien and Fulcanelli.

Ananke, she decided, as though the clutch of a strong hand was leading her there.

Chapter Fifteen

The next day, Penelope brought Fulcanelli a color wheel she found inside a cabinet in the kitchen—a simple disk with colors arranged clockwise in the order of a rainbow. She placed it on the desk before him to help cheer him up. Since their visit to the cathedral, Fulcanelli's complexion had turned chalky and pale.

"Look what I found. Optical contrast from the great magician Newton himself," she said and smiled, as she stepped back from his desk. It was Newton's gift to artists, his conceptual, circular arrangement of the colors of the prism.

"It's quite amazing. In Newton's color wheel, each 'spoke' of the wheel is assigned a letter," she said. "These letters correspond to the notes of the musical scale. He created his color-music arrangement as a concept to explain his belief that colors' patterns recur in the same way that musical notes recur octaves apart. When the disk spins, the colors blur into white."

He nodded weakly. A small bird fretted about on his hand.

She spun the disk in front of Fulcanelli, hoping its intricacies might spark some renewed sense of life in him, but Fulcanelli's spirit was cluttered with fears about the war and his sister Naomie, his glance perpetually evasive. He constantly wore his winter coat and his door remained mostly locked. Lately, he had even become unresponsive to the light and color that surrounded him. As she watched him, she wondered if knowledge could embalm a person as much as free him.

"What can I do to help you?" she asked, her voice soft.

"It's better I work alone, without distraction." His voice was worn down to a whisper. "Even in the best circumstances, it's far too easy to see in your scientific results what you want to see, rather than what is truly there." He seemed to her to be saying something else, and his words enveloped her with a kind of desolation, the way mercury moves in a silver shiver.

"It's okay to imagine though," she spoke out, gently grasping some of the papers on his desk. "Sometimes you must take action. You can't always just insist on the primacy of science."

"Yes, but it's dangerous. We build these dreams to convince ourselves that nothing can go wrong, but it does.

Look at Naomie. She's gone. This city is overthrown, and we have become part of the war resistance. The Nazis fear us. One by one, the soldiers will hunt us down and arrest us. They will give us a trial, and then they will decide whether to tear off our toenails or to burn us. Then they will cut us and pour salt into our cuts. They will starve us and beat us until we die. They live by a motto of 'by any means.' There are no limits to the cruelty of their imaginations and actions. The Nazis will do anything to anyone to meet their goals. Science can do only so much for the perils of humans." He spoke with grinding impetuosity.

Penelope argued, "But there is so much more to know. Have you forgotten that the Nazis need for you to believe your nightmares, and forget your instincts. If you do, they win so much more than this war. Look at me. I am here because I was told to come here to find my friend and bring this magical, ineffable necklace to people I've never known in a place I've never been. My father was a scientist. I am indebted to science. I don't have another place where I can return, there is no home for me to go back to."

Her soul thirsted for Fulcanelli to hear her and to see her, but when he looked up at her, it was in the way someone looks through a stranger. His despair was overtaking him. It was a mathematical sort of silence, painful and confounding yet also merely structural. His eyes bore the tone of someone indifferent to the light, the troubled and miscalculated intimacy of some deep loneliness. He was scared, and he wore his fear like a mask.

Penelope stared into him, trying to distinguish what was behind his armored face. She could see the fear crystalized within him, a calamitous and deep wounding.

"Why are you acting this way?" She spoke slowly and clearly, continuing in a mannered tone, "Though, in truth, I am surprised and confused that you are speaking to me at all because lately you often seem so reluctant to even acknowledge me in the apartment. It is like I am some ghost." She eyed him closely. "Some days you speak to me, and some days you don't," Penelope announced, stretching out her cramped and cold fingers.

Penelope could see his shoulders rise and fall with a brittle wave of emotion.

"My speaking to you is not the main issue," Fulcanelli began incredulously. "Enough of this. Penelope, we've got work to do."

She turned to face him, "Sir, there are no soldiers here. We have barely left the apartment. What is it precisely that you are planning to do?"

They both watched in silence as a car drove by on the street.

"Enough," Fulcanelli concluded and left the room.

She wandered into the main lab and found Lucien pushing papers around on his desk in frustration, in a desperate search of some mysterious scrap to finish his latest experiment. They had made so little progress in Fulcanelli's hidden attic lab since the explosion on the streets. Penelope approached his desk. Since their journey to Notre Dame, he also had become more brooding.

Lucien kept a winsome, wounded bird as a companion while he worked at his desk. He would often hum to it as he worked. Like Fulcanelli, he believed in the enchantment of music, of its magical ability to control emotions, to evoke and to tame the imagination, to bring about a soothing type of forgetfulness. The chattering bird was large like a jay but black and white. He had built a cage for it out of twigs and leaves and fed it scraps from his lunch.

Lucien struggled to calm it, reaching his hand inside its cage and offering it some stale crumbs.

"Have you ever noticed that your bird is different than other birds," she observed, smiling at the fretting creature.

"Outside of its wounded wing, how is it different?" Lucien asked, both surprised and distracted by her comment.

"It is silent," Penelope observed. "Your bird cannot sing." Lucien and Penelope could hear the other birds chirping and singing on the roofs and streets below.

"Give it more time. It was hurt and is still healing," he replied in frustration. "It needs to rest until its wing is healed."

Penelope shrugged, "Regardless, it is beautiful to look at."

"Yes, birds help make life beautiful." Lucien observed to Penelope. "It is in the artistry of their feathers and their language. You know, a bird's song is the oldest form of divination."

"How?" Penelope asked.

"It is both music and symbol."

Penelope watched as the magpie marched around, upright and authoritarian as a military officer. It tilted its beak upward and flicked its tail over and over against the floor of the cage.

"Through song and gesture and flight, the birds have so much to say about things, about the seasons and the weather and the fates."

"The fates?" Penelope asked. "What do you mean?"

"Their dreams and their destiny," he said. "People look to the sky for so many reasons."

Penelope thought of her own dreams, and as she glanced out of the window of the apartment, she realized the bird yearned to be free. She unfastened the cage door and petted the bird with her finger, soothing it.

Penelope put her finger to her smiling lips, "I am beginning to understand that freedom and love are similar."

Lucien looked pained and puzzled. He stared at her once again.

"I have been speaking with Fulcanelli about Newton's law of universal gravitation. In Newton's law, the force of gravity is proportional to the product of mass, and inversely proportional to the square of the distance between. Penelope, the closer we are, the more afraid I am of something happening to you."

"Do you really think love works the same as Newton's laws?"

"Perhaps they are universal. I can't think of anything more similar to love than gravity."

"Newton also stated that gravity always attracts and has infinite range," she said, her expression simultaneously redolent and harsh, her eyes hopeful. "But I am clear, crystal clear that the mathematical formulation of gravity has virtually nothing to do with falling in love."

He looked at her with grave desire. The intoxicating perfume of love had rendered him deaf, mute and blind. Fulcanelli's blueprints of the cathedral were sitting in disarray on the desk before him. Penelope stepped forward and opened one of them to a page with an extensive drawing of the flying buttresses of the cathedral.

"To think the structure would cave in on itself without them? They stand there quietly resisting the relentless pull of gravity on the cathedral," she said, smiling to herself. "Do you remember in your experiment with Fulcanelli how you thought that you had gotten the translation wrong by just one word? How you thought the symbol was an alloy, how you were mistakenly looking for two things not one."

He nodded.

"I have determined that you were right, that the translation was alloy. It was the gold from the tooth but also the blood from his mouth that combined."

Penelope sat down beside Lucien and leaned into the drawings, pointing to the buttresses that held the building in place. Lucien leaned in closely beside her.

After a prolonged silence, he said, "Do you really think so?"

She nodded and kissed his cheek.

Lucien continued, "I suppose this too is like alchemy. It is held together by antagonistic, opposite forces—hot and cold, positive and negative, and masculine and feminine."

She smiled, still looking down at the papers, "Do you think Notre Dame will survive this war?"

"Yes, I do," he concluded, pausing. "Do you think we will?" His voice gravelly and suddenly very deep.

Penelope turned towards him and breathed in his bright scent, which was so close and warm. The lavender perfume of this mystery, her love of Lucien, was so much better than the stench of their own measureless solitude. Both impassable and unseen, the power of their emotions within the context of the war was their grandest obstacle.

His hand grazed hers. She was fully aware of the difference between his touch and all of the rest. She wanted to raise her lips to his once again. But she did not.

Penelope looked out the window and watched as the sunset spread open like an orange blossom. She noticed that it too began as a lashing, red and expanding along the horizon.

She had been taught by the turns her life had taken that every border is a beginning point for some new end. She watched the flocks of migrating birds scattering in the setting sun from the snow. Without a home, they too knew they needed to stay in motion to stay alive.

"I have made a decision," she said as the last drop of sunset faded into the horizon.

He looked up at her with surprise.

Penelope's face held the prominence of wonder and a clarity found in unceremonious rain falling through the sunshine.

"Penelope, are you okay?" Lucien asked, and he reached forward and put his arm around her shoulders gently.

Her eyes became laced in the intricate red of sorrow that appears just before tears wash down the face into a sober weeping.

"What is it?" he beckoned.

"Call it circumstance. Call it chance. Call it *Ananke* or fate. It doesn't matter."

"Is everything okay?" he spoke with soft concern, reaching for her, leaning forward to touch his forehead to hers. He admired the subtlety of Penelope's quiet resolve, her slow breath, her confusion and discontent, and the ripples of her trembling hair as it fell down her back. He tipped forward even more, touching her cheek and neck with his lips. He grazed his hands down along the golden strand of her hair to her waist, pulling her to him.

Penelope mustered her courage, "Lucien, I think we can survive this war, but I need to talk to you and Fulcanelli about a plan that I have made."

As Lucien was about to respond, Fulcanelli called out to her from across the room.

"Penelope, I need you to come up with a new formula

for Philosopher's Mercury," he proclaimed with a fevered madness, explaining that he thought it was indeed an amalgam that would take root and eventually seed, ripen and grow into a tree, but he didn't know what to mix with the gold. He didn't realize yet the alloy was his own blood.

Fulcanelli now sat in the corner quietly weighing small things on his golden scales. She walked over to his table.

"I have made a decision," she stated with determination. "I need to talk with you both immediately."

Lucien followed her.

"What is it?" Fulcanelli asked.

"I feel like we are all decomposing here," she stated. "The timeline of our experiments is too slow. Naomie is held captive, and here we are stuck in this apartment, isolated, starving, and afraid. To be part of the Resistance we have to be out in the world, not hiding like hermetic scientists in this apartment."

They both remained in a thoughtful silence.

"Can I ask you something?" she turned to Fulcanelli. "I need you to tell me the truth."

He had taught her to seek out the simple truths that others had overlooked, to wait for the unexpected meanings to emerge. He had explained to her that the meanings become apparent later. After all, gravity itself was more about time and accumulated knowledge than the apple falling. Newton derived the Three Laws of Motion from prolonged scientific study. An object at rest tends to stay at rest, and an object in motion must tend to stay in motion, with the same direction and speed.

Fulcanelli nodded, "Of course, what's your question?"

She had been afraid of this moment because she was scared of what he might say. "Do you really think esoteric experiments in a homemade lab can end the war?" Penelope touched her fingertips to her face. They felt numb.

Fulcanelli looked dumbstruck.

"Please bear with me a minute and listen," she began. "I think I have a better plan. I need to leave Paris and go to London so we can get the money and resources we need. We are going to starve and be killed here if we do not do something," she continued. "Hear me out…"

Fulcanelli looked up at her while he was handing the bird a small cracker. The magpie bit down on it, causing crumbs to rain down to the floor.

Lucien stood behind her, listening.

"I am foreigner," she continued. "I can still move freely. I must go to London and work with the British *SOE*. They can train me and direct me. Perhaps the British can help us find Naomie. I will come back with money, contacts, and skills for the Royal Society. No one else can make this journey safely." She looked at him with an intent and grave entreaty. "You keep me here because you are scared, but I alone can do this. I am an American, and I am a woman. I need to go soon."

Fulcanelli stunned them all when he said simply, "I agree."

Lucien said nothing. He didn't excuse himself or say anything at all. He gazed at her ill at ease and pale, then turned and walked down the hall to his desk. She had never been so certain of her decision, and yet he walked away without a word, knocking her father's alchemy book from his desk in frustration.

"*Solve et coagula*: Dissolve and coagulate," the book said on its back cover. It was the alchemical motto. Metals and souls alike must be broken down to be reformulated.

Chapter Sixteen

"Fulcanelli!" A wild-card guy, an inventor, named Philippe called across the room. "I need you to come upstairs." He was building a death ray machine in Fulcanelli's study. Most of the time, Philippe was silent and still as a statue, fine-tuning the delicate instrument with the most potent and deadly name.

Penelope wandered upstairs and watched them talk intently together, wondering if his machine was real or just really some fantastical delusion.

Fulcanelli turned, stepped away from the machine and stroked his beard, thinking. He was holding a small and delicate bird in his hand, watching the birds outside feed from the seed he intermittently tossed to the roof. There were tons of birds, large and small, all huddled together, marching along the tiles of the eaves.

"The birds have suffered greatly this winter too," he observed finally speaking. "This one Lucien found with its feet frozen to the windowsill. We have nursed it back to health."

He uncovered his hand and showed her a new, small black and white bird. Its foot was wounded and delicately bandaged.

"What is it?"

"It's a magpie. They are mischievous birds with a profound intelligence."

The bird looked at Penelope and tilted its head to the side with an almost human-like self-awareness.

"Watch this," he pulled a mirror from his pocket. He held the mirror in front of the bird. It stared at its reflection with great curiosity. It fluttered its wings. It preened at itself and explored its body. It looked at the bandage on its leg then picked at the wrapped gauze with its beak.

"It can recognize its own reflection," Penelope's eyes gaped wide. Self-awareness or self-consciousness, Penelope saw her own reflection in the mirror behind the bird and saw that she had the tired and unkempt look of solitude.

From the corner of her eye she saw Lucien walk into the room.

Fulcanelli seemed to speak to the bird as much as to Penelope when he said, "Yes, and they also have great empathy. So, can you guess what it is thinking?"

The bird played in front of the mirror some more. It

waved its tail, twisting its neck from side to side. It examined its profile, then it stopped and looked at itself intently in the mirror. It fluffed its feathers. It stood tall. It seemed to feel strong and powerful, until suddenly its whole body shuddered in a giant shiver.

"Watch and you can see," Fulcanelli said as he adjusted the mirror.

Penelope bent down so that she and the bird were looking into each other's eyes. The look was prolonged and culminating, a dark paddle down some long estuary. Birds can't cry, she thought to herself, and she stood up abruptly, causing herself to fall backwards a little. The bird squawked and ruffled its feathers at her.

"The cold is lonely," Penelope said with cryptic solemnity. "It is a reminder of some other profound loneliness."

"Yes, it's profound, even for the birds," Fulcanelli replied and readjusted the magpie in his lap, cuddling it more closely. "They feel both the war and the cold."

She understood.

"They feel it all," Lucien added, his voice was raw and leathery.

Their conversation was interrupted by the clanking of a caravan of military trucks from outside. The trucks roamed savagely around the city. Penelope stepped forward to close the window, the glass still rimy with winter's frozen breath. She could see the snow coming down all around, ice swiveling down from the gutters in long, loose ringlets.

"It's like we live in two cities. We are up here, and they are there."

They watched as the infantry marched behind the trucks in formation below them.

"Look at them," Fulcanelli said with scorn. "They mistake that parade for strength. Man simply refuses to accept how really small he is within the scope of the universe." He turned to Penelope and Lucien. "We used to meet in the beautiful courtyard of the cathedral every Saturday to share our lessons as scientists. Now we hide here." He looked down at his feet and shook his head, "And if they find us, they will kill us all."

A man named Robert rushed up the stairs and called, "Fulcanelli! Sir, please listen. I did what you said, and I left nitric acid in the sun for two days, then added silver and copper. The reaction was strong and released nitrous gas, so I left it for fourteen days more. That produced even more of the agglomerate. I added water and left it eight more days, then I passed it over heat. I added more acid and then placed it in the sun. The agglomerate turned to gold, fool's gold. The major difference, I believe, was the sunlight. You were right. They are connected. It is my belief that it somehow influenced the action of the nitrogen."

Fulcanelli handed the magpie to Penelope and reached out to Robert, grasping the clump of fool's gold, rolling it around in his hand.

Penelope thought of Naomie's warnings about fool's gold.

"We need more time, more money," Fulcanelli muttered, stroking his beard. He looked distracted, dazed. He looked at Penelope as she held the bird so tenderly. "Penelope," he said, shooting his eyes to her.

She looked over at him. "What is it?" she asked.

"Do you know how Rome was built?"

She shrugged.

"Romulus would watch the birds," Fulcanelli said and took the magpie from her as he spoke.

"How do you know?" she asked.

Lucien stepped alongside her as Fulcanelli continued, "Because Rome was built by the wisdom of the birds."

Penelope turned towards him, confused.

He continued, "In 753 BC, when Rome was founded, Romulus and Remus used augury to determine which hill to build upon."

"But how?"

"Augury is divination. Quite simply, Romulus saw more birds on his hill than Remus, and so they built upon Palatine Hill."

"Just numbers alone?"

"And song, flight formation. They believed the birds could communicate the will of the gods."

"And you?"

"Yes, so do I."

"But why?"

"Because I speak their language," he smiled up at her. "Lucien does too. It's the Green Language, the Language of the Birds. It's all around us, and it teaches the most hidden and simple truths."

She looked at Lucien, and he smiled quietly back at her.

"What does it sound like?" she asked.

Fulcanelli paused as if enraptured by some song.

"Music." He stated flatly. "They touch sky and the earth, and so they see and hear it all, if you just take the time to listen. God's will. You cannot fully understand alchemy until you understand this. Language is the river of the spirit. If consciousness is vibration and light, language is its song. The birds have distilled it down to its most simplistic form."

Penelope took in his words. She noted to herself that living at 52 rue Laffitte was like existing in an exaggerated dream.

Lucien gathered the bird in his palm and handed it back to her.

"Here, you try," he said to her. "First calm him with play or food, then listen."

She closed her fingers around the bird in her hand and reached for a cracker. Instantaneously, the bird broke free and flew from her hand to a high shelf with a triumphant clatter.

Penelope looked at Lucien and frowned.

"What did I do wrong?" she asked.

"You can't hold on too tightly. In order for him to sing, he has to choose to stay and be free."

She sighed in frustration.

"Give it time," he urged, stepping closer to her. Since she had announced her plan to go to London, his tone had become dense and heavy.

"Look. The bird flew the coop!" Fulcanelli cackled, pointing up at the magpie.

"Not my greatest scientific triumph, I suppose," she retorted, embarrassed.

Fulcanelli shook his head as Penelope smirked. While she was frustrated, she loved the simple, freedom of the bird. She loved the feel of its feathers against her skin. The bird not only had freedom but a fierce resolve.

"It's a process that takes some patience," Lucien reassured her.

Fulcanelli stepped towards the shelf to retrieve the bird.

She thought of the prolonged years of frustration for Fulcanelli and Lucien in their translations and experiments. She was reminded of the frustrating and lonely year it took her in Sweetwater to create the mysterious golden pill, the final recipe in her father Thomas' magnum opus. She had nearly forgotten about the strange pill that she had sewn in the hem of her dress before she left Tennessee.

Penelope remembered that it had taken Naomie and her several days just to assemble the ingredients. "You must ingest my father's pill encased in gold." Penelope stated flatly to Naomie in her father's attic lab. Her mere presence was a graceful but forceful solicitation.

"Until then, I'm a prisoner," Naomie said and drew her lip into her mouth. "Time is running out. Soon, my family will sell me off and marry me to some old man," she frowned. Whenever she spoke, Naomie tipped her head to the side so that her long hair would perfectly fall across her left eye. The effect was demure.

Penelope was quick-witted and resourceful, but her face was crowded with worry over her friend's predicament. She was fixated on creating a golden pill for her beloved Naomie. Her father's alchemy book purported that the majestic pill could set a person free.

Naomie watched as Penelope pulled the apron over her head and delicately tied the strings behind her back. Penelope slid a pair of her father's glasses over her eyes for protection. Every subtle decision about the recipe was critical, no missteps.

Naomie thought she had nothing left to lose.

The girls gathered all of the ingredients over the span of several days, and everything was neatly labeled and splayed out before them, like a fan.

Naomie brushed the long hair from around Penelope's face and pulled it into a low bun along her collar. The girls were such close friends that though they didn't look much alike, they were often mistaken as sisters. Naomie was a few years older, almost fifteen, with long, tangled tresses like Penelope, but Naomie's hair and skin were tinted and her eyes held a swirling, twinkling gaze so much like the starry obscurity of the night sky. She was wrapped in dusty, silk scarves that flowed from her like a collection of meandering rivers.

The girls loaded the first ingredients into a large flask, creating a mixture the alchemy recipe book called king's water or *aqua regia*. King's water, the book described, was so strong that it could melt base metals. This mixture had no gears, no teeth, no pivoting wheel, and no engine to turn off. It was alchemy. Once the ingredients were set in motion, nothing could reverse it because, like seed to soil, things would begin to take root and decompose.

From the moment the ingredients first mixed, the solution started to react, so the girls had to act quickly. The bubbling liquid turned from clear to orange to red—all of their senses were alert.

Penelope leaned in to read the next step from its yellowed pages. The recipe warned to use extra caution, that the subsequent stage was the process of fulmination, and it was the recipe's most explosive and dangerous part. Adjusting her father's glasses, Penelope mixed a few flecks of the gold into the king's water, three parts hydrochloric acid, one part nitric acid.

She held her nose and turned her head away as she added the ammonia. Tangerine and fertile, like a cup of liquid from the sun, the concoction festered in rapt silence. It began to roll and boil as it transformed, and a misty bubble rose out of the liquid and landed on Penelope's earlobe, bursting into a corrosive vapor. Penelope screamed out in pain as the chemical melted away the thin surface of her lobe.

Naomie pulled her screaming friend away from experiment and yanked a colorful scarf from around her waist, soaking it in a bowl of water and wringing it out along Penelope's burning ear. Naomie washed the lobe of her friend over and over until the pain began to retreat. Naomie examined Penelope's damaged ear. Though the pain had mostly subsided, the bubble had left a deep ulceration, like a mangled thumbprint. Her ear was wounded so badly it would be a permanent and notable scar. She would have to wear her hair long to hide it.

Penelope was resolute and swallowed down her injury, still fixated on creating a golden pill to free Naomie.

She gathered herself and returned to the table. She lit a small fire in a large stone bowl, stoking it until the embers were a deep and pulsing red. Her father had taught her that fire was the doorway to alchemy, that without it, there was no hope for change. Carbon dioxide, water vapor, oxygen and nitrogen. The intensity and color of the flames depends wholly on the substance and its impurities. The alchemy book also described the stages of transformation, *nigredo, albedo, citrinitas* and *rubedo*. The fire was intended to marry the elements to a higher state of purification, a rebirth, a death, a rebirth, then another death. The fire was to burn hotter at each stage and fuel the transmutation.

The bubbling flask which had burned her ear calmed and reached a better equilibrium, so Penelope placed the dangerous, golden concoction over the fire to dissolve, then heat, and redissolve then heat again, as the recipe described. The gold began to crystallize into gold chloride. The cookbook said this was known as dragon's blood. There was a drawing of a dragon with its quilted scales, standing in a soggy garden. Penelope thought the crystals looked mostly like cinders.

She nodded to Naomie and together they carried the extremely volatile concoction to the high shelf with a great and shaking delicacy. It needed to sit in open air so it could decompose and dry out into a fine powder. It smelled like mud.

Penelope and Naomie returned to the book, arranging the remaining ingredients before them. Penelope uncorked a small beaker on the table in front of her. "Calcination," Naomie read, from the Latin root *calx*, which means bone. To calcine something meant to burn it until it turns chalky white, reduces to ashes or is cremated. It was more than a cosmetic affliction. After calcination, the substance was no longer affected by common fire.

They mixed the rest of the ingredients together in a glass bottle. They stoked the fire again and passed the bottle over and over the flame until the heat ignited the ingredients. They held it longer until the bottle turned black and the contents became a dusty ash. Penelope's ear hurt and her arms were taut with tension.

"*Solve et coagula*," Naomie read aloud from the book, dissolve and coagulate. The final stage meant that the mixture must be broken down before it can be built up. The book said the answer was "dissolution," dissolving the body and building up the spirit. "It was the most essential ingredient to the pill's freedom," Naomie read.

At last, Penelope climbed the stool and poured the white powder into the glass flask of *aqua regia* to dissolve, leaving it on the high shelf like a giant, soggy question mark. They had to wait at least a week for the full dissolution of the powder into the solvent.

The rates of time it took to break down varied, so a week and a half later, Penelope and Naomie returned to the lab. The two powders had dissolved into a liquid so they then soaked the liquid into small pieces of linen, which, once dried, they burned into a different powder. They collected the ashes with great care using only the dotted feather of a songbird and then they bound it all together by mixing the soot with a small amount of wine. The pill was then encased in gold. There was enough of the dusty ashes left over to make two, so they encased another pill in pure gold. The book said they had to let the pills age, so they stashed them in Penelope's bedside drawer. They had learned so much about waiting in their short life, and they knew they had to wait the full year.

Penelope reached down and felt the hemline of her dress to search for the distant object.

"What is it?" Lucien asked.

"I just remembered something I created years ago with Naomie that I still carry with me," she remarked. "Do you want to see it?"

Lucien nodded and leaned forward with a heavy curiosity.

Penelope smiled and reached along the edge of her dress, inching her fingers along until she found it, the golden pill. She squeezed it through the narrow stitching of her hem and handed it to him.

"What is it?" he asked, staring at the gilded oval. He gazed at its tiny shape. It was so small but looked like the sun coming out from behind a low hanging cloud.

"A golden pill."

"What is it for?"

She shrugged, "It took a year for us to make it. My father's book says it's a cure all. Perhaps nothing."

"It took a year to make?"

She nodded. Penelope recounted how she and Naomie had poured over the alchemy book for hours, trying to translate the symbols and codes. They had prepared the experiments through the night, scouring the woods surrounding her home to find the plants that resembled the diagrams from the cookbook.

Penelope explained to Lucien, "Naomie and I figured out that it would take a year or more to create the golden pill because the ingredients had to be distilled and cured and then aged almost until they decomposed and one thing became another. Then it had to be coated in gold.

The book said the pill was so strong that it had to be consumed at twilight because its forces were best endured in darkness and during sleep."

"What does the pill do?"

"My father's book proclaimed it sets fixed things free," she responded.

Lucien looked perplexed.

Penelope continued, "Before Naomie ran away from Sweetwater, my father told me that he created it after my mother died. He proclaimed that if my mother could have taken the golden pill when she was in childbirth, it could have saved her life," she paused.

"He said its effects were dramatic. All he said was that it could save a life and give a person back his spirit. But there were some losses."

"Like what?" Lucien asked.

"He suggested that there might be some unexpected side-effects from taking the pill. Nothing a person couldn't easily live with though," Penelope cautioned.

"Do you think it's real?" he asked.

Penelope shrugged, "I would like to believe in it, but I am unsure. My father was quite the dreamer."

She reached for the golden pill she'd worked so long to create. She held it in her hand for a moment and closed her fist around it in wonder thinking maybe she should swallow it down to see what might happen.

"I wish you weren't leaving Paris," Lucien said. "I am going to be lonely here without you."

She nodded in agreement, barely able to restrain her emotions.

Lucien was watching her so intently that she felt light-headed and overtaken. She also felt thirsty and reached for her water, fumbling. She sensed a helplessness in him she was unaccustomed to, and his words were liquid to her heart. She needed to be distracted, so, setting down her glass, she quickly tucked the pill back in her hem. She remembered how life's best things take time. The golden pill, she believed, had been her greatest scientific triumph.

Chapter Seventeen

The next day, Fulcanelli went to the cathedral. When he returned, he handed her some papers, "When you arrive in London, find a man named Charles and hand him these." He paused, "And Lucien has asked that you take his bird, the one he keeps at his desk beside him, with you."

She looked up at Lucien with a surprised glance.

"I insist," Lucien pleaded.

"But why?"

"So you can release him to fly back to me when you leave England for France. That way, I will know you are returning." His words had seemed electric. Even she felt the tingling static of the charge.

She leaned forward. His face flushed as he spoke, but he turned away. Human behavior still flummoxed her more than any math problem. She watched as Lucien left the room and reluctantly turned to her father's recipe book. *Aurum Potable*, it read. "Subtraction," the book continued, "the process of removing one matrix or vector away from another." That seemed to always hurt the most.

She fumbled through the pages of the book until she came upon the recipe for the golden pill. Penelope studied the complex diagram. "Gold never tarnishes," the recipe began, "It will not evaporate, rot, or crumble. It is strong and stable and can resist almost any acid. And when you pass it through fire, it becomes indestructible."

The page was stained by her father's fingers. It looked frayed and ancient, as any panacea should, the allure of a cure for all manner of physical, mental, and spiritual ailments that beset human existence. Someone had scribbled a quote from Paracelsus along the top margin of the recipe, though it was smudged and hard to read: "Gold receives its influence from the Sun, which is, as it were, the Heart of the world and by communicating these influences to the human heart, it serves to fortify and cleanse it from all impurities."

Penelope remembered how she had spent hours the night before she and Naomie attempted the make the pill cleaning and purifying her father's equipment. They could not dare to make a mistake.

She felt a similar influence as she prepared to leave for London, both of fear and of restless anticipation. From this point on, any mistake could set her back months, even years. She could die traveling and training this way. She gathered her belongings and read aloud to herself, "*Chrysopoeia* is the transmutation of other substances into gold."

Penelope remembered that the day Naomie swallowed the golden pill and ran away for good from Tennessee to Paris with her cousin Manfri. Naomie had said, "The only thing you can count on is change."

Naomie had gulped the pill down with mulled wine and offered Penelope a careful sip.

"Change more than love even?" Penelope had asked, tears scattered across her cheeks like a constellation.

"Change is love," Naomie had said. "Look at nature." She then swooped her spindly arms across the yard. The creek was bubbling over from the heavy summer rains, several trees had recently toppled across the main road out of town, and the seasonal shift was underway. "It's nature's force, like intuition," she added.

"Where are you going and when are you coming back?" Penelope asked, wringing her hands with despair.

"I am leaving my cruel family to go to Paris with Manfri. He wants to perform in the theaters, and I want to find Fulcanelli. He is my half-brother," Naomie responded as she held her friend tightly. Her voice was deep and raspy with conviction, and her words twisted sharply up through the eaves of Penelope's front porch.

With Naomie's bag already packed, Penelope knew her friend was serious this time.

"Here you go, then," she said pitching her prickling gaze to the sky as she dug into her pocket and offered Naomie all of her money. It wasn't much, but she thought it might help.

"Can I give you something too, for safe-keeping?" Naomie asked, as she stuffed the folded bills beneath her embroidered bodice.

Penelope nodded cautiously.

"Can you keep this for me?" Naomie pleaded, unclasping then pushing her beloved stone necklace into Penelope's hands. "Keep it safe and promise me you'll never remove it. One day, I will write to you asking you to bring it back to me," she said assuredly and swallowed another sip of wine.

Penelope clutched the necklace tightly. The stone was rough and, so much like her friend Naomie, it seemed to possess a mysterious potency. Penelope fixed the necklace around her neck. The stone flushed with strength and brought succor and emotional relief. It was damp but warm, and Penelope liked the weight of it along her chest.

"I promise," she replied.

Though they had sworn to find each other again someday, Penelope could not fathom how she could ever find her way to France to return the necklace.

Naomie smiled, then winced and drew her hand to her forehead. The effects of the golden pill were beginning to take hold.

"I am starting to feel a bit strange," she confided.

"Do you think it's the pill?" Penelope questioned, her gaze widening.

Naomie nodded and pulled the second golden pill from her pocket to examine it. Penelope could feel the same static that surrounded the pill begin to envelop her beloved friend. The pill was electric and glowing.

"I guess so. What did the book say?"

"The recipe said that the pill causes a transformation," Penelope cautioned. "It also warned that there are many side effects."

"Very good then. That means it's working," Naomie concluded and eagerly placed the second pill in Penelope's palm, but Penelope refused to swallow it. There was something reassuring for her in the not swallowing, in having it near, just in case she needed it later.

She wanted something to believe in. Penelope gazed down at her palm. The golden pill seemed to have a triboelectric charge. It sparked. It shone like the glow of an ember. She closed her palm and squeezed it into the hem of her dress for safe keeping.

The day Penelope left 52 rue Laffitte for London was one of the coldest on record. Animals froze to the ground and starved. Birds fell from the sky, their wings stiffening in flight. Lucien brought Penelope to the train station at Montparnasse and winced as she stepped up onto the train platform.

Penelope lifted her scarf and tucked her head into it to stop herself from crying. Lucien held her with an unquestioning, deafening gaze, crystallizing something deep and shared between them. She was flustered by his presence, but they couldn't do anything that would draw attention, so he reluctantly released her hand, discreetly passing her the magpie, and left quietly. He was awash with melancholy as he departed. Penelope had seen that heavy and clumsy gait before. It was the same weighted load that she had borne the day she discovered Naomie had left Tennessee for good, and then again on the day her father had died.

Penelope, too, felt bereft. The cold air inside the train station and her emotions within her heart felt jagged, almost unbearable. She found her train car and sank into silence. This was the first time she had left Fulcanelli's apartment since their trip to the cathedral. It was her first time since her arrival in Paris that she had been alone. She watched as the train pulled out from the station and moved across the earth's surface with a purpose that only a train fixed to a track can know and one that kept her anxious thoughts safely at bay.

She huddled in and could feel the undecorated strength of her body beneath her coat. All bone and sinew, her arms hung like rope. She traveled the long journey alone with Lucien's small bird, feeding it crackers, wiggling her finger like a puppet to entertain it, and listening for its song.

Part II

Chapter Eighteen

*W*inston Churchill had prescribed that the *SOE* was designed to "set Europe ablaze." It had nearly unlimited resources and stood ready to get behind any act of resistance to the Nazi occupation. It was the seat of the unorthodox war and also where Penelope had decided to go for training to become a formal part of the Resistance.

She arrived in London in late winter, alone. Fulcanelli told her to find a man named Charles who lived in an apartment beside St. Paul's Cathedral at the highest point in London. "I was told you should find the priest at the Cathedral, and he will take you to the *SOE*," Fulcanelli said.

Charles's apartment was beset by cigarette smoke and papers cluttering every square inch. The windows were shattered and boarded. Five other men also lived there, and when Penelope arrived, they all wanted to hear her story.

She shook their hands and gazed at their pale faces, wondering if perhaps they had become impervious to the sunlight. The walls of the room had endured months of the enemy's incessant bombing and were fractured with fine lines. Relentless was the word she heard most often about the bombs.

"Good evening," one man said with an awful squint to his eyes. "How did you hear about us?" He seemed deeply restless and suspicious, a cat stirred at his feet until he kicked it away.

"Someone at the Cathedral at Notre Dame sent me."

"And who sent you to Notre Dame?"

"A connection in Paris."

"I see," he said, and exchanged glances with the other men.

The man closest to her licked his lips and turned his gaze away. He seemed uncomfortable, as though he had hardly ever spoken to a woman.

"Are we supposed to believe," Charles began building some reasoned argument as he went along, "that an American woman who is a scientist with connections to Notre Dame in Paris and fluent French speaking skills would somehow land miraculously on our doorstep like this?"

"*Sprichst du Deutsch?*" Another man continued with outward disdain.

"Why are you treating me like some criminal?" Penelope's voice was magnified with frustration.

"Let's hear her out," another voice emerged from the corner of the room.

"Why? So the Nazis can dismantle us? She is an unverifiable unknown and is not worth the risk. What American would be willing to give up their life in this way, for this type of pursuit?" a fourth man continued.

"I appreciate your concerns, but they are without basis. I am here of my own free will with a desire to help, and I am also able to move freely between countries. I have worked with the movement in Paris, but those efforts are largely disorganized and without funds. It is hard enough to survive in Paris, much less actively fight the Nazis there. I have come here to seek help."

"You have to understand. It is just so . . ." another man searched for the word, "unusual . . . for an American to come to us this way." The man scratched the back of his neck the way a dog scratches fleas.

"Furthermore, you think that Paris has become a dreadful place. Well, London is even more so. The bombing is incessant. Why don't you just return to America? Why would you risk so much to be here?" another man asked.

At first, she couldn't think of an answer sufficient enough to convey her emotions, so she paused, gathering herself. There was no way for her to reasonably explain all that came to pass which had ultimately led her into the Resistance. Penelope considered Naomie and her gypsy spirit and Lucien's excessive devotion to Newton, and finally she said quite plainly, "My father was born in France. He was a scientist and taught me everything he knew. Now that he is deceased, my life in America is lost to me."

She thought of Paris and Lucien working in the apartment, waiting, willing the bird to return as some signal. She felt afraid and impatient to see him again.

She stared into the blank faces of these men. They looked unmoved and indifferent. She feared she hadn't said enough to convince them of her intent, but she also knew that what she said to these strangers and how she said it would either begin or end a conversation, so she tightened the waist belt of her coat around her and spoke again.

"Having left America to live in Occupied Paris, I have seen the true horrors of this war. How can I not fight against the Nazis in whatever way I can?" Penelope confided.

"So, tell us about your scientific knowledge," Charles continued.

Penelope told them about her father's scientific endeavors and her schooling. She explained, "I studied calculus, the study of change. It guided the laws of the universe, and yet humans were so imprisoned by their own convictions and the limitations of their own imagination, they could hardly bear it."

She told them about her love of Newton's *Philosophiæ*

Naturalis Principia Mathematica and how at the beginning of Book Three, there was a section called, "Rules of Reasoning in Philosophy." There were four simple rules, guidelines for dealing with mysterious, natural phenomena. "I believe the proper application of those rules could change the course of this war," she asserted.

"How is that?" another man asked, skeptically.

"Newton's rules are the basis of scientific reasoning. In using his methodology, I believe the *SOE* can subvert any limiting preconceptions or prejudices about the incomprehensible, unimaginably horrific actions of the Nazis." She paused and looked at their faces.

"Please continue," Charles urged.

"Ultimately the rules will allow our conclusions to be more sound because they will be based in evidence, reasoning, and logic, not superstition and fear. We will see what is, rather than what our minds allow us to see," she spoke precisely, articulating each syllable. "We will know exactly where to strike them from within France and exactly how. To defeat something, you must first understand the most basic truths about it, and Newton's principles offer a methodology."

"That is great for scientific discoveries, but tell me, what do experiments about gravity have to do with the war?"

"I understand your skepticism. As a scientist, Newton's rules were easy for me to memorize and understand and apply to my experiments," she continued. "However, human behavior is much more difficult to understand. I

have always felt I needed rules to govern my future inter-
actions with the world, and to guide me through the
mysterious human phenomena that surrounded me, so I
decided to create my own rules about human behavior,
based upon Newton's methods, from what I have seen up
close."

"Interesting," Charles stated.

"And what would those rules be?" another man asked,
with great curiosity.

Penelope continued,

"Rule 1: Humans always want more.

Rule 2: Humans like to talk about themselves.

Rule 3: Humans make the same mistakes over and over
again.

Rule 4: Humans don't like change."

The men in the room exchanged glances.

"And you think if we applied Newton's methodology in
a similar way to the reasoning of the Nazis, we could more
easily defeat them."

"Humans can be very predictable, especially in times
of stress. I am saying that you might even arrive at a place,
where you could predict their behaviors."

They looked around the room at each other, exchanging the discomfort of heavily felt emotions.

"*Dum spiro, spero,* while I breathe, I hope," she said, her
tone heavy and impregnable. The pallor of her words tore
at the stiff air that surrounded them.

"Yes, well, we have been looking for more women to

recruit to our cause." Charles intervened, nodding to the other men. "Please sit. Take off your coat. Would you like some tea?"

Penelope untied the belt of her coat and settled into a ratty chair along the wall. The questioning continued all night. Where was she born? How did she end up in France? And now London? What were her skills, her contacts, her interests?

"So, you want to be one of us?" Charles paraded her around the room the next day. "Recruits," he told her, "would learn survival, Morse code, demolition, weapons training, parachuting, map reading, security, and general organization of an underground circuit. Mostly, they needed to understand that there would be no recognition. They are invisible soldiers."

Charles told her she would need to learn how to become French. She would have to learn to blend, to not be noticed by the Germans. She would learn to speak perfect French. She would be Penelope, the ordinary Parisian. They would get her a job as a maid in a brothel. When the training was finished, she was to return to Paris to care for the prostitutes as their maid and caretaker so that she could spy on their powerful German patrons.

Chapter Nineteen

*C*harles had been the first to talk to her about the necrotic effects of power, "All of this destruction and affectation for power," he said. "Lonely power. And Europe is destroyed for the sake of it."

In phase one of her training, through a series of interviews, Charles was trying to determine Penelope's fitness of mind and spirit for the mission. He was French, working for the British government, and his suffering was strong and palpable in that moment.

He said he was afraid to go back to France, not because of the war, but because everything prior to the war felt like a previous life. Unspoken fears had now been expressed and realized. The *SOE* was constantly absorbing feedback from the war zone. Their only recourse was to continue to try to undermine the Germans through renegade subterfuge. Charles had fled France after the German invasion and saw the *SOE* as his best means of fighting back.

"I am afraid of what I might see, and what I will no longer find," he paused to sip his tea and clear the emotion from his throat so he could continue the interrogation again. He gathered himself to resume the interview. "What brought you to France to begin with?" he continued in his plain, clinical way. He was middle-aged with horn-rimmed glasses.

"I was invited there to study science under a man named Fulcanelli," she confided, though that time seemed mostly like a sordid dream to her now.

Charles shifted sideways in his seat, folding his arms.

She told him about Naomie's letter to her after her father's death.

Charles pulled out a notepad from his pocket and began to scribble on it.

He wrote something down and chuckled slightly to himself, shaking his head side to side.

"Yes, what is it?" she responded with irritation.

"So, you say that Fulcanelli was the connection in Paris who told you to go to St. Paul's Cathedral and ask the priest there to help you find a man named Charles who lived nearby. How could this be possible?"

Penelope looked speechless, as if she had nothing and everything left to say.

"Where was his apartment?" Charles continued, his

whole bodily frame stiffening with enthusiasm.

"Whose?"

"Fulcanelli's."

"What does that have to do with anything. I don't believe I should tell you," Penelope concluded, confused and scared by his amusement and disbelief.

"But why not?" he asked, his mouth hanging open in pained objection.

"I think the reasons are obvious," she responded, a look of reprobation hung in her brow.

"Just a minute," Charles gathered his notepad and stepped out of the room abruptly.

Penelope was exasperated. Why did he care so much about Fulcanelli's apartment? She squeezed her hands together in her lap, hoping her feelings of irritation would subside before he came back to the room. She was impatient and didn't want to lose any more time. She was tired of answering questions and needed to get on with her training, so she could get back to Paris, and Lucien.

When Charles finally returned, he brought another man she had never seen before, and he sat down across from her with a scowl. He wore the frozen face of a person who could not feign amiability, like some condemned criminal.

"This is Mr. Farragut," Charles buffered the awkward silence.

"Penelope," she said.

"People call me the Vicar," the man announced with

vexation.

Penelope sighed and took a long sip of water. This questioning involved so much patience, so much time waiting. She had also never been watched so much. She longed to look out a window, but they were all boarded up.

"Very well then," Charles continued at last, gathering some papers in front of him.

"You know," the Vicar said. "You didn't tell me this new agent was woman. It never occurred to me that the scientist you told me about was a woman, really." His voice rose up, as he looked Penelope up and then down again. "Very good."

She understood that the *SOE* needed women. The younger or more elderly the better. Clandestine was the word the woman had used.

"Clandestine," Penelope whispered out loud. The word hung in her mouth with a prickling taste.

"Penelope, we need to know where Fulcanelli lives?" Charles asked again.

"But why should it matter?" she retorted.

"This information is top-secret, but we cannot help Fulcanelli unless we know where he is." the Vicar said. "Can you please tell me the address of the apartment? It is very important."

"No, I don't think that I can," Penelope held strong. "I'm sorry to say. I am not sure I can trust you. The war, this training has taught me to mistrust everyone."

The men exchanged a long and then short glance.

"I see. Then can you tell me how you came to know Fulcanelli?"

"Well, I told you already, I was sent to France to be his apprentice. How have you heard of him?"

Their faces fell blank. They were unaccustomed to answering questions, as though it had never occurred to them, finding more in conversation than they could offer back.

"Or rather, how have you come to know Fulcanelli?" she narrowed her eyes.

Charles paused and smoothed his hair before he answered, "In fact, very little is known about him. We know he is a very mysterious figure, a legend. We know he is French and very educated, but it has been unusually difficult to establish any information about Mr. Fulcanelli— about his place of origin or his life. However, I'm sure you know that he is sought after by certain military branches of the Germans and the allies for his knowledge of physics."

Penelope shaded her eyes as she listened. She thought of Fulcanelli's revolutionary soul, both irregular and solid, charming, with a mustache and a most powerful mind. He had such a distinct, wild look and way in the world.

"We don't even know what he looks like. We have heard so many varied reports of him."

"Can you tell us anything about his appearance?" one of the men asked.

Penelope's mind turned, and she crossed her arms.

He continued, "Many have wondered if he even exists at

all. All we seem to have is a trail of books. No photos. No addresses. You are the first person we've encountered who claims to have met him in person."

"These are not mere claims," she stated and kicked her foot to the ground.

"We do not intend to offend you. It is just that we have often doubted his existence. To know his address, we might be able to protect him."

"And why are you looking for him so desperately?"

The Vicar leaned forward as if in some bodily distress.

"Charles called me over from the British Secret Intelligence Service. He brought me here because he knows that I have been hunting for Fulcanelli since the end of World War I." He said the words World War I with scorn and indignation, as though he was spitting in the face of some unknown distress. "I have heard many strange reports of him," the man concluded. "But you are the only person who has ever claimed to know him directly."

She thought of 52 rue Laffitte in Paris and of Fulcanelli feeding the birds, the magpies, that gathered on the windowsill outside of his office. She thought of Lucien beside him, frantically translating the important papers dug out of some ancient library. It was like a race of the mind over the war, a heavy mind, a transfigured life. She thought of the Nazis trolling the streets of Paris. She felt an urgency bite at her. She was terrified that like her father and Naomie, she might lose sight of them forever.

"These are my terms," she proclaimed, impetuously. "If

you train me to be a saboteur as quickly as possible and give me money to bring to them to support their work in Paris, then I will tell you everything I know. You are running out of time, and so am I. Fulcanelli helped me get here under the advisement of Notre Dame. I came here in hopes that you all would be able to assist us, and I need to return to Paris soon, but I will not give you what you want until I get what I want out of this." She pursed her lips and crossed her arms.

The men drew closer, whispering something between them.

Violence and loss, it was the guarantee of war, a simple and human equation. She could see in the Vicar's purloined pupils that he too had seen violence. She hoped these men believed her, though there was nothing to back her.

"Very well then," Charles began, and they both nodded in unison, exchanging a wide-eyed curiosity, mixed with relief. "We promise to expedite your training and funding, and we will send you back to Paris as soon as possible."

"Just before I head back to France, I will pass along the exact address of his apartment, but not before then." Penelope reached forward from her perch to shake hands with the two men.

Before she left London for her formal training in Beaulieu, Scotland, she said to Charles, "I have one last question."

He turned to face her.

"I have been told my friend Naomie is held in a German work camp," she began. "I am looking for any information that you have about her or her whereabouts now."

Charles blinked and tucked his arms behind his back, swaying from side to side, foot to foot, shaking his head.

"Penelope," he said with a distant smile. "Penelope," he said again and again. "To be part of us, you have to be willing to give up your identity. It's dangerous to ask questions about the people you love. She is your friend. She is someone for the Nazis to hold over you. To stay alive in France, you have to let these things go."

Her response was primitive, "I see," she said with a secret determination. She bit her lip and made it bleed to prevent the tears from rolling freely down her cheek.

"You have to be self-sufficient and very solitary," he concluded. "The fewer emotional connections, the better. We chose you in part because you have no family, no connections."

His words were like needles to the skin. It was true, that she had no one, but the words were ugly. She no longer wanted to hear him reminding her of these things, so she gathered her bags quickly and turned to leave.

"And one more thing," he tugged at her sleeve. "Take these with you." He gave her a handful of pills—benzedrine to keep awake and suppress hunger and a cyanide pill covered in rubber. "It must be bitten," he told her. "It won't melt in your mouth but it can kill you in less than two minutes. If the Nazis catch you, you can choose to die."

On the ride to the training camp, she had sown the new pills into the hem of her dress. She could hear them resting there, rattling against each other, along with the golden pill, the mystical one she had made with Naomie from a recipe shown to her in her father's book and sewn into this same hem the day she left Sweetwater.

Chapter Twenty

*H*er formal training with the *SOE* went on for months. They took her to warehouses outside of London and interrogated her, as a means of teaching her to be questioned and never to flinch. They taught her how to speak, to dress, what to eat, how to build a tunnel safely, how to build and defuse bombs. The list of ways to dismantle the German power was endless.

Charles helped Penelope swiftly graduate from the program. Her training had been a four-stage process. During the preliminary stages, when she was in London, there was a character assessment, a series of personality tests and interviews to gauge a person's ability to endure the stresses and strains necessary to function as a member of the Resistance. Then, the recruits headed to rural Scotland to the Group A schools where they learned Morse code, combat, weapons, parachuting, security, and map reading.

The training was relentless. She was taught hand-to-hand combat and how to fire a gun from the hip. She was pulled from her bed at night and interrogated. She was taught the necessity of completing the mission. She learned to be reticent and how to become another person entirely. With missions designed to disrupt the infrastructure of the German machine, demolitions and explosives were central. Penelope learned how to lay a charge then walk away and disappear. She was trained in endurance, and when she graduated, she moved on to the Group B schools.

Group B schools were also known as the finishing school. Professional actors, criminals, bank-robbers, and burglars, some even pulled out of prison, were recruited to teach her their craft. How to blow things up, how to steal things, how to lose someone who was trailing her. A professional bank-robber from Glasgow showed her how to blow safes. A career burglar, released early from jail, schooled her in the skills of picking locks. She was also taught tips for transforming her appearance, by changing the part of her hair, her gait, the way she ate and how she wore her expressions. She learned how to use make-up to create the appearance of a scar.

Penelope's final assignment of her training began in the small town of Beaulieu in the Palace House, a gothic country house that overlooked the Beaulieu River. The estate was built as a replica of the Beaulieu Abbey and was used as a finishing school for the last stage of *SOE* training. This mission lasted several days, and if she passed, she would be briefed then sent back to France.

Her mission was written inside a silk scarf that was delivered to her bedroom in a bundle of laundry. She unfurled it slowly, her emotions vacillating between excitement and sheer terror. Her test mission was to gather information from a restricted office in London. She was to meet a red-headed informant at St. Ermin's Hotel in West London for afternoon tea. He would hand her an address and a list of files she would need to locate and photograph. Once she had taken the photographs, she was to return to the hotel and hand the film over to the informant. She was given 72 hours to complete the mission and return to Beaulieu. She could not doubt herself. She could not waiver between actions and intentions. She gathered her sparse belongings into her bag and set out.

She caught the 5:30 a.m. train to London. St. Ermin's Hotel was located in West London along Claxton Street. The hotel was a cluster of brick buildings originally constructed as a private residence. At the turn of the century, the buildings were connected and the mansion was renovated into a hotel. The *SOE* had nested there because of its location, centered among the wartime intelligence offices and near the House of Parliament, Westminster Abbey, and Buckingham Palace. Penelope knew the hotel well. During the preliminary training phase, Charles had conducted many of his interviews with her in the rooms along the top floor.

She stepped off the street and into St. Ermin's front courtyard. The building had a Queen-Anne style brick exterior and elaborate gardens. The interior was equally as fancy, an elaborate neo-Baroque space with a gallery of balconies and a raised verandah.

She walked into the hotel where she saw a red-headed man sitting near the back of the lobby, quietly reading a paper and sipping tea. She wandered up to him, exchanging the phrase she had been taught that was used to identify all Resistance spies: "Is the fish at the market fresh on Tuesdays?"

The man replied, "But not as fresh as it is on Sundays."

She sat down beside him, and he poured her some tea.

He smiled, "It is a pleasure to finally meet you."

He was a middle-aged man with red hair and a stout build.

Using her cover, Penelope shared that she was a French maid, who had grown up in Paris. They talked for more than an hour as he grilled her on all of the facets of her pretend life.

"Become that person," she had been told her in training. "Let go of who you were before."

It was tempting to her but for Lucien.

She had come to West London in a state of full release. It was the epicenter of the *SOE* operations. The St. Ermin's Hotel at 2 Claxton Street was a regular meeting place for the British Intelligence. It was speculated by some of the spies that tunnels even ran between the staircase in the lobby and the houses of Westminster. As a bustling hotel, St. Ermin's was the perfect, discreet hub.

When the red-haired man was satisfied by his talk with Penelope, he slipped her a paper with the address of the office. "You are to find the files on a man named Fulcanelli. Photograph the ones that detail his biography, leave the building and return the film to me here at the Claxton Bar."

"You have got to be kidding me," she wanted to cry out, but she bit her tongue. Of course, Charles would ask her to do this for him. Then, he would get a picture of what Fulcanelli looked like as well as his address at the end of this mission. "Brilliant," she said aloud.

He passed her a small Minox camera the size of a pocketknife, and a key to Room 23.

"You'll find more directions in the room," he continued, "the night guards at the office work two shifts. The first shift begins at 7:00 p.m. and the second shift begins at 3:00 a.m. Those are the only times that the doors to the main offices are opened."

She looked down at the slip of paper. 54 Broadway, it read. She looked up in a flash.

"This cannot be correct," she whispered forcefully.

The man nodded, "It is."

"That building is as heavily guarded as Buckingham Palace," she exhorted.

"You have been trained well. I am told that you are

clever," he responded.

"This is the office of the Secret Intelligence Service, and some of the most seasoned intelligence operatives of our time work there. How can I possibly outmaneuver them?"

"You will find a way," he said. "Remember, you must be able to hide in plain sight," he concluded, gathering his belongings quickly and nodding her a curt good-bye before walking briskly through the lobby and out the front door.

The next morning, she left the hotel carrying a small purse and an umbrella. She felt nervous, so she walked to a bus stop several blocks away and decided to catch the bus to the other side of town. She thought that taking a circuitous and unexpected route would shake off anyone who could be trailing her. She got off the bus on the outskirts of London, took a walk along the Thames and eventually boarded another bus to travel back into West London.

She arrived at 54 Broadway in the late afternoon. The street was lined with mansard roofs and boarded-up windows. A cluster of radio antennae rose up from the roof of the address as well as a series of pigeon lofts. The building had a sturdy steel frame, and there was a plaque at the entrance that identified it as the Minimax Fire Extinguisher Company. She walked through the main doors into lobby where a retired military officer greeted her. The whole foyer seemed to be guarded by former officers.

"May I help you?" he asked.

"Yes," she proclaimed. "Feeling a bit fatigued. May I use your restrooms?"

He pointed in the direction of the restrooms. Because she was a woman, he barely looked up at her as she passed, so she quickly scanned the foyer and hurried through the door of the bathroom.

Another recruit in Scotland had told her that the SIS had little regard for the SOE, that they viewed the SOE's recruits as reckless and dangerous, so much so that the SIS believed the SOE could compromise their efforts in the war. This created a rivalry between the two organizations.

Penelope was surprised and confused that the SOE would send her to the main offices like this. Few buildings in London were as sought after and scrutinized as this one. In the bathroom, she tucked herself safely inside a stall and waited out the day until the noise began to quiet, and she could hear the loud clank of the main doors locking.

Having grown up in a small town, Penelope was used to being spontaneous and invisible, that fluid nature seemed to be one of the true marks of alchemy, transfiguration over obstinacy, pride, and ego. She leaned into the wall, melting into her memories of Lucien. Her feelings for him felt liquid too, transforming parts of her that she had never even known existed. If her mission was successful, then she would return to Paris to see him soon. Her patience was waning and she waited, impatiently eyeing her watch.

Just after 7 p.m., she heard the guards clearing the building. They opened the door to the women's restroom to look around, but it was more symbolic than functional, so they didn't think to check inside the stalls. When at last she heard the jangles of the guard's keys lock the exterior door, she peeked out the stall and moved to the door of the bathroom. The lobby was empty and dark, but the doors to the main offices in the rear of the building were likely locked as well. She scurried across the foyer and twisted the knob of the main door to the offices. It was frozen.

She pulled a bobby pin from her hair, inserting it partially into the lock, wiggling it around until she felt it yield. She pressed on the lever until it clicked in the lock. She twisted the knob and felt the door release. She bent the bobby pin and jammed it into the lock to prevent the guards from locking it again.

This was the restricted section of the building. She wandered up the staircase to the fourth floor. The third office on the right. One, two, three, she counted out loud in a whisper. She picked the lock again and twisted the doorknob open.

Penelope looked around the dark and formal office. There were two tall file cabinets standing side by side. She pulled open the first one. It was stuffed full. There was so much that she couldn't understand, that seemed to be written in code, Sussex, Wharf Nine, Whitefell—she couldn't determine if these were names of places or missions or people. Drawer after drawer was filled with folders, seemingly random. They were collections of people, names she had never heard of, places she didn't recognize. Hundreds and hundreds of people were collaborating behind enemy lines, unnamed and invisible too. She could see the rife paranoia of the war. The file cabinet contained impossible numbers of people and places. No intelligence agency could manage so much information, and these files were only a fraction of the volume of names and places from just one part of France. Fulcanelli was just a name among many mysterious names.

She had to start somewhere so she reached inside the cabinet. It didn't take long for her to find the largest of the files in the second file cabinet, and Fulcanelli's name was in bold letters. She wrestled it free and opened it on the floor. Inside was paper after paper with maps of places he had supposedly lived or visited. There were descriptions of experiments, interviews of people who had met with Fulcanelli or had seen him. A photo of a soldier from World War I was labeled "Fulcanelli," but she immediately recognized that it was not him.

For hours, she poured over the documents, whittling them down to ones her trainers at the SOE might think were significant and photographing them with her camera. *Relevant biographical material,* the orders had said. She now understood why the man with the frozen face thought that Fulcanelli didn't exist at all.

Penelope photographed the final documents, gathered

them all back together, and placed them carefully back in the cabinet where she found them.

As she was about to the close the drawer, another folder caught her eye. "Naomie Valentine," it read. "Naomie Valentine," she pronounced out loud. She was not expecting to see Naomie's name in this place. It was late. She paused a second and looked at her watch.

She had to know why there was a file on Naomie, hoping it might reveal information about her location. She pulled it from the drawer and opened it, spreading the pages on the floor. She was startled to see a photograph of a younger Naomie and another man who looked like a young Fulcanelli, his hands clasped around his waist, his skin tinted, and his eyes closed. She scanned his face for answers. There was another picture of Naomie with a man who looked like a much older Fulcanelli, perhaps their grandfather.

That's when she heard a noise on the street outside, and the jangle of the front door lock. It was 3 a.m., and the night guards were conversing. The shift was about to change. She stared at the documents on the floor before her. She wanted to know more, but her eyes were so blurred with tears she could not even read. She couldn't understand why this file was here. She heard the second door being unlocked.

"Something is wrong. The lock is frozen," she heard a man say. "My key won't even go in. I think we should call someone."

"Don't worry. It's an old lock. I'm sure it's just a fluke. I've been here all night and haven't seen a thing. Let's check all of the offices before we bother anyone. You start on the bottom floor and I will start on the top."

His voice clambered up the stairs and down the hallway. She heard the muffled frustration of his voice and then the sound of him coming up the stairway. Click, click, click. She had no more time, yet while she couldn't take it all in, she also couldn't quite look away and leave. She wiped her eyes clear and stuffed the photos of Naomie and a few papers in her pocket, gathering the rest of the file back together and tucking it away in the cabinet. She finally possessed a picture of her beloved Naomie and that gave her much-needed solace. She could hear the guard shuffling down the first floor hallway and the other guard pass up the stairs to the top floor. She knew they were scouring the building floor by floor, but that also meant there was no longer anyone guarding the front door of the building. She knew that time was limited and she needed to make a break for it, so she hurried out of the room, down the stairwell, and out the front door onto Broadway.

When she arrived at the Claxton Bar in the hotel, the red-headed man was waiting for her there. It was nighttime and the scene was much livelier than it had been earlier. People were drinking and loudly conversing in their seats below the fancy rococo plaster on the ceiling. She was eager to return to Beaulieu and the Palace House, distracted by the photographs now burning in her pocket. She quickly handed the camera to him.

"I think this should have everything you need," she said.

The man nodded and offered her a drink.

"I can't," she responded. "I must go. I am eager to return to Beaulieu. I am anxious to return to France."

"Be careful there. You must already know that the life expectancy of an *SOE* recruit in the field is only six weeks," he pronounced, nervous and a bit tipsy. "We have so little power."

She nodded back at him as she rushed out the doorway to find the next bus out of town.

Chapter Twenty-One

*B*efore she boarded the motor gunboat, Penelope opened her leather bag, lifted it to the sky and released the magpie, watching the bird wobble, perch, then fly off towards the lashing rain as if it knew exactly what to do. Her heart felt heavy with circumstance, and her thoughts ran truant. She had already learned so much about the stark consequences of letting go. *"Bon Chance,"* she whispered out loud to the bird as it flew out and up into the sky.

The word *chance*—it weighed heavily on her tongue. Tasteless and blind, it occupied the narrowest slot between what isn't and what might become. At the dockyard, the strain of war was audible and ubiquitous, in the high-pitched exertion of metal on metal, in the warships laid bare. The skeletal remains of the damaged boats had become the biting solemnities of a new, uncertain life.

Now she stood on the docks of the Devonport Royal Naval Base alone, waiting with a suitcase of money and a new network of skills and resources for the war. Months before, when she had left Paris, she had promised Lucien she would take his beloved bird with her. *Mail can be intercepted*, he had said with confidence, *but a bird is a thing of nature.* And yet, opening the bag and releasing the magpie had been so much more difficult than she could ever have imagined, all of her remoteness rising and gathering into one singular, austere moment.

Lucien had felt certain that the bird would know its way home, and when it returned to him, he would know that Penelope was close behind. Yet Penelope had gathered so many unchecked fears since she had left Paris. No matter what Lucien's intentions might have been in giving her his bird, the transcendent magic of possibility that a magpie could fly from England to Lucien's remote windowsill seemed too far out of reach for her to believe.

She doubted the magpie would even make it across the stormy channel. It seemed improbable. She worried that the bird would most likely starve along the way, filled with hope, instinct, and desire, yet overcome by its thirst and hunger, life's age-old and mordant companions. She wondered if the release of the bird had been its death sentence, questioning how such a small bird could ever find its way to anyone, and if Lucien was even still alive.

As a child in Tennessee she had learned to dance with gypsies, learning to shape-shift, observing that blending in was more than just a change in clothing and complexion, that it was more electric and alive than observable. She learned that melding was about the power of the mind, a current that could run person to person, making truths interchangeable. These lessons from the gypsies taught her to blend seamlessly with the Resistance. They appealed to her deep nomadic temperament, filling her with the true anthem of the gypsy heart and beseeching her with the enticing question, "what if?"

Living in London under the blanket of the war and training to be a part of the Resistance had been constantly disorienting. At night, alone in her small boarding room, she felt orphaned, sounds bouncing across the buildings like the walls of a dark cave. Occasionally, she heard a siren or the sound of laughter, an explosion or a scream from someplace unknown, followed by the long amnesia of silence. It was a silence that could make a person forget. Yet the city never cowered.

Seven months before, she had left Lucien in Paris and come to London to find the leaders of the Resistance. She had trained with them for months and was now ready to return to France. Everything had gone precisely as planned.

As instructed, Penelope stood on the dock, waiting watchfully for an unnamed soldier to meet her and take her to the communications office. Once there, she would be told whether she would be dropped into France via parachute or boat. Her training had prepared her to be told only what she needed to know, only when she needed to know it, and never more.

Bolt by bolt, the naval workers were engrossed in a willful resuscitation of these wounded ships. It was the blank stare of a submarine or battle cruiser, the boat's iron chest gaping from the lock and twist of a German warhead during a battle in the Atlantic. These boats had all come back to the docks like wounded animals, their entrails mangled and heaving. Steel plate upon steel plate, at all costs, the naval soldiers understood that they must withstand the war, repair the ships, and berm up the fleet. At the dockyard, the movement of troops and equipment was as constant and relentless as the broiling sea.

"Wait on the dock for further instructions on how to cross the channel," Charles had told her, and now she waited and watched the sky with an uncertainty that clouded over her eyes. The gusting wind was twisting her hair across her face, creating an uneasy, yet rosy countenance. She brushed the strands from her eyes and peered out through the rain. She thought she could still see the bird by a streak of white flashing from its wings. Without the ceremony of a goodbye, the magpie swooped down and then up again, its long tail trailing behind in the blustery air, never once looking back. This delicate bird, which she had faithfully carried with her all of these months, was more proof for Penelope, in war and in life, that not every-thing was as it seems.

She had named the magpie Beethoven because of the music he made while clinging to her shoulder. He too left a deep impression. She thought she would be too preoc-cupied to care for the bird properly, but instead, it was the magpie that had nurtured her during her long, torturous days training with the Resistance. She was learning that she could trust no one but the bird, and so she came to know him. Their room at the boarding house was their birdcage. They were in it together, comrades, chums, bonded in the willful ignorance that no one could deliver them from this destiny. When she returned every evening, he was in near constant demand of her attention, doting on her, singing her songs.

At dawn, before she left for the day, he fancied having her feed him from the palm of her hand. He was so fond of his own song he would nod and dance while he ate, curl-ing his feet in amusement. During the night, he liked to sneak out of her window and survey the city. He returned with shiny objects, stacking these gifts by her bedside: small coins, shrapnel and capsules he found on the streets of London. When the bombers came, he seemed to know before the sirens, chirping and pecking at her feet to wake her from sleep, so she would take him to hide in the cellar. He watched out for her, and nothing could curb him.

Her heart ached at the open sky as she watched Beethoven flying out across the southern channel. She hoped desperately that she would find him again in Paris with Lucien, though she had become secretly doubtful, convinced that these were illusions, delirious trappings of the mind in this withering time.

Now, the magpie was far away, a gypsy, tenacious and free. She watched as he seemed to outsmart the wind. Penelope turned back from the channel waters to the navy base's dockyard at Plymouth. The military infrastructure's reluctant symmetry reminded her of a churchyard, the cranes, and boats scattered like tombstones across an uneven fabric of cement and ocean.

She carried two suitcases with her. One contained 800,000 francs for Fulcanelli and his Royal Society. The other held a radio transmitter that she had been told to deliver to a certain pharmacist in Paris.

She felt the dock rattle beneath her feet and looked to see a man dressed like a postman approaching, his mouth screwed into a teaspoon of a smile. He was the British naval officer, coming to update her on her situation.

"You sure don't look like a Resistance worker," he teased as he led her off the dock, through the crowded causeways, and into the communications offices. British and American troops were scurrying in all directions.

"Do I look French, at least? That way they won't shoot me on the train into Paris."

Penelope stepped into a back office to finish her disguise. She wore a simple frock and some sandals. She pulled her hair into a low bun and secured a scarf around it, but her beauty was hard to domesticate. She had a slight build with large, sympathetic eyes, gilded brown and restive.

She gathered her documents. There was a *carte d'alimentation* (food ration card), *documents militaires* (military papers), *cartes de vêtements et d'articles textiles* (clothing ration card), *permis de conduire* (driver's license), *certificat de recensement* (census card), *carte de tabac* (tobacco ration card), *extrait de naissance* (birth certificate), *certificat médical* (medical certificate), *certificat de travail* (work permit), and *justificatif de domicile* (proof of residence). The Germans had made certain there was a card for everything.

When she stepped out of the office, she looked back up to the sky, thinking anxiously about her beloved bird. With him went anything comic about her life, anything dark or light to laugh off. There was only a bunched-up ring of questions remaining, dangling like distant keys just out of reach, far too many to count. She stood resolutely still in the wind and rain and tried not to cry.

The naval officer approached her again.

"There can't be much time," she cautioned, ready.

The officer smiled and nodded, "Yes, but we can't leave yet. Would you like to step back inside for a cup of tea?"

"No, thank you. Why can't we leave now? I am tired of waiting." Her voice was beginning to strain with irritation against the wind.

"We are waiting for two more," he said with a great twinkling in his eye.

She did not know she would be traveling with anyone else. With a sigh, she reluctantly followed the officer back inside the building. He offered her a hot cup of tea as she looked out at the choppy waters, tapping her foot on the floor with nervous impatience.

"No need to worry. We'll cross just fine. We're in a *MGB* 502. It's that mahogany vessel over there. It's more than 117 feet long." He rambled on, "We've got anti-aircraft guns, a couple of twin mount .5 caliber machine guns and a semi-automatic two-pounder."

The boat was smaller than the standard warships, but it bristled with weaponry.

"How long will it take to cross?" Her voice shook.

"With this high wind, six hours."

He explained that when they got close to shore, the three of them would launch off of the warship in a rubber dinghy and land at one of the remote beaches on the Breton coast. It was known as the red nose of France, where the air and coastline were most rugged. There were no shoals or offshore reefs, so they would be able to navigate their boat easily. When they reached the shore, they were to abandon the raft and separate. She would go to Paris. The other men would head towards Lyon.

She had already been told by Charles that once in Paris, she would need to reconnect with Fulcanelli and give him the suitcase of money for the Royal Society. She would deliver the transmitter to a pharmacy nearby. It had been arranged for her to live in a brothel as a maid, where she would listen in on the German soldiers who were patrons. If she heard anything of interest, she was to pass notes to a radio operator who lived above the pharmacy, and he would transmit the information to London. That was the plan. The rest was up to her.

There was a light knock at the door, and two men entered. Both were foreigners, but since they had been taught to hide the truth about themselves, she would never know them. They could only discuss the weather and how they planned to get in and out of the dinghy safely when they landed in France.

"Okay, it's time," the British officer stated at last.

The boat ride lasted almost an hour longer than the officer had predicted, and the wind made navigating the waters of the English Channel difficult. Penelope sat in the main cabin with the other men, though they didn't speak the whole ride. The less they knew about each other, the less chance there was of compromising their cover. When the boat began to slow to a crawl, the crew prepared the dinghy and quietly pushed Penelope and the two men off into a drenching, blinding rain. As they landed, Penelope fell forward hard onto the rocks of the Breton coast and cut her leg.

She stumbled out of the chilling water, fixing her eyes on the shoreline before her. One foot in front of the other, she clambered her way out of the rocky surf. The two other men attempted to cast the dinghy back towards the boat, then followed behind her up the banks of the shore. Her leg stung from the salt of the ocean water, and her fingers tingled and ached with numbness and uncertainty. It was pitch dark, and she touched each rock with a measured subtlety, as if her life depended on it.

Onwards, upwards, she chanted in her mind as they rose up from the frothy channel. They climbed higher and higher until the landscape flattened, and they crossed what seemed to be a gravel road. The three of them stumbled along the road until they saw the flickering lights of a house. Beside the house, in the distance, was a barn where they could sleep. They would part ways in the morning.

Penelope's leg was badly cut. She sat down in the barn and lifted her dress, drawing her finger along the jagged wound. She untied her scarf from her hair and pressed the seams of the cut together, wrapping the scarf tightly around the gash several times before knotting it against her calf. Her leg throbbed with pain and adrenaline as she curled up, resting her back against the wooden siding of the barn. She could barely sleep though.

So many rank and simple fears washed through her. She couldn't believe she was in France again. She looked around the barn. Who were these men? She refused to close her eyes and sleep out of fear of them. Though they were trained with *SOE* too, she still did not trust them. She watched and strained to hear their words as they huddled whispering together. They were close to her but just out of range, so she couldn't fully gauge why the taller of the two men watched her from the corner of his eye like a creep. In the darkness, her senses hummed with the static of fear.

She looked out the slats of the barn towards the house in the distance. The storm had blown over and the moon shone brightly across the fields. The lights of the house had gone out and she hoped whoever lived there was soundly asleep, unaware of the cold, hungry strangers huddled in their barn.

As the men finally started to drift off to sleep, her mind kept thinking about the uncomfortable hay beneath her head and how difficult it was going to be to remove the blood stains from her scarf. She was worried the Nazi soldiers would notice the substantial stain at the front of her dress and interrogate her before she could even make it to Paris.

Like everything in its path, the war had nearly consumed her. The next morning, without a good-bye, Penelope hurried to the train station in town and bought a second-class ticket for Paris. She sat down on a wooden bench to wait for the train.

Chapter Twenty-Two

As the train pulled into the Paris station, Penelope saw that all of the signs at Montparnasse were now in German. She had been in England for seven long months, and now Paris looked even more hollow-eyed and devastated than when she left. Even a banner that hung from the Eiffel Tower was in their language—*Deutschland Liegt auf allen Fronten*—Germany is victorious on all fronts. Members of the Resistance movement had cut the tower's lift cable so the German soldiers had been forced to climb up its iron girders to hang the Nazi flag and banner. An hour later the banner remained but the flag had blown away. The city of Paris may have been overtaken, but somehow its treasures held strong.

Penelope left the station and headed directly to the Jardin des Tuileries. Just a few steps from the park stood her new home, at 24 Rue Chambrement. Thirty women lived and worked there, and it was famous for its lavish rooms and extravagant sex.

Le Chambrement was a playground for wealthy and powerful men, one of Europe's most profitable brothels. Since the German Occupation began in 1940, Le Chambrement had been reserved by the military for the exclusive use of German soldiers and the French who collaborated with them. Though it was a simple six-story building, it was heavily guarded outside. The soldiers saw the country's brothels as a national treasure.

"Here, sex is not different from art," Madame Guerrain told Penelope as they stood in the building's opulent front hallway.

Madame had long silver hair that framed her face like the saturated curtains of a tall window. Her eyes were large and bright, watchful as a clock, and she moved with a slight tremor. The entrance was decorated to look like a cave, and inside the foyer was a magical grotto with dozens of paintings, sculptures, waterfalls, and exquisite chandeliers.

The rooms were even more fantastic. Artists had customized each with ornate murals of exotic settings to recreate lavish Moorish, Hindu, Japanese, and Polynesian ambience and decor. Art and solitude, it stood alone.

"This will be your room," Madame Guerrain said,

after guiding Penelope down an unlit hallway. It was a closet tucked away with no window. "Your room is close to the salon, so you can anticipate the needs of the women and their soldiers. Your job is to listen carefully, bring fresh towels, perfumes, chocolates, whatever is needed to make the most of each moment. This war is brutal. We offer a taste of civility, of the old life," she concluded.

The brothels and their singular devotion to sensual pleasure were a salve to the brutality of the war, and they were flourishing. At Le Chambrement, there were musicians in formal suits. There were flutes of champagne. There were silver platters, with chocolates and cheeses. As a courtesy, visitors were asked to bring champagne, chocolates, and cigarettes to their favorite girls.

Madame put her hand on Penelope's shoulder as if to instruct her. "We are patronized by some Frenchmen but also the most decorated figures of the war, and many more junior officers. There is a room for every vice. And the soldiers are insatiable and filled with them."

Penelope touched her hand to her face as Madame Guerrain led her upstairs and swung open the door to a Hindu chamber with a copper tub. A young woman was crouched beside it, filling it with bottle after bottle of champagne.

"Alice, you ought to eat more," Madame Guerrain said with disapproval.

She kneeled down beside the young woman and offered her a chocolate candy from her pocket. The woman lifted her hand cautiously to receive the treat. Alice had dusky, brooding eyes the texture of driftwood, and a pale complexion.

"Thank you," Alice smiled. Her teeth were dark and crowded, a bumpy rash was scattered along the palms of her hands.

"Alice, this is Penelope. She is our new helper and maid. She will be assisting you." Madame Guerrain turned towards the door. "I can assure you that no one knows this place better than Alice. You see, she has grown up here. Her mother worked as one of our most prized *fille de joie* for nearly twenty years," her voice rose up with pride and satisfaction. "Alice, can you answer any of Penelope's questions and familiarize her with the eccentricities of this . ." she paused, "place?"

Alice looked inquisitively at Penelope then nodded as Madame Guerrain strolled out the door. In the brothel, Madame Guerrain appeared to be in constant motion, never loitering, a mysterious woman of great responsibility and perhaps even greater secrets.

Alice stood and offered Penelope the chocolate.

"My stomach is very sensitive," Alice said apologetically, as if there were some error in her judgment.

"No, thank you. I am fine," Penelope said, refusing the candy. She didn't want to offend Alice, but she also didn't have time for candies. She was here to work, to uncover secrets and pass them along to the British. Surely, the pharmacist with the radio transmitter was already waiting for the first reports of intelligence from the brothel.

Madame Guerrain's abrupt departure from the room surprised her. It seemed implausible to Penelope that this aggrieved young woman would be her first friend at Le Chambrement. Alice seemed too sad and complacent to be helpful. As well, Penelope felt daunted by the coarse presence of the young woman in the midst of such lavish decor.

Penelope unravelled the bandage on her cut leg. She hadn't tended it since she wrapped it in her scarf in the barn in Breton. She needed to wash and re-cover it with a new bandage.

Alice grimaced as she opened another bottle of champagne.

Penelope moved closer and offered to help, "Actually, I will take the chocolate. I can save it for later." She didn't know what else to say, and she was impatient to begin her work and needed to find the right, tactful, yet disarming, words to make friends here.

Alice smiled and cleared her throat loudly. She seemed far too unhealthy to be deceptive. She looked like a knotted-up pile of necklaces. She wore all of the costume and parade of the brothel with none of the care, perfume, or polish.

"Madame Guerrain has the habit of giving me candies that I can never actually eat," she said with anxiety. "She thinks it will make me happy but they unsettle my stomach. She looked down at the gash along Penelope's leg. "Would you like some soap and water to wash your leg?"

"Thanks," Penelope mused.

"What happened?" Alice asked.

Penelope thought back to the high winds and the rocky shore along the Breton coast. Her re-entry into France was not without incident.

"I slipped in the rain. The cut is not as bad as it looks," she responded.

"You think?" Alice questioned, handing her the soap and water.

"It's like the candy. It is here now and will be gone the next moment." Penelope unwrapped the chocolate and popped it into her mouth, smiling. "But unlike a cut leg, candy can make you happy," she said with a full mouth as she tended her leg.

"No, it doesn't make me happy, but it is delectable," Alice said with a look of complete assurance as she pulled a silver pill box from her pocket. "These make me happy." She rattled the pills inside the box. "Try one," she beckoned.

Penelope thought of the pills sewn along her hem and shook her head again, "No thanks."

"Another day perhaps. They are the German's magic pills," she said. "The soldiers will give them to you if you ask. They make you feel . . . " Alice searched for the word.

"Delectable?" Penelope responded in a peevish tone.

"No," Alice chuckled. "Infinite." And she slipped one of the pills between her lips and returned the box to her pocket. She scooped a handful of champagne from the tub to wash down the pill, then another scoop and another.

She grasped Penelope's hand with affection as she helped her re-wrap her wounded leg, then they stood and toured the room.

"Each of Le Chambrement's thirty rooms is unique. This room is built to look like a Hindu temple. Each wall of the room pays tribute to a different Hindu deity." She walked towards the center of the room. "And a carving of Shiva hangs above the bed." She pointed across the ornate bedding to a carved panel. "Madame traveled all the way to India to retrieve these artifacts."

Penelope looked around the room. Four columns drizzled with copper paint framed the bed. The walls were adorned with Indian textiles and stencil designs. The pillows and bedding were all embroidered with ornate animals. A wood carved statue of a feminine deity stood beside the copper tub. A lavish leather stool sat in front of it.

"Madame Guerrain opened the doors in 1903. She brought in the best designers and artists to customize every room so that she might attract Europe's most wealthy clients. Throughout my life, I have seen politicians, actors, bankers, and aristocrats come and go from here."

A wave of muffled laughter could be heard from the floor above. Alice raised her eyes with a look of concern.

"What is happening?" Penelope asked, looking to the ceiling.

"Madame Geurrain will not be happy if she hears them. It's the women's quarters above us. It is nothing like these rooms. It is a common room where they all sleep and dress together. It is in shambles," Alice continued. "The noises infuriate Madame Guerrain but we like to have fun up there. You should come meet us up there tonight. It is like a party, and I will introduce you to everyone."

Penelope smiled and nodded, "Your mother too?"

"No, she's retired now. She doesn't come here any longer. She lives in an apartment above a bakery down the street. My mother never intended to stay at Le Chambrement long. She used to just spend her summers in Paris because as a girl she was never pleased with her family's life in the country. My mother had no money. She started working here so she could afford to stay in Paris longer. She was secretive, so her family never knew."

"And your father?"

"He was one of her regular clients, an aristocrat. I only met him once when she took me to his family house outside of Paris. There was a pond and flowers and lots of shrubbery surrounding his large house. He sat me on his lap and gave me a book. He had a wooden leg that my mother said had come from the war. "

"His leg was made of wood?" Penelope uttered.

"From his knee all the way down to his shoe. The book he gave me was a mystery," she answered. "Do you like to read mysteries?" Her gaze was becoming loose, her pupils pasty as if reverting to some distant place. Her hair was the color of dark pine.

Penelope shrugged. She had only read books about

math and science.

"What about your family?"

She squeezed Penelope's hand with affection and a girlish charm. Penelope felt her face burn. This was the first time since her training in London that anyone had asked her about the pretend life she had made up when she became a Resistance worker.

She stared directly at Alice as she spoke, "I grew up in Paris too. My family is deceased. Both of my parents died in an accident," she replied with finality.

"And how did you end up here?"

Alice stepped towards the tub, leaning forward to scoop another large handful of champagne into her mouth. She staggered a bit as she stood.

"What's the matter Alice? Are you okay?" Penelope asked diverting the question.

"Perhaps, I've had too much of the champagne," she laughed. Her feet were dragging as she stumbled forward into Penelope. Alice looked around her. "Don't be worried. Just promise me you will not tell anyone, because we are not supposed to drink the champagne."

Penelope nodded. Alice's eyes were grave with concern. "Madame is very strict."

"I won't say a word," Penelope assured her.

Alice pressed her hands into her belly. "I am starting feel sick. Before we finish arranging the room, let's go upstairs for a bite to eat." Her stomach looked concave. Penelope followed her as she ambled out of the room.

"Oh, and there is one more thing I forgot to show you," Alice said and swiveled, dragging Penelope down the hallway. She pushed aside an oil painting of a younger Madame Guerrain that hung along the wall. "Here you will find a set of keys that unlock every room in the maison, including the closet with the black market items," she winked. "Why don't you smuggle some fine item upstairs for the girls to enjoy tonight. They love to eat chocolates." Alice rattled the key with her finger and smiled mischievously.

Chapter Twenty-Three

*T*he only time Le Chambrement closed was when the military medics came through to examine the prostitutes. The commanders mandated these medical procedures and set the rates for the sexual services. Madame kept all of the black market items available at the brothel, and they were kept in another large closet beside Penelope's small room. One of her jobs was to dispense them in the club room, where the patrons drank and danced and where the officers chose their girls.

"Sex always increases before a large military offensive," Madame Guerrain observed as Penelope slipped out the door of the club room. "Don't hate the women who do this. They are desperate, and desperate people make difficult choices. You will come to love them and see them as I do. These women can make at least 100 times more money here, and most of them send it back to their families." She was uncorking a bottle of wine. "The Nazi soldiers love the dark-haired women and the red wine the best, the darker the better."

This was a dangerous assignment, to be embedded within the most powerful brothel in Paris, constantly surrounded by the most influential men of the war, caring for their women, cleaning their dirty rooms, and listening to what was being said, on the chance that she heard something important.

Penelope knew she had to become close to the girls. Her *SOE* instructor had told her that the prostitutes might have access to some of the classified intelligence. It was a matter of coaxing the stories out of the men. "They know the inner workings of the war. They can help you the most, if you become close to them," Charles had told her.

"The soldiers are the most talkative after sex," Madame Guerrain told her. "These women are their tonic. When the women put on their masks, the men take refuge. The soldiers want something exotic. They want dark hair and dark eyes. The girls color their hair and color their faces to please the soldiers. They become actresses. They are entertainers, and soon the officers begin to feel as though they are disappearing into that secret world."

Penelope wondered how Madame Geurrain had gotten involved in the world of the brothels. She suspected that

Madame hid here too, her true essence masked behind the colors painted on her face, and that, like many, she clung constantly to some silent grief that had not yet overcome her.

The women were told to walk briskly but quietly through the halls so as not to disturb the clients, and when they gathered in the parlor, they spoke in subdued voices.

Penelope understood that she was a non-essential accessory to this dream-like space and her role was to clean, prepare the rooms, and dote on the women, flank them, help them all while remaining invisible. She put on their make-up, styled their hair, folded towels, swept dust from the floors, carried basins of water and listened.

The women lived in a common room on the top floor of the brothel with thirty narrow, iron beds set side by side. The walls were covered with floral stained, peeling wallpaper. Make-up and costumes were draped everywhere. Penelope brought a weighty box of chocolates from the black market closet as an offering, one for each *fille de joie* as the women readied themselves for the nighttime visitors.

One woman, Elise, had endured a childhood illness and had been sent away from her family's home when they had run out of money. She was narrow as a toothpick and drew Penelope onto her bed for company as she dressed. She had a scar that ran along her cheek like lichen and tried to cover it with powder.

"I don't have a family either. My father deserted us, and

we had no money," she began. "I remember standing on the balcony of our tiny apartment as the soldiers beat and shot people in the streets. They would round them up and throw them into their trucks. It was one scene of horror after another," she said knowingly. "Then I came to Paris," she stumbled on her words for a second. "I came here to survive. Now I am sharing a bed with these same soldiers."

She sculpted her hair into a high bun and tucked a vermillion flower along the outer edge. "I've come to think of them as being imprisoned by the war too, locked up for years. We are all just happy to have human contact." Her skin had the mottled look of the scribbled map of some lost continent. "Sometimes, the men just want to talk, or for me to just to hold them. They miss human touch and a soft voice." She spoke softly. "So do I."

"Are you ever scared?" Penelope muttered, resting her vertebrae along the edge of the bed frame.

"Of course, all the time. There's always the chance they could turn aggressive. I have only been really terrified once though."

"What happened?"

Elise smiled and nodded, the sun reaching over her back. The verdure of the sun across her face made her look like a small girl. She draped strands of beads along her collarbone and gestured for Penelope to fasten them. She was at least thirty now.

She turned from the mirror to face Penelope and leaned her back against the dressing table, "One of our most frequent visitors to the brothel is a man named Andreas. He is very secretive about his role in the war." She bobbed her head as she spoke. "Over time, he has requested only my service, again and again. He is very jealous of my other clients. Then one day last summer, he came and told me he loved me."

"So, it was his love for you that scared you?"

"No, what scared me is that when he told me he loved me, he called me by my real name."

She swallowed down a dry gulp and continued, "I don't know how he discovered my true name."

She stood up from her bed and seemed almost embarrassed. "He fought in the first war and now this one; he has known only war." She hesitated, unable to grasp the words. "Believe it or not, some of the highest commanders in this war are impotent."

Penelope noticed after a while that the women who had been in the job the longest seemed the most embarrassed or ashamed, but it didn't take long for the women to come to love Penelope. She knew their favorite perfume and made sure to know their names and talk with them daily.

"What made you run away?" she asked a woman named Evie, pouring her a glass of wine.

She fixed her stockings as she spoke. "I married a man. He was a sailor. I was a virgin then." She began to laugh. "He was very sweet, but my family didn't approve of me marrying a sailor. When I got pregnant the first time, I moved to Paris, and he sailed to the Pacific and never came back. I haven't heard from him since. It was very hard because I was very much in love with him." She added quickly, "Have you ever been in love?"

Penelope longed to say something cunning, but instead the question caught her off guard and her eyes filled up with tears.

Evie gazed curiously at her, "You have," she said. "Penelope has been in love," she alerted the other women.

"Oh Penelope," another woman crooned.

The ten or so women in the room gathered around her.

"Tell us, please," Alice pleaded, tucking in close beside Penelope.

"Okay then," Penelope responded. "If I tell you, promise me that you will tell me all about the men you love."

They huddled closer. Truth and tact, she told them about Lucien, but in her story they had met before the war when the air was humid at a holiday resort during the off season. They drank rum punch and watched people in long, patterned suits play in the ocean. It was a long and detailed story she had heard a stranger tell another passenger on her first train ride into Paris.

Penelope exaggerated the size of the guest room and the bamboo bar and extended the length of the stay. The women huddled closer as she spoke and they posed so many unusual questions about the temperature of the water, whether he was an alcoholic, the color of the sheets where they slept, the feel of his kiss and touch. The women were so grateful and hungry for the fantasy that Penelope created. Penelope's heart raced wildly. It was the first time she had ever spoken openly about Lucien as her storied lover.

"And what did it teach you?" Evie asked.

"You know the term love can be used for many purposes," Penelope answered in a different kind of tone, low and timid.

Evie nodded.

"I suppose love is this formless, indefinite, and really indeterminate thing. Like the term infinity, it is difficult to even talk about. There are so many versions of it. For example, there is potential love and actual love," Penelope began.

The women chattered amongst themselves about which versions they knew.

"But what about Lucien?" Evie asked. "What type of lover is he?"

"Lucien?" Penelope questioned. She felt the pull of her emotions and paused for a moment. "He taught me about transcendent love," Penelope responded.

"What is that?" Evie asked broodingly.

She paused again, afraid her memories of Lucien might consume her. "It's is a profound type of love that centers around the relationship between same and other."

"Like strawberry and chocolate," a woman nibbled a strawberry coated in chocolate, offering it to Penelope.

Penelope smiled and continued, "It's difficult to find the right words. It's like a magnetic field, magnet to magnet, a draw to another person that feels both familiar and foreign and is virtually unstoppable."

"It sounds serious," Cleo chirped, rubbing rouge into her cheek, brightening her face.

"It is. It seems to overflow every limit placed on it. Nothing can constrain it. Like the concept of infinity." Penelope paused for an instant, reflecting. "In truth, they're basically the same thing, infinity and transcendent love, more fluid and better than liquid gold."

The women murmured amongst themselves.

"How can you tell when you find it?" Cleo asked.

"Because it defies logic and numbers," Penelope said. "I'm not sure what more to say than it's perceptible in the air around it."

The women surrounding her seemed to cling to her words.

"I have to go downstairs to meet my client," a woman named Anna stood abruptly looking at the clock. "It is the man I love. His name is Wilhelm. He is a Field Marshall of the armed forces." She added quickly. "Penelope, will you come hide in the room and listen to the way we speak? You seem to know so much about love. I need someone to tell me if he really loves me."

"Yes, and me too," other women chimed in.

Anna led Penelope down the stairs two floors to the Polynesian room to wait.

"You can hide beneath the bed," she urged.

Penelope felt a sick and empty sensation as she followed

Anna down the hall and climbed beneath the bed in the Polynesian room. Anna draped the bedskirt, blocking the light but not the noise. Penelope was grateful she did not have to watch and was careful to curl up frozen to a spot so that none of the floorboards would creak beneath her. When the stir and groan of the seduction began, she felt nearly overcome by an urgency to flee and wondered how long she would have to wait there. She had almost given up on the idea of hiding beneath beds or in closets until at last, Wilhelm began to speak.

"What is it Anna?" he asked.

"You have been gone so long," Anna crooned. "I thought you had forgotten me."

"No, never," he stated definitively. "I have been pleading with My Fuhrer. It is only out of my loyalty to him that I have made you wait, my love."

"To Hitler himself," Anna seemed pleased.

"I was pleading with him not to fire another Field Marshal over a battle on the Eastern Front."

"Did he listen to you?"

"No, he fired him anyway."

"What will happen?"

"I am not sure, but I have learned that I will never challenge his orders again," Wilhelm concluded.

Once Wilhelm had left and Penelope climbed out from under the bed and reassured Anna of his love for her. Penelope scribbled down a message about the Field Marshal, walked carefully down the street to the pharmacy to buy more cosmetics for the women and to pass her first note to the pharmacist in an empty bottle of hair dye. She also brought him the radio transmitter she had transported from London. Within hours, Charles would receive her first memo in London about the Field Marshal on the Eastern Front.

Chapter Twenty-Four

E stablished at the brothel, she couldn't wait to see Lucien any longer, so the next morning, she risked going to search for Fulcanelli and Lucien on her way to the pharmacy. When she arrived at 52 rue Laffitte, the apartment was empty of most of its furniture, papers were scattered on the floor, and the front door had sustained the cracking pressure of some hurried entrance or police raid.

She suddenly felt as if all the units of measurement the world provided had vanished—no map, no numbers, no Naomie, no Fulcanelli, and no Lucien. So much had happened while she was away. She felt the same as the day she had returned home to her empty home in Sweetwater the day her father had died. Penelope frantically looked around the vacant apartment in search of any clue to their whereabouts. The Royal Society seemed like an exaggerated, distant dream. She had gone to London in an effort to help save them, but once again she had arrived too late. Fulcanelli and Lucien were captured or were in hiding, and the suitcase of money she had brought back from London to rescue them was now tucked away beneath the floorboards of her room at Le Chambrement. It would have to stay there, for now. She felt a surge of anger and despondency rise up as she realized she was alone again, and she might never find Lucien.

She also felt afraid that someone might have seen her enter the apartment, that they might contact the Gestapo. Her eyes hurriedly scoured the room in hopes that she might find the stone or Newton's papers hidden away somewhere. She rushed to the piano pushed along the wall. She lifted the top of the piano and reached inside, feeling its rough edge bite into her arm. She imagined the contraptions Lucien might have hidden in there. She could feel a clip of hair, a feather. She reached in farther. It was like tucking her hand into a warm pool. Something that had been dormant was brewing inside it, so she stretched further. She could feel the edge of papers, and as she pulled them into the room and unfolded them, they seemed to reverberate light. Newton's papers! She re-folded them gently and tucked them in her pocket with a familiar intimacy. She circled her hand around and gathered up all of the items she could touch. She stuffed them in her purse.

She knew all of the hiding places, so once she had the papers, she walked to the wall above Lucien's desk and removed the clock that still hung there. She reached in and let her hands roam around the cavity of the hole in search of the mystical stone, but she couldn't find it. She wondered where Fulcanelli had taken it. Instead, she felt the thin edge of another slip of paper, so she retrieved it.

> *Dearest P,*
> *I thought I would write you a few lines before I*
> *leave. I am doing fine. Last night, I received informa-*
> *tion from the Cathedral about German plans to raid*
> *the apartment and arrest me. Someone has ratted us*
> *out to the Germans, and the police are trying to gather*
> *up the Royal Society one by one. I have decided to go*
> *into hiding for my protection and safety. L is in hiding*
> *as well. Be careful, they may have your name too. I*
> *think you know where L stashed the papers. Please*
> *find them, don't destroy them, but find a way to hide*
> *them until the war is over.*
>
> > *Best of luck,*
> > *F*

She folded the letter and the pages together and slid them into her pocket. It seemed to her that physics was no longer quite as silent on the war.

Penelope left the apartment and hurried through the streets back to Le Chambrement, a slender building with a blank facade. She was greeted by an African man wearing a turban and a tunic decorated in gold embroidery. His name was Abraham. He had keen eyes, angular features, and a quiet smile. His manner reminded Penelope of her father. She had seen Abraham play music for the patrons at night. He seemed to live a double existence as both a greeter and a musician in the salon.

"Good afternoon," he said, welcoming her with a deep, sonorous voice that echoed through the vestibule.

Penelope reached into her bag and handed him some hair dye and the bottles of wine she had picked up on the way to Fulcanelli's apartment, attempting to smile even though her heart was still reeling from the letter.

"My dear, you must at least pretend to be happy," he cautioned, gathering the items in his wide arms.

She stood as tall and steady as a pyramid and said, "Is that better?"

He chuckled, "You cannot be taught to be happy, but you can most certainly pretend. It is especially important here, now."

She was not an actress, and it was mortifying for her to be inauthentic in this way. Still she understood his admonition. Other sentiments could prove fatal to a person like him or her, because they were both constantly trying to overcome the distant barrier of expendability.

Penelope could feel the urgent heat of the papers seeping through her bag, but she understood that she had to continue to play along.

The brothel's salon was a strange and luxurious room

where docile soldiers usually prowled from sofa to sofa, one pretty girl to the next. Penelope worked in the salon as a server and a maid, and she had to step carefully because the soldiers liked to fawn over any newcomers. When she saw the soldiers on the street, they seemed dangerous, but here they were drugged by the magic of the place, their shattered humanity temporarily restored to life.

The courtesans in the salon were draped with scarves or were topless. They dispersed themselves among the couches and chairs, sitting upright with good posture and a coy smile. Penelope wore a short blue dress with a high waist and a ruffled hem, signaling that she was not for sale and was there to straighten pillows and serve chocolates and cheese and honey and wine on a silver tray. When the soldiers felt full, they would select a woman by signaling to her, and Penelope would set off to prepare a room for them.

She befriended all of the women. Over time, they came to think of her like a sister. Alice liked to hug in against her and caress her hair. For Alice and all of the women at the brothel, Penelope felt soothing, safe.

One of the courtesans, Cleo, had a burrowing and feather-eyed look of innocence. "He likes to say that we'll elope whenever the war is over," she shared. She was almost twenty and she sipped champagne while Penelope dyed her hair.

A greater obstacle than the war even was the harmful effects of the alcohol. Like many of the women, it was the only relief that Cleo could find from her loneliness, a careening and dangerous mixture that overtook her like a moldy spore. There were times when she would beg the soldier to stay for fear of the tearing, thorny bramble of her own thoughts. It was difficult for her to be with them, but she had no choice. She told Penelope she could no longer recognize her own reflection in the mirror and used the alcohol to subdue the men and herself.

"The one today was drunk and wild," she said.

"Why?"

"Because he's afraid of dying. He says the Nazis are preparing to for an invasion of Stalingrad next year. He is returning to his headquarters in Kleve, Germany to prepare the demolition squads. It is likely that he will not return."

Penelope went to her room and jotted a note, *"Lieutenant Voigner returning to Kleve to begin to train demolition squad troops preparing to invade Stalingrad next year,"* folded it, tucking it quietly away into her shoe.

All of the women underwent their own metamorphosis. They used make-up, perfume and hair-dye to paint disorder into order, trying to achieve whatever the men found most delectable. They sat before their mirrors for hours painting their faces porcelain with gentle rose cheeks, taking umbrage at the slightest blemish.

Penelope discovered that the more flamboyant the

woman, the more sensitive she could be, and she made certain to shower them with praise, to pepper them with soft kisses to the cheek. Her gentleness was balm to the many sharp wounds of the war.

The brothel was a shelter for the German soldiers. They came there to lay down the gun that hung over their shoulder and bury themselves beneath the blankets, unlace their desperate pallor and drop the untold wounds of their hearts to the floor. After all, they needed a common denominator. Sex. They needed their freefalling foot to land on simple, solid earth. Physical pleasure was the antidote for the prosaic day-to-day life of war. They wanted no more fore and aft, no more sleepless watch. As soldiers, they were taught a predictable pattern, a repeated design, an arrangement, a sequence. At Le Chambrement, they could wait still as timber.

The brothel was a carnival, a lonely, potent mixture of eroticism, alcohol and pain. Rose, Adele, Cleo, Elise, Greta, they told her anything she wanted to know about the soldiers, as long as she kissed their cheeks and dyed and braided their hair like a sister, and then she walked down to the pharmacy and exchanged her notes for bottles of more hair dye. If the sunflower pot was in the window, that meant the radio transmitters were in the back room. She hoped the information she was stealing from the Germans was helping, that it was getting to someone listening carefully in London who knew better than she did what to do with it. There was no way for her to know what happened after she transferred the notes.

She always returned to the brothel, greeted Abraham at the door, and found a pail of water and a mop to wash down the floors for the next night. In bed she cried and let herself feel the shrinking wonderment of her heart. Lucien had disappeared. She allowed herself to wither with the sorrow and friction of her loss. She could not let anyone see this, not even the other women. She had to feign delight and offer up stories of pretend things and pretend people who did not exist.

She was constantly vigilant. After all, she was there to eavesdrop on the Germans, and if she were caught, they would kill her. Now she had been asked to keep Newton's papers. Afraid of the constant military presence, Penelope tucked them behind an immense carving of Shiva that hung above the bed in the Hindu room. She felt that they would be safer outside of her room, hiding in plain sight. The Hindu room was for sex alone, nothing personal could remain there. As the maid, she dusted the paintings and artifacts and easily pulled the heavy carving from the wall a fraction and fit the papers snugly into the space between the wall and the Shiva.

The carving was an Indian relic, a wood wall panel of a dancing Lord Shiva. It was handmade from mango wood and depicted a deity with not two but three eyes and ash smeared all over his body. A snake was coiled up around his head and arms, and he wore a tiger and an elephant skin. Penelope traced the dancing figure with her hand

and then with her duster.

Through her loneliness and devastation, she realized she must remain asymptomatic. She wrapped her arms around herself and leaned into the wall. She could feel the heat of the papers rising up through the carving; Penelope understood that she too might be far more powerful than she had originally known.

Chapter Twenty-Five

*P*enelope's only time spent outside of Le Chambrement was her short walks to the pharmacy and back. The journey was several blocks long and meandered through a market and along a quaint square. As Penelope neared the pharmacy, she saw a group of Nazis gathered around a utility truck that was blocking the road and sidewalk. Men in uniforms with guns were scratching their heads and staring at the pedestrians walking down the street.

Penelope tried to walk cautiously past them to the pharmacy across the street, but one of the soldiers stood in her path.

"Excuse me, ma'am," the soldier said. "This street has

been closed. A parade will be coming through shortly. You are going to have to wait or find another way. If you go through the square and head over to the fire station up that block, you might be able get around it."

"How long will the parade last?" she asked.

"At least another hour."

She looked at her watch.

"Ask at the fire station, and they can tell you where to go," he said wandering away from her.

Penelope shrugged and tried to pass again when he turned the corner, but this time another soldier blocked her passage.

"*Nein*," the soldier said. "Do not cross through here. You cannot pass until the parade is over."

Penelope spoke up, "I just want to cross the street to get to the pharmacy."

"*Nein*." he said. "Go away."

She turned and walked into the square, sitting down at a bench and grasping a cracker from her satchel. A light drizzle was beginning to fall, beads of water were beginning to gather on her hair and the sleeves of her blouse.

She stared across the street towards the pharmacy. With a note tucked into the sole of her shoe, it was not safe for her to stay here too long, and yet she was so happy to be outside of the brothel. Though the crowds were gathering along the street, the parade had not yet arrived. She looked up at the large tree that stood at the center of the square. One of its branches grazed the arm of the bench beside her. Out of the corner of her eye, she saw a small bird climb down towards her, bouncing along the long branch. She glanced over towards it as it paced in little ovals, in and out, around and back. It was sort of like a waltz.

It made a move towards the cracker crumbs falling on her satchel.

As the bird approached, she slowly reached her finger towards it with her hand. When the bird perched upon her finger, she gasped, feeling an answer to a deep question cauterize within her. A silent chill rose up along her arms and neck.

"Beethoven?" she said out loud.

She had not anticipated this reunion and was trying to suppress her excitement. Her face was a tangle of emotions. Penelope wasn't good at handling restrained, dangling, ripe moments.

"Is it you?" she said, but she knew it was him. She recognized the pattern of the feathers along his body, the way he danced and moved, the shape of his feet.

Beethoven was in search of more crackers, and Penelope was in the way, so she crumbled more crackers into the palm of her hand for him to eat, and patted him gently on the back.

He ate the crackers slowly, pacing and strutting while he swallowed, but when the loud noise of the parade began, he grasped a dangling strand of her hair, flew up into the tree, and then off into the gray sky of Paris.

Several, fitful months passed for Penelope. Summer had moved into winter, and though she kept returning to the square, she had not seen Beethoven again. However, her encounter with the bird secretly convinced her that Lucien was alive and close-by, even though she had no way of knowing for sure. Penelope worried that if he was looking for her, he wouldn't likely find her if she remained hidden inside the brothel, so she eventually decided to risk going back to 52 rue Laffitte, to see if she could find any more clues to his whereabouts.

It was a dangerous curiosity to have, and despite the time that had passed Lucien now owned her heart in its entirety, and nothing pursued her so strongly as her thoughts of him. The streets of Paris were unpredictable and dangerous. The Nazis patrolled constantly, pulling anyone who caught their eyes to the side, asking "where are you going? Why?" She always carried her identification papers with her.

She waited until she needed to go to the pharmacy again and darted out into the vacant Parisian streets, only this time she veered away from the markets, east towards the distant apartment. She had only one uneasy hour to spare.

Penelope bundled herself under her coat. The Occupation kept the streets clear of people, so she hurried her journey along. When she arrived at 52 rue Laffitte, she stepped quickly into the building's familiar vaulted foyer and then rang the doorbell. She could hear a shuffling step approach the door and a barely perceptible, "Who is it?"

drift through.

"It's Penelope," she said, daring to say her name aloud. The *SOE* had warned her against it.

The door creaked open slightly, and Philippe, the man who had been building the death ray, peered through the tiniest crack. "What do you want?" he asked pointedly.

"May we speak alone?" she asked, looking over her shoulder.

Philippe reluctantly opened the door and motioned for her to come in and sit. The apartment was even more vacant than before, and his beloved death ray was nowhere to be seen. She didn't have the heart to ask what had happened to it. Nearly every scrap of metal in France had been hauled off to Germany to be melted down and made into weapons, and she feared that's what had happened to Philippe's beloved machine. His eyes flickered, barely lit. He looked bedimmed, almost unconscious.

"Please, be brief," Philippe said. He did not want to invite trouble, and his wounded, bent over body let her know that since she had last seen him, he had been interrogated and beaten, perhaps many times.

"I want to know if you had heard from either Lucien or Fulcanelli?"

"I have not," he stated blankly and shuffled in his seat.

"Nothing? No news whatsoever?"

"Fulcanelli, I have been told by one of the priests at Notre Dame that he has left Paris," he told her. "He said that Fulcanelli is trying to make his way to London then

America. But I have no way of knowing whether or not that is true. The same priest told me that Lucien was recovering from an illness but remained free. I was told at one point that he was taken out of Paris for his safety. But he may have returned. I do not know because I have not spoken with him myself. You know communication is so poor this could be nothing but hearsay from the Cathedral."

Penelope felt herself shudder. She wanted to rise up and scream with relief and delight, but she knew it would be unsafe, so she steadied herself.

"Do you know where Lucien is?" she continued.

"No."

"Is there anyone else I can talk to?" she pleaded.

"Perhaps if you could find that damn bird of his, the magpie. You know it returned after all that time with you in England. One day it just appeared, and Lucien could barely speak. He locked himself in Fulcanelli's office for days, talking to the bird, holding the bird, praising it like some lunatic." He shook his head. "It disappeared when he left. Though in recent months, I have seen it here again."

Beethoven had returned here to Lucien after all. He must have known that she had returned to Paris, she thought to herself.

"Then, if you would, can you do me a favor. If the bird comes back, can you tie a note with the words 'Le Chambrement' written on it to the leg of the bird."

"You are as insane as he is," he scoffed.

"Please, can you attach a note to the bird's foot?" she

pleaded.

She knew better than to reveal her whereabouts like this but she couldn't stop herself. Her trainers at *SOE* had warned her about this—about the risks of loving during a time of espionage.

"Please, Philippe."

His eyes widened. She hoped she could trust him.

"I will do what I can," he assured her as she rose and turned towards the door.

They quickly said good-bye, and she raced through the streets to the pharmacy. She had a note in her shoe to deliver about Germany's bombing campaign over Britain, and she needed to retrieve more hair dye before the courtesans came looking for her to fix their hair.

Chapter Twenty-Six

L ieutenant Hans Berger frequented the brothel and spoke in a trickling and sore voice that haunted Penelope's dreams, but he knew more about the war than just about anyone in Paris. "I feel sorry for the soldiers who don't fuck," she heard him utter, laughing, speaking in a caustic and broken French, as he stumbled through the doorway.

He preferred the decadence of the Hindu room, with its gold opulence. She was preparing the room just as he liked it, drawing the bath, burning incense, and fluffing the pillows when she heard him coming down the hall with his favorite girl, Cleo. She was round with velvet skin, and she wound her dark hair in a braid that was so long it grazed her hip.

Penelope quickly grabbed her things, then tucked herself underneath the bed so she could listen. She liked to close her eyes and pretend she was a shadow.

They walked into the room together, and he handed something to Cleo. "It's for the girl with long, golden hair," he said. "What's her name?"

It was chocolate.

"Are you speaking of the maid?"

"Yes, I think her name is Penelope. I saw her the other evening preparing my room, and I thought I should show my," he paused, "abundant appreciation."

"I will let her know," Cleo responded, setting the gift to the side.

He undressed and lowered himself into the ornate bath.

"Tell me about your life before Le Chambrement," he said sharply.

The men who came to Chambrement liked to visit first, to feign charm, civility, and familiarity, as if this were a mere social visit.

"My father was a scientist, and my mother was a seamstress," Cleo said. "They both died when I was a girl. " She traced her fingers across the water of his bath.

"So, your father was a scientist, you say?"

"Yes, a professor at the university."

"What did he study?"

"The ocean," she said, swirling her fingers into the pattern of a wave.

"And to think he had his most beautiful mermaid right with him the entire time." With that, he kissed her lips.

"Yes, science can be both beautiful and destructive."

"Yes, there are so many secrets left for us to discover," he unlaced her bodice with his hand. "And then once in a while, someone like Newton comes around and reveals the structure more fully." He examined her body. "Did your father ever study Newton?"

"Yes, I am sure he did, though we never spoke of it."

"Newton was a true scientist because he invented as well as discovered."

"Which do you prefer?" She let her words hang in the air.

The room quieted as he stepped out of the bath water. "I prefer to discover," he said, and Penelope felt the bed creak with the weight of his words above her, as he moved to the bed.

"I prefer to discover things that words can't describe," he continued. "Newton was the master–as were Hubert and Jan van Eyck."

"Who are they?"

"You do not know the Ghent Altarpiece?"

Cleo shook her head.

"It is the most famous painting. It was nearly burned, forged, broken, censored, stolen by Napoleon, and sought by great armies. It is the world's first major oil painting, and it is as mystical as Newton. It is one of the treasures of the world." He seemed to spit the words as he spoke them.

"And, needless to say, we are looking for it and will certainly find it."

"Is that why you are here in Paris?"

"No, I am in town to find another set of treasures. I am sent here with the assignment of hunting down several French Resistance groups in Paris. In fact, speaking of Newton, one of the groups even has the gall to call themselves the Royal Society. I am told they are a group of insurgents who call themselves scientists because they stole some of Newton's papers from a library a decade or so ago. It is completely absurd," he laughed. "A waste of my time really, but if I can track down criminals like them, life will be a lot easier for me," he said, tipping his head back on the bedspread. "We came quite close to the supposed Royal Society last year, but someone must have tipped them off because they slipped away before we got to them."

"Someone has Isaac Newton's papers in Paris?" Cleo asked.

"Yes, Isaac Newton. There are so many of his papers tucked away in various libraries throughout Europe."

"Do you have any leads on the insurgents?" Cleo asked in a weary and sorrowful voice.

"I get tips from time to time. Most recently I have been told to look for a blonde woman with a burn scar along her ear. Have you ever heard of such a thing, such an absurd thing as that, a burned ear?"

Penelope gasped and touched her ear, a terrifying

moment of self-awareness.

The lieutenant watched closely as Cleo undressed before him.

"No more absurd than a mermaid," she noted, batting her eyes.

"Yes, no more absurd than finding a mermaid."

He reached for her.

She fluttered her legs and he flipped her from her belly to her back. The bed rocked and pitched above, and Penelope closed her eyes and pretended she too was submerged beneath the sea, far away from the horrible shallows.

Later, after Lieutenant Berger left, Penelope pulled the sheets from the bed and smoothed the covers, before retreating to her room. Her whole body trembled with fear. He had already noticed her and had left her a gift. Had he noticed the burn along her ear as well? Her long hair could veil her ear for only so long. There was no way to heal that old and terrifying wound. Her teeth clattered.

Fulcanelli and Lucien had tried to tell her. The Germans were intent on hunting down every French saboteur. She thought of the British Intelligence files from London and realized the Nazis had a similar file on her in some stale intelligence office, *the blonde woman with the burnt ear.* She wondered what else they might know about her. She wished there were a way to heal her ear, some miracle cure, some alchemical balm or salve to restore the missing part of her.

She thought of the magic of Paris and remembered when the bomb went off in her bag. Lucien had showed her that miraculous place, the palm fountain at the center of the city. There was no way for her to find that park now. She thought back to Parc Verdun, the other magical park. She tried to remember where it was. Lucien had spoken of a mystical grotto with even greater powers. It was a long shot, but she saw it as her only chance.

The next morning when Penelope awoke, just before dawn, she pulled on her jacket and walked for miles trying to find the park. The war had contorted the city so much she kept getting turned around. Wandering from street to street, trying to stitch together what she remembered. Eventually she saw the gilded gates. She found the same refraction the hovering palm grove had held, like stepping through glass, only the gardens had been partially destroyed, and the sculptures were toppled too. She wandered through the park, past the grand rotunda, the windmill, and the pyramid. She could see the ancient wisteria weaving through the wrought-iron trellis, holding on for dear life. She followed the path to the grotto and waterfall. It was still there, though the water was frozen, encased in a calloused layer, like most of Paris. *This city had endured so much.*

The grotto was covered in a spongy, verdant but frozen moss and stood next to a massive waterfall. Another natural boulder waterfall cascaded from the rear side of the grotto into a stream bed. There was a small path that led past the grotto to the back side of the largest waterfall. She followed the path, climbing over the slippery boulders. When she stepped behind the frozen falls, she leaned forward to look through the water. It felt familiar, like looking into the mouth of her very own dark cave. She reached in to touch the frozen water and felt the ice's cold resistance. It wouldn't yield to her touch.

She put her face to the ice and looked through, like through the lens of a telescope. She saw tubes, like the glass tubes of a laboratory, cracked and configured into strange shapes and colors, the way a prism refracts light. She watched, enthralled, the way someone looks into an aquarium, seeing beautiful things they cannot touch. Even her tears could not perforate the frozen mass. They dropped from her eyes and scrolled along the surface of the ice.

She thought about Lucien. Happiness was not the only virtue. After all, loneliness wrote great symphonies and could paint masterpieces. It was the imperfections and miseries that necessitated the magic. Lucien had vanished, his touch was now a distant sensation. She had no way to find him. She had spent so much of her life waiting.

She put her ear to the ice and felt the cold bite down on her. Lucien had told her it heals wounds, but she didn't know if it would do so for ones that were old and distant. She could hear a vibration, the same muffled pulse and meter as when the moon passes from perigee to perigee. Her ear ached from the coldness. Winter was not the right time; she could tell the magic too was frozen in its icy spell. Her wound was not healing the way it had in the palm grove with Lucien, and she felt frantic. Perhaps the water needed to be liquid to properly heal the wound.

She traced her finger along the edge of the frozen water and looked back towards the path and the grotto. She needed to find a spot where she could safely stand where the frozen waterfall was thin. She pushed with her finger, but nothing would give. She stepped down the path and found a ragged and heavy rock that stood out like the arm of a statue. She lifted it off of the ground and walked back towards the falls, throwing it towards the ice, but nothing broke through. She tried with the rock again and again, until at last, a chunk flew free, and she was able to pull a small piece of ice from the frozen stream below. She placed the ice in her satchel. She had to hurry. The rising sun was marigold on the horizon.

Penelope covered her head with a scarf and ran across the city back to the brothel. The Nazi soldiers were milling around the entrance of Le Chambrement waiting for their commanders to emerge. The courtesans understood that sex was the soldiers' first allegiance. It was where they stood most naked and alive. The commanders understood this too, and any denial of sex would call forth pure revolt. War and sex were indelibly intertwined. There was no love in war, only sex and power.

She tucked her chin and pressed through the crowd of soldiers to the back hallway where Abraham greeted her. He shuttled her in the doorway. "It's not safe for you to be out so long," he cautioned. "Someone might notice."

She smiled and nodded at him and hurried to her room, gathering a small vase from her table. She reached into her satchel to retrieve the ice and dropped it into the glass vase. It was the size of an egg, and it clattered on the bottom as it landed. There was nothing numerical or rational about it, no theorems, propositions or corollaries to explain. The block of ice seemed to bubble as it melted into a puddle. Penelope could not conceive of any reasonable explanation for what she was doing. This was pure, harmonious magic.

Chapter Twenty-Seven

*P*enelope had worked at the brothel for over three
years. It was the longest she had ever lived anywhere outside of Tennessee. That afternoon, a group of
the courtesans at Le Chambrement wanted her to dye her
hair dark like theirs, but she didn't want to, so instead,
she hid on her bed and listened through the wall to some
new people who had moved into the small room beside
her. They were performers Madame Geurrain had hired
to entertain the soldiers.

"She's not a monster," a woman screamed.

"I don't care if she is an frog, as long as she can perform," a man said.

Penelope could hear a loud ruckus erupting over and

over again. There were several threats flung about. The fighting was awkward, loud voices and bodies thumping against walls. A crashing sound of some delicate thing erupted and a voice cried out in pain. Penelope felt compelled to run out of her room to see what was happening. The door next to hers was closed, but she decided to knock.

A bald man with leathery skin and a gap-toothed smile opened the door. He was wearing a hat, but she recognized him immediately.

"Manfri," she blurted out.

She was sure it was him because no one else could look like him. She could not remember anyone who looked more like a genie. He had that half-decayed look of war in his eyes, as if every object of value were hidden and locked away somewhere. He was more mangled and broken than she remembered. He clutched a book angrily. He looked petrified and was bleeding from his lip.

He gave her a solemn once over and then stared blankly at her face. He clearly did not recognize her.

"Whores go down the hall," he said, pointing his finger.

"Manfri?" she cried out. She looked at him with music in her eyes. She quite simply could not believe he was here.

"Just walk as far as you can see down the hall and knock on that door," he added impatiently.

"Manfri, it's me," she said, her words drifting by as he continued to look at her in silence. His pupils were dark as bullets, he was drunk and rundown with anger.

"It's me. Penelope ... your cousin Naomie's friend," she said, and she began to stir the air with her hands, leaning, arching and tilting her body around and around in a flawless pirouette, just as he had taught her.

Manfri's faced washed white, then brightened to a mineral beige.

"Lord, help me!" he shouted out, pulling down on her arm. "Penelope!" He hugged her waist, her neck, her arm. He held her face between his hands. She could feel the topography of his gnarled bones wrap around every facet of her in a desperate clutching of something.

"Show me again. Show me that again," he said.

He stomped his feet, and like a reflex, she began to pirouette around the hallway—only this time he saw quite clearly that she had the body of a woman.

"And again," he said, "It's just like I taught you." This time drawing the angry woman with the skin like an armadillo from his room into the hallway to watch.

Manfri and the woman watched as Penelope lifted her chin and stiffened her posture. One, two, three, four she calibrated a rhythm. One, two, three, four she continued. And once she'd remembered the coordinates of balance, she went off in the dance in an oval path around the hallway. It was all heliocentric, with Manfri as her sun. He had taught her that this was a problem of pure geometry, and it felt good for her to move this way.

He rushed toward Penelope and began hugging her over and over, tears melting down his face.

"You heard about Naomie's arrest I suppose."

Penelope nodded gravely.

"And what about Elodie? Is she here too?" she asked, peering behind the door, her words were pregnant with emotion.

Manfri looked down, shaking his head. "She's gone too." A trickle of blood slid down his chin from his lip. "You know months have passed since I returned to Paris without her, and it doesn't get any easier."

"But how?" she gasped.

"It was the Germans." He bit down on his lip. "Elodie and I had traveled to England to perform in a show. The money was exceptional. It was an offer we couldn't refuse. We thought we could outmaneuver the impact of the war. Just be there a few months before returning to Paris. We couldn't though. But if one of us had to die, I wanted it to be me."

"Die? Die? How?" The sound of her voice seemed to dismantle as it hit the air.

"It was a bomb," he said and he drew her into his room and closed the door. "Elodie was killed by a German bomb in London."

Penelope clutched her chest in despair.

"We were invited to perform at a theater in London. We were there when the invasion began. The music was playing and muffling the sounds from outside and Elodie was performing in perfect geometry. Dancing and running and spinning across the stage. It was captivating.

"Suddenly the air raid sirens screamed out and there was smoke, tons of it. We tried to run to the basement, but there was no time. The windows shattered around us. The doors blown clean off. The blast of a second bomb killed her." Manfri paused, his chest shuddering. "She was barely recognizable to me. A gentleman helped me carry her down to the basement, but it was too late. Elodie never understood the ludicrousness of the war. To her it was always in the being, not the having."

Manfri's companion spoke with a sharp tongue, "He'll never recover. He keeps asking me, why do rocks fall? Why do clouds rain? Why do fires burn? Why war?" She faltered for a moment. "He walks in his sleep every night, like he's in a trance with blank eyes and garbled words asking these questions over and over. I get no sleep. No money, no sleep. And he tells me I am too noisy."

Manfri furrowed his brow and said, "Love, solitude and death, that's what it boils down to."

"Bunyons, gray hair, and death," the woman smiled a crooked smile.

Penelope reached in her bag, pulled out the hair dye and handed it to her, smirking. "Magic," she said.

The woman laughed so loudly it floated down the hall.

"What is that?" Manfri said, grasping the bottle and admonishing the woman.

He looked down in thought and closed his eyes. Penelope parted her lips to say something, but before she could, Manfri straightened his jacket and looked at the hair dye in her hand and like a spark to a fire, an idea flashed before him.

"Penelope," he began in his impish manner.

She looked around cautiously.

He took the hair dye and touched her braid.

"You cannot dye these threads of gold," he said, reaching out once again. "Madame Guerrain," he then called out. "Madame Guerrain. I have it!"

Madame Guerrain wandered into the hall and leaned against his door, her arms crossed.

"What's all of the commotion?" she asked.

"Do you know who this is?" he said, his mouth agape.

Madame Geurrain nodded slowly.

"Our maid."

"She is not just a maid. She is a great dancer. I taught her to dance." he continued. "She should dance here. We should paint her gold. We will call her 'The Golden Girl,' a goddess, a dancing statue. The Nazis, they will love it."

Before Madame Guerrain could answer, Manfri had scuttled Penelope into his room. There, the armadillo woman painted her skin with a soft and glowing paint of gold. She adorned her with gold beaded necklaces and a crown. She pulled a sequined costume from her bag and fitted it tightly around Penelope's body.

Penelope was painted like a golden apparition, and when she looked in the mirror, she was astonished. She barely recognized her own reflection. Gold, Au, with the atomic number 79—she was pure, gilded and shining.

"She's ready to perform!" Manfri pronounced.

"But I can't!" Penelope objected. She didn't want to risk breaking her cover.

However, when Penelope looked up at Madame Guerrain, she saw Lieutenant Berger behind her, leaning against a wall, observing them from the hallway. There was no telling how long he had been standing there, listening. He paused a moment, licking his lips and looking her up and down.

He turned to face Madame Geurrain, "I couldn't agree more with the gentleman over there, and I expect to see her perform for me tonight in the salon. She is no longer a maid, she is a performer."

Madame Guerrain stiffened as he spoke.

"Indeed," she replied vacantly.

Manfri explained that the word "burlesque" was derived from the Italian *burla*, which means a joke or caricature. Penelope was to be a showgirl for the desperate eyes of the Nazis.

"You will have to consort with the Germans," Madame Guerrain told her, as she fixed her golden braid. "It is not the way I wanted it to be, but the lieutenant has demanded that he see you perform," she said with grave disappointment.

"But—," Penelope felt afraid.

"My hands are tied," Madame Guerrain concluded. "Just remember your commodity is seduction, and seduction is a form of magic. When they say higher, you lift your skirt but not too high. You have to keep them hungry. It is the decadent art of showmanship and illusion. A rare sighting, like the flash of a shooting star across a sky, a meteor, a rainbow, the moon.

"You bring the spell and keep them wanting more," she added. "The art of the striptease is baring first the ankle, then the calf and nearly the knee by decade's end. You never have to show it all, only just enough to stir the uncontrolled emotions." Madame Guerrain spoke with certainty as she handed Penelope a fan and nudged her out onto the salon's floor.

Penelope was practicing in front of the workers at the brothel. She was supposed to have fun with it, they said.

"Learn from the masters themselves," Manfri had coached her.

She gathered her hemline in her hand and watched the people congregate in the room. The frightening sting of the moment was clear, she was supposed to dance for the Nazis. The risk of them seeing her scarred ear was immense. She was crossing over to where the bullets were. From servant to the served, she could no longer fade into the shadows. She would have to learn to hide in full view.

She imagined herself as a mechanical ballerina placed in a box. The dial now cranked, the music began, and she walked slowly to the center of the room. She turned while doing the pirouette Elodie had taught her, falling backwards and tipping her chin to the gilded ceiling. She slowly, unlaced the shawl and then the long gloves and the even longer tulle skirt Manfri had fixed around her waist, until piece by piece, she was almost fully unraveled, just enough to leave them guessing. She swung her eyes and legs around and lifted the hem of her smaller, golden skirt to the highest and softest part of her thigh. She was mostly uncovered and fully painted in gold. She lifted her arms to her hair and pin by pin let it unravel around her.

She gathered her courage and traced the walls of the salon with her eyes, hoping to avoid contact of others—Cleo, Elise, Manfri, Madame Guerrain. She went along the chair rail trim, and no one moved as she traced the lines of their faces, person to person, until she saw him, or at least she thought it might be him.

She froze for an instant, thinking it must be some apparition, a stupidity of her mind's eye. But it wasn't. She looked again and his eyes were fixed upon her. It was Lucien. He was there, leaning against the painted wall of the salon, watching her dance and discard her layers, piece after piece right before him.

She surfaced for an instant, and her body shook, as he watched her with a familiar gnashing hunger. Day after day, she remembered the look of him. She imagined his warm touch at the fountain and craved the smell of his skin. She had realized soon after she returned to Paris that her passion for Lucien had carried her away to some place she thought she might never again return from. Even after so much time had passed, her emotions were unshrinking and relentless, and no amount of mathematics and discovery could exhaust these sensations.

Madame Guerrain grasped her hand, and they bowed low together. Then Madame Guerrain shuttled Penelope away. "Another performance in an hour," she said. "The swine will love it. They will love you. Only this time, you must look them in the eye."

Madame Guerrain licked her lips and smiled as Manfri danced down the hall to the door of her room. "You did it," he said eagerly. "Dance just like that again, only in front of the soldiers."

She was not listening. She could think only of Lucien.

Chapter Twenty-Eight

"What are you doing here? This is too dangerous," Penelope said. "Some of the highest ranking German officers visit here."

Lucien just stared at her. He touched her face and paused a minute, his eyes brimming over with love and affection. Penelope understood that he couldn't muster the words to speak.

The soldiers were filing in through the main entrance, and the crowds were coming for the show. She had just an hour before she was set to perform again, and so quickly and without thinking, she pulled him into her small room and closed the door. Her mouth was like dough. She, too, could barely shape her lips to form the words. She was both angry and incredibly relieved with Lucien standing before her in her tiny, windowless room. She wanted to hold him but could not. She was set to perform again, and she was still encased in Manfri's gold makeup. Everything she touched smeared gold.

"You cannot stay here. You will be killed if they find you. How did you get here? Who saw you?" She spoke quickly not moving.

"It doesn't matter."

"It means everything to me," she replied, her emotions liquid inside, boiling over.

He was noonday, nighttime; he was all things. He continued to watch her with a look of pain and rapture. "You and I together is a death sentence in this war," he began slowly. "So, you are supposed to be stealing information from the Nazis, but instead you are here to dance for their pleasure?"

Tears were forming in her eyes, though she barely noticed them. "I am only here to work for the Resistance. This place lives in a disturbing omission of time and place. These men let down their fears and talk openly when they come here. I learn secrets, important secrets, and I pass them along to the radio operators. The madame has asked me dance like this. Don't make me feel ashamed for the work I have done."

His neck and face burned with a deep, melancholy red.

"No man here has ever touched me," she said, "that was the promise." All of her passion and loneliness poured out through those words as she spoke them out.

Lucien paused then sat down on the bed and looked up at her with reverence and relief.

"Not ever?" he asked.

"Not once," she responded. "You shouldn't make assumptions about me like that."

Penelope looked in the mirror, frustrated. She could still hear the soldiers down the hallway and wondered if the lieutenant would be among them. When she danced, it was more difficult to hide her ear. She knew the Germans were looking for the girl with the burn scar along her earlobe. She brushed her hair with her fingers, examining the scarred tissue of her lobe.

With aggravation, she turned and stepped to the table where a covered vase rested. She removed the lid. The ice she had retrieved from the grotto long ago had become water, for months she had been trying to use it in different ways, hoping it might heal her ear. She examined the glass closely, and at last dipped the brush she used to powder her face into the vase, pulled it out and painted the water along her lobe.

She closed her eyes, hoping everything would fall into some artful order, all the broken pieces suddenly might fall into place. But when she opened her eyes, she saw that nothing had happened. She dipped the brush again, slowly painting the water onto her ear, hoping again for some change. She needed an orderly pattern, the way flower seeds colonize an empty space and sprout artfully. Again nothing.

Lucien watched her cautiously. He was trying to understand her strange behavior, assuming at first that she was performing some cosmetic procedure unknown to him, until slowly he realized what she was doing. Her eyes remained closed as tears started to fall. She slowly lifted the vase to her lips and drank the last tablespoon down. The flavor was complex. It tasted soft as satin and yet at the same time cold and metallic as wrought iron. She was the girl with the burn on her ear, and she had no other means of concealing her wound from anyone.

"A shot of alcohol?" he asked.

"No. It's from the grotto you told me about in Parc Verdun. They know to look for the woman with the burn on her ear, and now they tell me I must dance in front of the soldiers. I have no way to hide it."

She practiced veiling her mouth with a scarf like a belly dancer, ear to ear, but she worried this might draw attention away from her body and to her face.

She threw her handkerchief to the floor.

"I'm sorry," he said at last and watched as she moved toward the light of the candle.

"I am sure they will kill me," she concluded.

There was no reasonable way to explain everything that had happened, so much time had passed, and their emotions were dense and viscous, spilling out of the room and down the hallway. She wanted to howl with sorrow.

"I've missed you so much," he muttered. His voice was uneven and rife.

"Did you know that I had returned to Paris?" she asked.

"Yes," he responded. "The magpie arrived just before Fulcanelli and I went into hiding."

"Then why didn't you wait for me at the apartment?" she gasped. "I returned and there was virtually nothing left there and now years have passed like this." She gestured around the room, deflated. "I have missed you so much. I have never felt so alone." Her words broke open as she spoke.

She drew away from him. The elaborate painted costume she was wearing kept them apart in this moment. She still had to perform for the large-eyed soldiers, and she was afraid the paint would smear off on him. He pursued her nonetheless.

"It was the hardest choice of my life, but I couldn't risk it. Fulcanelli and I knew things that you didn't know," he said. "There was an informant in the Royal Society, and we were being followed. After you left, he warned me not to even say your name aloud for fear of what might happen to you when you returned. He worried they could set a trap for you." His speech was strained tightly. "Fulcanelli told me over and over again that it would be too dangerous to wait in the apartment for your return."

His whole body seemed to ache with emotion.

He continued, "It is, in part, why Fulcanelli agreed to let you go away to London in the first place. He knew they were coming soon to dismantle the Royal Society, and if they knew how I felt about you, they would steal you away and torture you like they had Naomie, just to break us to pieces."

Penelope shuddered, "So what happened?"

"We went into hiding. Then one day Fulcanelli stepped out for an errand, and, out of nowhere, they took him off of the street and into an interrogation room."

Penelope closed her eyes as if doing that would make this sound less awful.

"And then?" she asked, bracing herself.

"And then they said to him, 'we have some questions for you.' And Fulcanelli laughed and said, 'Only I have no plans to answer them. I'll be leaving soon,' and that night he somehow escaped his prison cell. He had the stone with him. It is my belief that it somehow the strange stone protected and aided him in his escape."

"Then what?" she asked, her forehead knit with emotion.

"He made his way to the cathedral, and the priests sent him to London, then America to hide with the stone until the war is over."

"Where in America?"

"I have no way of knowing. I have not heard from him."

Lucien's words were sparse and confusing. She felt herself becoming more circumspect. At first, she didn't like it, her memories of the potent stone pricking her neck like nettle. As a young girl, the stone had clung to her like a small animal. It seemed to be alive, and its warm touch had nearly gutted her. Then, she had been starving not only for knowledge, but for touch, and the stone had been intoxicating. It reminded her of Naomie. She had learned to press it against her heart to help her fall asleep at night. She squeezed it when she was nervous or scared. During her time on the ship crossing the Atlantic to France, for company she had stirred the necklace against her skin like warm soup. There was a word for it. It was the opposite of loneliness, but she could no longer find it in her tired memory.

"Do you think Fulcanelli is okay?" she asked.

"I do," he said. "I think he is as surprised as I am."

"At what?"

"That he did it," Lucien said.

"Did what?" Her voice was low and controlled.

"Transmuted –," Lucien smiled as he spoke.

"How?" she asked

"I don't know precisely. I can only guess. But I know it had something to do with the importance of the stone," he said.

When she arrived in Paris to give the stone away, Fulcanelli had told her a story that in the eighth century an Islamic alchemist named Geber had first understood the concept of *material prima*. He understood the principles of hotness, coldness, dryness, and wetness—two of them interior qualities, two others with exterior qualities. Geber believed that alchemists could rearrange these qualities in metals, turn the internal external, achieving enlightenment, both physically and mystically.

Her mind spun. Since her voluntary submission to

the study of these magical, mathematical principles, her world had turned upside down. She had brought the necklace across an ocean to France and now she was hiding Newton's ancient papers.

"He escaped the Nazis," he said. "They thought they had cornered and trapped him and then he disappeared with the papers and the stone."

When Lucien had described the stone's many magical properties years earlier, he had mostly focused on its ability to transform metals into gold, nothing about it giving people the ability to become immortal and escape from prisons.

"No, you are wrong," she whispered. "Fulcanelli doesn't have the papers."

"I went back to the apartment and they are missing from where I hid them. The stone as well," he said.

"Fulcanelli has the stone, but I have the papers. When I returned from London, I found a note from him in the apartment and he asked me to keep them safe with me."

"Good, then make them disappear like Fulcanelli until this horrible war is over," he cautioned.

She secretly wished he would take the burden of the papers away from her.

"And you? Why did you disappear? You vanished," she declared. "But not because of some mythical stone like Fulcanelli. It was your choice. Even after Fulcanelli had gone into hiding, you never bothered to contact me or find me until now."

"It is this war. I thought it was the right thing to protect you, don't you see?" he pleaded.

"And why now? We are no safer than before. There are Nazi soldiers waiting right outside that door. Why now?"

"Because the magpie brought me a strand of your hair, and I no longer had the strength to stay away from you." His words were tense, a tight and knotted rope.

She felt confused and deeply alone. She looked at the clock and sat down in her chair, beginning to refresh her make-up for the show. She knew she would have to perform soon.

From the moment she had opened the door and found him there, she had felt the shrill air of his words wash over her. His explanations buoyed her for an instant, but she also worried they could wash her away completely.

The war. It had been this elaborate matrix of letting go. She was not angry at him. She was angry at life and for his insistence that their life together be perfectly harmonious or separate.

He knelt down beside her as she gathered her hair into a braid and pinned it on top of her head. Madame Guerrain had told her to do that so the men could watch her let it cascade down her shoulders and back like some waterfall. She clipped large earrings to her ears, hoping they might mask her deformity. She clipped them both high on her ears, creating a symmetry that would seem more artful than deceptive.

Lucien watched her restlessly. He too wanted to touch

those parts of her. He leaned forward and kissed her neck, and she felt all the passion in her body poured into that spot.

She looked at him, his lips now touched with gold. There was a knock at the door as she wiped them clean with her bare thumb.

"That's the madame. I have to perform. Please wait for me here," she said. "Please stay."

She was dressed in a sequined bodice with a small, embroidered skirt. She wrapped a longer tulle skirt around her waist that was both golden and sheer. Her nerves quivered and hummed inside her body.

Once again Penelope stepped out of her room and into the salon. This time it was filled with people. The lights dimmed, and the music began. Just as Elodie had taught her, she breathed deeply and placed one foot directly in front of the other, dragging the toes of each foot as she went. She stood in the center of the room, slowly raising her arms, tracing the contours of her body with her fingertips. Arching her back and swiveling her hips, she pirouetted across the room, taking in the soldiers all around her.

She had been told to undress down to the bare essentials, to molt, Manfri had said. He had also told her to make eye contact with the men, but she found she wasn't able to do that, and instead, she tipped her hips into an acrobatic leap or twist or tumble and grazed the walls with her eyes as she dropped each layer of clothing. She was in a state of perpetual delirium, part trance, part wakeful sleep.

First the tulle, then the stockings then the shawl, then her hair tumbled down around her. Elodie had taught her the mesmerizing geometry of a woman, so she knew well how to swivel as she rolled. She was flexible, and so she liked to grasp her leg in her hand and pull it up to her head to stand and spin. It was a lyrical dance. It told the liquid story of Circe, abstract and intricate, a cross between ballet and jazz. It was burlesque, the suggestion of something not really there.

She progressed through the room, her scarves and ties deciduous, sculpted and well-powdered. Manfri smiled from the doorway. When she tipped her head to the back wall and let her hair fall down around her, once again, Lucien was there, watching her. His eyes beckoned her with the rank, perfect tonic of love and jealousy, and he made her flush even through her gold.

Seeing Lucien standing so close to these monstrous men frightened her, so when her song ended, she bowed quickly and hurried out of the room and down the hall, terrified by the cruel accusations that could now be levied against her. She had crossed over into the "art," as Madame Guerrain had called it. They would scrutinize her now— her perfections, her flaws, her burned lobe. It was a fine tightrope to walk.

Chapter Twenty-Nine

*M*anfri ran after her, grasping her arm. "They loved you," he said, but his words felt sharp. "Elodie would be so proud."

"Would she? That I have now danced for the very people who killed her." Penelope felt a surge of sadness and noticed that he had not yet released her arm.

"Yes," he paused, "she would."

She saw deep craters of pain in Manfri's roughened gaze. She felt his hurt deep in her elbows and straightened her costume to disperse the sensation. While she seemed to want to move on quickly from it, he decided to stay there a moment intentionally expanding the silence and discomfort in the space between them.

"Penelope?" he asked.

She wasn't sure how much longer she could endure.

"Penelope, what's wrong?"

Elodie, her parents, Naomie, all of the names were just hung up in her throat.

"Is it about your dance? Is everything okay?"

Penelope heaved a shaky breath and leaned her body heavily into his shoulder to steady herself.

"It's nothing new. It's really nothing," she responded. She had so many questions but instead focused on his scribbled, frozen look of pain and merely stared back at him. He kissed her hand then released it and turned quickly away. He hurried down the hall back towards the salon to collect the tip jar.

When she returned to her room, Lucien was there once again. She said nothing to him. She was angry he had risked so much just to watch her dance, but she was also afraid of the love she felt for him. She sat at her table, pinning her hair and gathering rags to wipe away the paint from her skin. She hardly recognized her own reflection. She wiped a coarse rag along one arm then another, mopping away the golden illusion.

Lucien seemed angry too and moved to her side. When he glanced at her in the mirror, he could see she was afraid from the trembling of her mouth.

"I don't understand why you went out there," she said, looking up at him. "You stayed away from me for years, and now you stand among the soldiers to watch." She drew in a deep and shuddering breath. "These Nazis who come here. They come and they go. That is what people do," she said. She closed her eyes and looked down at the smeared and golden paint still shimmering on her skin.

They stood staring at each other, held in their spots like stakes to the ground. Love, nature, and math. There was no equation. She was held in place by an overwhelming fear of loss, and she turned inward, closing her eyes.

And though Penelope didn't have family, a home, or even a plan to get her away from here to anywhere better or safer, she did have her loneliness. She realized that loneliness was the only place she had truly known. It was always there, and it had become her most prized and secret indulgence, like a cave, no light nor embellishments. Only a steady temperature.

Lucien was heated and restless. He had closed the door behind him. They each had too much to say, but she had learned long ago about the yielding potency of silence.

He knelt down beside her and began quietly tracing the contours of her arm with his breath. "I felt like I was going to die watching you, watching those men watch you."

"It wasn't me. It is a ridiculous costume, a stage, a show."

"You undressed."

"To this," she pulled at the remainder of her costume. "I was covered. No one could touch me. They told me to do this. This was my assignment. These men, their hearts are tinted by the war. They will not give up anything unless they get something in return."

"I saw them devour you."

"I am a decent woman. I am like a stray dog to them. I am here to learn their secrets."

Lucien had a melancholy look. "What do you expect? I am still angry."

"I am only doing what you and the Resistance demands I do. Isn't this all about ending this horrible war?"

He was wrestling pure emotion, no logic, jealousy. "The thought of another man touching you . . ." he began. "I may never sleep."

She was watching him in the mirror, his eyes flaring with anger.

"You turned away from me. You left me there alone," she said at last. "And now here I am in this cage. This is what you asked of me."

There was a swift knock at the door, and Penelope stepped out, closing the door behind her.

"Mademoiselle, in several weeks, Lieutenant Hans Berger will be back," Madame Guerrain's voices hummed through the door. "And you will be performing for him privately. He has requested you."

"But Madame Guerrain, I'd rather stay with the large groups in the salon."

"Well, what you'd rather do is not one of the choices this war gives us," Madame replied.

Penelope nodded and returned to the room.

Lucien gasped, his face and chest reddening in despair.

"So now you are dancing for them in private?" he said,

jealously.

"I have no choices here," she looked around the tiny room. He looked into her frightened eyes and at her quiet yet trembling hands. "And you? Why did you disappear? You were supposed to be waiting for me in Paris." She asked and then felt the urge to know the answer vanish. She already understood how war and violence necessitated disruption.

Lucien's anger and distance in her small room only exacerbated the hollow feeling within her. The room was so self-contained, he was everywhere at once. She tried to keep her head down for fear of his mercurial gaze and the intrusive thoughts and shame that would rise up in her. He was close, and then more distant. There were moments of acute connection followed by great canyons of despair. Inconstant, that was the word, and she couldn't understand what she had done.

"The explosion scared me," he said. "It made me think it was too dangerous for you to be close to me. The soldiers might come for me and kill me for my work in the Royal Society, or even worse torture and kill you. I never wanted to hurt you. I have loved you from the moment Naomie first told me about you. The thought of you in pain was unbearable. I was trying so hard to protect you."

"But you did hurt me so badly."

Without saying anything, he moved beside her and tugged at her cold hand, beckoning her to stand in front of him. She stood and threw her face onto his shoulder clutching the back of his shirt in her fingers.

"This all seems so endless. I'm so tired," she said.

"I know. I left because of my love for you, and I couldn't stay away because of my abundant love for you. You possess every part of me." His words perforated the air around her. "I have thought of you every day. It has been nearly unbearable."

She felt the breath of his words along her neck. She smelled the sweet, licorice scent of his shirt as he traced the bodice of her costume with his finger until he found the end of the string. He played with it gently, tickling her back with the loops and ribbons, until at last he tugged at it and it unraveled to the floor. She leaned back to look up at him.

"Please understand," he beckoned.

"I have no other choice . . . " she confessed.

He touched his hand to her mouth once again, tracing his finger up along her jaw to her ear. Her skin felt metallic, and it turned his finger gold. He felt the tug and pull of the makeup on her face. He traced the lacy edge of her costume. She felt his hand shaking. When she closed her eyes, none of this had happened. Nothing. No war. No loss. No danger. When she opened them, he was pushing her down on the bed. He was undressing her, pausing to touch her fleshier parts, smelling her neck, licking her face and ear.

He bit her lip, and she felt waves of shivers go up and down along her body. His mouth tasted like hunger. He was hovering over her, and when he drew away for a second, she could see the gold paint smeared on his cheek and arms. She felt even dizzier. She was naked now, and she wanted him to be naked too. She grasped at his clothes, "I want to see you," she said. She wanted to feel his skin. She was unbuttoning his shirt, his pants. She bit his cheek and kissed his eyes. She felt him ripple. He tipped her chin up to his, a stranger but all known. Wasn't this the thing with human existence—loving, breathing secret passwords through kisses, so much known and unknown.

All movement and pleasure, he used his finger to draw ellipses on her belly as they moved together. Her ancient book with the naked picture of men and women's hands entwined had taught her that it was Kepler's laws of planetary motion, an ellipse more than a circle, that it took Mercury three months to circle the sun, Venus only seven, Earth one year, Mars two years, Jupiter twelve years, Saturn thirty . . . she felt his fingers continue to slowly trail Kepler's ovals of pleasure along her belly. She knew the mathematical equations of the planetary motion, and yet none of the astronomical data she had studied could explain what she now experienced.

She was a string taut with pleasure of an infinite variety. Lucien hovered above her. Smoke, fire, water, his love was liquid in the same way. He was everywhere but nowhere all at once, only small circles and marigolds. And with that thought she came the entire distance and Lucien too. She wrapped her legs around him. With the sun as her focal point, she loved him fully. With love and sex, no matter how far the distance, the sum of pleasure was always the same.

Chapter Thirty

"It's so easy for humans to blame God for their misery," Manfri said. "Really, it's mostly of their own making."

Several days had passed since Penelope had last seen Lucien, and her emotions had taken hold of her like a flu. Every time she danced she scanned her eyes along the wall of the salon hoping to see him there. She had not slept because of how much she missed him. The profound uncharity of their love consumed her long days and even longer nights. Daily, throngs of soldiers now stood in lines around the block to see the Golden Girl perform. Their smoke and noise only heightened the reverberant anguish of her sorrow.

She was beginning to understand why Newton avoided love, the heart often aiming higher than the actions of humans. Lacking control and discipline, love's mobility could be a cruel and unresponsive companion, particularly in the face of loss and war. No amount of powder could mask her sorrow.

"I can't stay here. I have to leave," Manfri explained, his breath smelled faintly of liquor.

"But why?"

"Because of the money," Manfri confided. "I'm hungry. I'm broke. I can't even afford a proper drink. I don't see any way for a man like me to make money in this brothel. This place is for beauties like you. Madame Guerrain told me that I could keep the tips from the performances, but all of that money has now been confiscated by the Nazis. There is nothing left for me."

"Please stay, Manfri. I can give you money," she said, a familiar feeling rising up in her. "I have some stashed away." She felt bereft. She thought of the SOE's money hidden beneath the floorboards of her room. Perhaps that would make him stay.

"You're a maid at a brothel, what money could you have? Plus, it's not just the money. I cannot stay here. Paris reminds me too much of Elodie and Naomie. I am a gypsy, Penelope. I have to be free. I miss the large crowds," he continued. "I would prefer the godforsaken circus cage to this place. Le Chambrement is like a prison. The more I stay here, the more I realize its confinement. How have you remained here for so long?" he asked, looking around.

Penelope had lived at Le Chambrement for three years.

She had not seen Manfri in over ten years. He looked the same but his body had deteriorated some. Penelope could see his misconfigured emotions, his forward slouch, his textured face, his filthy trousers' legs, his stained scarf knotted tightly at this throat. He was a perforated sponge to sorrow.

"Where else could I be?" she asked with sincere curiosity.

"Come back with me to America," his voice beckoned. "We can find a band of gypsies. You can leave this place behind. You have to. I insist. We can take your golden dance all the way to the Grand Ole Opry. *Straight from Paris,* the marquee would read . . . Penelope, you dreamed of it as a young girl. Don't you remember?" He waved his gnarled hand as he spoke. "Ever since I returned to Europe, I've been starving, barely scraping by day to day. I'm tired of being hungry. There's nothing more for me here." He paused and continued, "And you? You'll die here too. What's left here in Paris for a girl from Sweetwater?"

His voice was aching, wistful.

She paused, swallowing back the unrequited words of her heart, words like love and providence, "It's the emotional attachments that keep me here."

"And what are those?" he asked.

"They are deeper than any hunger," she concluded quietly.

"Are these attachments more powerful than the war? You are lying to yourself that you will not be killed. Don't you feel afraid?" he questioned.

She thought of Lucien and Fulcanelli, her eyes brimming with tears. She wanted to tell Manfri about all that had happened to her, but she knew that she couldn't. The *SOE* had warned her about the risks of telling anyone anything. She had likely already told him too much.

"Yes, there are so many lies I have to wake up and tell myself every day to go on . . . This is my life." She gestured around the room.

He sighed, nodding, "I lie to myself every day. Some days, I pretend that Elodie is still here. Some days, I pretend to eat a beautiful meal. I am a con man, anything for an audience and a dollar. Every day a man like me enjoys a slow dance with truth," Manfri said matter-of-factly. "I think the word for it is deception."

"That or self-deception," Penelope smiled faintly back at him.

"That's my secret, if I hide my truth from myself then, no one else can see it," he laughed, circling his foot on the floor. "You wanna know how to tell when someone is lying?" he asked.

"How?"

"Watch their nostrils flare, their blinking, shifting eyes. You have to look closely at these things." He smirked, enacting all of the traits at once like the mask of a clown.

"*Nullius in Verba*," she said.

"What is that?"

"Don't take anyone else's word for it," she pronounced.

"Never, once," he said smiling broadly. "Penelope, don't

be foolish. Come back with me to America. I'm leaving tomorrow at noon."

"I wish I could, but I can't," she said.

"Think about it," he winked and turned the lights out to return to his room.

That night, she couldn't sleep so instead she pulled Newton's papers from behind the carving of Shiva and read them. They were yellowed and hand-written. They were filled with odd symbols and coded language. Newton was always trying to understand a world he could not see. But he was stubborn and never settled for the perforated, incomplete view his eyes offered up. His vigorous scientific method mixed science, imagination, and a mystical sort of faith together to derive what was unseeable to the naked eye. Yet, while these formulas were readily visible to him, physics and Newton were silent on the topic of love, and now she understood why. The depth of the papers helped numb her pain.

Newton had avoided love his entire life by insisting on the primacy of science and scientific method. Penelope felt frustrated that her love of Lucien could not be expressed with numbers, equations, or reason. She lacked insight about the patterns and intricacies of it. Like math, love had been cultivated from time, immemorial. It was universal and involuntary. But, unlike the fastidious nature of physics, love was incendiary and deceiving, advancing everywhere and nowhere at once. She looked down once again to the papers, pulling them into the light so she could see them more clearly.

The Tree of Diana, Newton began, works. By immersing an amalgam of silver and mercury in intro acid, an alchemist could produce a tree of silver that possessed the shiver of life. The papers went on to discuss the Tree of Life as seen within the Temple of Solomon, and its sacred geometry, spirals, cone, orthogonal projections and whole areas of gold. It was highly technical, alchemical, religious and scientific. It was all about proportions. Newton saw it all as a mathematical problem he could solve, a story about God's relationship to humanity. God's blueprint.

Newton's papers contained drawings of a Gothic cathedral. He saw the cathedral as a harmonious, intentional structure, a metaphor for the metaphysical world. Inside the mathematical structure of the temple, he felt sure, resided the secrets of the universe. Newton believed that an alchemist had hidden all that sacred math there to be discovered. He felt theories and equations were also encoded in the Bible, in Genesis, Job, Psalms, etc . . . He felt he was chosen by God to interpret God's secrets, the macrocosm and the microcosm and the transmutation that occurs between. *Chryspoeia*, the transformation of base metals into gold. It was both scientific and religious.

Newton noted that transmutation was a chemical process, the disintegration of atoms, involved the transfer of energy. Decay. One thing becoming another. The particles from one transmutation are used to transform another atom. Nucleus to nucleus, a nuclear transmutation. Newton wrote that through nuclear transmutation it was possible to turn lead into gold. He saw that something else might be possible because he theorized that transmutation was occurring all the time in the stars. Manipulating metals can just as likely dismantle as create. The sacred geometry of a few grains of metal contain incredible life and when split apart, could destroy cities.

Penelope set Newton's papers in her lap. She thought of self-deception and transmutation. The transmutation was not what was relevant, Fulcanelli would have told her. He liked to say that it was always more about the transformation of the person than the element. It was therefore less about the papers than what she would ultimately decide to do with them.

According to Fulcanelli's logic, it was all up to her. She reflected for a long moment, running her hands over and over again across the ancient edges of the parchment, a lattice of worries knitted across her brow. She thought of calculus and the distance she had traveled, from Tennessee to France to England and back to Paris. She sat up and reached toward her side table. The papers told her nothing about what to do in this moment. The vase of water that she hoped would magically heal her ear was long gone. Nothing scientific or alchemical could save her. She grasped the drawer of her table and jerked it open. Inside was only a quill and a stack of envelopes she used to deliver her notes to the pharmacy. She pulled out an envelope, slipped Newton's papers inside, and sealed the bulging package.

The next morning, she stepped into the hall and handed the envelope to Manfri.

"I can't come with you to America," she said.

Manfri listened intently.

She continued, "When you leave here, can you take this with you?" she asked. "Protect it. The papers inside it are very important."

He nodded and tucked it into the pocket of his vest. "Anything for you," he confessed. "But then how will I return it to you?"

"If I survive the war, I will come find you. Keep it hidden until then."

"In Nashville. The Grand Ole Opry—that's where I will be."

"Then I will meet you there," she smiled weakly. "You must not lose it. I would rather you burn it than give it to the Germans."

"I promise I will keep it safe and hidden."

She clutched his hand with the deepest gratitude. She knew that as a gypsy, Manfri would be able to move more freely and fluidly between the shadows. Beyond song or dance, hiding and transfiguring were his greatest art forms.

Chapter Thirty-One

That afternoon, Penelope gathered her satchel to leave for the pharmacy. Abraham called out to her. "Madame would like to see you before you leave." His voice rung out through the grotto-style entrance of Le Chambrement.

Penelope nodded as he led her into a back office where Madame Guerrain sat counting a box of money. Her eyes were focused, her mind spinning like a lathe.

"Good afternoon," Penelope greeted her.

"Yes," she replied. "Please have a seat."

Penelope settled into a velvet chaise.

"Your dancing has become quite popular," Madame Guerrain waved the bundle of money in the air. "An officer will be by shortly to collect your tips. He wants to discuss with me the possibility of sending you on some sort of tour across Germany to entertain the soldiers."

"The Nazi soldiers?" Penelope's nerves were singing out. She shifted her feet beneath her several times over.

Madame Guerrain nodded, averting her eyes.

"You wouldn't send me there, would you?" A noxious wave surged up in her throat behind her words.

"I am not sure that I will have a choice, Penelope. You see I have been forced to do many things that I would have never thought possible. I suspect your friend Charles from London would be very excited at the prospect of it."

"You know Charles?"

"Of course, I do. How do you think you ended up here?" She became taciturn, glancing towards the door, nodding to Abraham who promptly closed it. Then she continued, "It would be very risky to send you to Germany, but the intelligence you could gather there could be transformative to the efforts of the *SOE*. Not many people have been able to embed that deeply within the Nazi infrastructure. On a trip like that, you would be very well-positioned to help us. We would have to think through the mechanics of it very carefully. For example, how could you safely deliver the intelligence messages back to London?"

Madame Guerrain gave Penelope a ruminating stare, her eyes narrowing as she sipped a glass of water.

"All of this time here, and I never knew." Penelope felt startled, shaken even. "Why didn't you tell me that you were working with Charles?"

"For your safety and mine."

"And Manfri? Was he involved in this?" Penelope drew her hand to her chest, an old habit from when the stone necklace prominently hung there.

"No, he was not involved," Madame Guerrain decreed. "Just Abraham and me."

"I see," Penelope sighed.

She needed to understand the breadth of her circumstance. Her mouth was bone-dry, her breath rapid.

"I am certain that Manfri said good-bye to you before he left," Madame Guerrain commented, her hand grazing the wad of money.

"I was able to speak with him this morning," Penelope responded.

"Penelope, I was hoping you would return to America with him."

"Why?"

"For your safety, my dear. When our friends back in London inquired about the possibility of you coming here to . . . " she cleared her throat. "Work," she nodded as she enunciated the word. "I told them how risky it would be. They assured me that you were the right woman for the job. They told me that you had no living family and no other attachments." She drew open the drawer beside her and placed the cash inside, pushing it shut. "Still, I urged them to make it a temporary appointment, perhaps a year or less before you returned to America. That way, none of the clients would become curious or attached to you," she paused. "What the *SOE* and I didn't understand was that you loved someone in Paris already and that you were coming back here, in part, to be close to him. What is his name again?"

Penelope watched her wide-eyed and cautious.

Madame stared at her, screwing her mouth sideways with impatience.

"Lucien," Penelope responded.

"Yes, that's it," her eyes widened. "I presume you were headed out the door to go to the pharmacy. You must know that radio operators in Paris are being picked off quickly," Madame Guerrain said, handing her an extra list of items to acquire. "There have been several raids in the neighborhood already this month. Be watchful. The Gestapo follows operatives like you to the destination and moves in quickly, arresting some and shooting others on the spot. Be careful, the Nazis are clean and very organized," she continued. "It seems as though they have a new informant."

"Who else here is part of the Resistance?"

"As I said before, just me, and Abraham," Madame responded.

"Then do you know what happened to Lucien, the man who came to see me here? He has still not surfaced again and so many days have passed. I am worried. Do you think you could help me find him?"

"Yes, I saw him. I remember him. I remember watching him leave your room and walk down the hallway to the entrance." She paused, "I saw him but so did the lieutenant."

Penelope's mind was whirling. She felt angry Lucien had foolishly risked so much to see her dance again.

Madame Guerrain pulled a handkerchief from her pocket and wiped the lipstick from Penelope's mouth. "You cannot set yourself apart in this war climate. If you wear red lipstick, it is enough for them. They will send the officers to seek out the woman in the red lipstick."

Penelope wiped the smudge of red from her coffee cup.

"Your friend has been captured, I believe," Madame Guerrain said.

Penelope's stomach dropped.

"According to Abraham, he was captured in a raid several days ago."

Penelope looked at Abraham. He stood stoic and steady by the door.

"What?" Penelope gasped.

"I am not certain, but I think this is so. The pharmacist may be able to help you," Abraham said as he smiled sympathetically and reached to open the door.

Chapter Thirty-Two

Penelope took Madame Guerrain's shopping list, gathered her satchel, stepped outside, and hurried down the street to the pharmacy. She was Penelope the ordinary Parisian once again, finding her way back to the pharmacy, and she carried with her a note about troop movements in Northern Germany and a question, "Where is Lucien?"

When she walked through the entrance of the pharmacy, she stepped directly to the back of the store. "I would like to speak to the pharmacist myself," she stated to a store clerk. "May I go in the back?"

The man looked at her for a long time. They knew each other, but words had barely passed between them. The man responded, "Is the fish at the market fresh on Tuesdays?"

"But not as fresh as it is on Sundays," she replied and immediately he ushered her into the storeroom.

The pharmacist was a middle-aged man with a large mustache and reading glasses. His name was Hugh. "How can I help you?" he asked.

She handed him the note from her shoe. "And I need some information," she said timidly.

"About what?" he replied, adjusting his glasses to focus on her. "I have been passing your notes regularly through the transmitter. Your information has been critical to the Resistance, especially the information about the movement of the troops towards Russia. We have been able to dismantle several positions as a result of your work. I hope you are not tiring of it. Some say we are nearing the end of this nightmare." He looked at Penelope with the pleading compassion of a longtime friend. The Resistance brought about that kind of intimacy.

"Yes, I am pleased with my work," she said. "My question is not about that. I have a question about a dear friend." She felt her emotions scrambling within her, and for a moment, she couldn't find the words, any words at all, just a burning red flush that raced up along her neck into her face. Her hands were shaking. "Please, I am begging you. Do you know a man named Lucien? I have heard that he has been captured by the Nazis. Do you know what has happened to him? Where is he? Is he alive?"

She felt anguish as she spoke the words aloud.

"You know it is very dangerous to ask about real people," the pharmacist said, with an alarmed look. "To name names can be a death sentence. It is highly discouraged."

"I realize this," she said, with tears shining like gems at the edges of her eyes.

"Are you willing to assume the risk?" he responded.

She nodded.

"Then who is it that you love?"

"His name is Lucien Delvaux. I heard he has been captured and sent to the prisons."

The pharmacist flinched at the mention of his name.

"I know him. Fulcanelli's apprentice," he responded. "I will inquire and get back with you."

"Thank you, thank you," Penelope was relieved.

He smiled at her over his glasses, pouring a bottle of pills on the table. With that, he waved her away.

As she walked to the front of the store, she saw a flash of something metal through the window, as a group of German officers ran swiftly into the pharmacy with their guns drawn. Penelope and the other patrons of the pharmacy were instantly surrounded.

"Rats, rats," the soldiers cried. "Put your hands against the walls."

The French called it a *rafle*, a raid where unlucky souls would be taken away for mandatory labor in Germany. The officers screamed and shouted at the patrons. They overturned elixirs and bottles from the shelves. The patrons' backs were pressed against the wall, and one by one, they were forced to show their identification papers.

Penelope reached into her satchel and handed her identification papers to the young officer. He paused to look at her face. She thought she recognized him from the brothel.

The officers took the papers out on the street and held onto them for an hour, a long hour of cruel silence. Then they dragged away the people they suspected of illegal resistance activity. Hugh was taken and crammed into a truck along with his transmitter. His glasses were broken. Penelope could see a bottle of poison peeking out from his pocket. She knew he would distribute it to the prisoners. During her training, she had been taught to always keep the pills with her to take just in case, as a last resort. More time passed until she was the last person in the line, but instead of being dragged to the truck like the rest, she was hustled into the pharmacy's back room and told to wait.

"For what?" she asked. "I need to be home before dark."

"Until an officer can question you," the familiar soldier said as he closed and locked the door.

She looked for a window where she might escape, but there were only rows of shelves holding bottles. She could see no farther than the shelves in front of her. "I am innocent," she replied over and over again. "Please, release me." She closed her eyes as she screamed through the door.

She was in the room for at least an hour, until she heard a loud car pull up in front of the building. She heard keys rattling at the lock, and as she looked up, she recognized Lieutenant Hans Berger as he walked through the door.

His gaze was cold and mineral, his gait relaxed. He immediately recognized Penelope and walked up to her to touch her face.

"What are you doing here?" he said, accosting her.

"I am here to buy hair dye for the madame," she said, shaking the black, inky bottle towards him. "Madame gave me a list of items." She handed him the list. "I came here and became caught up in the raid. I am sure Madame Guerrain will be worried about me. Can someone escort me home?"

"Ha," he responded. "That's the thing about whores and spies . . . they don't have a home."

She attempted to steady her breath as he grazed her hair with his hand.

"My golden girl, your eyes are hollow," he said to her. "You always look straight ahead. You never look at anyone. Please let me see those sad and beautiful eyes."

She looked up at him from the corner of her eyes.

"I am here to buy hair dye from my friend the pharmacist," she said. "Please release him. He is a good man."

"Is that so?" he said.

She nodded.

"I guess you did not know that this was a hideout for the Resistance. That there were radio operators upstairs and that the pharmacist was a traitor and a spy." His frozen voice rendered her speechless. "And what about your boyfriend? Did you know that he worked for the Resistance too?"

"Who do you mean?"

"The Frenchman."

He looked her up and down. His mouth emitted the putrid smell of decay.

"Ah yes, you Americans and your French boyfriends. I saw him leaving your room, and so I checked on him. Lucien Delvaux. It turns out that he is a very dangerous man. I sent him to the prison to do some work for the war, so he would not distract you from your dancing. Though you are not a French maid as you portrayed yourself to be, you are an American dancer, and you have so much talent," he smiled to himself and stroked his chin.

His crooked smile reminded her of a fishhook.

"Normally, I would send someone like you to a work camp," he continued. "But you seem to have so much promise."

She turned her face away from him. He grasped her chin and examined her. He reached forward to pick a gold sequin from her hair.

He turned to the officer beside and spoke to him. "You see, this is the sweet dancer that I remember," he said. "And I think we can make an arrangement." He placed the sequin on his tongue and swallowed it down. "You do not need to think of Lucien anymore."

He touched her breast with his hand and pulled her hair back, staring directly at her scarred ear.

"Then I cannot dance," she said, her tears betraying her.

The lieutenant paused, considering her words.

"Well your dilemma might not be as grave as you think," he began.

She gulped.

"It depends on what you are willing to give me," he said, tracing his finger up and down her chin. "I think I might be willing to spare you and your Frenchman."

She shuddered at his touch.

"Let me think this over. I will release you now, but soon I will come find you at the brothel to make a business arrangement." He turned to a guard, "Escort her back to Le Chambrement."

When she arrived back at the brothel, Penelope lay down on her bed, closed her eyes in distress, and gazed at the abundant darkness. She understood that out in space, light rays passing near very massive objects such as stars are seen to travel in curves. In each instance, light-bending has an external cause: for water, it is a change in an optical property called the refractive index, and for stars, it is the warping nature of gravity.

Penelope knew that light could also bend along a curve, the optical illusion of a stick when it is seen in a glass of water. It was always an external mechanism, gravity, water. "My every impulse bends to what is right," she said, as she drifted in and out of sleep. She knew what she must do.

Chapter Thirty-Three

*O*rganization was everything. Lieutenant Hans Berger would arrive precisely on time two days later. She knew he expected her to greet him at the door. Madame Guerrain had told her this. Penelope looked out the window, waiting for him, polishing the windows with vigor and a hint of sour nausea.

She had spent the last days reclining on the Roman couches asking the prostitutes about Lieutenant Berger. They told her he had held several positions in the Reich. He had been a flying ace who had led the Air Force. He then became an economic adviser, a leading advocate of "Aryanization."

"You can almost taste the blood in his breath as he

kisses you," Cleo, his favorite, reported. They told her he bragged about wanting to create an economic empire. He liked to come to the city because he was an art lover.

"But he really came to plunder the homes of his Jewish victims in order to build up his personal collection," Marie concluded.

As the women told her about the lieutenant, she looked above them to the series of vignettes by Henri de Toulouse-Lautrec, male and female centaurs copulating. This was a room where all of the financial transactions occurred. Abraham managed all of the finances. "Berger is like a ghoul. He thinks he'll live forever, even with that gammy leg," the women chuckled.

She learned that he loved his revolver. He called it his *punta*, or prostitute, and he laid it on the table beside them like a prop. He wore a Madonna medallion under his shirt and never took it off. Penelope already knew a great deal about his preferences because she cleaned and prepared the room for him and his *punta*. He liked the Hindu room with its enormous copper bathtub. She filled the water to exactly 104 degrees. He always expected to have a long, lavish bath before sex.

He was fastidious in all ways. She knew he would expect her to dance for him while he bathed. She also expected that next time he could tell her about Lucien. This was a simple mathematical equation and with the horizontal and vertical axises in place, she could construct her geometry and execute her plan. It was all just a variety of data points along an x and a y, she reassured herself. She was concentrated and silent as she sat on her stool waiting for him to arrive.

"He is coming," Abraham pronounced. "Be careful."

They looked out the window and saw him from a long distance away, the lieutenant walking down the street with a thick and awkward gait. He wandered through the artificial rock walls and waterfalls and came in, as usual, through the front door. Penelope met him in the mirrored Pompeii Room.

"Sir," Penelope called out loud to him, making sure to look him in the eye.

"Ah, my gilded girl," he replied, looking upon her.

She waited for his eyes to surrender, but they stayed unblinking and reptilian.

Soon the heavy doors swung open, and the beautiful, serene Madame Guerrain, with her smile and round, elegant face, swept him through the doors and down the hall with Abraham to secure his payment.

Penelope slowly climbed the stairs to the Hindu room, where the golden and carved bath was already drawn. She felt the bubbling crackle of her nerves. He was a man of fetish, and she was his latest fixation. She knew what the exchange would be, and she was ready when he stepped into the room and paused to examine her. She offered him some food.

"I am not hungry," he responded, still watching her expectantly, pushing the plate from between them. He looked powerful and frightening in his uniform, and she wondered if he would look less menacing without clothes. "I am not interested in the madame's sweet treats. Have you already forgotten why I am here?" he asked impatiently.

She shook her head and closed her eyes. As she danced, she thought of Naomie and Elodie, destroyed by the German bombs. *I can do this,* she thought to herself, steeling her shoulders and arms.

She slowly raised up to her tiptoes and looked down at him with blinking timidity. He wanted her to watch his eyes, but she found that she couldn't, so instead of watching his eyes, she watched lines of sweat drip down his face. It was all in close proximity and the subtle difference did not seem to stir any notice by him. The line of sweat along his brow continuously reformed, falling between the creases and shadowed valleys.

She thought of Manfri and his ruddy face. She thought of his music and of Elodie dancing beside him. She felt envious of them now and wished she had another to lean on in this moment. She wished she could share her life with someone. She continued to move to the rhythm of the background music. Elodie came to her again as she swept the scarves around her face and slowly tipped backwards. She kicked her legs to the sky and let the scarves fall down all around her with her hair. Piece by piece, discovery by discovery, she let more layers of scarves drop from around her, and when she finished, he had already discarded his own clothes and had awkwardly stepped into the bath.

"Even if you did not go to bed with me, I would ask you to dance for me alone," he began. "I'd kill a man for this." His words vaporized in the steam around him.

She paused and watched him close his eyes.

"So, you've killed a man," she asked gently. The words stood alone in the room, like a flickering flame.

"Come closer," he whispered. "Yes, so many," he continued, looking satisfied as she stepped close enough for him to stroke his finger down the line of her bodice. He began telling her how he had gone to Berlin to order the Gestapo to increase the "productivity rate," laughing as he spoke.

Penelope felt the searing heat of terror rise up in her.

"Tomorrow, I am leaving, but I will be back, and I will kill any man who has touched you," he stated blankly, licking his lips like an animal.

"There's no reason to," she said. "No man here touches me. I am here to dance and clean."

She soaked a soft towel in the warm waters. She dabbed a scented oil on the cloth and bathed him slowly with the gentle touch of the towel.

"The travel makes me tired," he said at last.

She could sense his deep fatigue.

"For me to kill them would only be in self-defense." He had an air of awkward humor about him. "Am I not here to touch you?"

She was afraid but felt a sense of inner boldness. "Well, I suppose that depends," she said.

"Please continue."

"It depends on what you are willing to give me." She too had learned the art of negotiation, of trading things for things. She looked at him with a particular sadness. With the soldiers, there was always something given and something taken.

"Give something, to you?" He looked genuinely confused, almost bereft, and paused for a moment to think. "Ah yes, you are not like the other girls here. No illusion of simplicity. An eye for an eye," he caressed her face. "I suppose you are referring to the Frenchman."

"I am. And no, I am not a prostitute. I am a dancer."

She began to unfurl the laces of her bodice.

"I don't want to tarnish our time with such matters," he concluded licking his lips. "I shall tell you later."

She shook her head and dropped the string of her bodice into the water before him, "I think you should tell me now." She turned and stepped away from him.

"Then, I think you have some things to give me as well. One thing for another," he said with a sharp and grafted tongue. "Lift your hair for me. I would prefer that you wore a bun."

She turned her ear away from him, lifting her hair as slowly as the unraveling of a morning flower, the way Elodie had taught her.

"Come close . . . Nice, now let me see your other cheek," he said.

She tried to let her hair drop, but he reached out and

held her arm.

"Your hair up," he smiled. "It looks so lovely."

She could not suppress her fear as she turned her cheek to him, revealing her ragged lobe.

"Yes," is all he said as he traced the burned lobe of her ear. "Then I was right."

Penelope tried to look perplexed. "I don't understand," she said with a feathered voice.

He didn't look at her at first. When he broke through his thoughts, he looked at her with a frozen aggression.

"Don't play games with me."

She tried to hide her astonishment and fear. She brought the lieutenant another golden cup full of her wine, and he drank it down without speaking. "I know you are part of the *so-called* Royal Society," he yelled at last. "They are criminals. Somehow they even stole Isaac Newton's papers from a library."

"I don't know what you are talking about."

"You are a liar then."

She shook her head and brought him more wine. He gulped it down quickly and without hesitation. He closed his eyes and leaned back into the water, "If it weren't for me, you'd be torn to shreds. Your boyfriend told me all about you. He told me that you had even gone to London to train with the British." He pinched his eyes with disdain. "He told me so much."

His words clung to her. She felt a heavy, cold loneliness set in, like a statue cemented. She was trapped. Lucien had spent so much time hidden away from her, allegedly protecting her, and now, within a matter of days, his confession was her death sentence. She couldn't bear to think of what mangled cruelties he must have suffered at the hands the Nazis to exact his betrayal of her. Anguish ripped through the center of her, but she fought to remain stoic in the face of the evil man in front of her.

Betrayal, it was the most solitary word of all, beyond abandonment, beyond torture, beyond hatred. It was the human act that cut the most deeply, splintering north from south and east from west.

"Then, he must have mistaken me for someone else."

"Has he? He has told me how you spy on the soldiers who come to the brothel and pass your notes to a radio operator. That was what you were doing at the pharmacy that day, wasn't it? That's how I knew to find you there. It was so easy," he grimaced. "And to think, you told me you were there to buy beauty products."

He reached to touch her face.

"You can tear my room apart. You will find nothing."

He remained silent and continued to sip from his golden cup, staining his teeth vermillion. He was soaking in some distant and dark thought.

When he spoke at last, it was with an insincere tone of praise. "Your Frenchman is stronger than I expected. He was arrested outside of Paris. There was a raid on a doctor's house where the Resistance was meeting. He was interrogated and tortured at my personal request. I thought he would surely be dead, but when I inquired, I found that he was not, and so I asked that he be put on trial and sentenced to death. For now, he has been sent to the Soufriere prison, outside of Paris, and has been placed in solitary confinement. Soon he will be shipped to Buchenwald. He told me everything, that the blonde woman with the scarred ear works at Le Chambrement and I felt certain that woman was you. The soldiers are going through your room just now. I would check on them, but I am . . . diverted."

It was worse than she had thought. Not only was Lucien tortured and dying, he had betrayed her, out of madness, out of desperation. The Germans had made an art out of pitting neighbor against neighbor and friend against friend, family against family, and now lover against lover. They understood the formula perfectly. First divide, then conquer. Few were immune. What did they do to him that would lead him to that choice? She could not know in this moment.

Regardless, the penetrating reality of Lucien's betrayal pursued her. Since she was a young girl, Penelope had understood that humans can harm one another. Betrayal was a dark line along the human succession of power, beyond a throne or crown, the opposite of loyalty. Betrayal and its ugly spawn, "an eye for an eye" tore through humans, sharp as ice, and like some cold liquid, Penelope's dizzy thoughts circled and then slowly descended into a new darkness.

The lieutenant stirred the water with his fingers and

watched it swirl around him. "He told me you were a whore now," he cackled. "He had so many unkind words to say about you." He was trying to break her down. Betrayal, violence, and love, it was a toxic blend. For her, far worse than the danger she now faced was the sensation of the conflicts within her heart. It was like a chain reaction. She could feel the chemistry of his words overcome her limb by limb, first an unbearable, flu-like pain, then a blinding numbness, then a release, like her heart dividing from her into two or more fragments, a type of excruciating combustion, the relation of mass and energy.

His words whipped at her, as if they were more judgment than observation. Shame coursed through her vessels. Lucien had told them everything about her. Shame, the worst kind of thing, like some abrogated treaty held against her, one she had signed and sealed with a waxy coin. She wanted to curl up and expire. She didn't know what to believe. She closed her eyes and tried to think of some guiding principle, some equation to help her understand the excruciating pain of Lucien's torture and his ultimate betrayal of her identity. She also knew the lieutenant would say and do anything to hurt her.

"Once he started talking, I couldn't get him to stop," he chuckled aloud.

The *SOE* had warned her about the dangers of love, and yet here she was. She needed something to take shape in her mind, something she could hold onto. She knew humans are inclined to make the same mistakes over and over again, and that terrified her. The lieutenant sat before her now. He was ready to hurt her, kill her, or even worse. She swallowed her devastation and sorrow over Lucien down in a giant gulp.

What did she know to be true? She went through her list of human behaviors that humans always want more, that they like to talk about themselves, that they don't like change, that they like to believe they are in control of things even though they are not, that they are forgetful by nature because life is hard and forgetting is a survival skill, that they are lonely.

She looked at the water in the tub, still swirling around the Lieutenant Berger. There could be no other natural conclusion than this. She decided to add another hard-won rule.

Rule 5: Humans will betray you.

It was a simple truth. She thought of Lucien and of his love of Isaac Newton. She remember Newton's deeply held mistrust of people. He was an introvert and a private man who never traveled far from his birthplace. While Newton experienced so much celestial wonder, he mostly kept to himself. In fact, it was believed that throughout his life, he never fell in love. While he could imagine so much of the world's magic, love eluded him. Or perhaps, this was his choice, and he eluded love by design. Penelope wondered what Newton would have thought about betrayal and the physics of human behavior.

Her vision faltered. Perhaps Newton understood how

blinding love could be. It had never occurred to Penelope that Lucien would endanger her in this way and, even worse, leave her in the hands of a monster.

Perhaps Newton understood that it was better to avoid love, and yet he had also never traveled across an ocean or tasted the breath of another. Eventually he lost his mind and went mad. The numbers eluded her.

The lieutenant let out a sigh of relief and pleasure, chuckling to himself. "It does not even matter what he said now though. For surely, he will be dead soon," he concluded, triumphant. "In fact, I may do it myself."

Penelope felt the heat of fury rise up in her. In an instant, she felt divided. Division, a self-sustaining process, a chain reaction in which one reaction initiates the next, and a part of her evaporated forever.

Her whole being burned with scalding anger. It was the heat of transmutation. Alchemy is most often understood to be a belief that lead can turn to gold through a process called transmutation, four elements blended together. Aristotle said the four were wetness, dryness, heat and cold. Everything on earth was alive, and everything contains these four elements. Through heat and wet, a leaf can become soil. Water can become steam through heat. Similarly, a mind could overheat, the tears cool it. But patience was also a key ingredient to alchemy. She would never let Lieutenant Berger see her cry.

She gathered her emotions, the heat of her anger, the wetness of her sorrow. While she could not yet make gold, she could make stone, and Penelope made herself stone.

Frustrated by her lack of visible emotion, Lieutenant Berger pulled the drain from the tub and let the water swirl down and away. He stepped from the tub and stood still while she dried him.

"Undress for me," he said, as he walked slowly to the bed. "But before you begin, fill my cup again," he barked at her, thrusting his empty cup towards her. "And to think, you were a part of the Royal Society, and you don't even know the importance of what is said in those papers. Do you even know who Newton is?" he cackled, leaning forward to steady himself and climb into the bed.

She grasped the cup from his hand and stepped across the room to the dresser. As she set the cup down beside the wine bottle, she reached down to the hem of her costume and traced her finger along the edges until she found it, the unmistakable circle she had sewn into the hem of the skirt the previous night. She pulled the plastic pill between the stitches, her hands shaking. She dug her fingernails into the plastic, slicing it open. It was the same size as a small pea. It was covered in rubber and filled with cyanide. She poured the powder into his empty cup then filled the cup with more wine, carefully swirling the poison around and around until it was fully dissolved in the liquid.

She stepped across the room and handed him the wine, then turned her face to a mask of amusement, as she danced for him and dropped her skirt to the floor. She knew she must forget his cruel words and his intentions and beguile him. Her satin stockings fell to the floor, as she lingered in their unfurling. Like some half-opened blossom, she rose up and tipped her chin to the sky drawing her hands down along her waist and hips. As he drank down the poisoned drink, he watched her, petal by petal, piece by piece, transform until she was standing naked before him. Her cheeks flushed with intent. His face turned sallow then ashen. Reaching for her hand to pull her to the bed, he slowly fell forward to the floor.

"Now we will see if you are immortal," she muttered.

War breeds war, corruption breeds corruption. She could tell by the way his eyes stiffened and his cheek pressed against the hard wood, he was dead.

Penelope stepped quietly away from his body. She could not waste time with her anger or disgust. She pulled her satchel from beneath the bed, slowing dressing and buttoning her dress to the very top button.

There was no time to waste. She grabbed his revolver and reached under the bed for the briefcase of SOE's money she had hidden there. She had to leave. The soldiers would soon be scouring the place in search of the lieutenant. She had to warn Madame, Abraham, and the women. This was a magical and twisted world. She hurried out the door and down the stairs, along the fake rock walls, past the waterfalls, through the mirrored room towards the door.

"Mademoiselle, mademoiselle!" a voice cried out. "Please, please . . ."

Penelope turned back to look at Abraham. "He is dead,"

she cautioned.

"Okay. I will handle it. Be very careful," he said to Penelope with an enduring tenderness as he handed her a bag that contained hair dye and a scarf. "From me and Madame," he whispered, kissing Penelope gently on her forehead.

Chapter Thirty-Four

*F*reedom, it was a profound and delicious silence. Penelope had escaped the brothel the previous afternoon and hidden at 52 rue Laffitte. She didn't know where else to go. She dozed fitfully there, until the howling song of a wounded animal pierced through the quiet and awoke her. She sat up disoriented and unsure where the noise was coming from. She rubbed her eyes and looked around.

She was hoping that Philippe would be at rue Laffitte, so that she might find have someone to talk to, but Philippe was gone. Instead she had dyed her hair black in the kitchen sink. She had been unable to look in a mirror to see the result because all that was left in the apartment was the piano, trash strewn across the floor, and the crushing question of the moment. What should she do?

She was a criminal in the eyes of the Gestapo, no longer sheltered by the brothel. With her scarred ear, she was still easily identifiable. She felt astonished at how quickly her life had shifted. In an instant, everything was different. The lieutenant was dead, the women at the brothel had likely fled or been captured, and this apartment felt unfamiliar and stifling. A fugitive now, she felt a familiar, dusty darkness envelop her. She had buried her father in Sweetwater, had joined the Resistance, and had been trained in espionage in London. Now, she had poisoned a Nazi lieutenant.

All of the sharpened depths of her sensations slid into place around her. She felt tension, anger, and repulsion. To be a fugitive was a new type of brokenness, but she was also free from the tyranny of the brothel. Just as her life after her father died, both anything and nothing was possible. The piercing howl of a wounded animal that had woken her, echoed through the long shadows of the empty rooms once again.

It was still dark, but she managed to sit up and feel her way to the Lucien's corner window where the sound was coming from. She thought of the hole in the wall above where his desk used to be, and she reached her hand deep inside the wall secretly hoping she might find the howling rock, her distant companion.

The hole was empty, but the sound still rang out across

the room. She withdrew her hand and moved towards the window, unlocking it and swinging it out into the summer sky. The air felt soft and cool. She leaned out the window to see if she could spy the moon. The sky was barely lit by a blazing sliver. As she was drawing her head back inside the window, she noticed a bird huddled against the edge of the sill beside her. It was Beethoven, and his left wing hung almost flattened from his tiny frame.

Penelope reached out the window and carefully grasped the bird, drawing it into the darkness of the apartment. She stumbled across the floor to her satchel and dug around in her bag until she found a matchbook. She lit a match and saw the bird's eyes flicker with fear and pain in the light. She let the matchstick almost burn into her skin as she stared at the animal. Stubborn and loyal, it was most certainly Beethoven.

As the match light fizzled into darkness, Penelope drew the bird to her chest. His howling song grew quiet. She felt his heart beating with the confusion of pain. Careful not to touch his wounded wing, she clung to him with devotion and resolve. While everyone else had fled, she was left alone to deal with the aftermath. These sensations were not some anomalous storm that appeared out of nowhere. Rather, they were hauntingly familiar. The lieutenant's words about Lucien had damaged her. Planted in her mind like dark seeds summoned up from the dank earth, they fed upon her fears and doubts, unfurling from soil to stem to vine and binding her. She could not find a way free from the pain.

Beethoven was broken too, but he had come back for her. Penelope would sleep holding him close against her chest where the stone necklace had rested. Love had always been both intractable and clarifying for Penelope. Her thoughts rambled through all that had happened. She knew that she could not safely leave the apartment, yet she dreaded the stale solitude of the empty space and her wild, dark thoughts.

The warmth of Beethoven made her miss the comfort and companionship of her distant necklace. It had hung around her neck for years, its rope frayed along the edges as if it were just beginning to show its age. The necklace had always been her most prized and secret indulgence, like love, a gift she had given away so readily to the Royal Society. It had been an orb of inestimable connection, a friend. She missed the necklace. She missed her family and Naomie too. And most of all she missed Lucien. Love was not reasonable. Penelope undressed her mind, untying her sweet memories of him. She let them fall freely down all around her, wild and protracted.

Having sat before a mountainous fire with the French gypsies, and watched it all night, fully aflame, its flames reaching for oxygen and life, Penelope had also seen it dwindle down, down, and then down some more. *Deficere,* Latin, the alchemy book had taught her, to fade. Penelope knew that soon she would have nothing of Naomie left other than memories, nothing tangible and permanent like the numbers in the alchemy book. Then, like the fire, the memories would dwindle down to cinder, then on into dust. Penelope understood nature. Germination to decay and loss. Such a perpetuated cycle of loss was written in her plasma.

Beethoven shook against her chest. She thought of how she might be able to find the mystical palm grove or Parc Verdun and revive him in the daylight. She tried to remember the way to the palm grove, her thoughts shifting from there to the cathedral. She drifted off to sleep trying to remember the view she had held of the city, standing with the Lucien, Fulcanelli, and the gargoyles at Notre Dame, the mosaic of the Paris laid out before her.

When she awoke again, just before the early morning light, Beethoven lay dead on her chest. She wept as she wrapped him in her handkerchief. For Penelope, the bird's death was a terrible omen. Time was running out, and she was out of choices.

In spite of his distant betrayal of her, she had to find Lucien. She shot up off of the floor, gathered her bags, and ran out the door of the apartment. It was early morning, the sunrise grazing the tops of the buildings. Penelope walked south through the city towards Soufriere. Madame Guerrain had told her once that the prison was eleven miles south from the center of Paris.

With the lieutenant now dead, it was not safe for her to travel on the trains. Nazi soldiers were on most street corners. They all seemed to leer at her as she walked by them. As she crossed the Seine, she was forced to stop as two soldiers got into a drunken fight in the center of the bridge. A crowd formed. They thrust their fist and hands and legs through the air, and she couldn't help but imagine them arresting her. She felt trapped there. Soon they settled down, and the crowd dispersed. Penelope swept her face and hair into a scarf before she passed by them.

She needed to become more unrecognizable. The girl with the long hair, she thought she could hear people on the street murmuring. News traveled fast in the city. She tucked herself into a park and twisted her hair into a bun, releasing strands just long enough to cover her damaged ear.

Paris was a weird communion of displacement, somewhat like a party but with summer fumes, and soldiers. No one looked her way as she quickly walked from the park back into the city streets.

As she moved south through the city, she could see the green woods emerging from the cityscape. She hadn't been near a forest since she left Sweetwater. It seemed so normal and natural until she noticed the rubble and the burnt-out buildings. The war had rendered Paris' surroundings almost unrecognizable. She stopped to rest and eat at a market. As she crouched among the crates behind a flower stall, she heard high pitched laughter. She couldn't discern if it was a noise of pain or delight.

She heard a cackle again and looked behind her into a warehouse. She could see someone in the far-off distance.

Her eyes focused on a woman sitting behind her with binoculars. She was looking past the markets and south up at a hillside. Her knees were to her chest, and she seemed to be anchored there.

Penelope had become so accustomed to not talking to people that it didn't occur to her to ask questions. But when she heard the noise again, she realized the sound was coming from the woman, and it was so bizarre and gleeful she had to say something to her.

"What is that noise?" she began.

"I am sorry. It is me. I am watching the birds."

She handed Penelope the binoculars, and she saw the immeasurable blue depth of the sky, always there, blanketing her sorrows. She drew the binoculars down to the tops of the trees and saw a group of long-tailed tits take off from the tree and land together again and again.

"What's so funny?"

"I am crying tears of joy," the woman said. "The birds are making me laugh because they are so free, and they don't seem to know what to do with so much freedom."

Penelope frowned back at her.

The woman was smiling but looked like a person who thought the worst of things. She had large eyes and a large mouth. Her lipstick and the words that flowed out of her were so joyful and red that her mouth looked almost orange, burning like the sun before it drops below the horizon, at times both scary and awesome. Her lashes curled prettily around the corners of her eyes.

"Dear," she said, patting her leg sweetly and speaking to Penelope as if they were old friends. "I know this has been long and brutal, but you have got to get it together." Her eyes were on fire. "I have heard something on the radio this morning that has made me cry for joy . . . for joy," she said again. "Can you keep a secret?"

Her gestures were sweet and her words were filled with enthusiasm.

"What is it?" Penelope asked. Penelope gazed at the woman and met her silver eyes that glimmered in the light like the blade of an axe before it falls.

"The Americans have landed at Normandy. They are coming to free us!"

Penelope was afraid of what the woman said. Locked away in the brothel, she knew nothing of battle plans and freedom. Penelope felt a strange mixture of love and fear, like standing at the edge of a cliff and reaching out. No one else seemed to be as excited as this woman. The market was crowded with people, and they all seemed oblivious to this woman's joy.

"I haven't heard a word about this," Penelope said. "Is it true?"

The woman paused and tried to catch Penelope's eye. "Yes, it is. Most people don't realize it yet, but I do. I have been a part of the Resistance. I have never given up. Some people like to leave things unfinished. Not me, dear, I never quit too soon. Let me tell you," she continued. "The Nazis will fall. The end is coming soon."

Penelope cast her eyes to the warehouse floor. She wondered if she could trust this woman.

"I didn't know this."

"Yes, isn't it funny how the most important things are often what you don't know or can't see?" Her hands and face were brimming with expression. Her silver blue eyes were intense, and she wore a brocaded dress that hung much more like curtains from a rod than a dress from her lanky, feminine form.

She was close talking and ornate, "Look at me. Please look at me." She enjoyed her decorated authority.

She continued, "If you listened to the radio, you would know that they announced *Blessent mon coeur d'une langueur monotone* on the *BBC* this morning," she whispered.

"What does that mean?"

"*Wound my heart with monotonous languor,* the radio had announced. It is the signal from the *BBC* radio announcers that the Normandy invasion has begun. The Americans and the British have landed on the northern shore of France. They have come to free us. Soon all of France will be free!" she sang out in a whisper. "They have been preparing for a surprise invasion for many months. We have been waiting and waiting, and now the time is here. The Germans don't stand a chance. Soon they will be running scared."

Penelope felt a panic surge through her. If the Allies were coming, she would need to hurry. The Nazis would begin killing their prisoners. She needed to free Lucien before they killed him outright.

"I have to hurry then," Penelope gasped, gathering her belongings and racing out of the warehouse and through the market.

Chapter Thirty-Five

*S*oufriere Prison was eleven miles from the center of Paris, and when Penelope arrived at the village that surrounded it, she wandered its perimeter and decided to rent a room in an inn with the money the *SOE* had given to her. She needed to engage with the town and get a picture of who was who. So much of her life had been about waiting. It was a patience that gave her time to gauge circumstances, and before long, she realized an entire day had evaporated. In the village, she was occupied with staking out the prison, planning how she might get to Lucien, and waiting for her moment, impetuous as any gamble of chance and circumstance. With the Normandy invasion underway, time was running out. Any day, the

Nazis could ship off or execute the prisoners inside.

Though she could feel Lucien near, the prison was an enormous obstacle. It was a large compound that consisted of four rectangular block buildings and a detached hospital. With over eighteen hundred cells, it was the second largest prison in France, and the Germans had taken it over and used it to torture and hold fellow members of the Resistance. She needed to find a way to enter the building, retrieve Lucien and leave. So, she waited and watched from the lobby of the hotel, contemplating her choices and hoping for some distant stroke of luck, or even a miracle.

She knew the village surrounding the prison was small, so she asked the innkeeper's daughter for help. It was a risk, but she felt she had no time or choice in the matter. The woman said the prison had an infirmary, and that some of the doctors who worked at the prison liked to drink heavily in the restaurant of the inn some afternoons. The restaurant was hot in the summer, and she said they liked to sit by the window and drink her father's homemade wine. She reported that the men liked to call themselves physicians, but really they seemed to be retired doctors. Penelope wondered if perhaps it was these men who tended the wounds of the tortured prisoners. She decided to station herself at the restaurant.

On the third day, an older man she had heard the others call Dr. G passed by her. Before she could formulate a plan or ask the innkeeper's daughter any questions, he noticed Penelope sitting alone at a table and, thinking she was pretty, asked if he could join her.

"You are very lovely," he said and offered her some wine. He looked lonely and told her it helped him digest his dinner better to drink before a meal. He had an extreme tremor in his hands that made it difficult for him to sip the wine without staining his shirt. He was red faced from drinking and appeared to be ready to retaliate at any infraction, so she spoke carefully, chatting with him about the weather and the wine. He enjoyed the attention and her idle chatter enough that he offered her another drink.

"Do you mind if I smoke," he asked, lighting his cigarette.

"Not at all," Penelope replied, placing her hand along the sill of the window beside them. They sat there for several hours, chatting and drinking until he became more talkative and comfortable with her.

"The truth is I need to get out of this town," he confided at last. "I am tired of this pathetic life of mine," he cackled.

"But you are a medical doctor. That is a very respected and helpful profession, is it not?" She watched him as she spoke, feigning ignorance and innocence.

"That's what I used to be." His words slurred. He poured himself another glass of wine and started to talk about his life. His story was filled with platitudes about the Hippocratic Oath. He told her about his work as a medic during World War I. "The heart and brain are the most important organs but I have come to believe that the soul outranks them all."

He exhaled the smell of burnt cinnamon, a combination of mulled wine and cigarettes.

"Do you like working at the prison?" she asked.

"No. Never," he shook his head. "Can I confess something?"

She nodded, filling his glass once more.

"My soul is forever broken. The Nazis are very systematic in their methods," he leaned in, bumping the bottle of wine with his arm, almost spilling it. His speech was badly impaired. "The truth is I hate them all."

"Who? The Nazis or the prisoners?"

"The Nazis. If I could figure out a way to release all of the prisoners, I would. But I don't know how. If I did it, they would just shoot us all down, me and the prisoners just the same." He turned his gaze back to the cup before him. His face looked burnt and deserted.

"I have heard word that the Americans are coming very soon. If I had money, I would just get out of here and forget this whole nightmare," he continued.

Penelope leaned forward and met his gaze more fully.

"I think I can help you." she said.

"You?" he knit his brow together. "How? Penelope, I must confess, you are far too beautiful to be helpful in a war."

She put her hand on the doctor's shaking arm, steadying it and gathering her courage to speak. "Hear me out," she began. This was her chance. "Have you ever met a prisoner in Soufriere name Lucien?" she asked him with urgency and a racing heart. "He is my husband."

When she said this, the doctor pulled his arm away and tried to stand up to leave, but the fog of his stupor was too great. She reached beneath the table into her bag of money. She shoved a bundle of cash across the table at him. The silence between them was deafening and prolonged.

"Please," she begged. "I need your help. This is more than enough to get you out of the country."

He considered her offer for a moment, doing unknown calculations in his secret soul.

"Yes, fine," he agreed as he grabbed the money. "I do not work with your husband, but there is a doctor who does. He is his primary caretaker. We call him Dr. Blome," he said.

She grasped her satchel from beneath the table, and they stood together.

"He knows your husband," he said, and they walked out of the restaurant. He stumbled to his car, and they drove down the road through the gates of the Soufriere Prison without speaking.

When they arrived in the prison hospital, Dr. G led her down the hall to another man. She had almost two million francs remaining in her satchel, along with Lieutenant Berger's pistol.

"Dr. Blome, there is someone here to see you," Dr. G said, as he drifted off down the hall towards his office, his bundle of money bulging from his pocket. "Can you do me a favor and hear her out?"

Dr. Blome looked irritated, but motioned her to take a seat across from him.

Penelope and the doctor sat in silence for a few moments as he shuffled paperwork on his desk. She dug her nails into her crossed arms, attempting to stifle her emotions. She watched him gather some of the papers into a pile and shove them into a file cabinet.

His face looked like a contorted mask. His office smelled thoroughly sanitized, like a hospital room. It had the distinct and overwhelming glimmer of citrus.

"What is it, young woman?" he gave the impression of an irritated child.

"What can you tell me about a man named Lucien?" she began. "He is my husband."

The man cackled and leaned forward on his messy desk, crossing his arms against his chest. "I think I know him, but he is just a number to me. With the Allies progressing towards Paris, we have been given urgent orders to kill them and leave," he said with a wicked smirk. He pointed to the numbers on the charts. Lucien was one of these numbered prisoners. Penelope looked at the paper and nodded. She could tell he was trying to hurt her. She had been inoculated against this pain before.

"You will likely not get very far outside of Paris without any money," she cautioned. "And if they catch you, the reprisals will likely be just as brutal."

The charts, this monster, and his horrible office were too much—she pulled the gun into her lap and opened the bag of money for him to see. If he could not help her the for fear of Allied retribution, she thought, he might help her for money. It might surely give him choices to leave or disappear. They sat in a prolonged silence as he gazed at the money.

There was no trace of emotion or understanding in his countenance as he spoke at last, "This is fine then. Your husband is in the prison. You will have to find him yourself. There are thousands of prisoners. Most of the guards have fled. A few remain, and those might try to kill you. I will give you several hours inside while I excuse myself for dinner. It will not be easy," he said and motioned for her to follow him out of his office. "I can take you to the entrance, but you are on your own once you get there. This is a volatile time for the soldiers and the prisoners. A prisoner might confuse you for a soldier even. You are totally on your own here with your own judgment. And remember, you cannot un-see what you see," he warned. "This place has broken many before you. It can happen in only an hour."

She handed him the money. The doctor smiled and led her out of the hospital and to the entrance of the prison. Penelope reached into her bag and grasped the revolver to steady herself. She felt her skin pale as she stepped forward.

"Good luck," he barked out, more laugh than warning as he turned on his heel and walked back towards the hospital. "I will give you a clue, I believe your Lucien is in the basement level, solitary confinement. His room is no longer even locked," he cackled. "You realize that since the Normandy invasion that all of these prisoners live in unlocked cells."

Chapter Thirty-Six

*P*enelope walked down a long, clattering alley, through a door, and down a long hallway of cells. She had three buildings to scour. She hurried from cell to cell, person to person. Multitudes of prisoners cowered silently into the spongy shadows of their cells. This type of fear held a strong and polar charge. It was the opposite of a magnet. The place smelled of death and allegiance. She stopped abruptly as she stood before a small cell in the lower level of the second building. Something familiar caught her eye.

To see if she could find Lucien, she looked at the face of every prisoner before passing by. In one cell, a man was dangling inches from the floor of the cell from a rope, his head hung, spine draped over as if in verse or prayer. She recognized his face. It was Philippe. She gasped. He must have been arrested too.

She wandered farther into the dark basement until she came across another cell with a familiar face. She slowed, stopped and waited for a moment.

"Penelope?" the woman asked.

It was Madame Guerrain. She was advancing from the shadows. Penelope pushed three times on the gate of the cell, wrestling with the door until it gave way. She was surprised when the door swung wide. "Madame," she said, "please come to me. Come out of the cell. It's me, Penelope."

Madame Guerrain lifted her head and spoke, "Penelope, it is you." Her voice jangled, and they embraced.

"Hurry, gather your belongings," Penelope said. She grasped Madame's hand and continued through the maze of cells. She felt like she was walking through the halls of the dead. There was no solace in this place, no light, no flame, and fear was king. The other prisoners came to the bars having heard their voices, waving in and out of the darkness. She wanted to touch them all but when she came close, they all slipped away. At the end of the long alley, they turned a corner and dropped into a stairwell. She felt certain that this path was taking her to her own long death.

It was like forgetting how to see, the darkness slowly enveloped them. The world felt upside down, and she wanted to forget everything they were now experiencing.

She couldn't scrub off any of the inky commotion of the prison and darkness that had congealed around it. The sensation of it crawled onto her along the tips of her fingers and between her toes, an almost geometric parquet of muck and grime. She couldn't stand the subversive grip of it any longer. All the many facades of suffering gathered in Soufriere.

There were three levels of cells below her branching left and right. She would have to find Lucien, and then find her way back out. Even though she was scared, she could still feel Lucien's presence and so she rushed forward into the darkness of the corridors. The prison reminded her of a cave. Her eyes adjusted to the dim lighting. The prison was the only place she had ever been that was nearly devoid of color, only the molten red of the blood stains against the floor.

At last she and Madame Guerrain came to the lowest level of the first building of the prison. It was like a basement, only worse. There were a handful of doors clustered together and she tried each one. These were the solitary confinement cells. Madame Guerrain waited for her in the threshold of the stairwell, her eyes scared and unsteady.

"I don't think I can go any further," she said.

Penelope handed her the gun from her satchel and looked around to get her bearings. She felt something in the air, the impression of some unnamable sensation. She braced herself, choking back the tears. She thought she could feel Lucien in the air around her. He was near, but she worried that perhaps she was too late.

"Keep watch, please," she asked Madame.

Solitary confinement. It was a 10x8 room with no heat or windows. When she opened the last door and saw Lucien, she thought he too must be dead because his body was still and on the floor. She knelt down beside him to touch his back. He was asleep but jumped at her light touch. She fell to her knees and reached out to gather him close.

He didn't recognize her at first with her dark hair, but realizing who she was, he pressed his head against her chest. She could feel his breath faltering. She looked around the dark room, afraid, making sure there wasn't anything there that might hurt him more. Penelope couldn't fully disarm. She felt she needed to close her eyes and truly hold him, but she couldn't stop her vigilance. Her heart and mind were ill with worry.

She looked around. The walls were covered with poems, timelines, and mathematical equations, and diagrams of the sky. There were sketches of structures and machines as well as drawings of long-haired women, so many pictures of a long-haired woman. Penelope read the images like a book. She reached for them and reached out, tracing them with her finger wondering who else could have made a home out of this cave. Perhaps calculus and art had saved him too, given him a place to go in his head that the Germans could not invade.

She looked down at him, and he opened his eyes. They

were so much more transparent than before. She wanted to reach out and touch his face with her hands, but she was afraid he might retreat in fear. Many people have died here, she thought to herself, and he was barely hanging on. With her dyed hair and disguised clothes, she wasn't sure if he really recognized her. He seemed to look through her as his body started to tremble with fear or sickness. He appeared to be wrestling his way out of some nightmare.

"Lucien," she said. "It's Penelope." She felt she had to remind him. He looked at her, his whole being placed in a latency by this cruel abyss. "No, you are not. This is another cruel trick. She is dead by now too. The soldiers told me."

"No, it's really me," she said.

He pulled her to him and touched her damp skin, holding her tightly. All across him, she could see the bruises spread like lakes and ponds on the landscape of some continent or ocean. Her body shook in a disorderly sort of way against what she saw and felt. She wanted to reshape this pain-filled world. He fell away from her, and she hunkered down on her heels and touched the water pooling in the wells of his eyes. She was squatting and balanced on the tips of her toes pretending she was in the ocean rising and falling in the waves, not in the basement of Soufriere.

As she turned to set her satchel on the floor behind her, Lucien struggled to sit up. She met his eyes with hers, his hair was wet and clinging like cold fingers to his face.

"I can't believe you've come here for me," he said at last.

"I thought you were dead. The lieutenant told me that if he could find you, he would use what I said to kill you. I'm so sorry Penelope. I thought you were long gone."

"What do you mean?" she asked.

"He had already hurt me beyond what was imaginable," he continued. "But worse, he was going to find my mother and sister and kill them if I did not talk," he choked back at her, crying. She wasn't sure they were even talking about the same thing anymore. "What else could I have done?"

She looked at him, confused.

He watched her with his irregular eyes. "I'm sorry."

Penelope tried to hide from Lucien that she was crying, but he discerned it almost immediately. Lucien had always been able to easily winnow the truth of her emotions.

"Can you ever forgive me?" he proclaimed. "You were supposed to have already left for America with Manfri. When I left Le Chambrement, he promised me that he would take you with him." He was exasperated. "He promised me he would take you out of the brothel and out of France forever. I thought that you were gone and my words wouldn't matter. I spoke them out to save my mother and my sister."

All she could do was listen. She was bound by her tears and thirst to understand.

He continued, "But then the guards told me that you had stayed at the brothel, and the lieutenant had gone there. It was the worst day of my life. Beyond any of the cruel moments that have come before."

She winced, remembering the events at the brothel. She feared that if Lucien knew the true details of what had happened, he would scorn her.

"Did you really think that I could leave you?" she said. Her words tasted sweet to Lucien.

"Penelope, can you ever forgive me?" he asked, drawing a long, heavy breath.

She wanted to forget everything that had happened at the brothel. In Sweetwater, as a girl, when her loneliness and fear would overtake her, she would make a bed of leaves and flowers in the fields beside her house. The leaves and petals that made up her pillow were also sedatives: poppy, valerian, and passionflower—botanical properties that would bind her to that spot until the excruciating loss would fade away.

"Lucien, I am here in spite of the betrayal. Love does not differentiate, people do," she said and huddled around him like a tree. "We can talk about this more later but we have to leave now. It is not safe here."

He felt the syllables of her words along his fevered and aching skin.

"You were supposed to return to Sweetwater," he said.

"But I couldn't. You see, you and I are an alloy. We are bound," she said and pressed her lips together.

"But it would have protected you to separate," he said. "I thought you would leave. It was a miscalculation, and you should have never come here. It is too dangerous."

"You underestimate me again then," she replied.

The words hovered around him like jagged static in the air, and they seemed to nip at him with great ferocity as one skillful tear traveled down his dirty cheek to the ground. He was so weakened that his eyes no longer reddened when he cried. Penelope closed her eyes, feeling trampled by the weight of the war.

"If only we had the stone," Lucien smiled weakly.

"Yeah," she replied. "You know I have come to think that I was wrong about the stone. I believe it was the love and not the blood that completed it." She paused and continued, "It's the invisible sum of things, beyond math, beyond the reach of Newton's rational mind."

Lucien drew his hand along the dirt. The look of love in his eyes swirled and twisted around her like a whirlpool. He coughed, his head weaving unsteadily. She felt scared in spite of her resolve.

He coughed over and over again and put his head in his hands and started mumbling something about the rain. A fever rose in him, and he faded in and out of lucidity as he told her convoluted stories about how he was interrogated for nineteen days, tortured for ten of them. First, he was hung by handcuffs with spikes. They asked over and over again about the whereabouts of the papers. They tortured him with water, nearly drowning him. They called him a beast and beat him over and over again.

"My love," she said, reaching out to caress his face.

"I'm sorry. I'm so sorry. That wasn't what broke me," he said, "It was the solitude and my fears about you."

"We have to get out of here," she pleaded.

But Lucien's fever rose and his thoughts slipped away again. He fell away from her to the floor of the cell.

She looked at him. His face had the checkered look of a stray dog, his eyes a faded echo of gray, then blue. There seemed to be nothing to grasp onto. He looked the same as her father looked when he was dying. Nothing could have prepared her for this desperate pain.

When he pulled his hand away, she turned quickly and a memory flashed up her neck like a hot needle. It was a memory of something long forgotten, something she needed to say, or maybe she needed to ask. She touched that place along her neck. Her face tingled, and the lights began to waiver, her vision darkened around her into a tunnel.

Dead, dead, dead. It was an unbearable sort of desolation, and Penelope felt her fever rise. She felt her emotions swarm, rank buzzards come to take away the rest of her. She could not let him die. Lucien was thrashing and spitting at the air.

Penelope's head was now throbbing. She had expected this journey to be hard. She had come with so little and yet managed to be leaving with even less. She stood staring at this broken-down man until the nails of her tightly held fist began to cut her hand. She knelt and grasped his hand once more. It was rough and clammy. Fission, she could feel him splitting apart. She could tell he was dying. She was desperately afraid.

She looked around but couldn't find anything to comfort him—no blanket, no food, only a glass bottle of water. Then she remembered and began to tear at the hem of her dress with her hands. She reached out to grasp the water and once again ran her fingers along the seam of her dress, searching for the two pills left, one benzadrine, one golden. She grasped the wide oval one and pulled it between the stitch of the cloth.

She had carried the golden pill with her for so long, across and ocean, a continent, and now a war. She held it in her hand, and it felt hot to the touch. She sat him up and placed the pill between his lips. He closed his eyes and pulled the pill into his mouth.

"Swallow it down," she urged.

He gulped down.

"It's gold."

She pulled the last pill from the hem of her skirt. Benzadrine, it would suppress her hunger and nausea. It would give her energy. It would suppress her deepest desires. She swallowed hers as well.

Chapter Thirty-Seven

*H*er father's book had taught her that *chrysopoeia* was from the Greek *khrusos*, "gold," and *poiēin*, "to make." This was the full-blooming perfection alchemists sought in all materials—to turn lead into gold, to turn base metals into noble ones, the transmutation of matter, the completion of the great work.

Penelope was unsure how the pill was going to affect Lucien, and Naomie had warned her about its unexpected side effects, so she knew there was no time to waste. She grasped his hand and led him out of the cell. Madame grasped his other elbow, and they steadied him up the stairs down the long, dark hallway opening the cages as they moved through.

When Penelope arrived at the main door of the building, a soldier blocked their way.

"Where do you think you are going?" he said, reaching forward and grasping Penelope by the arm, pulling her away from Lucien and Madame Guerrain. "No one leaves here alive."

"Move aside," Penelope said with fury and exhaustion.

He spat at her face.

"Coward," she cried out.

Penelope simply narrowed her focus and closed her eyes. She could hear Madame Guerrain screaming, "Leave her. Leave her. Let her be." Penelope faltered as the guard stepped forward. She heard the sound of his raspy breath. She looked down and and saw his fingers clasping a gun.

"Leave her," Madame Guerrain screamed even more loudly.

She felt her heart beating against her chest as his other hand reached towards her. She could see the flash of his crooked smile rising as he swung the butt of his gun at her and almost hit her. She took another step backwards, this time losing her balance, almost falling backwards onto the dark floor. He swung again, hard, more focused, this time cracking the metal barrel of his gun into her shoulder. She yelped.

He swung again and again, over and over, using the gun as a blunt object and hitting her hands, arms, and head. It was vicious, and his screams of anger and pain rang out through the prison. Finger by finger, in his rage, he lost his grip on the weapon and it flew out of his hand. There was a pronounced and hollow clatter as the gun hit the wall.

He reached forward and yanked her by the hair towards him and grasped her throat with his large hand, squeezing her, choking her. He started to shake her the way a wolf shakes its prey, lifting her off of the ground.

Penelope gasped for air and clawed at him. When he threw her to the ground, she felt a strange splintering in her throat. The world began to close in around her in waves, curtains closing and then opening and then closing again. Her vision flickered in and out. He was no ordinary villain. His moral ruin was tragic and complete. She felt her tongue flaming with pain. He picked up his gun again. There was nothing that would prevent him from finishing her off. She tried to scream and she couldn't. Her vocal cords wouldn't function. She closed her eyes and braced for the next impact.

"The war will soon be over," Madame Guerrain pronounced and shot the soldier with Penelope's pistol once, then twice again to ensure that he was dead. The noise rang loudly through the hollow building. Madame Guerrain wept with relief as she ran to Penelope, grasping her, steadying her, leading both Lucien and Penelope out of the prison.

As they walked through the doors of Soufriere, the fingertips of dusk were gathering along the horizon. The streets were empty. *Solve et coagula.* Alchemy had taught her that the word *solve* meant to break down and separate and that *coagula* meant to come back together, the wounded skin healing anew. Things had gone so unimaginably wrong during the war.

The golden pill. She hoped so desperately that it wasn't some game of her father's imagination and that she had mixed it properly. It had been so many years ago, before the death of her father, before the war. It seemed like another life entirely. As Penelope, Lucien, and Madame Guerrain walked slowly back to Paris, her throat felt the pain of a thousand bee stings. She was afraid to speak or swallow. She looked over at Lucien. His whole body was now twisting and writhing. She wondered if it was the freedom of the light and the air that was affecting him or whether the golden pill was taking hold.

She thought of Fulcanelli and their tour through Notre Dame. He had noted that the famous rose windows utilize geometry on three levels: physical, hidden, and symbolic. The visual impact was physical. It was geometric and numerical, circles, squares, triangles, stars.

Lucien was mumbling about the cathedral, saying he could see all of the glass panels, and then, suddenly, he spoke with total clarity, "It's like looking at the constellations. I can see them, but I can also touch them."

Madame Guerrain looked weary.

Penelope turned towards Lucien, placing her hand upon his. He seemed aflame from the inside, the way a window draws the eye, heaven and earth, matter and spirit. It was all involved, every space of him defined by a golden, geometric figure. His eyes flashed with the colors cinnabar, verdigris and red oxide of iron. There were so many uses for color in life.

Lucien's face bore the look of punctuation, replete with both pain and joy together, and she wondered for a moment if she had made a mistake, that the war had quite simply changed him forever. She had learned so long ago that there was no turning back with the golden pill. He swallowed it whole and the effects must take hold on their own time in their own way.

They walked all the way back into Paris and took Lucien to Madame Guerrain's apartment on the top story of the brothel. Abraham greeted them at the door, embracing Madame Guerrain with a passionate kiss. Penelope had not realized they were lovers too. He was alone in the brothel. The soldiers and courtesans had dispersed, Le Chambrement was boarded up and empty.

"What shall we do?" Madame Guerrain asked.

When Penelope tried to speak, she tasted blood and couldn't. She gestured to her throat. The bruised prints of the soldier's fingers could still be seen there. Abraham brought her glass after glass of water to drink, but that did not help her speak.

"Give your voice some rest. It will come back," he reassured Penelope.

"Rest," Madame Guerrain urged. "Your throat will heal."

Penelope lay down beside Lucien, and they slept for

days. She held him close. He seemed to radiate an after-glow, tremoring light out of every fissure. Her father had never explained the effects of the medicine to her. He had only twice explained its complexity, but Penelope had her ideas. She had read her father's book cover to cover. Now she studied Lucien closely and remembered that the pic-tures from the book had portrayed the pill as both a seed and a medicine.

The pages that followed the recipe were a series of drawings of trees with drupe-like capsules each drawn with a single golden seed inside. The drawings depicted the fruits of the tree developing rapidly and then ripen-ing gradually, only a few at a time through seasons. There were pictures of fruits ripening and budding flowers simultaneously. In the drawings, fallen fruit budding into new trees were scattered beneath the ground below.

Penelope felt the notion of the pill as a ripening, cycli-cal agent was essential to understanding its effects. First lead to gold, then death to life. That was the progression of the scientific logic. The pill was no doubt redemptive, a transformative exchange of opposites, but at what cost? She watched his energy rise and fall with his sleep. When his energy dropped, it was as though he released a blue, green light. When his energy rose, his cheeks reddened. He did not eat or drink anything.

After four days, Lucien finally awoke and with-out opening his eyes, he mumbled something about the papers. When he awoke again hours later, he said he was almost blind, and Penelope could see that his eyes were translucent and appeared almost gelatin. "What have you done to me?" he beckoned to Penelope, but she could not speak in return.

She brushed the hair from his eyes, deciphering his every movement. His skin was smooth and clear. His eyes twinkled with the glinting sequins of a child's, but they saw nothing before them. His movements were smooth, his manner a broad and sweeping tide.

"Your vision will come back," Madame Guerrain reassured him, but as the weeks passed, there was no improvement. Later in August, as the Allied soldiers were readying themselves to free Paris, Lucien was still not able to see. Penelope, who still couldn't speak, asked Madame Guerrain to read a note to tell him that Penelope had given Newton's papers to Manfri and told him to take them to America. Instead of calming him, this news concerned him even more.

The pill had saved his Lucien's life, but Penelope wondered if they could ever regain their senses again.

Chapter Thirty-Eight

*I*n late August, the skirmishes outside the brothel escalated between Parisians and their German occupiers. As the Allies drew closer, these fights were happening all over the city. The chaos and street fighting went on for nine days. Then abruptly, after four long and brutal years of Nazi occupation, Paris was free.

Rumors spread that General de Gaulle would greet the city and march down the Avenue des Champs-Élysées and then pay a visit to Notre Dame. As the bells of Notre Dame tolled throughout the city for the first time since the occupation began, Madame Guerrain insisted that Penelope travel with her to watch the celebration. While Lucien stayed with Abraham, Penelope and Madame Guerrain hurried out the door of the brothel and across the city, to wait for the general on the steps of the cathedral with a crowd of Parisians.

Madame Guerrain squeezed Penelope's hand, "Notre Dame is the soul of this city, the essential place for this."

Penelope looked up at the enormous cathedral, remembering her mystical visit there with Lucien and Fulcanelli during the early part of the occupation. She thought of standing with them amongst the ever-watchful gargoyles and looking out across the city. She traced the towering architecture with her discerning gaze to find lonely statues looming above them. When she found them and shaded the glare of the sun from her eyes, she thought she saw a shadowed figure lurking behind one of the statues. She worried her eyes were playing a trick on her, so she looked again and saw a Nazi soldier positioned beside the statues. Penelope reached for Madame Guerrain to warn her but she was so swept up in the carnival of the moment that Penelope wasn't able to get her attention. Madame Guerrain wore a hat that framed her face. Her dress was solemn and plain though she also wore a red, white and blue armband of the French flag.

General de Gaulle's car was arriving. People were crowding in around them. Penelope looked up again and thought she saw more movement from behind the gargoyles. Perhaps two soldiers were there, but Madame Guerrain was transfixed by the moment, as though living in another space entirely. She stood on the tips of her toes like an excited little girl as the car approached.

"He's here; he's here!" Madame Guerrain cried out, squeezing Penelope's hand.

As soon as General de Gaulle stepped out onto the street and turned to face the large crowds, a shot echoed from the gargoyles. More machine gun fire came from across the street as Resistance fighters shot at the soldiers among the gargoyles. Penelope pulled Madame Guerrain to the ground. As they crawled towards the church, chaos rose, and the crowds pressed in around the general and through the main doors of the cathedral. The mob reminded Penelope of the pull and flow of floodwaters, pulling and thrashing at every part of her and yet moving forward in a confluence of people and noise as they squeezed through the narrow opening. She was terrified by the sound of the guns, but miraculously no one seemed to be hurt by the gunfire.

As they entered the cathedral, a few more shots echoed from the within the church. The shots seemed to be coming from behind the organ and the gallery near the vaulted roof. Madame Guerrain and Penelope dropped low, inching across the floor towards one side of the cathedral. Penelope looked up and spied more Nazi soldiers hidden. Stone bits were flying from the impact of the bullets, but the mobs of people didn't seem to care. Again, miraculously, no one was hurt.

Penelope and Madame clutched each other and huddled behind a pillar watching as Charles de Gaulle marched down the center aisle of the church, his head high and his shoulders back as though nothing strange or dangerous were happening. A strange mingling of incense and gun powder choked the air. The general stepped resolute and undeterred.

In spite of the chaos, a group of elderly women and others spontaneously sang out the Te Deum hymn as the general arrived at the altar of the cathedral. Penelope watched it all, cowering and awe-struck. When the hymn ended, General de Gaulle walked out in a state of tranquility, as though nothing was happening. Madame Guerrain and Penelope huddled together in the back of the cathedral until Madame felt it was safe enough to return to the brothel.

Chapter Thirty-Nine

*P*aris was free and the golden pill had saved him. Lucien could not believe he had been in Soufriere Prison only weeks before, barely able to stand, making friends with the rats and roaches in his cell. He had watched them scavenge for just about anything, and he assumed one day they would eat him as well. The effects of the pill were miraculous—except for the blindness and the transmutation.

Penelope wanted to find another word other than transmutation for his body's response. Undeniably, there had been a fundamental change within Lucien. Maybe it wasn't only darkness and light that had inverted for him. It was like being born anew. His rules of logic and understanding too would perhaps be new, a type of dynamic enlightenment, the ever-ripening evolution of consciousness, like a fruit ripening and unfolding to a sun it never knew was there. It was both exciting and terrifying for Lucien, making it difficult for him to make sense of the world or stay awake for long periods. It was a type of transmutation but of things moving from darkness to light instead of lightness into dark.

The golden pill was more solvent than medicine, dissolving self, reversing the tide of opposites, like only knowing the alphabet from finish to start, z to a.

Penelope wondered what love would feel like for him now. She thought of Fulcanelli, how he seemed to struggle with love. He wore his emotions at the surface of his skin.

"And Paris is free? I wish so badly I could see it with my own eyes." Lucien's voice wavered as he spoke. "It is so hard for me to believe. I want to see the colors again." He craved the light. The golden pill was supposed to set him free, but it had anchored him in darkness and he felt stuck in the past. He was an artist and a scientist, taught to lead with his senses. The pill had given him his life and an increased capacity to see with his heart and not his eyes, but he had not accepted this shift the way Naomie had. He didn't want that meeting of dark eyes in a light world, where he could intuit more than he could rationally see or experience.

Penelope brought him painting supplies so that he could return to his art. He had told her one time that he would only paint again once the war was over, but he still refused. "I cannot," he would say. "I feel as though I don't know myself anymore. Who can paint without their vision?"

Though his body was becoming strong again, he felt that he could not move through life in the same way. He had not yet embraced his transformation, and without clear sight, he could not see the notes that Penelope had left for him explaining that Fulcanelli could have more vision, that in the darkness there was more sight.

Often, when Penelope was in the room, unless she touched him, he would not notice her. Be he could sense other things of a more esoteric nature, specters of candle-light and tinsel, the geometry of the sky pulsing. Penelope recognized this range of thought and feeling. She had read her father's book and Newton's papers. Her father and Newton spoke this language fluently. As well, Lucien was nearly consumed by his questions about Newton's papers, upset that Penelope had sent the papers away with Manfri so far away to America.

When Lucien's body became strong again, Penelope took him out into the streets of Paris, hoping to soothe his fears. The voiceless leading the nearly blind, they wandered across the city, avenue to avenue. They wandered street to street, trying to find Parc Verdun. She wished she had some map to guide her there. The effects of the war had changed the landscape of the city.

Were it not for the geography of the mansions that surrounded the park, she might have never found it. She saw
a group of familiar-styled mansions clustered in a neighborhood, and she followed them round and round, past the
library, past the Deschamps mansion and straight through
the gates of the park. Once again, the change upon enter-
ing the park was subtle, like passing from one climate to
another. With his tinted eyes' vision, Lucien noticed the
transition most dramatically, a refraction of temperature,
sound, and feeling. For him, every unseen change was
now most pronounced.

"Where are you taking me?" he asked, squeezing her
hand more tightly. The gardens were even more unkempt
than when Penelope had been there last. Several of the
sculptures had been pushed to the ground. The plants
were overgrown and misshapen. She led Lucien past the
grand rotunda, the windmill, and the pyramid. The flowers moved through the wind like chimes, with feeling and
sound that regular flowers in regular parks could never
embody. They traveled down the path to the grotto and
waterfall. The water flowed freely from the massive falls.
The mist glistened on their faces.

Following the path, they stepped carefully over the
slippery boulders to get to the backside of the falls. As he
stepped behind the falls beside her, Lucien leaned forward
through the water, opening his eyes. No longer ice, the
water yielded perfectly to his touch. Penelope could feel

the thunderous power of the liquid pouring down around them.

"It's like a show of lights," Lucien cried out in relief as the water transformed his vision.

The water was garbling his words. By his count, there were sixteen colors. His eyes sparkled with wonder and relief. He counted and described them all to her as the transformation continued.

When he finished, he cupped his hands, filling them with water and offered her a sip. Penelope drew the water into her mouth and swallowed, feeling it slide down her throat, slick and silvery. She hoped that something healing and magical would happen for her as well, but nothing came of it. What at first was a small tingling was perhaps just the coldness of the water passing down. She drank more and more until her stomach ached, and tears ran fast from her face. She waited and watched Lucien revel in the miracle of his newly recovered sight. She felt as though she had spent most of her life in waiting.

"For heaven's sake, why can't you speak?" he said, his eyes sparkling with the same translucent liquid from the golden pill, like fruits ripening. "I promise you that we will come back here every day until we find the correct potion." He looked around the park with a voracious curiosity. "There are other magical elements here that might help heal you," he said, reassuring her.

She nodded, standing in silence. With Lucien there was always a deep longing for more that stood in the space between them.

As they left the park, Lucien led her back to the front door of the Deschamps mansion. He traced his finger along the wall of the building until he felt a rock move. The key was hidden along the stone facade of the building. He pulled the key from its hiding place, unlocked the door, and led her inside. Lucien had lost his boyish complexion but not his intensity, and he still looked exquisite to Penelope.

She wanted to say loving words to him but could not utter a sound. Instead she laced her fingers in his and wondered how his heart felt towards her now that he had taken the pill.

The house had been emptied of all of its art. It was unclear whether the art was hidden for safe-keeping or if it was stolen by the Nazis. Lucien had not heard what had become of the Deschamps' daughter. The walls were blank but the furniture remained. It was covered in blankets, the shades and windows closed tight. The air had the stiff and dusty odor of an attic. Lucien smiled quietly at Penelope.

"My vision is only partially returned. I will keep going back to see if I can make more improvements," he said and looked down at her.

She nodded.

He touched her throat gently with his hand. "Perhaps the loss of your voice has more to do with your heart than your throat. The grotto's water can only fix wounds of the flesh that are unhealed, not wounds of the heart. Trust me.

I have tried to heal my heart there many times." He winced as if in pain.

The sound of his voice was full and achingly articulate, the timed and rhythmic cadence of someone or something closing in on some greater story. She was trapped in the inward resonance of her emotions. Like some fossil shaped by the sediments in which she remained, the betrayal and her fears remained buried within her, yet pervading all.

She wanted to ask him when and why, but she was not able to say anything.

He led her up the stairs of the mansion. Lucien's face still had a square brow with handsome, amiable features, but his cheeks were pale, almost parched with a mask of sorrow.

"The guards at Soufriere told me that Naomie was killed at a concentration camp." He was poised and statuesque as he spoke.

She felt a pervasive, damp sadness take hold within her. If she had not known the contours of his face so precisely, she might not have noticed the change, or she might have mistaken the sorrow for fatigue. Penelope had studied him the way a painter studies his portrait, and she knew the latent face of melancholy. She hugged him tightly, holding him in the dark hallway until she felt his sorrow reverberate through her.

He led Penelope into the main bedroom and opened the curtains, letting the light pour into the room. The Deschamps' family tree remained hanging in its spot above the bed, the only decoration that remained. Lucien sat down upon the bed and gazed at Penelope in the light.

"My vision is still somewhat shadowed, but I can see enough of you in the light. Would you please dance for me like you did for the men in the brothel?" he asked.

The question startled her. It was not what she expected, but he spoke with affection and sincerity, so she obliged.

She thought of Elodie and Manfri. Their dances always told a story. She remembered their dance of Circe of the Golden Tresses. She closed her eyes and lifted her arms in the air.

When she felt brave enough to begin, she opened them again. She swiveled her hips and began to tuck and roll her belly, her arms rising and then falling. She raised her arms again and turned, pirouetting and tipping her throat to the ceiling. She felt a spiral of pain in her throat but continued. She slowly, unbuttoned her blouse and drew it open, unraveling before him piece by piece until she was almost entirely naked. She tipped her chin to the resplendent sky once more as he quietly drew in beside her, tracing his finger down along her wounded throat.

There was nothing to hide behind, no golden paint or shawl. They were alone, truly alone, for the first time since they had last been in this house so long ago. She gathered her courage to continue the dance with him right beside her. She was almost to the part where Odysseus confronts the enchantress Circe as she draws her light from the sun, but before she could pull her chin back down to reach her arm up, Lucien kissed her. The kiss had all of the yearning and passion of before, only this time there was also the marbled flavor of loss, the bitter price of life and love.

As she stood nearly naked in the empty house, there was no agreement as to what might come next. Yet just as the Seine flows northwest through Paris before emptying into the English Channel, for Lucien and Penelope beyond everything was their love, one soul mixed in movement with another, and love alone could expiate their losses—his vision, her voice, and the distant betrayal. The Deschamps' mansion and its main bedroom was a paragon of art, beauty, and love, a testament to the fallibility human life and its ideals. Lucien looked her at her a long time before saying anything.

"A person can say so much without saying a word," he commented.

Once again, they discovered how deeply a heart could break within the arms of another, that gravitational space called love between two hearts, bodies entwined with body, souls intersected. Love possessed them, though, both liquid and gold, it could not yet explain the path of the rivers, tides, and comets. And it could not undo life's losses.

Chapter Forty

They returned to the brothel to find a frantic Abraham. "A group of ranting men came here and searched the place. They said they were looking for whores and dragged Madame into the street. They called her a pig. They undressed her, shaved her head, marched her up and down the avenue, and beat her. I couldn't stop them."

"Where is she now?" Lucien asked with great urgency.

Abraham led them to her bedroom. Madame Guerrain's head was covered with a scarf, and her face was bloody and badly bruised. "They stole our records. One by one the women of Le Chambrement will be hunted down and shamed, if not killed," she told them.

"Alice is in hiding with her mother. Elise has fled to the countryside. Cleo has gone missing. They are calling it the 'horizontal collaboration.' Some are calling for our executions. It is a disgrace. These women were not the ones most responsible for collaboration. They were trying to survive. What about the government officials? The financiers? I can give them long lists of those French men who came through these doors arm in arm with the Germans." Her eyes were blazing. "Revenge is a weakness of the mind."

Abraham continued, "It took almost no time for the joy to give way to violence. Some of these men believe that such reprisal will divert attention from their own wrongdoings. It is an act of degradation and humiliation. If only they knew the information that these women passed along to the British. Lives saved. Battles not fought."

Madame Guerrain broke in, "But it is not really about that. It is about power and control over women. In towns outside of Paris, I am told that truckloads of women, teenagers, are being driven through the streets. One woman was a cleaner at a military office," she looked at Penelope.

The mobs of shearers were called the *tondeurs*. Their victims were mainly women who lived on the economic fringes, who traded services and goods with Germans for money to buy food for their children. It was a separate means of survival for them.

"I was told that often the shorn women are paraded through the streets in the back of a truck, some painted with tar," Abraham added.

"They are hunting women like animals. I am told Anna

was nearly kicked to death," Madame Guerrain's voice choked. "Penelope, I have contacted Charles in London and arranged with the *SOE* for you to leave Paris immediately. You must return to America. They will hunt you down. They have your name too. They will be back before long."

"This cannot be," Lucien bellowed, panic-stricken.

With her voice broken, Penelope could say nothing. Misinformation and patriotic bombast had a coarse complexion. The cruel and insipid reality of his words washed over her painfully.

"Lucien, don't be foolish. It is urgent. They will be back soon. Paris is too dangerous. She will die at the hands of some angry mob. Look at what they have done to me. I have decided," she said. "I have already made the arrangements for her to leave. The plan is in motion," she said and shut the door on them abruptly.

Penelope stayed in Paris until a telegram from London arrived later that week. Abraham handed Penelope the note from the *SOE*. *Penelope,* it read, *A car will be waiting outside for you at sundown tonight. We have arranged for you to be picked up in New York City and taken to Sweetwater. Best Wishes, Charles.* The message was clear.

Penelope walked into Lucien's room.

"Come with me to Tennessee," she wrote on a slip of paper and handed it to him, while leaning her head against his shoulder, drawing him close with her arms.

He had been seriously injured in the war. The scars were visible on his hands and arms. Though his vision was better, his eyes still churned with pain. He strained to read the note. The golden pill was still very much in motion inside of him.

"I cannot leave France yet," he said. "When my vision improves, I have to return to my home in the north to find my mother and sister. I need to make sure they are okay. I have written to them and have not heard anything. I am afraid the Germans hunted them down because of me."

She had so much that she wanted to say but couldn't. She had lost so many loved ones along the way, and she understood the frantic fear of not knowing.

She laced her fingers around him, kissing his face, two cloistered souls, a long humming embrace, and the desperate solitude that the war had left behind.

She wrote another note of paper for him with her address in Sweetwater.

That night, as they then wandered hand in hand down the staircase to the entrance of the brothel, she heard Naomie's words ring through her memory, telling her that often yearning can so readily lead to despair. The brothel, like the Deschamps' house, held luxuries Penelope had never seen or conceived of before she traveled to Paris, with its needlepoint chairs, fine silver, and tapestries.

In this brothel, so saturated with art and emotion, she wondered if Lucien would ever come to America to be with her. She worried her memories of his touch might soon turn to despair. Perhaps it was all just the cruel loneliness of her imagination. Maybe she just needed to believe he was a good man and that unlike everything else that moved her heart, he would not disappear.

Through the window of the main entrance, she felt the cool moonlight pouring in, like a spotlight all around them. She could see the flickering headlights of the car approaching.

She gathered her belongings and stepped into the car that waited outside for her, not sure if she would ever see Abraham, Madame Guerrain, or Lucien again. As the car drove her out of Paris, she gazed out the window at the moon and the labyrinthine mazes of stars, much like the words on the pages of a dictionary that keep turning and turning.

Chapter Forty-One

"*Je t'ai attendu*," the woman waiting for her at the bus station in Sweetwater said. I have been waiting for you. Her long dress was covered in lace, and there was a spaciousness about her. Her complexion was chalky, and her long hair was braided and woven many times around itself into a crown upon her head. Deep veins were strung along her arms like the contours of a fine and delicate instrument, and her eyes were translucent, the same tint as the ocean.

It was Naomie. She grabbed Penelope's hand and held it in the delicate way someone holds a fine piece of glassware. Penelope felt rapturous, thinking perhaps that it must be a dream. She had felt certain Naomie had been killed and had spent so long searching and waiting for her beloved friend.

As they wept together, Naomie told Penelope of her journey, how she had escaped from a train into Buchenwald and made her way across the Atlantic and on to Sweetwater in hopes that Penelope would be there. Naomie was living in a rusted-out wagon parked against the side of a hill on the far side of town. A trail of smoke was coming out of a make-shift chimney, and there was a large boulder beside the wagon. The boulder was split into two, the veins of minerals circling its center like the rings of an ancient tree.

An older man stood watching them.

"You two are the sum of so many things," the man said at last and smiled with the ebullience of a child, handing her a crumpled envelope.

Penelope knew his smile.

"Is that Manfri?" she wanted to ask Naomie as she grabbed the envelope.

Naomie seemed to understand her thoughts and nodded moving her hands to Penelope's face and then down along her cheeks and chin, all the way down to her belly.

"It's him."

Penelope began crying tears that were heavy with fatigue.

Naomie's eyes moved across her like a steady drizzle. As always, she was lit from the inside, and Penelope wrapped her arms around her, the excitement still crackling inside of her.

Penelope was overwhelmed. It was too deeply painful

for her to contemplate all of the time that had passed in her life without Naomie and never really knowing if she would find Manfri again. The war had rendered her friends almost unrecognizable to her.

"Time has moved so slowly," she thought she heard the Manfri say, and then, in her excitement, she turned from Naomie and ran to him the way a frozen person runs to a fire.

She grasped the papers he had given her and felt afraid of their potency. She was worried what might happen next, that there must be some new and natural calamity coming, some new illusion, and so she held on to them for dear life.

The next morning, Penelope woke up burning with the light of a fever. She was concerned that this was both a beginning and an ending. She thought in her delirium that she had seen Fulcanelli peeking out from somewhere so she went to look for him.

Naomie knelt next to her and touched her forehead. "You are feverish, my dear," she said. "You are very sick." Tears pooled in her eyes.

Penelope felt her vision waiver and she dropped her head. She could no longer carry the weight of her journey. Penelope fell into a deep and feverish sleep that rattled her like wine to her veins, the intoxication flickering in and out like a candle.

Naomie tucked in beside her and curled herself around her, tenderly resting her head beside Penelope's.

"Where is Fulcanelli?" Penelope wrote on a slip of paper.

"I miss him terribly, but he has returned to France. His home is there. Love can be so lonely," Naomie said, "but he left this for you," she said and handed Penelope the bluish tinted stone. Naomie's hand seemed to rattle as she placed the potent rock in Penelope's palm. "He said it is yours to keep forever." She smiled, caressing her friend's feverish cheek. She continued, "There is your imagination, and there are the things life brings to you. You have to go and leave some memories behind."

The air seemed to buzz around them.

Penelope wondered if this was what love does. She squeezed the beloved rock tightly in her palm and it warmed to her touch. She felt like a woman badly in need of things, mostly of love. She needed a place to rest, and beyond all else she thought she might finally have found that place. It was sparse and downtrodden, but so was she, and she thought it might just make do. A place among her people to hide and lick her wounds.

She missed Lucien and disappeared into her fevered thoughts for days. She was exhausted, and she spent all of her time in bed, as if in some great stalemate with life. She wrote him letter after letter about her life and travels, about her longing and love for him. She still could not speak and could barely even eat or drink. Penelope refused plate after plate, but Naomie knew better. Naomie understood right away that Penelope was pregnant and not sick.

"Rest. You are sick because there is a baby," Naomie told her. "Sulphur and mercury united," Naomie continued pointing to her belly.

Prima materia, pure, raw emergence. Penelope knew that having a baby was the most potent transmutation, lead to gold, something from nothing. She never envisioned this for herself. Would-be gold-makers were mothers, not her. She had never aspired to this and had no visions of how this could be.

"Who is the father?" Naomie asked.

Penelope could not speak. Naomie came to realize this and offered her some tea. Naomie filled her cup full.

"Lucien," Penelope wrote in the dirt before Naomie and grasped the cup, tipping her head back all the way. The tea tasted like smoke and bitter apple. She offered some to Naomie, who smiled and finished it down, tears of joy pouring down their cheeks.

Home. It sounded nice. Home, sweet home sounded even better. It had been several days since Penelope had eaten. She was dehydrated, but her eyes were damp with hope and the gentle fog of emotion.

"When I was escaping the camp, I heard a rumor that you and Lucien had been killed," Naomie said in a low, sad voice.

Penelope's throat still hurt and ached all the way up through her mouth and head, but she was trying not to think about her broken parts. They remained silent together. She remembered a time in her life when such protracted silence was unsettling. Now she gave it plenty of slow melting room. She even savored it like a sweet candy to her tongue. She had learned that silence, like a deep cave to the heart, had depth and resonance. The deeper the silence, the deeper the truth could come humming on through.

Her stomach burned with hunger and grief.

"Life will hurt you," Manfri chimed in. "I know you miss Lucien, and I miss Elodie every day. But you, me, and Naomie have each other now."

Penelope nodded. Her lips were tight with tension, her eyes marbled and distant.

Manfri smiled back at her.

Penelope looked up at the sky. There was a sameness in the resplendent blue of the sky. Penelope took another sip of the tea, trying to gain hold of some real thought or feeling. When she finally drifted off to sleep again, she held her beloved stone tightly, lovingly and dreamt of water. From small creek to river to ocean of salt, she had plunged headlong, so deep and so dark now than she could no longer see the bottom.

Chapter Forty-Two

*M*onths later, she could smell the baby coming, but when she walked outside, there was nothing there, no wind, no angel, only the slow sucking sound of the wet ground saturated with the waters of the churning rains, and because no one was there to offer her a hand, the chunky heel of her shoe sunk as easily to the wet grass as a pushpin to a hem, and when she tried to step forward, her heel sunk even more. Her foot stuck and she swiveled, landing hard on her back. Naomie came to her, helped her up, offering her a warm drink made of wild cherry bark, draping a blanket over her.

"It is supposed to speed the delivery," Naomie had said, but Penelope refused it and wandered down to the creek to be alone. She made a bed of leaves for herself and plunged her feet into the creek to cool the heat of the pain. It was a sculpted sort of pain that took the shape of a poultice, spreading across her entire abdomen at once.

Birth was a labyrinth of things, sulphur and mercury, blood and water. The product would take shape, the most perfect melding of things, namely gold. Birth was capable of changing most fully one thing into another, a woman to a mother.

Penelope thought of the loss of her own mother after childbirth. The labor pain was a relief to her deeper sorrow.

Penelope moaned in agony. She watched the inky rain clouds circle above her like buzzards. Her memories were large, indistinct and random, bulging out like some hernia. Since the war, her mind was continuously caught between forward and reverse, though lately, she was mostly stuck in reverse, always looking back, the weaving from memory to nearly lost memory. She missed Lucien so badly. She wished he could be with her, but he had vanished. All she knew about the future was that she was having a baby that day.

Penelope lived with Naomie and Manfri in a wagon on a mountainside overlooking Sweetwater Creek. There, large boulders hung to the steep banks like the crooked teeth of a wide-open jaw, vines and trees and laurel woven down along its gullet. The creek was hidden, and like Penelope, it was abrupt and asymmetrical in its beauty, a swirling soup of things, life draining down and pooling there with nowhere else to go.

Gravity pulled everything down to the valley below. There was no stopping it. All of the watery ions buried deep beneath the fibers of her sinewy form were drawn up and out and rolled down her cheek and on down even farther into the belly of the valley to the creek that resided there.

And yes, she had yielded to the gravitational pull, the slumping down of things. Now, here she was, on her back, on the day of her child's birth, all the way down to the ground.

The winds picked up, and a large limb snapped off a tree and fell down beside her with the giant weight of a gorilla. She looked above her and saw the maze of branches braided and swinging wildly in the squalls of the wind. The limbs dangling above her like some distant firing squad, her eyes boiling and darting with the strong tonic of raw and undiluted fear.

Birth was limbic and settled into the sky, downburst after downburst of air bursting free and pouring over her. She thought again of her mother. The gusts of labor were painfully overpowering. The baby was coming, yet her body was too tired to move, and Penelope had no choice but to bear it fully.

In one volcanic breath, the baby was born. It was a girl, and Penelope ceremonially plunged her into the creek. A fiery comet, like her father, pure gold. The baby chewed Penelope's hand and squinted her eyes open to the blue sky. Her arrival coincided with the appearance of Venus, the

evening star in the sky, and so she named her Vesperale—
French for little star.

For many years, Penelope wrote letters to Lucien about
the baby's arrival, about finding Naomie and Manfri,
about the stone and Newton's papers, but, one by one, they
all returned from Paris unopened.

The End

Acknowledgements

*L*ife is never just one thing, so it is important to note that I started this book the year my daughter was born. I spent so many sleepless and delirious nights dreaming of how I would feel at the book's completion. Now that I am here, I know that what I feel most thoroughly is love and gratitude.

I have dedicated the book to my family because, without a doubt, I could never have done this without them. They speak the language of unconditional love and support so fluently. I also needed my dear friends. There is no question that Yael and Liz have read the book more than anyone. I would attempt to explain how much their attention to this project has moved me, but I cannot find words adequate enough. So much gratitude and devotion to all of my dear friends who have helped me believe in myself, persevere, and understand the story better.

Many thanks to Henry Ferris who labored over this manuscript with humor, kindness, and abundant editorial wisdom. Thanks to Stephanie Koehler and Jana Good for helping me see it through the finish line.

And finally, to the brave women of the French Resistance whose courage, passion, and sacrifice inspired this story. Liberté, Egalité, Humanité.

About the Author

Sarah Patten grew up in Chattanooga, Tennessee. She lives in Asheville, North Carolina with her husband and three children.

Made in the USA
Las Vegas, NV
01 March 2021

18815991R10247